Daughter of the Manifold

David Maxwell

Zem Publishing

Remember, Daughter of the Manifold

Sing me a memory

Chapter One

C alendra is at the heart of the world. The worldtree.

The packed hall is warm, but the hair on her arms stands on end. A chill rolls down her spine.

She perches on a cabinet not designed for perching, absorbing the majesty and chaos of the Descension. The Hall of the Announcer is at capacity. The simple granite dais at the center provides a focal point for the crowd, jubilant at the first sighting of their immortal leader since before Calendra was born. Calendra knows she should be elsewhere, but she wants the best view of the big event and there are so many people that nobody will care. Least of all Uncle Mal, who stands beside her.

She gazes around the Hall with its circular wooden walls and concentric rings on the floor and ceiling. A hall inside a tree. She has heard her whole life of the worldtree, but to hear of a tree fifty paces across and hundreds tall is not to witness it. It feels wrong that some ancestor carved an entire hall, indeed a palace, inside such a magnificent thing. When she voices this to Uncle Mal, he assures her that only the outer part of the tree is alive and, aside from the small door at ground level, the worldtree never felt a thing and is a happy and healthy tree.

It is a sight to behold and she beholds it with Uncle Mal. It is a rare treat. He even formally invited her! He has only been her new father for two years, most spent with her tutor, so it is her first chance to see where this father works. Maybe even to get to know him.

While her homeland is a place of bitter cold, the sacred lake in which the worldtree stands is warm year round. She feels an energy flow through her. The world gains a texture it once lacked. She tries to blink it away. It is an odd experience, like suddenly noticing the canvas after years of staring at a painting.

Calendra's new sense registers a change. It feels like something is being added to this canvas, the material on which reality is painted. No, she realizes. Like the canvas itself changes, so that the addition that was never part of the old canvas has always been part of the new canvas.

"He's here," she whispers.

Uncle Mal twists his head to look at her, about to say something.

The Announcer materializes on the dais, silver robes flowing. A cheer erupts and the ecstatic crowd hurls party streamers, but Calendra's eyes are pulled to the right. A man leaps towards the Announcer. The Announcer's Protectors notice, late, and the man twists mid-air between their blades. The assassin's own blade stabs towards the center of the dais. Towards the Announcer.

Calendra's new sense registers the canvas change once more, but not to add something. It feels as if the canvas loosens its hold on the Announcer - as though some force that fights to slow all things has lessened its grip on the Announcer. He does not change his location. He moves. *Fast*. He is a Speed Artist!

Calendra knows it should not be possible. One cannot have multiple powers. Each person is limited to one Art. The Announcer is a Spatial Artist, not a Speed Artist. His own histories are clear about that. He learned the ways of this world by teleporting to every corner and eventually ascending to become one with it. He is a Spatial Artist. She saw him teleport not a moment before.

Her new sense knows the truth. With that certainty comes an awareness that she can do the same.

Calendra slows the world.

The movement of people is slowing. Stilling. Streamers unfurling with glacial slowness. The roar of the crowd a note held. The assassin's blade still moving fast. But the Announcer is moving faster. Taking a step to his left. Avoiding the blade easily. Stepping back to his position of practiced ease. His Protectors are not moving as fast, but are faster than anyone else. The closest Protector is leaping. Stretching his sword towards the assassin's neck ...

Calendra gasps as her new sense is cut off and a shudder goes through her. The world resumes normal speed.

"So fast," she gasps in the moment of shocked silence as the assassin's head is removed from his body. Total pandemonium erupts.

In an instant, she is spun and held over Uncle Mal's right shoulder. He runs towards the exit, weaving between people faster than she can make out. She wonders if he can slow the world too, but her head feels too light. Her eyelids droop.

She looks back before losing consciousness. The Announcer stands tall in a pool of the assassin's blood, chuckling as he looks into Calendra's eyes.

CHAPTER TWO

"Welcome to your new world. You are a remnant of a remnant, but humanity will rebuild. The world of green and blue you once gazed up at will now provide everything you yearned for in your dying world."

The Traveler's Welcome

Written record from the Eightieth Year of the Great Transference, Library of the School of the Manifold, Sanctum

Calendra's eyes snap open. Her back hurts. She vaguely remembers waking, only to pass out from the pain. Uncle Mal's face appears above her, shadows scampering over his face from a crackling fireplace. He speaks in his soothing baritone, so familiar yet so seldom heard.

"Rest, Calendra. I had little choice but to run. We're still not safe, but the danger is far enough to let you recover tonight. You are safe here. We will leave tomorrow by kinder means."

Calendra shivers as her uncle walks to a table, pulls squares of paper from his pocket and starts arranging them.

"What danger?" It hurts to talk.

He continues with his squares. "You saw something that few had imagined, fewer suspected and, as far as I know, only you and I outside the Announcer's inner circle know for sure. Dangerous knowledge."

She considers for long seconds. Much has happened, but little of it is unique to her. "The Announcer is a Speed Artist."

"He is. Good. Why is that dangerous?"

She thinks about this for some time. To have two Arts is weird, but dangerous? The tone of her uncle's question makes it feel like a test. Uncle Mal ran from the Announcer to protect her. She will do her best.

"You can only have one Art. And he's immortal. Is he the Traveler?"

Uncle Mal looks up at her, finally. He smiles. "No, child. No, the Traveler is long gone. He gave his life to bring our people to this planet from the Twin." He points out the window at the waxing moon that forever hangs in the sky. "The Announcer may be something almost as important. The first person since the Traveler to access multiple Manifold Arts. If that is natural, it means something important for the Arts. If he gained these abilities, there are people who would kill to learn how, so they might do the same."

He pauses, his expression softening into something more fatherly. Calendra's head spins. She knows some basics of the ten Arts and humanity's history, but she struggles to keep track with her uncle's breathless pace and unapologetically formal language.

"I tell you these things as it's your right to know why I've taken you from your home. I do not say them to frighten you. We fled in case someone heard you identify his second Art. The reaction of a man who has just survived an assassination attempt will seldom be calmer than that of a man with time to consider his next move. I needed to ensure that he has that time. I do not believe the Announcer is an evil man, nor even one who would hurt a child to achieve important ends. He would not hesitate to take your freedom though, and of course I may underestimate his ruthlessness. As I told you, there are also others that may wish to use your knowledge, or eliminate it. But that's not a worry for today."

Imprisonment? This is no game. "You're not a kid. Are you safe?"

"No, child," he laughs and turns back to his puzzle, moving and rotating squares. "I'm not safe. The Announcer knows now that I'm a Speed Artist. If he knows what you know, he knows why I fled with you. I was not forthcoming about my Art when I sought and gained permission to live in this land, as he does not allow foreign Artists to enter Chalveno, let alone enjoy diplomatic privileges. I have betrayed the trust I was given. For that reason alone, my liberty is forfeit. Given my Artistry, he would probably give me the choice to serve him fully or languish in prison. I would not choose the first of those options."

Calendra shakes her head, trying to clear her fogging mind. "I don't understand."

Her uncle curses and looks as if he will sweep the squares from the table, before he catches himself.

"I've put too much on you today," he says without looking up. "Your father and I grew up together, but in another nation. He moved here with your mother after meeting her in our land. I moved here after your mother died to support him. When your father died and I agreed to adopt you, I was granted citizenship. But I had another reason for coming to Chalveno. The leaders of my homeland long suspected the Announcer has access to multiple Arts. Arts of the Manifold, specifically. His Spatial Artistry was known, but there was sound evidence he could also manipulate gravity. They sent me to confirm this, along with the likelihood that he could manipulate his speed. Knowing he can all but confirms that he can access all three Manifold Arts, which is extraordinary, though less confusing than if he could only access two."

"All the powers of the Manifold?" Calendra is happy to focus on something simpler than her family history. "So ... he really ascended?"

"I don't even know what that means," he scoffs.

"Is he immortal?"

"I doubt it. We know of no use of the Arts that can make a person live forever. If you mean impossible to kill, certainly not. Even just to never give in to the ravages of time? No, we think not. To age at a slower rate than others though? Yes. For the right kind of Artist, that's a simple trick. You did something similar yesterday."

"I did?" She stops to consider. "I made the world slow down. Except the Traveler. He was too fast. How?"

"You're a Speed Artist, of course, like the Announcer." He grins at her. A rare thing. "Like me. You can change the rate at which you interact with the world. You are a Manifold Artist and your Art is a particularly useful one. You are not just able to see the world slowly, you're able to move faster than it."

A Manifold Artist! Calendra has learned of the ten Arts, but the three Manifold Arts are almost legends. Physical Artists are common to her, people who can use Spirit - the energy of life - to boost strength, endurance and other attributes of the body. She even met an Artist of the Mind who visited their treetop town and claimed to remember everything she ever experienced. Never a Manifold Artist though. Well, except for her uncle, apparently.

"But how does the Announcer being fast make him immortal? I don't understand."

"What did it feel like when you were fast?"

"I could think fast. See fast. I'm sure I could have moved fast."

"Good. And did it feel like a matter of the pace at which you did things, or the pace at which time passed for you compared to others?"

His language trips Calendra up but, on reflection, it is clear. "The world slowed. I was normal. But my normal was faster than other people's normal. It was the second thing you said, I think."

"Good. When I ran with you, Calendra, I was going anywhere from five to ten times my normal speed for the first half hour. After that, I ran at maybe triple my normal speed for eighteen hours. To do so is normally impossible. Almost nobody alive could do it, and even I prepared for years to achieve it. I set up the right contacts and funds to provide me with some very special types of food. Even then, my Spirit almost ran out several hours before we arrived here. I had to conserve the last wisps."

"You almost lost your Spirit? My tutor said that running out of Spirit is dangerous." She considers. "I guess that's the chill I felt before I became Fast? Spirit?"

He smiles. "Some Artists don't realize they can manipulate their own Spirit and practice an Art until late. Others do it as babies. We don't know why, though it seems the ones who learn later have more power. Not more Spirit. Just the ability to fuel their Art more with the same amount of Spirit."

"Why can't I feel it anymore? I felt so close to everything while I was Fast."

"You burned through your Spirit in the time it takes to blink." He grins at her. "Even as underdeveloped as it is, you must have been living twenty, thirty times your normal speed to use it up so quickly. Thing is, few Speed Artists can live that fast for any amount of time, not without years of dedication to improving their capacity and power. So it seems you have appallingly little Spirit, or a prodigious ability to burn it up. To improve your capacity and skill is far easier than improving your power, so that's useful, but both require the discipline and will that few children possess."

His eyes twinkle as hers widen further, horrified that she burned through her first Spirit.

"Anyway," he continues, "I spent many hours at triple speed, short periods at many times normal speed. You won't notice it, but I am older than I should be because of that. Not by much, but the faster you fuel your Art, the faster you age. And the faster you burn Spirit. One minute at thirty-speed is not fifteen minutes at double-speed. And, of course, it applies in the other direction. A Speed Artist can speed up the world."

He stops talking, seeming to give her time to think about this. She does. He goes back to his squares.

"So, the Announcer ages slowly by living Slow?"

He somehow smiles in her direction while scowling at the squares. "Good. How he does so boggles the mind. Living Slow takes as much Spirit as living Fast, and even powerful Speed Artists cannot live at more than double-speed or less than half-speed for long. To have lived so long..."

Uncle Mal chews on this for a while, moving squares faster and faster, before tearing himself away with apparent effort. He smiles.

"The important thing is that you can do the same. Now you know your ability, you will burn away your years living fast. We all do. You will need to be disciplined with this throughout your life. I'll leave you to rest. We will leave tomorrow, but eat, think and sleep knowing you're safe here. Our host will visit you once more in the coming hours to continue your healing. His position is sensitive so he won't introduce himself. It's best if you avoid even looking at him. The fewer people who know his role, the better."

He walks to a bench and returns with a tray with a glass of infused water and an unappealing lump of brown-green processed food, muttering at his squares as he goes.

"Calendra, it is important you eat every scrap of that meal. I'll explain the details later, but you must do so while thinking of the feeling you had when you became Fast. Was there a feeling, an impression, that you can focus on?"

"I felt a change just before the Announcer arrived. It made me think of Dad's painting lessons and how he told me to think of the canvas I paint on, not just the paint. It felt like the canvas changed to fit the Announcer. And when he became Fast, I felt a different change, like he lifted off the canvas a little. I guess that seems strange."

She looks up. He is staring at her, slack jawed. He quickly composes himself.

"Why, that's a wonderful interpretation of the Manifold. My brother was always subtle. Now, I need you to think carefully about this. Are you certain you saw a change in the canvas before he arrived, and before he became Fast? Might you have seen him teleport, seen him move Fast, and then interpreted how that would have looked on this canvas?"

She stares back, confused. "But you heard me. I said he was coming and you looked at me. That was before I became Fast." She shrugs. "Unless he was Fast as soon as he arrived? But I'm sure I felt him go Fast after I said that."

"Yes, I remember that. I had hoped my memory was distorted. No matter. There's a lot here for us both to process. We'll talk tomorrow. Eat. Please, try to empty your mind of questions and just think of the canvas, as you call it. Try to picture the world around you, especially the food you are eating. Try to see behind it, not just as you eat but as you digest. This is the most important thing. If you need to think through things first to clear your head, do so. If you even must sleep, do so. The sooner you eat, the better, but only if you properly meditate during the meal. Do you understand?"

She nods firmly. She was normal just yesterday. Ordinary. Now, she is an Artist. One of the rarest types. To be the best Artist she can be, she only has to ignore her pain, deny herself sleep and think about one thing for a few hours. Easy.

"I do, Uncle Mal. I won't let you down." She looks down. "Thank you for rescuing me."

He smiles and comes to her, leaning forward to kiss her on the forehead. "You are my daughter now."

He winks, kisses her again, and walks off. Calendra closes her eyes and savors the moment. Her uncle has always provided for her, but has been absent for much of the last two years and has never been open or loving. But he saved her, and he named her his daughter. Daughter!

She determines to show him that the only daughter of Malnor, Artist of the Manifold, is worthy of his love.

CHAPTER THREE

"Life resonates, billions of lifeforms singing in harmony as one. It has welcomed you. Repay its generosity with respect."

The Traveler's Welcome

Written record from the Eightieth Year of the Great Transference, Library of the School of the Manifold, Sanctum

C alendra eyeballs her meal. She tries to remember what it felt like to look at the canvas, not just what the metaphor put in her head. She tries to picture the substance that links her and the food, even before she touches it.

She rubs at her temples and turns away. Thinking feels like wading through maple syrup. Besides, her curiosity gets the better of her. She gets out of bed with a groan and makes her way to the table her father's squares still cover. Dozens of tiny squares with markings on one side. Series of lines and squiggles forming some kind of overall pattern, like a puzzle. Calendra cocks her head and stares at them, seeing only the squiggles.

It is a pattern. Calendra sees the type. Lines almost straight, but not quite. Lines branching and entwining. Flows. Hierarchies. It is that which links leaf to branch to tree, that which links the dozen streams of the Chalvstrom oasis to the crashing waters of the Spine River below. She occupies some minutes trying to picture the pattern before giving up. Was the puzzle his? Why did he cut the squares so small?

Calendra returns to bed and her strange meal. Meditate.

She relaxes her eyes, trying to see ... behind the food? Through it? To see it not as a thing itself, but as paint on a living canvas that can be separated from the canvas - its relationship to everything else dependent upon its relationship to the canvas. This triggers a hint of a memory. Songs her father would sing. Her first father, now. She pushes it aside, all her youthful determination focusing on the canvas.

She weighs the food brick in her hand. It feels firm, squishy, and heavier than she expected. She thinks about it in her hand. Its texture. Its weight. She tries to think about its mild aroma, though her sense of smell has always been weak. She thinks about the canvas and her place on it, now she knows she can change her speed.

She takes a small bite out of the meal and begins chewing, somehow holding all these things in her mind. She gulps down the food. The effects are immediate. She feels a surge of tingling as she had the previous day, like it is inside her and part of her, but not the physical her. It is short-lived.

She breathes deeply and calms herself. The canvas. She tears into the remainder of the meal, chewing quickly while maintaining focus. As she eats, she feels she is beginning to see the canvas, not just picture it in her head.

By the time she has finished, she thinks she can feel the change in the canvas directly - from the canvas on which the meal had been to the canvas on which it is part of her. She feels a slight bump in the canvas where she is painted, like a pressure waiting to be released.

Does she feel something else? Maybe not, but she feels certain that the food has made her more in tune with the idea of speed. Then she reminds herself to stop overthinking it. To just keep thinking about the canvas and how her place and image have changed.

She keeps focusing but lies down properly, eyes still closed. Getting herself comfortable, she relaxes her mind on the picture before her, clear as a real painting, of herself on the canvas. All else ceases to exist as she stares at a vivid mental picture of a bruised, glowing girl lying on her back, her image painted on the living, moving, evolving canvas of reality.

An unknowable time later, she hears a knock. This frustrates her.

"Yes?"

The door opens and she hears boots on wood. A soft voice speaks, male but effeminate, with no accent she can place. "Am I too soon? Did you eat recently? Did I disturb your meditation?"

She nods her head, eyes still shut. "I ate right after Uncle Mal left." With sudden delight, she corrects herself. "After my dad left. He said four hours. I think I can still see it, but let me finish before it leaves me!"

She almost shakes with frustration. There is a long pause.

"Young lady, you've been alone for nine hours. If you've been focused for that long, you should be very proud. Do this throughout your life and your Artistry will be greatly rewarded, or so the legends say. For now, your food is enough a part of you that further meditation won't likely make a difference."

Calendra allows herself a moment of pride at his words. Nine hours! It felt like two.

"Meanwhile," he continues, "you have bruised ribs and I fear for your future abilities as an Artist. I'm a Resilience Donor. I can give you my Spirit. It will help you become physically resilient, enabling your body to focus solely on repair. Do you understand?"

Calendra nods. She has heard about the Resilience Donors that work at the Chalvstrom hospital.

"I will place my hands on your shoulders," he says, "and you'll feel my Spirit change you. It is not yours, so you cannot use it. Let it fortify you. Do not try to control it or direct it. The effort can only hamper your healing. You need not continue your meditation, though if you choose to I recommend you focus not on the Manifold, as Malnor no doubt instructed you, but on your physical self and how my Spirit changes it. Questions?"

Calendra shakes her head. He places his hands on her and Spirit floods into her soul. He is right. It is not hers, but it becomes one with her as the food did. She feels the tingling from earlier, but far stronger. Then it settles and she feels physically tough. Not strong, but like nothing can damage her. Like rubber. Her pain remains, but it dulls to a slight itch. She lays back and thinks about how the Spirit is changing her.

She remains unsettled. After some time, she rises and goes to the table with the patterned squares. She stares at them and flips over the squares that are face-down. She stares some more, circling the table to get different views.

Then she sees it. The pattern. The flow. She moves and rotates dozens of tiny squares until the picture is complete. It is a map of Chalveno, but like she has never seen. It seems to map waterways. That, or something with a branching pattern like a waterway.

She smiles, goes to bed, and falls asleep in moments.

CHAPTER FOUR

"By chance or design, life here is compatible with humanity. The air is clear, the water sweet. Plant life is prolific, varied, nutritious, and rarely toxic or hostile."

The Traveler's Welcome

Written record from the Eightieth Year of the Great Transference, Library of the School of the Manifold, Sanctum

C alendra wakes to the creaking hinges of the room's only door. She opens her eyes to the orange tint of dawn light. A spicy burned oil aroma triggers pangs of hunger. Uncle Mal - her dad! - walks towards her, grin on face, tray in hand.

"Daughter, you look rested. How do you feel?"

Calendra sits up, prods at her chest and stretches her back muscles at different angles. "I can breathe and sit up and twist without it hurting. My ribs are sore and I'm tired, but better I guess."

She suddenly remembers her meal and meditation. Her dad starts to talk but she holds up a forefinger, causing him to pause. Calendra quests inside herself, looking for her new Spirit. She unfocuses her eyes and looks for the canvas. What others call the Manifold. She can feel no Spirit. No tingling sensation. She was to have her Spirit back! Has she not done her best? She cannot see the canvas with her body's eyes, nor her mind's, but she thinks she can feel it. She cannot see the connections between things, the fabric of reality, but maybe ...

"Quick, use your Art! Be Fast, then Slow."

He stares for a moment, then becomes Fast. As he does, or before he does, Calendra feels a change. She cannot see it directly as she did at the worldtree, but she can feel the canvas change. She can feel what changed and she thinks she can identify that the change relates to speed. She breaks out in a grin of renewed hope, feeling the change as his speed manipulation halts.

At that moment, her dad becomes Slow. She feels this in the same way as before, but flipped. She feels the canvas change to hold him more tightly, weighing down his motion more aggressively than normal. Her dad watches her reactions and grins.

A laugh leaps from Calendra's mouth before she closes it. "I can still feel it, Dad. I have no Spirit, but I could feel the canvas change both times and I think I could feel that it was Speed Artistry. I think I'm still a Manifold Artist." She pauses. "What can I do without Spirit?"

"Stop jumping to conclusions about mysteries as complex as regaining depleted Spirit. It is a dangerous thing to do, and consumes time and resources, but it is not an uncommon thing. It is done accidentally, negligently or deliberately by many people, all the time. If you expected to be bursting with Spirit less than a day after eating and meditating, that's my fault. I didn't want to flood you with information, but I hadn't realized you would think this way."

He sighs and softens his expression. "Calendra, the soonest I've regained my Spirit fully after draining it - yes, I have done that, multiple times - is around four days. With food of the right type, I regained enough after two days to feel the first wisps of Spirit. I experienced the same nervousness you are feeling. Now, a person doing it for the first time, not understanding the meditations that focus it, not possessing the resources to accelerate it, but just naturally absorbing Spirit in their comings and goings ... I've seen such people take fifteen weeks to feel the first wisps."

Calendra gasps. Fifteen weeks? She cannot imagine it. Despite never having felt the Spirit inside her until this week, it is now inconceivable that she would be without it for almost half a year!

His eyes grow warmer. "You are still presuming. You are not one of those people. You had guidance on meditation. I can't know how focused your meditation was, but I expect from your reaction that you worked harder on it than you have on anything in your brief life, and feel you deserve the reward." He laughs aloud.

"And the food? I won't tell you what that meal cost. I had it prepared recently, anticipating that I would need it myself. Possibly under desperate circumstances. Once I learned you share my Art, the choice became simple which of us would benefit most. Some scholars theorize that the first 'reseeding', as they call it - I hate that word - is even more important than the Spirit you are born with. I'm not sure about that myself but, in case there is truth to that, I wanted you to have the greatest chance possible at your Spirit being broad, deep and clear."

Calendra shakes her head to clear it. It is never easy to understand her dad and that much harder when he is excited.

"No," he continues, animated, "I will eat the bed you lay upon if you don't get your Spirit back. Given your advantages and strength of will, you should already have the seed. One which will generate faster than for most. Now rest. We leave at the sun's shrouding, if you can walk. I'm proud of you, my girl."

"Can't you just call it truenight like everyone else?"

He laughs and gestures towards the table. "How did you know the pattern? When did you do this?"

"It just popped out at me. Only after I ate that meal, though."

Her dad nods slowly and leaves. Calendra lays herself flat, smiles softly, closes her eyes and thinks of Spirit. Her thoughts become dreams minutes later.

They leave at truenight, not long after the sun has set. There is no farewell. They walk at a steady pace along random paths through sparse undergrowth beneath the thick jungle canopy, always heading west or north. They hide during smalldawn under towering maples, when the reflected light of the Twin interrupts the night, to avoid detection.

They break at dawn and sleep in a cave, one of thousands nestled into the ridge they keep to their right. Calendra cannot become comfortable. She feels the spikes and bumps of dark stone barely cushioned by her thin bedroll, sees the eerie glow of fluorescent yellow and blue mushrooms, and is kept on edge by the frequent but irregular dripping of water seeping through cracks above.

She tries to feel her Spirit. Dreams take over before she does and she wakes tired and bitter. Until she calms herself and reaches inside ... and feels it! The tingle for which she has been waiting. They walk that night at a better pace, a bounce in Calendra's step. An Artist she remains!

They sleep within new caves the following day. Calendra is once again unable to rest her mind, lost in thought as she stares up at hundreds of stalactites of myriad shapes and sizes. She has felt the Spirit inside her growing all day, but its regeneration slowed and then stopped shortly before dawn. She asks herself what she did wrong, as she knows that regeneration takes days or weeks. Her body finally wins over her mind and forces it to switch off.

When they wake, and her dad sees her dark mood, he asks what has changed. Calendra explains. He laughs and laughs, eyes alight. His massive hands grasp her tiny shoulders before sweeping her into a hug that makes her gasp. He puts her down, winks at her and snaps his fingers. He becomes Slow.

Calendra whoops with delight. It is as clear as northern ice-waters. The canvas. She cannot see it at will, but sees it the moment her dad manipulates his speed. As lightning provides a split second of light in the darkest forest and the image burns into the mind enough to picture your surroundings, the image of the canvas changing flashes before her and burns into her mind.

She suddenly realizes why he is laughing. She takes a deep breath.

Calendra becomes Fast.

Calendra is running circles around her dad. Feeling she can soar in the air like cloud-seeds. She was not expecting the exhilaration. The joy of moving Fast. She only watched Fast the first time. Now she is moving Fast. It is a delight! She is seeing the change in the canvas. Seeing from her own eyes at the same time as seeing herself lift from the canvas in her mind's eye. It is almost breaking her mind. Her joy is too great to be thinking about it.

She stops. Briefly worried, she checks her Spirit and is surprised to feel it almost at the same level as before she used her Art. She is not certain, but she is confident. She can feel how full her Spirit is, roughly at least. It is quite different to physical energy, the depth of which is difficult to tell until it flees entirely. She reports this to her dad and he suggests she try living at half-speed. She does.

Living so slow ... disconcerting ... running so slow ... her dad's breathing too fast ... her Spirit ... feeling diminished but ... mostly there ...

She stops. He suggests four-speed for a minute, though he frowns slightly as he does. She becomes Fast.

She is glorying in the motion. Running. Dancing. Twisting. Turning.

She stops. Her Spirit feels diminished but still abundant. Finally, he tells her to cut off all diversion of her Spirit and rest, meditating on the Manifold, but instructs her to tell him the moment her Spirit is full. The moment it stops regenerating.

Twenty minutes later, she tells him it feels full.

There is no laughter this time. There is only joy. Calendra feels it radiating from her dad. Relief. Astonishment. Smugness? And unrestrained joy. With a smile that should split his lips, he embraces her once more.

He holds her in the air and celebrates her. He shouts the name of her birth father, her mother, and the Traveler himself, and tells them of the pride they should have in Calendra, Daughter of the Manifold.

Calendra knows he is overdoing it, but that day, and the next, and for the following weeks of endless walking, it does not matter.

She is an Artist. She is a Manifold Artist. And her dad is proud of her. And those are wonderful things for a girl to know.

CHAPTER FIVE

"There is an energy to this world, a primal power borne of life's interactions. Focused, filtered, it affects physical essence, thought, even relationship to the spacetime manifold."

The Traveler's Welcome

Written record from the Eightieth Year of the Great Transference, Library of the School of the Manifold, Sanctum

"Run to me, Calendra. Double-speed."

Calendra stretches, stifling a yawn. She squints at her dad halfway down the snowy hill from the shaded entrance of the hilltop cave they have called home for days. The steam from the hot spring below fuzzes the image, but Calendra can see he has cut rough steps into the snow.

"Too old to climb a hill now, Dad?"

Her call cuts through the still winter air, the violet Twin beaming down at them through a deep blue sky and making the ice look like water. She can feel his glare at thirty paces. She sighs and readies herself.

She is excited about her Art, but the tests make her weary. After weeks of trekking without using her Art at all, she has done nothing but practice and submit to testing since this valley became snowed in.

She has not done this test. Her dad has pushed her to use her Art with subtlety, practicing with changes in her speed to learn how much Spirit certain uses require. He has pushed her to practice her movement, to handle the jitteriness of moving Fast and the suffocating feeling of moving Slow, but she has done these things on level ground. She anticipates the challenge of doing it downhill.

"Down the slope first, girl. Don't use the steps yet."

Calendra becomes Fast.

Calendra is pushing off with her left foot. She is looking at the point on the hill at which her mind expects her to land. She is watching the ground drop as she sails past it. She is practically flying. The ground is sloping at the same rate as her fall. She is becoming nervous, slamming shut the flow of Spirit ...

Calendra's body lurches as she returns to her natural speed. Her right foot hits the ground unexpectedly. The snow protects her from breaking anything but her knee buckles, she tumbles headfirst into the snow and rolls down the hill. She comes to a stop in front of her dad. Bruised and grumpy, but unharmed.

"Again!"

He beams at her like he has just given her the most wonderful birthday present for which a girl could wish. She makes a mental gesture at him she would never dare physically.

As she trudges back up the hill, she resigns herself to a long day. She might resent him being upbeat when she just wants to sleep, but he is right. They can go nowhere until the snow melts or freezes. She wanted to be the best Artist in the world before weeks of walking without her Art made her just want a nice bed. What does she think, anyway? That she will never need to use her Art on a slope? On steps? She had better learn this well.

Her second try is better. She lands halfway down the hill before cutting off her Art.

After thirteen attempts, face covered in snow and ice, Calendra manages to run the whole way down at double-speed without falling and can still arrive at her dad's side smoothly before she cuts off her Spirit. She whoops, jumping in the air with her forefingers toward the sky. Her dad laughs warmly and pats her on the back.

"Nicely done. You'll need to practice at different speeds, of course, or your muscle memory and instincts will only learn to calculate your movement at two speeds."

Calendra sighs.

"Calendra, don't be melodramatic. That's my thing. I won't have you change straight away! No, you're used to double-speed. You need to keep working with it. Time for the steps! Let me just ice them again." He claps his hands together and grins.

Calendra shakes her head as he walks up the hill towards the hot spring, whistling, bucket in hand. Confirming her Spirit is still virtually full, she follows him up the hill, scowl half-hearted, heart light.

She is far worse on the icy steps but starts to win back the thrill of perfecting a new skill. She practices, and practices, and practices. She runs at different speeds up and down hills, up and down steps, training the instincts of her body and mind to adapt to her dynamic relationship with the Manifold.

They leave the valley three days later under the cover of truenight. Calendra is exhausted, but feels a thrum of excitement at her new abilities. They continue their trek west and north along the lower parts of the Iceteeth, the great mountain range separating the three nations, sleeping in caves during daylight. They forage their food from the bountiful forest at the base of the great dividing range to make basic but nutritious meals of tubers, mushrooms, vegetables and fruit. Calendra is thankful they stick to the lower areas where food and warmth can still be found. Her muscles grow stronger and her stamina deepens until she is able to bear the weight of her own equipment rather than continuing to weigh down her dad. He seems increasingly tired.

In the afternoon of the fourteenth day since they left their temporary home, they reach a road. They follow its course at a distance for several hours until they spot a crossroads. Her dad pauses and scans their surroundings, frowning behind his growing beard.

"We have a choice to make. We are within days of the border between our two lands, Chalveno and Tolgarlo. That way," he gestures towards the setting sun, "lies Tolgarlo, the nation in which I was born. Actually, we're even within a week of the Free Cities, but in the wrong season. And while those lands hold the least chance of discovery, they also provide the least protection. They are on the far side of the mountains, that way." He gestures north-east. "Calendra, my intention was to take you straight to Tolgarlo. To our capital. The information we have must get to our leaders, both the civilian government and the Council of Artists. You'll usually just hear the Council of Artists referred to as the Nineteen. Not only has reporting back to the Nineteen been my mission for years, Sanctum is probably where you will be safest."

He pauses and looks to the sky. "Though that is not certain either, and we still need to get through the border undetected. The Announcer keeps this border closely guarded. Anyway, this is no longer my decision. It is our decision. You are my daughter, not my ward. When we began this journey, I thought of you as I might see a bowl of pristine crystal. Of great value and greater fragility. I no longer see you that way. Your skill with your Art is advancing. Your power and regeneration of Spirit is almost frightening. You are not defenseless or fragile, though you still have years of training to become all you can be, though." He shrugs, putting his full body into the motion.

Calendra has no idea what to say, so she just nods.

"So. What say you, Daughter of the Manifold. Continue to Tolgarlo, where you will be protected, attend the School of the Manifold, even be famous if you wish, while facing unknown dangers from those who discover what you know and what you can do? Or remain in Chalveno, with your Announcer hunting you, but otherwise living quietly in obscurity?"

Calendra sits on a nearby rock, eyes down, chin on fist, thinking.

"What would you do, Dad?"

"That's the wrong question, Calendra."

She considers further. The right question. "Which one will make me a better Artist?"

"Almost there."

She furrows her brow at this. Is that not the right question? "Ok. Which option will make me a better Artist in ten years' time?"

Her dad laughs, arms spread wide. "That's the right question. If we return to my lands, I will be required to resume my duties. You will attend the School of the Manifold, where you will learn about the Manifold and uses of your particular Art. You will be trained as well as any Artist in the lands and better in pure Artistry than anyone in Chalveno." He grins at her. "But you are no ordinary Artist, Calendra. Not even an ordinary Manifold Artist."

"Because of my power?"

"Sure, but that doesn't affect education, just your ability to maximize it. Education, however, is institutional. It is established to bring everyone to a minimum standard, but in doing so can fail to maximize opportunity for exceptional students. Especially for those students who think outside of the rigid structures of a universal curriculum."

Calendra nods politely. She loves that her dad does not speak down to her, but sometimes she wishes he would speak a little more plainly. She has noticed his language becomes more technical the more excited he is about a topic. She understands the point, though.

"You," he continues, "think differently. You see differently. I attended the School of the Manifold for years. Some of your thoughts are, I believe, unique. I've never heard your canvas metaphor. It's excellent. But that's neither here nor there. They will expect you to answer questions using their analogies, but will not discourage you from thinking your own way. It's your vision, this Manifold sight, that I worry about. It is like nothing I've heard of and I worry their rigid thinking will confine yours and make you somehow lose that ability."

Calendra is confused at this. What ability? "I don't understand. What makes me different?"

He smiled at her, brown eyes twinkling. "What do you think I sensed when the Announcer became Fast?"

"The same as I did? A sudden change in the canvas as he lifted off it slightly."

He laughed. "No and no. First, that is not what you described. You felt the change before he became Fast. Second, that's not how it works. For anyone. Nobody sees the canvas, as you put it. We use the idea as a way to conceptualize the shaping of our Art to achieve an effect. Far more importantly, nobody sees a Manifold Art's use before it takes effect. A normal Manifold Artist is just someone who can use an Art, not someone who can read changes in the Manifold before they happen."

Calendra has heard things to indicate this before but did not take them on board. She does now. It thrills her.

"So!" He continues his speech. "On to Tolgarlo and you can be relatively sure you'll be safe and become a top class Speed Artist. Or ... we remain in Chalveno. Near the border in case we must flee, but not so near that patrols may stumble upon us. If so, I'll leave you for a day to deliver my message, but then we hide. We will live on constant alert. Live off the land. I will be your only company, maybe for years, but you will have me at your complete disposal. I will train you far more intensely than the School of the Manifold would. I will train you, Calendra, not just a generic student. I will help you develop whatever extraordinary gifts you've been granted. You will have a chance at becoming the greatest Manifold Artist since the Traveler."

His grin widens. His eyes dance.

"You will hate it. You will hate me! You will be lonely. You will probably become an odd young woman, lacking foundational social interactions all others take for granted. But you will do things, Calendra. Great things. Things important enough to be immortalized in song. And things too important to ever be known, to ever be celebrated."

He takes a breath, halting the flood of words and emotions. He leans forward, grasps her shoulders and looks into her eyes. His mania has subsided, but his eyes betray his thrill.

"What say you, daughter? Will you be comfortable and safe and great? Or will you dance on the knife's edge and suffer and be extraordinary?"

She looks unblinking into his eyes. She closes her eyes and hums softly. She calms herself and drops into a meditative mindset, letting herself feel the canvas and her place on it.

She opens her eyes. Every sense experiences a pulse as the Manifold seems to flex around her.

The world unfurls, like half a heartbeat, as if waiting on her decision. Her heart stops with it.

Her glazed eyes clear, her jaw closes, and her nostrils flare. She looks at him. Through him. The world closes back in on itself as she makes her decision, completing its beat. Her own heartbeat resumes.

"Extraordinary."

A Memory of Kolan

One hundred and eighty years ago

K olan surfed the waves of time, feeling the undulations of reality itself. He needed more moments. He had wasted too many.

Kolan could use his Spirit - his life energy - to manipulate his relationship to time. It was a rare power. He could not change the fabric of time itself, of course, but he could change his position in the different rates of time's flow. He could move to a different Time. One of a limited number of discrete Timestreams.

He visualized it as grabbing a board and surfing along the top of a wave to make his way to where the waves were smaller, or larger, then jumping off to bob in those waters. Even that metaphor was not ideal, but it helped Kolan picture the changes he needed to make.

His master disagreed. He insisted that time was like a wide river, deep and swift in the center, shallow and slower towards the edges. The world and almost everyone in it experienced the flow of time at a consistent rate, by this thinking, bobbing along in a middling time current.

It was an inlander way to think. Kolan grew up by the shores of the mighty Ergaut Sea, not by the banks of some mangrove-lined river. Water flow rates were hard to picture. He was a child of the waves. He rode a waveboard before he could walk. The flow rate explanation bothered him, anyway. If you dropped into slower moving water, then came back, such mechanics would have you enter World Time behind the world, forever living in the past. Kolan was certain the Manifold itself would collapse before it permitted time reversal.

No. For Kolan, time was the undulations of waves created by varying winds. The larger the wave, the faster your clock ticked, like widening the hole in a water clock. Everyone moved forward through time at the same rate, but those bobbing in larger waves moved farther up and down than those on smaller waves. The distance you moved vertically determined your personal time flow, while everyone, irrespective of personal time flow, moved inexorably towards the shore at the same speed. How did that not make more sense?

He knew the waters of time, even if he saw them differently. He didn't need to understand the other Manifold Arts fully, but his master tested him on the fundamentals of the Manifold - the superstructure of the reality within which everything existed. And he had a test tomorrow!

Kolan had surfed into big seas to provide some extra studying time. He had learned a lot. He had lived eighteen Kolan hours in maybe six world hours. It was time to return to Human Time.

Feeling the rush of winds that did not exist and the taste of salt only in his mind, he diverted almost all of his remaining Spirit to surf back to waves of his world and his friends. Rejoicing in the freedom, distracted, he saw his destination arrive … and pass by.

Shocked, he mentally tried to surf back. *Fool*, he thought, *it's not an actual wave. Divert your Spirit!*

He drained his free Spirit and tried to turn the imaginary board. He slowed but drifted further before finally coming to a rest. He bobbed in waters so calm that he could barely feel any vertical movement. He tried to divert more Spirit but had none left to divert. He was told to never empty his Spirit.

After untold minutes of terror, he calmed. He had no clue what Spirit actually was, but he could always feel it thrumming with life inside him and he could use it to fuel his Art. He had learned the theory, though. Spirit fed itself. Keep a relatively full Spirit and you could constantly feed a small amount to your Art at the rate it regenerated. Lose half your free Spirit to the hunger of your Art and the regeneration rate would drop substantially, requiring the cessation of all active or passive use of your Art. Let your Art consume it all and you would be in trouble.

No free Spirit meant no Spirit regeneration. The Spirit that made up your being was bound and could not be diverted. It would slowly, through some kind of osmosis, generate a seed of Spirit from which regeneration could begin. He was stranded for now.

He was not concerned about dehydration or starvation. He was not in some void. The world, including its rivers and plants, existed in this Timestream. It was just things not of this world that were absent. Buildings, tools, furniture, humans. The world seemed to be anchored to all Timestreams, but separately. He could eat a melon here and it would not disappear from the world in Human Time. He could not interact with anything in Human Time, but he could live off the land here.

Kolan closed his eyes. He was alone. For the time it would take to reseed and generate enough Spirit to guarantee his safe return, he was alone. And time was stretched. Probably by a lot.

Kolan suspected he would miss his test.

Chapter Six

"I suspect that humanity will be enough a part of this world after a few generations to benefit from the effects of this life energy. Your grandchildren's grandchildren will be faster, stronger, smarter, and more connected to this world than you are. If you lay the ground-work."

The Traveler's Welcome

Written record from the Eightieth Year of the Great Transference, Library of the School of the Manifold, Sanctum

As Calendra sees the first hint of sunlight in hours, her dad puts his arm in her path.

"Stop, Calendra. You can only once experience a thing for the first time. Unless you're a Memory Artist. There are some things memorable enough to wish I'd been prepared for my first experience. Around the next corner is one of those things, all the more so as perspective is key. I would ask you to close your eyes until I say, but I do not trust your ability to delay gratification!" He chuckles at his own wit. "So, turn around, my daughter, and walk backwards. I will guide you."

Calendra looks blankly at him as he snuffs out the lantern. She turns and walks backwards. Her dad, walking in front from her perspective, guides her around one bend. She feels a stiff breeze and the sun on her back, and sees the cave wall illuminated. After a few dozen steps, more sideways than backwards, he halts her.

"Turn around."

She does. She understands. Perspective.

She stands in the center of a small plateau above a slope covered in long grass moving in rapid waves, the cave entrance behind her and to her left. Several hundred paces ahead stands a redwood, its two hundred paces of trunk mostly obscured by rich foliage growing almost to the ground, its crown lower than the plateau.

It is not alone. Behind it stand two more, together forming an almost perfect triangle. Behind them, three more, then four, and so on. Thousands of trees form a wedge. That wedge encircles a verdant, steamy jungle nestled at the bottom of the wedge-shaped valley. The far side of the valley is steep, formed by the roots of tall, jagged mountains. The Twin frames the image, casting the world in its soothing blue-violet light.

Calendra gapes at the order. She would not have seen how symmetrical it is from the cave entrance, how perfectly the forest nestles the jungle.

"How? It can't be natural."

"No idea how," her dad replies, "but I don't see how it could be unnatural. Unless someone long ago selectively destroyed trees to make the pattern. That wouldn't explain the even spacing between the trees. Someone could have planted them in this pattern centuries ago, but I would still expect some variation."

He shrugs at his own musings as Calendra walks forward. A step away from the edge of the plateau, she is driven forward by intense winds and begins to topple off the edge before her dad seizes her flailing arm and pulls her back.

"Either way," he goes on, "the shape of the forest channels the intense winds entering from behind us around its edges and out the broadside of the valley, protecting the more fragile jungle at the base."

A fragment of a memory surfaces.

"My … my mother used to bathe me in a river, I think. She would kneel over me, her back facing upriver. The current was strong, but as long as I was directly in front of her, I was protected from it. Is that what the forest is doing?"

"Good. Yes, your memory is probably right. Your father told me the house you lived in while she was alive backed on to a stream. You were very young then. I'm surprised you remember that."

"I can't, really. Just a flash of a memory. I guess that means it will be calmer inside the forest? We need to get there, though."

Her dad grins, walks past her to the far end of the plateau and descends from view. She follows and sees steps leading to a trench dug into the hill. The trench is around two paces deep, enough for the long grass to obscure it from view. Once inside, she only feels a stiff breeze rather than a tempest.

They pass through the grasses and the wall of redwoods. The wind stops in short order, at which point the trench slopes up to become level with the forest floor. The redwoods within are completely bare of leaves, except at their very tops, which form an interlocking canopy that blocks most light.

The ground is a world of mushrooms. Mushrooms of every color and combination of colors, some glowing softly in the still twilight world. Mushrooms a finger-width tall. Mushrooms taller than her. Branching patterns of spreading fungus.

With the undergrowth sparse, it is not long until they reach the jungle. It is wilder and unchecked, but not so strangled with life as to make progress troublesome. The air becomes warmer and more humid as they continue their descent. Sweat stinging minor cuts from close encounters with unseen branches, Calendra follows her dad through a particularly overgrown section and finds herself in a clearing.

She scrunches her eyes to squeeze from them what must be a hallucination. A circular lake lies at the center of an elliptical clearing dozens of paces wide. Steam flows upwards and outwards from the lake's surface. The area around the lake is packed with white blossoms. Nestled amongst the hundreds of blossoms, a blanket of snow-white life, is a simple wooden cottage. She turns and stares at her dad.

"How many houses do you own? Or are we visiting another friend?"

"I see my efforts to use less formal language around you are too little, too late. No, this is not my house. It belongs to an acquaintance. One who built it as a sanctuary. He gave me his blessing to use it should the need arise." He shrugs. "Not sure if that extends to a long-term stay, but if he shows up, I doubt he will be too upset."

"How did he find it? Those caves seemed to go forever. I couldn't count the number of other ways we could have taken."

"I'm not sure. When I asked, years ago, he looked wistful and told me, *I just listened, Malnor*. Strange fellow. I don't think anyone else knows about this place. He brought me here to recover from a pretty nasty gut wound. This all makes it the safest place I could think to spend a few years."

"And the flowers? I haven't seen them before. Why are they the only thing that grows here?"

"They are interesting. They're the results of an experiment he was conducting when I was here. Those flowers are vanishingly rare. They only grow in several places, and very slowly. My host - Vrailen's his name - believed they would thrive in this place. He planted some fifty seeds here, ten years ago. Seems his hypothesis was correct! Amazing. They are soulblossoms. Their exact effect and nature are not well understood, but when consumed, they seem to nurture one's connection to the Manifold."

Calendra's breath catches. She has felt the effects of eating the right things. There are thousands of them!

"They are rich in Spirit," her dad continues. "Spirit that is closely aligned to the Manifold. A Manifold Artist that consumes them should enforce their Spirit, improving their capacity and perhaps their power. Some of this is uncertain. They're rare and costly. They should be very valuable for any Artist, most of all for a Manifold Artist. Which leaves us with something of an ethical quandary. From the even height of all these flowers, I assume their owner has either not been here in years or has felt no need to harvest them. We could be here for some years. If these flowers grow as quickly as I suspect, we could benefit from them and still let them grow back by the time he needs them. If he ever does. On the other hand, we're already staying without welcome and they represent significant wealth. What are a couple of Manifold Artists to do?"

Calendra tries to contain her excitement. She looks around the clearing and notices the entrance to the cottage is a dozen paces from the outer edge of the soulblossoms. She smiles.

"We have to get to the cottage, right?"

"Must be forty, fifty that we can't avoid trampling." He winks. "Gentle, though. It's important to remove the entire flower, roots and all. Dig around the edges carefully, with your finger if you need to. Lay each one out, petals up, as you go."

Eager, Calendra walks to the point closest to the cottage and begins removing soulblossoms with care. Her dad gestures when the path is wide enough. She continues as he lies on the ground, eyes closed, a soft smile on his face. She continues until the sun's light becomes faint. Her dad starts gathering the flowers into delicate bundles when she is almost at the cottage.

Finally, with over two hundred soulblossoms gathered, they open the door to their new home. It is simple but adequate, with two narrow beds, a table with two chairs, a wood stove with cooking space and chimney, and a series of general purpose benches. With further exploration, Calendra is relieved to discover a basic squat toilet dozens of paces from the cottage. She happily removes enough soulblossoms to create a path to it as daylight turns to twilight.

She settles in. After a short time in thoughtful silence, they eat a basic dinner of local ingredients foraged and grilled by her dad. She retires to her bed holding a soulblossom. One a night for now, they agreed.

Calendra meditates. She thinks about where she is and the life around her. She thinks about the canvas, trying to see it without diverting Spirit. She settles her breathing, steadies her mind and puts the entire blossom in her mouth. She grinds it evenly, then swallows. She closes her eyes and reaches out to the world around her.

The world expands and contracts in a brief pulse, during which she sees an image of the canvas and her place on it. She sees the soulblossom's place on it as it becomes one with her.

She feels a thrum. A brief connectedness to the life of the valley. Then she falls asleep, thinking of the canvas once again.

CHAPTER SEVEN

"Learn to be part of this world. One with it. It is our nature to shape our surroundings to suit ourselves. This place has a finely balanced perfection. It is yourself that you must shape, to become a part of this balance."

The Traveler's Welcome

Written record from the Eightieth Year of the Great Transference, Library of the School of the Manifold, Sanctum

Calendra reclines on her lounging chair with eyes half-lidded and meditates on the soulblossoms. Under the branches of a beautiful tree to which she has taken a particular liking, she feels the warmth of the lake as she sips fruit-infused cooled spring water and nibbles at leaf-wrapped spiced tuber.

Over many weeks at her new home, her dad has focused her efforts on learning the valley, especially its sources of food, and focused her mind on processing her new environment. Her daily dried soulblossom helps her mental focus, but she is getting restless.

Her dad lounges beside her on his own chair. The mysterious owner of the residence apparently made the chairs before dismantling them and putting them in storage. With the tools in the cottage, it takes little time for her dad to assemble them. She throws a piece of tuber the size of a knuckle through the thin fog. It hits him in the ear.

"I'm bored!"

Her dad leaps out of the chair. He claps his hands loudly, cups them around his mouth, throws his head back and booms to the heavens.

"The day is here! Zem, Traveler, the Nineteen, Announcer, hosts of the heavens - harken to me! It begins!"

He runs triple-speed down the blossomless path towards the cottage, fog swirling, and disappears inside. Seconds later, he emerges with a small bag and returns, holding out a series of cushioned pads with straps attached. The local materials and craftsmanship show all the signs of his 'better than good - good enough' philosophy.

"Put these on, oh listless child of mine. Large ones covering chest, midriff and back. Medium on shoulders and knees. Small ones on elbows and ankles. Gloves on hands. Helmet on restless noggin."

Calendra considers looking bemused, but the source of her dad's excitement is not mysterious. Combat training. Finally! Her first father's wonderful stories of her mother's days as a young martial scout patrolling the border with the Free Cities sounded fantastical as a child, but now ... well, maybe she should have been bored earlier. She dons the equipment as her dad straps on his much larger pads. Once they are done, her dad addresses her.

"No becoming Fast for now. One point if you make contact with me. Two, if you hit me with something decent. Three, if you gain an advantage over me, somehow."

Somehow? Calendra vows to hit him in the face. "And what do I do with these points?"

"Do with them? Why, you gather them up, walk about a thousand miles to Sanctum, find a town crier and have him report your successes to the waiting crowds. Oh, they will come. Bless us, they'll wail! Lay hands upon us in blessings, in the name of ..."

She cuts him off. "When I break your nose, Da, it won't be because I don't love you."

He leans back, arms held over his stomach, and mimes laughter, before adopting a fighting stance and staring at her, eyes blazing.

"Come at me then."

She does. To play to her advantages of speed and agility, she launches off her left foot and angles towards his weaker left side, but changes direction as her right foot lands. She ducks as she angles towards his right side. With his weight already moving to his left, he seems caught off guard as his eyes dart down to her feet and he lashes out with his right fist.

Calendra comes in low and plants her left foot just in front of his right. She spins to circle behind him as she launches her left fist towards his unprotected back. A smile flashes over his face as, lightning fast, he pushes off his right foot and spins. Her blow misses by a hair, leaving her overbalanced.

Laughing, he bends at the waist and his right arm rockets towards her. It comes to a halt just before her face. His index finger extends and, almost tenderly, pushes against the center of her forehead. It is enough, with her angular momentum and shaky footwork, to send her sprawling in the fog.

"Very good," he tells her as she rises and rubs her bruised butt. "How did you do that?"

Calendra cocks her head. "I pictured it and did it. It was only a few steps."

Her dad stares at her. "Ok, but how did you move so smoothly? It was like you've been fighting all your life. Did they teach you in school?"

"I don't know, Dad. I planned it, emptied my mind and my body followed."

"Your father never ..." He shook his head. "Never mind. Good. That was a clever move. Using your brain in combat is half the skill. Of course, you can only plan a fight one or two moves ahead before you need to adapt, but it's a good start. A thousand more of them and hopefully your body will keep up with your mind. Again!"

Calendra charges. Her dad does not move other than to trace her path with his eyes. Her second step, off her left foot, becomes a jump. Her third becomes a leap. She flies towards her dad. He does not move. She unleashes a right hook at the last moment, aimed at his smug grin. At the last moment, so quickly Calendra would need to be Fast to see it, his right arm rockets up and catches her fist an inch from his face. It is like punching a moss-covered rock. Her hand moves no further,me, but her momentum, forward and angular, causes the rest of her body to shoot forward and to the right.

Her dad casually steps back and to the left, letting her lower body shoot past him while he still holds her fist. He releases before her arm snaps and she lands butt-first on the ground. Again. On exactly the same part of her butt.

Her dad laughs a long, hearty laugh. "Should've made butt pads, huh? Again!"

"Are you sure you're not Fast, Dad? You're so quick. How can I match this without my Art?"

"I promise, Calendra. I could, in the name of your education, but I'm not. You need to see what the body is capable of without Spirit. Too many Artists become so accustomed to using their Art that they forget about mundane training. Wasteful. Not just for the times in which you cannot use Spirit. It is wasteful of power potential. Speed Artistry multiplies. Mathematics does not get more simple. So once you are quicker than me we'll start throwing your Art into the mix. Not before. For either of us. Agreed?"

Calendra nods slowly. "Agreed".

Her dad spreads his arms wide. "Again!"

It is weeks of going to sleep bruised, though somehow waking up fresh, before she earns a point. She is only somewhat surprised at how natural it comes to her - most skills have in her brief life - but her dad is always just ahead of her. Her first points come from a decent kick to the back of the knee. For the following weeks, she gains a point every few bouts without getting close to gaining an advantage.

It is not until a dozen weeks later that she receives her first three-pointer. The cost is a bloodied nose. In a proper fight it would have been a broken nose, as her dad clearly pulled the punch. She does not care. She accepts the blow for position. Her dad's fist makes contact a split second before she sweeps his legs out from under him. She slides away and finishes with her knee on his neck, her thumb on his eyeball and her blood dripping onto his forehead.

"I wid!" she screams in his face, afternoon rains falling about them.

Her dad beams, pushes the thumb away and motions for Calendra to remove the knee.

"Superb, my girl. Superb. Not just the move, and your improved reflexes, but your willingness to accept pain to be great, and your judgement in knowing when it's required. I'm very proud of you."

He continues talking for a time, but Calendra's head is ringing from her dad's pride. And from getting punched in the face by a man-shaped bag of muscle.

It is another few weeks until he finally allows her to use her Art. By this stage, she has fulfilled her sacred vow by punching her dad in the face, though only once, and scores multiple points each bout. She even gains a three-pointer every ten bouts or so.

"Let's try some Speed Artistry, Calendra. Double." In fighting stance, he beckons to her. "Come at me, foe!"

Calendra becomes Fast.

Calendra is exploding forward. Ten paces. Five. One. Her dad is sidestepping. She is swinging. Her fist is hurtling through the air ... two paces past her dad. Calendra is stumbling. Stopping diversion of Spirit ...

Calendra becomes Normal. She hits the ground.

"Again!" comes the cry from behind.

She rises and walks slowly towards her dad. Two paces out, Calendra becomes Fast.

Calendra is moving. Swinging. Her dad is moving his head. She is missing. Completing a full spin. Falling forward and to the right. Her dad is stepping back. She is jumping up. The height of her leap is surprising. She is throwing a left jab. He is pivoting. Her arm's momentum is throwing her off balance. She is hitting the ground. Ceasing flow of Spirit ...

Calendra becomes Normal. She frowns. "This is harder than I thought".

He nods, not joking around this time. "People don't realize. Some Arts just improve you with little effort on your part. People think Speed Artists can just do normal things, faster. That is not true. When you're Fast, you're not doing a normal thing quickly. You're doing a new thing. Your body, having spent years learning to match your reflexes and muscle memory to your natural attributes, takes time to adapt. You found this while running. If your speed is doubled, a punch with your normal effort will move twice as fast, but it will not carry twice the force. It seems more like the distance between you and other things is halved. This requires mental adjustment as neither mind nor body expect to reach the same place in half the time. You must retrain your body to adapt to any speed multiplier in effect. This takes repetition, experimentation and focus." He shoots a toothy grin at her. "So. Again?"

Calendra rubs her bruised hip. Repetition. Alright. "Again."

CHAPTER EIGHT

"This world has welcomed you. Repay its generosity with respect."

The Traveler's Welcome, Fourth Refrain

Excerpt from a transcription of the Canonic Oral Traditions of Chalveno

C alendra flies from tree to tree, catching each vine and using her momentum to launch her to the next. After six years in the Valley, it has become second nature. It teaches her to balance momentum with short bursts of speed. And it has become her favorite way to burn off some energy.

She is not supposed to do it without her dad there. Especially in the afternoon, when the daily rainfall would make the branches slick. At the speed she flies, a bad slip could leave her crippled and without help. Then she would face a long and painful recovery, during which she would be unable to escape his lessons when she got bored.

Well, he is not due back for another day from 'checking his mail' and need not know. After a third of her life spent in the Valley - learning its rhythms, walking through it, meditating on it - she feels such a oneness with her jungle that she cannot imagine harm coming to her.

Besides, her mental state will not allow for a slip. Her meditative mindset has seeped into her everyday life. *Try not to try*, her dad told her. *Once you know the world and know yourself, you will not need to think. You will flow.*

Flow she does. Her senses paint a picture below the level of awareness, and her body follows her will. It has been her painting that has helped that the most, rediscovering her childhood love for color and texture, feeling closer to her Valley home with every painting. She has long given up on figuring out where he got the materials.

Just as she releases one vine, moving at pace, she feels a lurch and sees the world bend, flex, and revert in an instant. She lands hard. The canvas changing is no surprise. She sees it every time she or her dad become Fast. But this is not her, and it is not him, and it is not Speed Artistry. She only has one data point, as her dad would call it, but it feels similar to her experience at the Descension. A Spatial Artist!

After a moment's consideration, she runs towards the cottage. This is her home. If she must flee, few can catch her. She is a Speed Artist. She is the Daughter of the Manifold. This is her jungle. Still, she is circumspect enough to slow as she arrives and approach quietly.

She peers through vines and sees a tall, slim man, blonde, maybe late thirties, lounging in her chair. Her chair. Under her tree. The tree she feels closer to each week. Her tree. She grabs a thick branch and squeezes through a gap in the vines.

Calendra becomes Fast.

Calendra is running. One step. Two steps. Three steps. Calendra is slowing. Skidding. Turning. Extending her branch. Halting in front of the man. Holding her makeshift sword at his throat.

Calendra becomes Normal.

The man slowly raises his left eyebrow. "Who in the name of Tolgan's sacred balls are you? And why in the name of Tolgan's sacred mem..."

Calendra cuts him off. "You first. How did you find me?"

The man chuckles, shaking his head. "I have no worldly clue who you are, girl. I came here hoping to find Malnor."

She lets out a held breath. "Malnor is my father."

The man's brow furrows before realization seems to dawn. "Ahh. The brother's girl. I see. I'm glad you inherited his Art. A useful skill indeed." He grins at her. "Not as nifty as mine."

Calendra's eyes are down, briefly caught in a memory of her first dad painting with her. Helping her move the brush. Helping her capture the face of the mother she can remember in fact, but not in her mind's eye. She pulls herself out of it. She walks to a lounging chair and sits.

"Thank you. And it may be fun to teleport where you want, but I'll take an Art that brings me closer to the fight, not far from it." That earns her a chuckle.

"Very good. Though it's certainly gotten me into a fight or two. Your father told you about my Art? No, I guess he needn't have. How else would I have arrived without being seen? Or you saw me. You got to me quickly."

"I felt you arrive." She waved her hand dismissively. "This is my Valley. My home. I know when it changes."

"Your valley? Your home? I discovered this ... What did you say? Felt my arrival? Nonsense. But I appreciate your love of this place. I still haven't found something similar."

Calendra's nostrils flare in response. "Don't call me a liar."

The man looks into her eyes, studying her. She stares right back, defiant. He finally speaks.

"You're certainly earnest. Are you telling me, to be clear, that you didn't know I'm a Spatial Artist, you didn't see my arrival with your eyes, hear it with your ears, smell it with your nose - yet you knew when I arrived, where I arrived and which Art I accessed?"

"Yes. I felt the change in the canvas. The Manifold. I felt the Manifold change. I felt the world redraw itself to include you in this place. It's different from the change that's made when my dad or I use Speed Artistry."

The man's eyes widen as she speaks. They look like they might split as she finishes. He takes in a slow breath and releases it.

"I don't know, daughter of Malnor, if you understand what you're saying. Well, if you understand the context within which you're saying it."

She shrugs. "My dad told me it's not something people do."

He shakes his head, a strange smile on his face. "It's not something anyone does. I developed an interest in the Era of Settlement during my youth. I've read more about the Manifold than most people alive. I've never read an account like this. Your father will help you understand this gift. I have no time. Where is he? Actually, what's your name? Maybe we'll do that first."

"Calendra." She dips her head towards him.

"Pleasure, Calendra." He returns the gesture. "Vrailen."

"How do I know you're a friend of my dad?"

Vrailen frowns, then adopts a different air. "Calendra," he announces in an uncanny imitation of her dad's tenor, "harken to me! Do you not yet see the advantageousness of caution? Be cautious, for threefold are the reasons! The wise loiter, it is said. And while the other reasons are lost to time's caress, the message is clear. Now, run over there and retrieve to me the sun, for I desire it!"

"Good enough," she says with a grin. "He's a bit better these days. Sometimes he talks to me like I'm a person rather than a packed theater. He's checking his messages. Outside the valley."

"Bah! Of all the times. Can you tell me, in detail, where he would be?"

"I haven't been there. He calls it a 'dead drop'. He goes from time to time."

"Blight and pestilence! When is he due back?"

"Tomorrow."

Vrailen holds a hand to his temple and strokes his chin. "Ok. I wait. I considered teleporting outside the valley and either searching or waiting there, but I can't afford the Spirit. I'm low from getting here and I may need it, depending on your father's decision."

"Decision? What is this about? I can use my Art to try to find him."

"No, Calendra." He shakes his head vehemently. "Depending on your father's decision, you might need all the Spirit you can keep. A day is frustrating but not fatal, depending on his next move."

"What. Decision."

"Whether to run for election to the Nineteen."

"The Nineteen? Who are they?"

"The Nineteen are a collection of Artists and Donors who represent the various Arts. While they don't hold formal power - that is in the hands of a popularly elected government - they control the direction the Schools of the Arts take, they have enormous influence in the Artistic economy, and they unite Artists across the nation. There have been periods in the past that have seen the subjugation of Artists. The Nineteen was established to ensure protection of Artists in a way that does not threaten the civilian affairs of state. The history of their establishment, the need for it in the first place, means they seldom make decisions that directly affect the nation. But if they do, and if Artists side with them, no government can oppose them. Still, internal divisions within, and between, the Arts rage on."

Calendra stares at him before answering. "And this relates to my dad, how?"

Vrailen looks at her, eyes tinged with sadness. "Your Grandmother has passed from this world and become part of the Manifold. She was a member of the Nineteen. She represented Speed Artists. Her death is a great blow to Tolgarlo's stability. She helped bridge differences between Manifold Artists and Mind Artists and was ... well, was really the only representative of the Manifold Arts in whom I held any faith. Your father must know, grieve and decide."

Calendra's grandmother? Dead?

"Your grandmother was the glue that bound them. The kindly fingers with an iron grip. There are very few Speed Artists and even fewer with the experience and wisdom to sit on the Nineteen. Your father's been away for years, but his mother's radiance shines from him and he's made few enemies. He's the most likely candidate to maintain unity, which makes him the best candidate to unite the Speed Artists, and then the various voting blocs."

Calendra breathes out slowly, trying to process the river of information. "Do I have any family left to meet?" She does not mean to say it out loud.

"I'm sorry, Calendra. She was a mighty woman. I think she would be full of joy to see the woman you are becoming. She was looking forward to meeting you, but she approved of your father's decision to stay hidden in Chalveno. Didn't he speak of her?"

"He spoke of her as a mother, but not as a woman, and not in the present. He speaks so reluctantly of family, and they ..." Calendra struggles with the words, feeling them to be a betrayal.

"They are far, and you don't know them. I understand. Don't feel guilty about this. Once Malnor decided to remain here with you, I think he would have avoided dwelling on matters beyond you both. That's his nature. Thoughtful but decisive. Once he decides, he doesn't let sentiment stand in its way."

Calendra, to her shock and shame, cries. "It's my fault. He let me decide. I chose to stay so I could be the best. And ... and so I would have him to myself, not have to be without him for weeks at a time. But I cost him the last days with his true family."

"Calendra, don't take this on yourself. He knew when he moved to your nation that he might never see her again. Had you never needed to flee, he would still be in Chalvstrom and wouldn't have seen her. More than that, he isn't a hesitant man. If he gave a child the choice, it was because he believed in you. His message to the Nineteen only spoke of your Art, your prodigious power, and your dangerous knowledge. It didn't speak of the thing far more wondrous. Far more dangerous."

"That I can see the Manifold?"

"Malnor is no fool. He knows such a thing cannot be discovered by the wrong people. The Announcer may want you captive to protect his secret, but there are people in Tolgarlo and Chalveno who'd stop at nothing to find you and exploit your ability. I suspect I'm the only other person on this planet to know your truth."

He smiles, lightening the mood.

"I need to rest. My Spirit is low and regenerating too slowly. I must recover it before Malnor arrives. I hope you've realized something he really should have drummed into you. Never mention your ability. Not unless you trust your life and the lives of everyone you love in that person's hands. And only if you are beyond certain that no other can hear. This applies to your ability to detect a change in the Manifold before it happens, and to your ability to see its nature. You'll need to trust someone eventually, though. Choose carefully."

He rises and starts plucking soulblossoms. "Have these helped?" His grin indicates they should not have helped themselves to his priceless possessions, but that he is not upset.

"They're incredible. I feel an immediate connection to the world around me from just one and I feel closer to the Manifold every day."

"Good. I ask that you use them carefully, if you stay. They grow in only a few years in this place, so it's easy to pick and plant by rotation. Malnor can do the math, but I suspect you can easily consume ten of these a day."

Calendra's heart soars as he walks away.

"Oh, and Calendra?" Vrailen turns to her. "I have two more gardens of these. Please use them carefully, but if worse becomes worst - if this valley's discovered - do not let them fall into enemy hands."

He retires to the cottage as Calendra grabs her supplies, reclaims her chair, and paints the night's soulblossoms.

CHAPTER NINE

"I believe the spiritual energy created by life can be shaped to a far finer point by humans. If you develop a means to generate and control it."

The Traveler's Welcome

Written record from the Eightieth Year of the Great Transference, Library of the School of the Manifold, Sanctum

C alendra and Vrailen lounge on their chairs shortly after smallnight. The old tree seems more and more important to this place, especially when she is meditating on the canvas. This is her favorite spot as the view of her tree is perfectly framed by the waxing Twin above.

It is her favorite day of the year. The Spawn. She never feels quiet so close to her trees as when the air itself is alive with life. It is only for two days each year that the flowering plants of the world - every one - release their pollen into the breezes. Two days of pollen and seeds of every color and shape spinning and dancing through the air, looking for the perfect place to land. Two days of coughing and wheezing, to be sure, but to wear a mask is to reject nature. Calendra embraces it.

The sound of snapping branches comes from outside the clearing. They both leap to their feet, pollen flying, as Calendra's dad pushes through a thicket. He sees her and smiles. Then he sees Vrailen. He freezes before grinning broadly.

"Vrai! I thought you'd never come!"

He walks towards Vrailen, arms wide. Vrailen embraces him with a warmth that seems more than that of acquaintances.

"It's good to see you, old friend. Please, I am here with sad tidings and urgent timeframes. Your mother …"

Calendra's dad freezes once more. He sighs and moves to an empty lounging chair. He sits on the edge, looks up at Vrailen and nods once.

"Your mother, Malnor, has become one with the Manifold. I am so sorry. She lived a full life, but to lose one of the greatest of her generation is grievous. She will be sorely missed by all who understand what she did and saw who she was."

He bows his head, hands clasped white-knuckle on his knees, eyes closed. Tears start to form and flow down the sides of his proud nose, like a once dry waterfall after an upstream flood. She has never seen him cry. He is silent, though. For a minute he says nothing. Finally, he wipes his eyes with his sleeves, opens his eyes, and stands.

"Thank you, Vrai, for breaking the news. I'm grateful to learn of it sooner than I might have. Surely sharing news of her passing isn't the reason for urgency. I assume you'd have me replace her?"

Vrailen gives him a sad smile. "Who else, Mal? Golndil? The man's been living Slow for thirty years! He would rather live centuries alone than decades with purpose. Narelda? She loves that school. Loves her kids. Even if she would give that up, she knows only the school. It's her whole universe. She probably doesn't even know who's on the Nineteen! Or how about Yaldon, yes? He's the next most likely. Can you imagine? Yaldon speaking for your Art and making decisions with the like of Alvertus."

He gives a visible shudder. Calendra's dad grimaces.

"No, Mal. There are others that might do, but will they gain the support of the Speed Artists? Even if they do, will they have the sway within the Nineteen to hold things together as your mother did? I think not. If you are not in contention, Yaldon will win. Speed Artists are accustomed to having a strong representative. They will not trade that for someone weaker, even if they worry about the Nineteen's composition. You must run."

Calendra's dad rubs his eyes, weariness writ large. He looks back up at Vrailen. "You've met her? Seen her talent? You understand what I'm doing here?"

Vrailen nods, expression solemn. "I know more than you realize. More than I should. She told me what she sees! Dammit Mal, did you not impress on her the importance of keeping it quiet?"

Calendra watches with surprise as her dad's eyes widen before he adopts a guilty expression. Something she has also never seen.

"It's my second time away in half a year, Vrai. We haven't seen another soul for years. I trust you with this, of course. I wish it weren't your burden to bear, but I trust your discretion."

"Of course I see what you're doing here, Mal. You're protecting an asset of unquantifiable value and making sure it is as valuable as possible in the future. I ..."

Her dad holds his hand up to silence Vrailen. "Vrai, I know you mean no offense, but she is my daughter. Named. Loved. I'm protecting my child, who's of unquantifiable value to me, and teaching her to protect herself from a world that will see her as an asset rather than a woman."

Vrailen bows his head. "Apologies. As you say. So yes, I see what you are doing, both as a father who wants the best for his daughter, and as a citizen of this world protecting a person who might improve it. I admire your personal sacrifices. Were the choice between stabilizing your country and protecting your daughter, I would still ask, but not push. But is that the choice, Mal? Or is it a false dichotomy? Might you be able to protect her, help her development, even spend time with her, but in Sanctum? Can you protect the future and preserve the present?"

Calendra watches her dad as he listens to Vrailen's pitch. His expression flickers between sadness, consideration, anger and surprise. Once Vrailen finishes, her dad laughs for the first time since learning the sad news.

"Worked on that for a while, eh? You didn't use one conjunction."

Vrailen bursts out laughing, the tension released.

"My rehearsal was a bit more formal, but more emotive. I had to use the word dichotomy, Mal. Dichotomy! I rehearsed so much it poisoned my mind. I was speaking to poor Calendra like a historian." His eyes flick to her briefly. "She seemed to understand it though. Do you talk to your daughter in speeches, Mal? Do you teach her words like dichotomy?"

Calendra's dad really laughs this time. He calms himself eventually and takes deep breaths until his smile slips into the start of a frown.

"Maybe, Vrai. Maybe I can do both. She could go to the School but I fear they will carve her into the same shape they did us. They will chip away at her genius until it is blunted. I want to keep teaching her myself. Perhaps I can do that in Sanctum. Or perhaps my duties will prevent it and she will languish. And, of course, the chances of someone discovering her talent increase. She's no fool, but the tiniest gasp, the smallest movement of the eyes at the wrong time ..."

"How about this, Mal. If you win, I'll provide a tutor for her. She can enroll in the School, learn what she can from them, train with you when you are able, and every other moment she will have the resources to train. I can't promise a dedicated Speed Artist but we can put together a group of trustworthy combat soldiers and Physical Artists for the rest. If she even needs any of it. Maybe she'd do well in a more traditional environment after years of your training?"

"Hmmm. That could work. Your financial fortunes continue?"

Vrailen waves away the question. "I have a sizable income from previous finds and some substantial assets that no market can yet price. I'm not worried about minor expenses."

Calendra sees a change in her dad. He starts to agree with Vrailen.

"You make a good case, Vrai," he says, as Calendra feels a vibration in the canvas. From his decision? Like when she made the decision to stay in Chalveno? "We still need to figure out transportation," he continues, as Calendra's focus draws within. "The valley is a long ..."

Calendra stops listening. She sees it. Not around her, but beyond her. The world stretches towards the Valley's entrance, but upwards. As if the canvas has been pushed up in one spot, leaving the surrounding canvas sloping up towards it. A change in the Manifold she has never seen. It is not stable. But if not speed or spatial ...

Calendra becomes Fast. Very Fast.

Calendra is feeling the canvas. Watching. Seeing it more clearly at such speed. Like a bubble forming. Expanding. The canvas is stretching further. Like a finger poking a rubber sheet. The stretching is increasing. The bubble is popping. The canvas settling. She is picturing the location of the bubble on the canvas. It is at the entrance. And ... up ...

Calendra becomes Normal.

"... Sanctum. We need to ...".

Calendra cuts off her dad's musings. "Stop!"

Both men freeze, colorful pollen drifting past their wide eyes. Calendra speaks like her mouth is full of sap-covered pebbles.

"Artist. Above the Valley entrance. Gravity Artist in the air." She gasps, unable to say more. She is more terrified than when they fled from a god.

Her dad growls. "Now?" he spits. "They come now? Whoresons! I'll kill them. Every one of them."

He trembles with anger. Calendra's fear rises. She has never seen him like this. She does not know whether her dad has changed or revealed an anger long held within.

"Still your rage, Malnor!" Vrailen snaps. "We need data before we act." He closes his eyes for a moment. "I'll check. My Spirit will suffer, but I can manage two at short range."

Calendra feels the same flex of the canvas as days before and Vrailen disappears as the canvas changes to show him painted elsewhere. High. Very high. Half a minute later, amidst total silence, she feels it again. Vrailen appears where he left.

"Rot and decay, Mal. We're screwed." He looked wrung out. "The Valley is gone. There are too many. No way to kill them all. With that many, including a bloody Gravity Artist, we'd be fools to think the ones here are all who know."

Calendra's dad looks at him, eyes and lips showing calculation replacing the rage. "You're able to leave, Vrai?" Vrailen nodded. "Then we get Calendra beyond their reach, above all else."

Calendra objects but her dad silences her with a gesture. "Daughter, I swear to you I'll do what I can to get myself out. I have no desire for a heroic death, but nothing you say can change my will. Do not sway me on this."

She nods in understanding, determined to help. He addresses Vrailen again.

"Thoughts? What are their positions? Their numbers?"

"Gravity Artist fifty paces above the entrance. Forties, male, dark hair, light tan skin, blue coat. Not sure if any others are Artists but I saw twelve more, varying ages, all wearing deep green. All crowded around the entrance, out of the wind. Watching."

"Hmmm. Take it to them? We can use the ditch. It may prevent them from seeing us until we're upon them. Or we lure them into the forest, separate them and take them down one by one. If they're Physical Artists, things could get dicey."

The Spatial Artist rubs at his brow, considering. After a short time, he addresses them both. "My Spirit won't get me to Sanctum, but it will get me to a colleague who can get me the rest of the way. As that journey is considerably shorter than the one I'd planned for, I have two more short range jumps in me. I can think of two ways I can use them. I can disguise myself as you and surrender while you two sneak past, deal with any guards and escape. I simply jump away once you do. Or ..." he grins, his eyebrows bouncing, "I can take out the Manifold Artist."

Despite his world crashing down around him, Calendra's dad grins back. He rubs his hands together. "Oh, that would be fun to watch. I don't know, though. That's a lot left for me."

"You know I can't fight. What serves you better? A distraction, or taking out the Gravity Artist?"

He spends some time chewing on this. "If our aim was just to escape this place, I'd say the distraction is better. It's not, though. It's to get Calendra safely to Tolgarlo. That Gravity Artist can't do much to bar our passage, but he might be capable of stopping her from reaching the border. Greater chance of escape now against greater chance of safety outside the Valley. Not to mention taking an enemy Manifold Artist out of the picture. That is worth something." He turns to Calendra. "What do you think? What is the wise thing to do?"

"How do we know they're enemies? How do we know the Manifold Artist deserves death?"

Her dad jolts back as if struck. "Rotting luck. Blessed with a daughter ten times the person I am. That is the right question, Calendra, though I forgot to ask it. I thought of myself as an outsider while with your people, but they're still people. You're right to pull my focus away from black and white." His eyes dart over to Vrailen. "False dichotomies."

They both laugh until Calendra snaps her fingers at them.

"Anyway," her dad continues, "whether the individual men and women are enemies, or deserving of death, if they work for someone I deem a threat to your life or liberty, they're an enemy. If, whoever they work for, they represent an immediate threat to us, they're an enemy. And if, no matter who they are, they won't let us pass unmolested, I'll do what I must to overcome them. But we can't know any of this unless we ask."

Calendra lets her eyes defocus. The sounds of rustling leaves. The sensation of the world humming. The smell of moss and mush... well, no, not mushrooms. Had there been fewer in the Valley than when they first arrived, now she thought of it?

She realizes she is being distracted and lets her mind relax again. The smell of moss. The sound of the wind. The sight of blurry white, punctuated by darker shapes.

Her eyes snap open. Blurry white. How could she forget? They literally surround the three Artists. Soulblossoms.

"The blossoms! We can't leave them! You said, Vrailen. They can't fall into enemy hands." She throws her stare at both the men. "I haven't explained how important they are to me. The difference they've made. Just here and there. To leave this many ... Please. You say you need to talk to them, Dad. So, talk to them. Buy us time. If," she points her forefinger at him menacingly, "you're sure of being able to use Speed Artistry to escape. If your escape closes off, I'd rather keep you than some blossoms."

Calendra's dad smiles and starts to respond when Vrailen interjects.

"He can't guarantee that, Calendra. Not with that many of them there, Arts unknown. But I can. It's not likely these people have met your father. They'll just have a description. One of them will have seen him coming back from the dead drop. They'll have realized who you are. They may not know your face though. So, I will go. I assure you that at the first sign of genuine danger, I will selflessly escape and pray for your survival. Thankfully, it's very, very hard to trap a Spatial Artist or kill one on their guard. Also, I can talk the bark off an ironwood. I'll buy you time. You won't know how much, though. I'll have no way to warn you." He rubs his hands together, looking excited.

"Oh, I'll know when you leave," Calendra told him.

"Ha," Vrailen replied, "you will too. Baffling stuff. Good. Best case scenario then, other than them turning out to be adventurers of no threat to us, is that I tangle them in riddles for twenty minutes before they come at me. Then I run into the forest, where Mal will wait, and run madly in one direction, keeping away from the jungle and clearing, while Mal picks them off. If they get too close, or enough of them overtake us, he uses his Art to get to you in time. You both do your little speed thing, circle back around them and run. I return here, punch a hole in reality and step out the other side with five thousand of one of the world's rarest items. Everyone wins. Except my poor valley, of course."

"That's a plan!" Calendra claps with enthusiasm. "Don't forget that I can kick some ass out there. My dad taught me a few things and my Spirit is stronger than when we arrived here. Much stronger. I know, I know. My freedom comes first. I promise. If I must, though, or if you're in danger and I can tip the scales, I'll get in there. Do some harvesting."

"Ha! She really is your daughter. Alright, Calendra. My suggestion is to strip the petals with your fingers. They detach easily. Forget about the roots. Stuff them straight into the spare traveling sacks, tight as you can. When it gets dicey, we all grab what we can. If we're occupied, take what you can and throw the rest in the spring. Oh, and let's each eat as many of the damn things as we can. Stuff your face and your pockets, Mal."

Vrailen grins at Mal like they are children about to play with a new toy.

"It's time to break spacetime."

The two men run to the cottage while Calendra uses fingers and thumbs to strip petals, stuffing some in her mouth as she goes and washing them down with water when needed. The growing carpet of multi-colored pollen is disturbed wherever she kneels and she inhales lungfuls of it, requiring more water. The men are back out in minutes, mouths full of soulblossom petals. Their pockets overflow with them. Her dad takes a drink and drops a pack next to her.

"Put on the gloves in the heavy pack before you strip your fingers to the bone. Knee pads as well. You could be here for two hours if we can buy you that. Take two minutes to setup right so you can run like the circle winds when you need to. Fill the bags as much as you can. There's also water in there to wash down what you eat. Be fast, not careful. And please, Calendra, conserve your Spirit. You might need it."

Calendra nods. She has practiced extensively at her dad's direction to figure out how Fast she can live while the lost Spirit matches the rate it regenerates. Her dad has told her that most Artists do this permanently, especially Physical and Mind Artists. Speed Artists do not, of course, as they age faster by doing so. She knows she will conserve nothing, but what is some lost time against the benefit of thousands of soulblossoms?

Calendra dons the equipment. Her dad pulls her up and embraces her.

"I think we'll be alright my girl, but know this. Burn it into your memory. I love you, daughter of mine, and I am proud of you beyond measure. The years of just you and I have been my most joyful and I ... I regret it took a crisis to make that happen. If it goes poorly, get to Tolgarlo. To Sanctum. Do not identify yourself to anyone unless you're arrested. Say you're a refugee from Chalveno otherwise. Find Vrailen. Be what you were meant to be."

He kisses her on the forehead and steps back, flustered. Vrailen hands her a folded sheet of paper.

"This is the location of my colleague, near the border. He is a thing beyond rarity. A Spatial Donor. He can teleport others. He can get you to Sanctum."

He bows to her and walks to her dad, who addresses her one more time.

"Calendra, we won't be able to communicate. If you finish before I'm back, run to the exit. Don't wait for me. I'll lead them the other way. If you hear me shouting, run. Stop for nothing. I love you."

He turns and runs. Vrailen follows.

Calendra goes to her knees and strips petals with each hand. Strip. Store. Strip. Store. Strip. Swallow. Strip. Store. She finds a rhythm. Her eyes lose focus. Her hands move by feel.

The minutes pass by. The endless pollen of the Spawn starts to fall like iridescent rain. Petals fly. She begins to feel the world match her rhythm, pulsing in time with her hands. Her hands matching the rhythm of the world. She aligns her Speed Artistry to her Spirit's increasing regeneration rate. She continues her movements to the world's rhythm, eating as she goes. Her chest feels as if it is expanding. Her limbs feel a need to stretch, to disperse the energy that courses through her. Her pace increases.

Strip Store Strip Store Strip Swallow Strip Store.

The world's rhythm matches her accelerating pace.

StripStoreStripStoreStripSwallowStripStore.

She sees the canvas through closed eyes. It thrums and pulses to the rhythm of her work. The rhythm of the world. She feels like her tree is in the center of the pulses. Faster.

After time unknown, so deep in the rhythm that nothing could break it, she cracks open an eye. She gasps. She has picked over half the soulblossoms! The tree branches move glacially in the strong winds. She watches thousands of individual pieces of pollen slowly descend. How Fast is she? It does not matter. As long as her Spirit stays full, it does not matter. Move!

Calendra's pace picks up again. The world beats like a taxed heart. The canvas flexes with it. The muscles on her arms weigh a ton. She speeds up. Her Spirit is still full.

A change in the Manifold distracts her. She detects a sudden alteration of gravity, marked by a stretching of the canvas near where the forest begins. A few moments later, she feels another change. The redrawing of the canvas that accompanies spatial manipulation. The person appears above the ground. She hears a faint scream echo off the mountains. Seconds later, she feels another spatial change as the canvas again removes a Spatial Artist. She does not feel the canvas redraw them.

Her work has not slowed and she allows herself a smile. That madman must have teleported into the sky, exactly where the Gravity Artist was hovering, grabbed him and let gravity pull them both down. He teleported out of the Valley just before he hit the ground. Calendra acknowledges that maybe spatial tricks are pretty cool. She also realizes her time is almost up. With a Manifold Artist dead, there will be no quarter. With Vrailen gone, there is only her dad to buy her time.

Her mind has become distracted. She focuses. She accelerates, as does the rhythm of the world. Accelerates more. The colorful pollen is falling so slowly that she could pluck it from the sky. She still feels her Spirit regeneration rate increasing.

She is so full, so full, but continues to force blossoms into her mouth as she goes, dislodging scratchy petals from her throat with yet more water.

The world is pulsing so fast it feels like a single note.

StripStoreStripStoreStripSwallowStripStore.

She cracks an eye open again. Her heart almost stops. She is close to done! Minutes remain. She closes her eyes, deep in meditation, and listens to the rhythm of the world.

She closes her eyes ... no, they are already closed. She can see the world as though they were open. She can see the canvas so clearly.

Hands flying, she feels the rhythm crescendo. As she strips the last soulblossom, the pulsing stops. Completely. She feels a ... collapse in the canvas. As if the lungs of the Valley have deflated.

She feels a wave pass over her, over everything, centered from her tree. The tree that feels like the essence of all trees. The tree on which the jungle might have been modeled.

Suddenly, with a spike of alarm, Calendra feels her Spirit diminish. It regenerates, but not as quickly. Far quicker than normal, but not as fast as when the world was pulsing. She eyes the three full bags of soulblossoms and the field of naked stems.

She stares at her tree. It has changed. Not visually, but in her mind's eye. She feels it with the sense that sees the canvas and feels the connection between things.

She has loved the tree because it feels so anchored in reality. It is more like the canvas emerges from the tree than the tree is painted on the canvas. Now ... now it is dead. Spiritually, at least. It is on the canvas but not part of it, somehow.

And the Manifold around it, the part of the Valley that has been so full of life, sound and movement since she arrived in the valley, seems to curl like the leaves of a tree with severed roots.

The rhythm. That beating, pulsing rhythm. Her tree. Both lost. At the same time! At ...

Realization crashes into her like a flung boulder. She runs to the tree, frantic, tearing at the soil, tearing at its bark, soil flying, pollen flying. She is too slow.

She runs to the cottage, trampling soulblossom stems, batting pollen from the air, and returns with an axe. With all her might, she slams it over and over into the base of the tree. Even with the canvas now still, she remembers the source of the pulses. The center of the last wave of power from a dying tree. She throws all her weight into the axe, her bones shaking from the force of the blows.

Wood chips fly as she hacks away at the beautiful tree. Lightning strikes above, slow enough to see it form, fork and vanish. Calendra's axe flies. Finally, with a deafening crash, the tree falls. Calendra realizes her lack of thought as it falls on the cottage. So be it. She knows her time is up, now her existence and location are known.

She looks at the stump. Nothing! It cannot be. She hacks away at the sides of the stump, despondent, on the verge of tears. It must be here. There is no other explanation. The thunderclap finally hits, a slow rumble.

Finally, she feels the axe sink in farther than it should. Her breath catches. Becoming even Faster, she hacks away at the edges until she sees the top of it. Hard, deep-brown, crinkled skin around an object the size of her hand.

A treeheart. She has not heard the word, but she knows it to be true. Her tree contains some type of heart, a thing that pumps Spirit? Calendra has a treeheart. She does not know what it means, but she knows it is special. And she has thousands of soulblossoms to go with it. A treasure beyond all reckoning or hope.

Her joy is cut short by yelling and the slow cracks of breaking branches. No! She is out of time.

"...NNNDDRRAAAAAAAA! RUUUUUUUUN!".

Her heart stops. Minutes more. She only needs minutes more.

Calendra becomes Faster. Much, much Faster.

Her dad's voice is slowing. She is grabbing her knife. Hacking at the root-like structures connecting heart to blood-like vessels. Hacking. Slashing. Stabbing. Her dad is entering the clearing. He must be Fast. He is slow to her. His eyes are widening. Run Calendra! She is looking at him, tears staining her dirty face. She is holding up a forefinger. Staring into his very soul.

Oneminutepleaseoneminute, she is screaming.

Her dad's expression is changing. He is skidding to a halt. Scooping up a branch thicker than his biceps. Calendra is still hacking. He is turning back the way he came. An enemy is emerging from the tangled bushes. He is sprinting towards her. The woman is reaching the clearing. Her dad is swinging the branch. It is connecting with the woman's face. The nauseating sound of cracking bones.

Calendra is turning her eyes back to her work. She is sawing. Hacking. Concentrating. Severing the final root. Grabbing the heart. It is coming away freely. Throwing it in a bag. But the shell is disintegrating before her eyes. In seconds she is holding a soft, squishy object like a fruit. White, viscous sap is oozing from it.

She is looking at her dad, surrounded by five enemies with swords, wielding only a thick branch. One is running towards her. Need more time!

Calendra becomes even Faster.

Calendra, deep in a haze, switches off her mind. She is too Fast. Even her sped up mind cannot keep up, or will not, with her father seconds from death. With her seconds from death.

Her speed is unfathomable. Pollen hangs motionless in the air, a fuzzy rainbow. The enormous man charging at her is moving so slowly, but is so close. Still, she is paralyzed by indecision. Her Spirit is almost empty, so reckless is her speed.

Run? Fight? Help her dad?

She balls her fists together. White sap leaks down her knuckles. Sap that feels exactly like congealed blood, but snow-white.

She looks down at it. Up at the enemy. Down at the heart. Up at her dad.

Nothing to lose. She feels what she must do. She lifts the heart to her mouth. The world seems to exhale.

She tears it in half with her teeth. Squeezes the sap down her throat. Tears chewy chunks out of the heart. Swallows them all.

Her enemy is two paces away. She washes down chunks of heart stuck in her throat.

Her enemy is one pace away. Her Spirit is so low, so low, from living so Fast. So Fast. The chunks of heart enter her stomach.

She feels something click into place, like the world snaps its fingers and suddenly things that were separate are now one.

Calendra screams a scream that seems to come from the world. She feels a rush as her Spirit is forged anew. It is like when she ran out of Spirit and ate the meal. But the power! Paralyzing, bone-shaking power floods through her.

The little Spirit she has left is overwhelmed by the influx of something more pure. Calendra feels it all snap into place.

The heart becomes part of her. The soulblossoms become part of the heart and part of her. The tempestuous Spirit inside her aligns in an instant. The world inhales.

Calendra moves.

She picks up her knife and side-steps the enemy with ease, then slides the knife through his ribs. She does not think. She runs over crushed flowers through a haze of hovering pollen.

She faces her dad's opponents. His face is covered in blood, his eyes are losing focus and his blood soaks his clothing in several spots. Two enemies lie on the ground.

His eyes flick to her. He is Fast, but barely. His eyes widen. He does not see a sword darting towards him from behind. Calendra is there. She slashes her knife blade at the fingers holding the blade, sending the sword off course. She follows with a strike to the woman's neck.

Calendra is a blur. She moves like she has never moved. All her lessons, training, meditation and practice snap together for these sublime moments. She has no fear. No doubt of the result. She is the Daughter of the Manifold. She is reality itself. She cannot be stopped.

In around twenty seconds, by her reckoning, a fraction of a second by theirs, they are all dead.

Calendra becomes Normal. Bodies land in the carpet of pollen. The Spawn resumes.

The lovely clearing, once a picture of snow-white blossoms, of dreamy steam and warmth, of a cozy wooden cottage and crackling hearth, is obliterated. The cottage is in ruins. Broken flower stems soak in pools of crimson.

Calendra stares around her. Her dad limps to her and collapses to his knees. She silently hands him a water canteen. He washes the blood off his face and hands. He lies down on the broken ground. She lies next to him.

"Is it over? That was really all of them?"

"Yes, my girl. That's all of them. We cannot linger long in case others are on the way. But we are safe for now. Rest."

Calendra nods shakily. "Ok. Are you alright, Dad?"

Her eyes are already closed. Calendra hears his reply as if from a great distance.

"I was dead, Calendra. I knew it. I accepted that whatever you were doing was worth the cost of fighting. I have never, ever seen someone move like that. Truly the Daughter of the Manifold."

Calendra smiles as her mind shuts down.

"My girl. My girl is becoming a god ..."

Chapter Ten

"I have a plan for you, to split your collective focus then recombine it, like light split by a prism merging through a complementary prism."

The Traveler's Welcome, page 31

Written record from the Eightieth Year of the Great Transference, Library of the School of the Manifold, Sanctum

*R*unning.
    Running.
Sun setting.
Still running.
Sun rising.
Still running.
Spirit churning. Dad slowing. Spirit too low, he is saying.
But still running. Jumping. Weaving. Stepstepstepstepstepstepstepping.
Always running.

Stopping?

Calendra becomes Normal.

Her strides do not stop. How can they? For a day and a night and a day she has run. The exhaustion is compartmentalized, thrown into the box of tomorrow.

One foot. Another. Forever, with no hope of finishing. Only in this way can her mind animate her body.

Running is breathing. To not run is to not live. Pain is not relevant.

So she ran. Did run. Has been running. She cannot keep track of then or now or soon. She flows with the energies of the world. She does not focus on ignoring the pain. She just runs, clothed in pain. Just running. Running.

Stop.

Her legs start to slow. She looks at them and cocks her head. She turns her half-lidded gaze and sees her dad far back. She looks at her legs and commands them to stop.

The command breaks her out of her flow. She gasps as pain and fatigue burst from tomorrow's box into today's, locking her legs. She falls immediately, bangs her elbow and grazes her cheek. She gets to her hands and knees and looks back at her dad.

"We're here." He beckons her. "Almost time to rest."

She rises and stumbles towards him as he drops bags and soulblossom sacks. He peers at the base of an unusual conifer, a type she has not seen before that is completely out of place in the surrounding jungle. It stands at the bottom of a modest hill of pale rock. Seedcones litter the ground.

Her dad sweeps away the cones and uncovers a large, flat rock. He runs his fingers between bark and stone for a few seconds, then grins. With little apparent effort, he pulls the rock towards him to reveal a hole with a rope ladder that leads down into the darkness. He looks at Calendra and points at the entrance. With a sigh, she starts to climb down. They reach the bottom after a minute.

Calendra's dad leads her through a long and winding cave system. After ten minutes of walking, having heard nothing but soft footsteps and dripping water, they arrive at a heavy wooden door that blocks their path. Her dad knocks with increasing force. After a minute or two, they hear a sliding metal grate and a voice emerges.

"Who comes this way? Identify yourself!"

"Friend Torland, I am Malnor and with me is my daughter, Calendra. We come in great need at the urging of a mutual friend. He told me to request that you honor your second debt to him by assisting us. He was not sure whether that debt would cover your services for both my daughter and I, and so left it to your judgement."

There is a brief pause before the clink of metal and creak of wood signals the door opening. An older man with an enormous snow-white beard and hair to match invites them to seat themselves with a wave of a hand from voluminous pink robes. Calendra and her dad sit on two inelegantly carved chairs facing a crackling hearth that sends smoke through a ventilation point in the ceiling.

Torland pulls a chair over and sits to face them. "Do you know what Vrailen did for me to create this debt?"

"I do not," her dad replied. "I did not ask. It is not the nature of our relationship. He offered this freely as he hopes that I reach Sanctum as fast as possible. I will greatly appreciate transportation as the walk to the capital takes time. My haste is of Vrai's making, and damn him for it."

At Torland's inquiring look, Calendra's dad adds, "The Nineteen requires a new Lord Speed. Vrailen believes it should be me. He should already be in Sanctum, nominating me."

"Oh," Torland says. "I'm not happy with these tidings. Farellia was a bedrock. A brilliant woman and a masterful Artist. Still, it's quite a debt to call in just to get you to a place to which literally all roads lead. He must consider this important. He always did like to pull strings. Who are you to him?"

"I'm Farellia's last surviving child. I share her Art. I am ... quite talented. I have been in Chalveno for years, away from the politics of Sanctum. And I don't want the bloody job."

"That'll do it. The last two reasons more than the first two. Very well. I would have honored his request, but only to the letter had you not satisfied me. The letter would have been to send you without your daughter. I think Vrailen has shown some rare wisdom. I will send both of you. Where is best?"

"Vrailen's private living room, if you're capable."

Torland laughs at this, huge belly bouncing rhythmically. "I was still on the Nineteen when he made his fortune and built that garish monstrosity, which means I was invited to see it, which means I have been there, which means I can send you there. I must warn you though, it can be challenging for me to determine how much Spirit to use when transporting a Manifold Artist. Some require less than I expect. Some require much, much more. I will send you. I will then send your daughter. If either of you takes more Spirit than I expect, I may have to shift your daughter's location to somewhere easier at the last moment. It will take weeks to regenerate and there's no room for her here. If I do, she will be safe, but may take time to get to you. Understood?"

Calendra's dad nods at Torland and turns to her. "Calendra, if you are sent somewhere short of Sanctum, get there fast and safe under another name. Please don't use your Art. The urgency is mine, not yours. I would not see your life's moments used up prematurely just to ease my worry."

Calendra smiles up at her dad. "I'll be fine. I'm hungry though, what do you …".

Without warning, Torland touches her dad's shoulder. The canvas stretches, twists, pops out of existence, and pops back in. It no longer includes her dad. Even the bags he held are gone. She gasps. So strange to see the same change that Vrailen and the Announcer made, but done externally to a different person. It was as though Torland had reshaped the canvas with his hands.

"Woah," she says, "that was different to last …". She bites off the words, realising it might reveal the way she sees the canvas.

It does not matter. Torland reaches for her. He touches her shoulder. She feels the massive influx of Spirit that is not hers. Spirit that does not infuse her but seems to flow through her, using her as a conduit before smashing against the canvas and tearing a hole in it. Into this hole pours her own Spirit, her mind and her body following. At the same instant, her body, mind and Spirit burst through the back of a different part of the canvas and stick to it, embedded as if she has always been on this part of the canvas.

She turns from the wall she finds herself facing and sees Vrailen and her dad grinning at her. Her dad comes to her and embraces her in a spine cracking hug.

"I'm so relieved, my girl," he whispers. "I feared where you might end up. Bless Torland. Such power. Such control! You'll soon realize the rarity of his ability."

Vrailen interjects. "You've no idea. I've only known of ten Spatial Donors in my time and none have his control. Spatially shifting another person must be so, so much harder than shifting yourself. When I use my Art, I can make micro-adjustments to my entry as I shift through the Manifold. He can't do that, as far as I know. He must visualize where to send you. Perfectly. The man has only visited this room twice! Amazing."

He seems to notice their exhausted looks. "Sorry, I can talk shop forever. I'll show you to your rooms. I think your journey here was harder than mine."

In a daze, Calendra follows the two men out the room and down a short corridor. She walks through a door Vrailen opens for her, veers to the bed she sees and collapses face down. She hears her dad clomp over and feels him remove her shoes. With great effort, she turns her head to the side to look at her dad and Vrailen.

Vrailen addresses them both. "Mal, Calendra, you're safe now. I guarantee nothing can touch you here. There are only three bedrooms in this wing, which is all but inaccessible. Rest. Recover. Mal, we'll need you tomorrow, but sleep all you can. Calendra, sleep. If you need anything at all, pull on the cord to the side of your bed several times. You are my guests and will want for nothing."

Her dad draws closer and looks into her exhausted eyes. "You're safe now, Calendra." He is half-conscious, but his tone is confident. "No more running. Sleep."

She smiles. No more running. Her mind drifts away. Safe at last.

A Memory of Danald

Two hundred and thirty years ago

S uspended between the dreamscape and the waking world, Danald felt one with all.

Eyes shut, he breathed in, chest rising, shoulders falling, muscles stretching. Behind his eyelids, the world sparkled and twinkled. Lights of changing colors burst and flowed in rotating geometric patterns.

He breathed out, chest falling, shoulders rising, muscles contracting. The shifting colors reversed their flows, tracking back along their curling paths and falling into blackness.

Danald opened his eyes after some minutes, maintaining his paraconsciousness. The dancing lights remained, mapped onto the verdant jungle surrounding him. The trees, plants and mushrooms swayed and swirled back and forth, in and out, to the rhythm of his respiration. Their movement followed the looping, geometric patterns of the light bursts.

The jungle itself danced to the beat of his breath, adorned with rivers of rainbow fires.

Danald's thoughts were clear. He did not mistake his perception for reality. He had done so once before - a terrifying experience. Watching reality bend is not as whimsical when one thinks it is real. Those were the early days of experimenting with his Art, when he had been unsure how far to sink into the dreamscape. It was not unheard of for Artists of the Paraconscious - Dream Artists, as was becoming popular - to lose their tether to the conscious forever and fall into a dream from which they never wake.

Danald had danced this dance many times. He knew his limits. He retained enough consciousness to know the irreality of his perceptions. What a joy, though. The others could have their Arts. He did not need to be strong, fast or tough. His memory was just fine, and his instincts served him well enough. Even the Manifold Arts were nothing. Who cared if you could get places fast or even fly? He could experience something they could never know. A different level of reality. Danald would take experience over utility every time.

Besides, his Art had its practical uses. He listened to the jungle. He heard its call and felt its flows. The patterns made by the transcendent lights changed as he traveled, as did their intensity. He had spent years following these variations, advancing where they intensified and retreating where they diminished.

When he found a local peak in the intensity, he would spend several weeks in that location, eating the local food and sinking deep into his para-reality. Each stay had seen him feeling more connected to life and boosted physically and mentally. He felt hopeful about this one. The energies here seemed stronger than he had ever seen them.

Mentally drained and ready to see blackness behind his eyelids, Danald halted his flow of life energy. His Art ceased and his waking mind exerted itself once more. The afterimage of the light bursts remained for a time, as did his brain fog. Finally, alert if melancholy at the loss of connection and visual beauty, he was clear-headed enough to set up camp. He really should have done this when first settling on a site, but he could never resist dropping into the irreal immediately.

Fully conscious but half awake, he started staking out his tent. It was a light-weight, foldable wonder made from woven silksap threads. Crucially, it came with a waterproof cover made from one vast sheet of dried sap from some native tree. Often as not he slept on the jungle floor as the Twin waxed and waned. He felt closer to nature that way. It was seldom too cold as he kept within tropical jungles, but sleeping was difficult when it rained. He had worked for a snotty rich brat for a year to afford the tent. With it, he had absolute freedom.

He prepared three small walls of rocks, layered some dried twigs and leaves from his bag, and squeezed several drops of oil onto them. He created a pyramid of scavenged branches on top, careful to leave spaces for air to flow, and laid out his cast-iron stove on the rock walls. Reaching in with the fire-sparker that cost him two weeks of work, he ignited the oily leaves. There was a fine art to generating enough heat in these small fires to smoke and ignite wetter branches without wasting precious oil or dried wood.

After several minutes of careful tending and blowing, Danald was confident it had enough heat to handle what he threw at it. Two hundred breaths later, the drops of water he flicked at the stove sizzled instantly. He picked, peeled and sliced several fruits and two tubers before throwing them on the stove, along with a range of nuts, berries and some hauntingly beautiful silver flower petals he had never seen.

One could never starve in the tropics, though he had learned the need to balance his diet. Man could not live on fruit alone! He occasionally stopped by a town to enjoy a night or two in civilization and eat meals prepared by another, but rarely. He enjoyed decent food, but did not really care. He carried salt, spices, oil and crushed nuts, but did not concern himself with balancing or perfecting taste. Throw it all on a hot grill, mix it all up and get it in your face. Anything else is ceremony.

As always, Danald sunk into paraconsciousness while cooking, for no particular reason he could identify. He finished cooking and smashed through his meal. Quickly enough that it all seemed to enter his stomach at the same moment. He immediately knew this meal differed from all others.

Danald gasped as his consciousness expanded. He still hung between the real world and the dreamscape, but he experienced both with startling clarity. The transcendent light he had only seen deep in the paraconscious sprung forth before his open eyes as trees and plants jerked into motion, all moving to the rapid rhythm of his heart rather than the slow rise and fall of his chest. It had all the hallmarks of the usual trip in reality he felt when using his Art, but with an intensity and clarity that stunned him. He chuckled to himself.

How long would it last? He sat down, readied himself, and released a torrent of life energy. Danald's paraconscious mind leaped to the surface and the world whipped into a dizzying frenzy of movement and color. Blinded, he closed his eyes and loosened the tether to his conscious mind, drifting further.

Behind closed eyes, Danald saw a thousand rivers and streams of fire-like light flowing around him. Where larger streams intersected, they formed the vaguest of outlines. He did not need to open his eyes to know they corresponded to the enormous trees around him. He saw streams of lights beneath him, branching along the jungle floor like tiny river deltas. As he turned, he realized there was an overall direction to the flowing fires. Many of the largest streams flowed in and out of one particular source. Perhaps some kind of local chief tree.

Danald noticed something else strange in the flows. Three intense sources of the transcendent lights were in a triangle, but the center of that triangle was

completely dark, one of the few spots on the jungle floor that was not connected
to the rivers of fire.

Danald opened his eyes. He could still see the lights mapped onto the plantlife.
He gazed up and down at the huge banyans that seemed to be the sources of the
flows. He could feel their power. Then he turned to the void - the tree surrounded
by radiant giants but with no light itself.

It was the gnarled, dead stump of a coconut palm. It was at least five paces wide.
He could scarcely imagine its size when it had been alive. He went up to it and
peered into the shattered stump, increasing the flow of life energy to sharpen his
paraconscious vision. As rivers of light swept around him, he saw a hint of light
from the center of the stump.

Dizzy, Danald wound back his use of life energy and slid back into full consciousness. He walked to his tent and returned with a small hatchet. Within
minutes, he had hacked away the rotting wood at the center of the stump. He
pulled back as he felt the hatchet slide into wood that felt fresh and yielding.

Danald peered into the hole and saw the strangest thing he had seen in his
twenty-four years of life. He had hacked into roots that seemed to form a spherical
cage. Inside that cage was the thing that had felt fresh. A brown-green lump of
wood that looked like a ball of muscle. With great care, Danald sawed away at the
cage of rotting roots with his knife until he could remove the strange chunk of
wood. It felt springy yet tough, like an uncooked vegetable.

He stood, held it in front of his eyes, fueled his Art like he seldom had before
and sunk into a trance. This strange piece of wood, this heart of a dead tree,
glowed like the sun. It did not sparkle with fiery lights nor emit energies that
connected it with other trees. It was the glowing coal of a fire no longer burning.
It brimmed with life, yet was no longer a part of the world.

Danald had long been certain that some foods could affect one's life energy
and one's Art, despite the mockery of the elders. His ability had drawn him to
areas rich in life energy. He always ate ingredients from those areas. It was the only
explanation for his remarkable increase in power over his years of wandering. The
meal that let him find this thing, this heart, was proof enough. It was probably
those strange petals. It hardly mattered now. He had a greater opportunity.

Danald used his knife to pare away thin strips of the heart and chewed them
as he went, washing them down with water. In minutes, he was done. He felt the
fibrous strips settle in his stomach. He lay down and readied himself.

Danald released life energy like a broken dam in flood waters. He gave everything he had to his Art in one instant. He saw transcendent lights burst out of
his core and watched as they formed streams and rivers that flowed into those

from nearby trees. As his life energy burned away in a dazzling moment, he cut the tether to his conscious mind completely.

Danald transcended time, space and body. He felt the forests and jungles of the world like they were part of him and he was a part of them.

And he felt something wrong. Part of themself that was wrong, like an infected finger. An infection that needed to be cut out. It was disrupting and diverting energy flows through themself. It was ...

Danald crashed back to reality, his life energy spent. He felt the void where his life energy had once been. Last time he ran dry, it took weeks to recover.

Moments later, he felt a burgeoning fire deep within. Moments more and he felt life energy grow inside him. His Art became accessible. It had taken seconds. He wondered what he had forged himself into.

Danald looked south east towards the infection that his world was excising. He had a direction. He lay on the jungle floor and passed into dreamless sleep for the first time in years.

A Memory of Djulita

Fifteen years ago

"Welcome! Ummm ..."

The man shuffled through his papers. He was tall and slim, but muscled, with the face of a warrior. Conspicuously large hands. He looked like a carving of himself.

"Oh, Djulita. Hi, Djulita! Can I call you Djulie?"

"I would prefer not, Candidate Malnor."

He beamed at her and threw his arms wide. "I like you already, Djulie."

"Djulita please, Candidate. Even should you appoint me, I am professionally and ethically obliged to remain politically neutral. It is best if we remain at arm's length. Particularly until a formal appointment is made."

"Of course, of course." His weathered, deep-brown cheeks cracked into dimples as his grin widened. "You will find, Djulita, that I abhor formality. If successful, you will need to get used to that. But you're quite right. This is a formal selection process and I will make sure to weave an appearance of neutrality."

The man winked at her, something her bosses in the Department of Artistry would never do for fear of harassment allegations. As it should be. Yet she did not hold this against him. It was the same wink her father, may the Announcer keep him, once gave anyone from child to Chief Minister. The facial equivalent of a dad joke. You rolled your eyes but inwardly chuckled. Outwardly, if the delivery was good enough. This wasn't.

"So," the man continued, "why do you want to work for me?"

Djulita cleared her throat and straightened her back. She had practiced her answer to this question a dozen times.

"Candidate Malnor, I am an experienced bureaucrat. I have worked for multiple departments of state, from desk work to secretarial work for executives. I wish to serve the public whilst ..."

She stopped. He had closed his eyes and put his feet on his desk. "Candidate?"

"Oh, sorry Djulita. Please finish your rehearsed answer. It's well worded." His eyes remained closed.

"I ..." Djulita was at a loss for words. She was never at a loss for words. She had been interviewed fifteen times and been the interviewer five times. It was humiliating. Of course she had rehearsed. Certain criteria need to be checked off for an appointment to be lawful and unbiased. Not everyone could just speak off the cuff.

The man finally opened his eyes. His face fell. "Please, Djulita. I apologize. If you knew me, you would know my comment was in jest. But you don't, which just makes me a jerk. Of course you rehearsed your answers. Who wouldn't!" His expression softened into a genuine smile. "Djulita, I don't care about the formalities. Yes, yes, I understand there are processes. Always processes in your line of work. They vetted you for this position, correct?"

She nodded.

"You know the procedures of government and how they intersect with the world of Artists? You understand the legal and bureaucratic relationship between the Nineteen and the Governing Council?"

She nodded again.

"I do not," he continued, "but I trust you do. Unlike some of my potential colleagues, I have enormous respect for the work of the mundane - sorry, non-Artistic - bureaucracy, whatever I might think of the elected leaders of the day. You people keep this nation running in all the small ways, continuing the day-to-day matters that can so be easily overlooked yet would paralyze society if not done well. I'm not interested in your answers to these things, as I trust you are amongst the best."

He took his feet off the desk, stretched his back, leaned forward and looked into her eyes.

"What I want, Djulita, is someone I can trust. Not to do anything beyond the scope of their position, but to allow me to be myself around you. As you've seen, being myself can cause hurt. But to do my job, I must be able to be myself. I also need to understand you. So. Why do you want to work for me, Djulita?"

Djulita was not sure who to be. She had not expected this. It was her first try at becoming an Artistry Liaison. She wondered if they were all so strange. Her shoulders slumped in resignation. No point is second-guessing the man. She would be herself.

"Candidate Malnor, I want to get right in amongst it. The world of government is insular. We do our best, but it is often in a vacuum, divorced from the decision making of elected officials. We are also told to respect the constitutional boundaries between Artistry and civilians. We do this too eagerly, I fear."

She paused and finally held his gaze.

"I want influence, Candidate Malnor. I'm good with patterns. I understand trends and movements. I find connections and gaps. I think I can make a difference. I pay attention to the affairs of the Nineteen. You are not like the others. They are career officials, deep in their politics. Unimaginative. Conservative. You've been away from Sanctum for many years, living in a different culture. You bridge the old and the new, the familiar and the other. You will win. I want to be by your side when you do. Not because I have a particular agenda, but because I believe in myself and my judgement. I back myself to shape the decisions of one of the most important people in the world. The only thing you lack is familiarity with the current environment and civilian politics. I will be that bridge for you."

Djulita took in a few deep breaths, exhausted. Influence? She wondered if she'd gone mad. How would he react to such a proclamation of self-interest?

He smiled. "You're hired."

Djulita stared at him. "Candidate, you don't want to ask me anything else? What about the other interviewees?"

"Other interviewees?" He laughed. "I've been absent from Sanctum for years, but I still have access to information. I knew as much as I needed to about Djulita the bureaucrat. It was only Djulita the person I needed to know. There are no other interviewees. If I didn't like you, I would have found some. No need now."

"But ... Candidate ..." She couldn't believe she was arguing with him. "I'm not even an Artist! And I'm ..." She looked down, afraid of his reaction.

"You're what, Djulita?"

Djulita steeled herself. "My mother is unwell, Candidate Malnor. There may be times in the coming weeks where she needs me. I may not be capable of serving you completely. Should you win, and I remain your liaison, I will need to take time off when ..." She cannot finish the sentence.

"Stop."

He looked at her, stone-faced. Here it was. He had his needs. She could not blame him. Maybe she would find a role the next time they held an election for one of the Nineteen. In however many years that might be. Her eyes fell.

"There is no more precious thing than family. We were once a remnant of a remnant, only thousands remaining. We are now a civilization. All from so few. Every life is precious. Taking care of those who came before us influences who we will be in the future. No, you will be my liaison. You will take any time you need, anytime you need it. If your contract does not provide for your salary during any absences, I will personally. If your absences leave me short, I will pay for someone to fill in as needed. Whoever you recommend."

To Djulita's horror, water pooled in the corners of her eyes. "Thank you, Candidate Malnor. Truly."

"Then that's that! You start tomorrow. If your bosses have a problem with that, they can come here to discuss it with me. Don't worry about the future. Look forward to it. I'll see you tomorrow."

He rose, walked to the door, and opened it for her. Djulita left in a daze. She was at home before she knew it. She ate a quick stir fry she didn't remember preparing, lay down on her thin mattress and looked at the dripping ceiling, vibrating from the kids partying above. She drifted into sleep, smiling. He would be the most important person in the world, and she would help him navigate his course. She would even be paid more, though that excess would go straight into the next experimental treatment for her mother.

The first few days were hectic. Mal, as he insisted on, knew nothing of the bureaucracy and next to nothing about the current Artist-civilian political environment. She had to go through everything step by step. He listened attentively and never interrupted, other than to ask the right questions. He treated her with respect bordering on deference and seemed to consider her the expert and he the student.

She ensured all the necessary forms and authorisations were prepared and duly executed. She would not see him disqualified because of some technicality. With his political opponents wielding power over parts of government, procedural tricks were not beyond plausibility. Despite all that needed doing, he asked that she take his daughter out for a day. She protested, of course, but his insistence that they meet early for his own comfort and trust let her really enjoy the day with the thoughtful young woman.

Mal met regularly with the obscenely rich Vrailen. This had concerned her at first. She worried she had misjudged Mal and that some kind of financial influence may be involved. This notion disappeared during the first of their meetings she attended. They were clearly old friends. Their politics aligned, and they both had strong concerns about the political balance of the Nineteen. This seemed to be their sole motivation. Besides, Mal seemed to care nothing for material wealth, and Vrailen had so much of it that to commit crimes for the chance at a little more would be absurd.

She got the impression Mal did not even want to be one of the Nineteen, which astonished her. Who would not want to wield that kind of influence? Yet their conversations made her sure that Vrailen had convinced him to run. Whatever their motivations, they tested her ability to remain professional.

Mal was determined to start his campaign the next week. While Djulita could not help him with this - as a matter of direct politics, she could only help coordinate any arrangements with the civilian government - she was allowed to hear his discussions and attend his engagements. It was Vrailen with whom he discussed political tactics.

"Start with the Guild, Mal. They're your base and the people that actually elect you. But you won't, will you? Idiot man." Vrailen's words were cutting, but his tone was relaxed.

"Course I won't, Vrai." He turned to Djulita. "What would you, as an impartial observer, say my biggest political strength is?"

"You're a connected outsider. You bridge the gap between tradition and modernity."

"Ha!" He pointed at Vrailen. "There it is. Going cap in hand to the Guild is the old way. Yes, they elect me, but they're not the future. Artists must unite in the way non-Artists have. Through popular representation, not through the backroom decisions of old men and women. No, Vrai. I will head towards the future before circling back to the past."

Vrailen chuckled. "Circling back? The bureaucrat has you speaking like her already. Probably got you using the word 'synergy' unironically!"

Mal laughed until he cried, holding his sides. "Their terminology is infectious, I'm telling you." He calmed himself. "Manifold School first, Vrai. They are our future. They'll also be the ones screaming in their parents' ears about that future. Then the School of the Mind, then School of the Physical Arts."

"The schools?" Vrailen scrunched up his face.

"Yes, Vrai. The bloody schools. They're all our future, not just the ones that vote for me."

Days later, Djulita stood next to Mal in the Great Hall of the School of the Manifold, the hallowed institution that shaped the rarest of talents. He was wearing ... well, it was absurd. Memorable though. She waved at Mal's daughter, who was standing near the corner with a plain, bookish girl with spectacular silver hair. Not gray. Silver. It caught the light like polished silverware.

Mal turned to her. "Go. Take a seat. I have to prepare myself. I'd rather take on five Strength Artists than give this damn speech."

Djulita watched Mal as he seemed to withdraw and mumble to himself. How odd that he disliked public speaking so much. He seemed so at ease with conversation. She thought it entirely possible he would rather fight five Strength Artists.

Students and faculty filtered into the Hall over the following minutes and Mal took a seat at the center of the row facing the students. Djulita walked quietly to the side of the Hall and stood. A bell sounded, the Hall filled, and the School Head stood. Everyone quieted.

"Silence," he announced to the already silent crowd. "We are honored, students, to hear from Candidate Malnor, who is up for election as the representative of the Speed Artists on the Nineteen. This is the first time a candidate for the Nineteen has requested to speak to the students of this School, rather than just the faculty. You might also be pleased to know that this is the first official engagement of his candidacy. Give him the attention that warrants."

He sat, and Mal rose. Mal grinned at the watching audience, showing no sign of the nerves of moments ago. She could see a number of students struggling to contain themselves at Mal's attire.

"Young ladies, young men, those who are both and those who are neither. It is my honor. It's been many years since I studied here. I feel like a student again, made small by the scope of history, wisdom and beauty in this place. When I was young, a man in will but not in body, I thought of myself as the future. I came to this place of rules and lessons and discipline and thought of it as the past. I come back now, much older, hopefully slightly wiser, and know I was wrong, and I was right."

He swept his gaze over the students, ignoring the faculty.

"I was wrong about rules and lessons and discipline being of the past. These things feel insulting as a young adult, but I look back and see them for what they are - the foundation stones upon which my successes as an adult were built. But I was right that I was the future!" This raised some eyebrows. "For I was. But now I am the past. You are the students, now. You are the future, now."

He gave a warm laugh, grinned ear-to-ear, and shrugged.

"That's why I'm here. You folks can't vote for me. I'm not here to convince you that I should be elected. I'm here to tell you that you matter. You feel small now, but you are not. You are giants. You will change the world. So I ask you for only two things. I ask that you own that future. Be young and have fun, but remember that every effort you put in now, every good habit you form, will make you better equipped for that burden of privilege. And I ask you to guide me, to help me steer our present in the direction of your future. If I'm elected, I will listen to you and help usher in the future you want."

The room was silent.

"That's it." Mal clapped his hands together. "Speech done. That leaves us forty minutes, if I'm not wrong, for the most important part. Listening and answering. Ask me anything."

There was silence for several seconds, then the applause started. Djulita got the feeling these kids had never been spoken to by an adult like that, let alone one of the most powerful Speed Artists in the world. Mal waved down the applause. Then the questions started.

How quickly did his Spirit regenerate? Had he killed anyone? What the merry hell was he wearing? When did he go to the School? A girl who looked far too old to be in school asked, voice husky, if he was married. He answered them all with friendly ease, while almost never actually answering them.

For someone who hated it, he was a natural politician. No. He was naturally what a politician should be.

The Schools of Body and Mind went even better. Those students had no direct connection to his election and seemed to be even more surprised that such an important person would be so warm with them. It was only once he started visiting civilian schools that the news sheets picked up the story. Some stories praised him as the powerful Manifold Artist who cared more for children than adults and more for popularity than tradition. Others derided him for those very reasons. Either way, they spread news of the election to the corners of Tolgarlo that had Speed Guild members but little connection with the affairs of Sanctum.

He visited orphanages and trade unions and even civilian government departments. He met with civilian leaders. Last of all, on the day before the election, he visited the headquarters of the Guild itself. His speech was brief. He promised to build bridges, not just within the Nineteen but between Artists and non-Artists, and between Sanctum and the regions. He answered questions openly and was not distracted by sour opponents with gilded words.

He won, easily, though not without drama. The votes in Sanctum, counted by the following day, were inconclusive. He received fewer votes than Yaldon, though not by much. It was still enough for Yaldon's supporters to declare victory. Votes from outside Sanctum had never accounted for much. A week after the election, once all votes from all corners of the land were delivered by boat or Endurance Artist, the result was clear. Mal had received votes from outside Sanctum like nobody in history. Yaldon declared the election a fraud. Nobody cared.

After Mal's inauguration, he came to Djulita's home. She was aghast. The tiny box she lived in was chaotic, all tidying and maintenance deferred through the election period and tense days after, with any spare time spent with her mother. Still, she could hardly deny entry to one of the most powerful people in the world. He seated himself at her gesture. She perched on the edge of the bed.

"Congratulations, Lord Speed."

She grinned at him. Her smile broadened as she realized what a weight had been lifted. Thanks to Yaldon's posturing, she'd refused to believe Mal had won until they inaugurated him.

"You are what we've needed for a long time. I'm so privileged to have been a part of it."

"You were my anchor in the storm, Lady Djulita. Thank you." Malnor, Manifold Artist, member of the Nineteen, bowed to her.

"I came to talk of the future, not the past. Your appointment as my liaison to the civilian government is not over, but it is not enough. It prevents you from advising me on certain matters, and it restrains me from rewarding your service as it deserves. Be my Chief of Staff."

Djulita's mouth hung open as her mind seemed to leave her body. Such positions were for the most influential, informed and intelligent people in the nation. For Artists, at least. She was just a mundane civil servant.

"I know, I know," he continued. "Politics isn't your thing. I'm not asking that you do dirty political work. I'll leave that to Vrai. He loves it. There's something wrong with him. Some sickness of the mind. But you know the system, you know the people and, whatever you claim, you know politics. So here's your chance. Join me. Influence me."

Djulita could not answer for several seconds. Not as she needed to decide. There was no decision to make. It just took time for her mind to drift back to her body.

"Yes, Mal."

Her emotions came back at last. She started laughing and tears actually flowed this time. What a difference a few weeks could make. He walked to her and cautiously grasped her shoulder, as if afraid of being forward.

"My one condition is that you move out of this ... efficient housing. I do not believe this place is conducive to your best work. Vrai has an investment property that needs a tenant for complicated taxation reasons and has asked if you and your mother might reside there. She will have a full-time carer. For his sake, of course. He worries, and this will ease his mind."

Djulita nodded, mute.

"Then it's done! Vrai's representative is already downstairs to help you move. Welcome to my team! You and I are going to disrupt things, Djulita."

She grinned at him.

"Djulie."

Chapter Eleven

"This plan must be enacted at all levels - individual, family, community, civilization. You must separate into different collectives."

The Traveler's Welcome

Written record from the Eightieth Year of the Great Transference, Library of the School of the Manifold, Sanctum

Calendra wakes as the sun's first light drowns out the soft glow of the waxing Twin. Her nostrils flare at the scents of caramelized fruit and spiced flourcake, motivating her to rise without her usual dithering. She stretches sore muscles, cracks stiff joints and walks to the door. Behind it waits a feast that could fill a family. A note has been placed under her plate.

Gone to register my candidacy. Enjoy the estate but please don't leave. I'll arrange for a tour in a couple of days.

She puts away the enormous meal like she has not eaten for weeks. Which may be effectively true, she realizes, given how Fast she lived the previous days. She washes the food down with some kind of fermented milk drink.

As she gets up to change, she notices the small mirror on the back wall. A silver metal sheet beaten as thin as paper and polished to a sheen. How long has it been since she saw herself, other than in the shimmer of water? She has not cared about her appearance, alone in the wilderness with only her dad.

Calendra goes to the mirror and gasps. The girl she stares at looks so many years older than the one she last saw back in Chalvstrom. She only lived six winters there but looks ten older. Is it adolescence? Yes, she first started using sanitary cloths shortly before her flight from Chalveno, but it is not only that. She lived so fast, for so long. Her dad had warned her. She has borrowed many tomorrows to spend today.

Calendra laughs at her own concerns. She is alive. Her dad is alive. She would have borrowed thirty years of tomorrows for that.

Calendra cleans up in the nicest bathroom she has ever seen, then opens her wardrobes and flips through the extraordinary range of fine clothes provided by Vrailen. She settles on a bright yellow dress, black leggings and a small golden hat with a large bow. She has no idea what the fashion is in Sanctum, or anywhere really, but she will wear what she likes until she knows.

She grabs a bright silver knee-length coat in case there is a chill. She has been told that the weather is milder in Sanctum, and it is spring, but it never hurts to be prepared. She is accustomed enough to the extreme cold of Chalveno to know the penalty for under-dressing. She does not select any of the jewelry in the drawers. She selects a pair of silver ankle-high boots with thick but flexible soles. Beautiful, but suitable for rougher terrain and any need to flee.

Ready to explore her new city, she goes to check the view from the room's only window. Before her, through the clearest glass she has seen, is a garden filled with plants she has never seen. Her wonder grows as she watches.

A silver-blue shrub with violet flowers that bud, grow and wither in half-minute cycles, like it is living Fast. A golden broad-leaf fern with branches that flow in the breeze, apparently unaffected by gravity. A tiny fig tree with iridescent fruit that teleports between five different places at random but frequent intervals. It is a garden filled with the visible manifestation of life aligned not just to a Domain - Mind, Body or Manifold - but to particular Arts.

Calendra stays transfixed for some time before she realizes she is only using one sense. She draws on her Spirit without altering her speed and unfocuses her eyes and mind. After a time, she feels the energies of the garden and begins to see the canvas on which it sits. The canvas is a riot of pulsing movement, plants rich with Manifold-aligned Spirit manipulating their own speed, gravity and location.

She realizes that this is her home now and she can enjoy the view any time. She tears herself from the garden and rings the bell. There is a knock at the door moments later and a pretty boy in serving robes introduces himself.

The house is beautiful, but Calendra finds its size lonely. So much space with so little life. Oh, there are small trees and plants and flowers of all kinds, but the floor beneath her feet is dead. She already misses the feel of soil between her toes. She returns to her room in short order to watch the plants, asking the attendant to bring meals to her room until her father returns.

After two days of eating, sleeping and meditating, she hears a knock shortly after lunch. She opens the door to a slim woman with sharp features, a little younger than Calendra's father.

"Hi Calendra," the woman says with an effervescence that contrasts with her bookishness. "I'm Djulita. Your father asked me to show you around town today. Are you ready?"

"Oh yes," Calendra says, eager both to get out of the place and to put an end to the poor woman's hand-wringing. Calendra finds it a little odd that a woman twice her age should be nervous.

Djulita offers a hand and Calendra shakes it firmly. Djulita's eyes widen slightly.

"Quite a grip you got there!" Djulita's fingers feel like they are crumpling. "Been chopping wood?" She chuckles at her own joke.

"Yep."

"Oh." She appears momentarily flummoxed. Suddenly, the baffling tension breaks. "Of course you have. That man!" She rolls her eyes.

Calendra laughs. She may not know Djulita yet, but the woman clearly knows Calendra's father.

"Thanks, Djulita. It's nice to meet you. I'm sorry about my dad. Generally. I'd like to see the famous sights if you don't mind. The Great Schools, the lake, and whatever others I don't know about. But can we go through regular areas to get there? Seems I should see what normal life looks like before seeing how the fancy live."

Djulita seems to like this and beckons her to follow. They exit the guest wing through a thick metal door with several locks and, a few turns later, leave the house through a guarded entrance. Calendra realizes the house is in an elevated position as she looks at the sprawling city from above the surrounding rooftops.

There are patches of buildings with gaps between like winding rivers. The buildings house a blend of residences and businesses, mostly two or three levels high, in an incongruous mix of wood and stone. From her vantage, she can see several broad alleys, curved at the sides but flatter at the bottom.

They walk through the nearest rounded alley, teeming with people of every age and color. Well-dressed ladies mix with soil-coated farmers, grubby children with older merchants. She sees nobody dressed in yellow and silver, but clothing styles and colors are so varied there is no fashion with which to conform. The people wear a riot of colors. The smells that drift down from restaurants above are as diverse as the sights. Far more varied than in her homeland, never mind in the wilderness.

The alley descends below the level of the buildings into some weird half-tunnel sunken walkway. Most foot traffic is on the stone floor but people occasionally ascend to the ground level above by way of stone steps placed every fifty paces or so. They encounter a temporary market where two of the trenches intersect with vendors selling food, clothes and trinkets from market stalls.

After some time, they walk up an incline of slopes and steps to reach flat ground. Elevated above the tops of the trenches, Calendra turns and realizes the entire area is built into a shallow bowl, perfectly round at the rim and curving down to a mostly-flat bottom. The trenches look like a god ran the tips of her fingers through clay in twisting motions. All the elevated land is occupied by buildings and the trenches form a network of walkways. She looks at the alien landscape in wonder.

"First time in a big city?" Djulita smiles at her.

"Yes," she replies, "but it's not just that. It's such a strange landscape. And where are the trees and plants and flowers? Is it all like this? Just … rock and dead wood and people?"

"Oh, the city isn't that big. There's nature everywhere outside it. Some people go for walks there. I do, when I find the time. There are also public gardens. Some of the richer areas have trees planted along the roads, but everyone wants to live close to Lakeside, so there's not much room for trees."

"Richer areas? Isn't Vrailen rich? Why doesn't he live there?"

"Vrailen is from here. He's very well known. He built his first house on that little hill in the Trenches. That's the nickname for Outer Sanctum, by the way. He just kept making it bigger and never left. He seems to like it here. The people here seem to love him as their own. Come."

They walk along the crater wall towards a modest hill that is completely barren and crowned with a narrow stone tower. When they arrive, Djulita hands a coin to the guard and they climb a stair on the outside of the tower to a platform above. The tower continues to rise high above them from the center of the platform.

"What is it for? War?"

"War?" Djulita chuckles. "This is Sanctum, the heart of Tolgarlo. No war comes here. They watch the weather."

"The weather? Just get inside if there's a storm. You probably don't even get blizzards here."

Djulita looks surprised and points east towards the Trenches. Calendra stares for several moments before realizing.

"The rain has to go somewhere. That's why you don't build in those channels. If a storm comes, people need to get to high ground. Where does it drain?"

"That's right. A big enough storm can also make the lake spill over the wall and flood straight into the crater. There are dams, but the folks of the Trenches have long memories. We get indoors at the first sign of a storm or, Traveler forbid, the alarm warning for overflow. The water drains into a huge natural well in the center of the crater, which empties into some underground reservoir, but you don't want to be down there."

"You live here?"

"Born and raised. It's a long walk to work, but I wouldn't leave it even if I had the money."

Calendra is starting to like this woman. She realizes she has not yet looked around. Her eyes widen as she turns and takes in the landscape of circles. Behind her, the huge circle of the crater. Before her, an endless circular lake stretching beyond view. To the south, untamed jungle from horizon to lake's shore. To the north, a large, perfectly round hill covered in buildings ornate and grand. Lakeside. Beyond it, the jungle.

The whole scene is cast in the ethereal blue-violet light of the Twin, an ever-present palette to the world except during smallnight, but one that is so much more noticeable in the sweeping expanses of Sanctum, where the view is unencumbered by soaring trees or majestic mountains.

The size of the hill on which Lakeside stands looks similar to the size of the hole in which the Trenches lie, like an inverted mirror image. In geography and in privilege. Calendra chuckles at the sad irony. Her dad would call that "metaphorically apt".

"On top of the hill," Djulita tells her, "is the Great Palace of The Revered Traveler, though everyone just calls it the Palace. It's where you'll find the Parliament and the Chamber of the Nineteen. Below that are the three Great Schools. Each level below is less well-off until the second lowest level compares to the Trenches. The lowest level can flood, so nobody builds there. They keep it as a public place, open to all, whether you're from the Trenches or high up on Lakeside. They have festivals on Days of Reflection."

"Days of Reflection?"

"The designated days each year that we celebrate the Traveler and the founders of our people. You don't have them in Chalveno?"

"We have a three-day festival each year to celebrate the Traveler, and the Descension of the Announcer is quite a thing when it happens. Descensions can be years apart, though."

Djulita looks aghast. "But when do you rest? Aside from the two days of weekends, of course."

"Two day weekend? How do you people get anything done? We have a one day weekend but we get our annual break for communion with Zem."

"Zem? Oh, I heard this somewhere. Your name for this planet, yes? You get a break to talk to a planet?"

Calendra is impressed with her efforts to make the question sound innocent. "To commune. The heat here must warp your mind. Every Chalvenan is expected to spend two weeks each year in nature. Becoming closer to the life of Zem helps us understand this world and is our way of revering the Traveler by doing as he once did. We take turns looking after each other's work while in communion."

"Huh. One long break does sound nice, though two weeks off doesn't make up for thirty-six days lost. What if people don't like nature?"

Calendra stares for several seconds. "What are you talking about? How can anyone not like nature? We live in paradise!"

"Oh, I love it, but many city dwellers don't. It's also not the easiest here. We might live in paradise, but around here it's a paradise for plants. Not only is the jungle untamed, we're forbidden from taming it. Sanctum was built where life won't go. Our founding words forbid interfering with nature's domain in this area. That's why there are tens of thousands of people living in the Trenches. We have no room to expand."

This gives Calendra something to consider. Such different cultures from people who started in the same place. Such different views on this world's life. She wonders whether it comes down to different perspectives, or just geographical and ecological variation.

"I think I'd like to go home now, Djulita. I'm more tired than I expected."

"Of course. You'll see enough of Lakeside soon. Would you like to watch the smallnight first? I find the heavens inspiring. The changing light is very pretty from here."

Calendra nods and they sit in silence as the Twin starts to eclipse the sun. As the minutes pass, Calendra sees she is right. The effect is striking, oranges and reds accentuated amongst the blues and purples of the Twin as the light dims until the smallnight arrives in full, blackening the blue lake and softening the jagged rocky landscape into flowing contours. She is accustomed to more closed environments. Or at least ones where much of the sky is obscured by her trees.

As the sun continues its journey behind the Twin, Calendra gazes out at the myriad lamps that light up the Trenches and Lakeside, and listens to the distant noises of people and industry. Light eventually pours around the planet that occupies so much of their sky. Djulita rises.

"I never get bored of that. The beauty of the changing light. The glow of lights as the sky goes dark."

They descend the tower and walk to the Trenches, and Calendra's new treeless home.

CHAPTER TWELVE

*"Become a part of this world, body, mind and soul. Meditate on life
- on its substance, its energy, the reality in which it exists."*

The Traveler's Welcome

*Written record from the Eightieth Year of the Great Transference,
Library of the School of the Manifold, Sanctum*

Calendra awakes to firm knocking and throws on a coat before answering the door. A tiny woman walks in and grins.

"Calendra, we're going to have some fun!"

Calendra does not think a woman so old and so small should be this bubbly. Her gray hair is dyed with streaks of emerald green and an extravagant necklace hangs over her deep green tailored pantsuit. Calendra suspects she should have stayed in bed.

"Cat got your tongue?" The woman winks at her.

"I'm sorry, I was lost in my own head. And ... a what got my tongue?"

The woman waves this off. "Nevermind now. A strange old family saying. Probably a child's name for a snapvine. So, so, so!" She claps her hands together like a delighted toddler. "Your father asked me to personally assess your abilities before you enroll in the School and I 'set out to destroy you like I once did him', as he was delighted to inform me. Which shows why the boy needed a hard hand. Ha! Well, boy or not, he put up his own hand for that silly council when I would not. Still a boy, but a good boy. I was already here to speak with him, so I granted his request. So! Some testing first? Good!"

"I'm sorry," Calendra interrupts, "but who are you?"

The woman, old enough to think of Calendra's dad as a boy, laughs aloud. "I'm Narelda, soon to be your teacher at the School of the Manifold."

"You're a Speed Artistry teacher?"

"I am the Speed Master. There are few Speed Artists and therefore few students. There are only around two hundred full students at the entire school at any given time. Usually fifty or sixty are Speed Artists. Across eight years, each of my classes has only seven to ten students. There are two Gravity teachers, as that Art is more common. Only one Spatial teacher. Spatial Artists are even rarer than us! So yes, I will be your teacher, as I have been to two hundred other Speed Artists, Malnor included."

The woman really is animated about her students, Calendra notes. Or about numbers.

"So, some quick tests. Any data on your knowledge and abilities will help me to determine which class to place you in when you join our school. Run on baseline Spirit, please."

"Baseline?"

"Baseline Spirit. Our term for fueling your Art with exactly the right amount of Spirit to allow one-for-one Spirit regeneration during active use. In other words, divert only the amount of Spirit that you can maintain forever and let's see how fast you are! Go to the far end of the room, start diverting Spirit, then walk to me, please."

Calendra does so. She thinks she is at least at triple-speed. She feels no Spirit loss at all. Narelda frowns.

"I'm sorry. I can talk too much - use many words when I could use few. I might not have been clear. I want you to only use as much Spirit as you can regenerate permanently. Not a burst of it now that will regenerate once you stop using it. Try again. Remember, only as much Spirit as you would be able to use if I forced you to use your Art permanently, without rest. Understand?"

"Yes. I understood the first time. I didn't know your term for it, but I know what you mean. I've used my Art enough to know what Spirit use I can sustain, but I can go slower if you want?"

Narelda frowns, all whimsy gone. "Are you trying to impress me, girl? Or yourself?"

"No." Calendra's anger is rising. "I did as you told me. I can go faster than that. Besides, what's impressive about a lot of Spirit? That doesn't take skill or practice. I thought I might impress you with the things I've worked so hard towards, like control and use in combat. I'm proud of those things."

Narelda's face plays out some internal argument. "Peace, Calendra. I believe you. Your father told me your natural abilities are extraordinary. He is, however, known to exaggerate. I now wonder if he was underselling it. Hmmm. Ok. Your Spirit is strong. No need to quantify it yet. You're right, we'll test your movement and cognition."

Without warning, Narelda reaches into a satchel and throws a dart at Calendra. Calendra instinctively becomes Fast and dodges it with ease. Narelda throws darts faster and faster and Calendra increases her speed more and more until the darts seem to run out. She nods at Calendra.

"Good. You can read?"

"Read? Of course. Can't everyone?"

"Most people, yes. Not all. I wasn't certain of literacy in Chalveno and didn't want to shame you, were it unusual there. Of course, I should have remembered that no child of Malnor would go uneducated, no matter the culture they are raised in. He did teach you, yes?"

"Geography, history, botany of course, even mathematics. Between practical things."

Narelda looks at her skeptically. "Read these cards to me."

Narelda begins to flash cards at her with short written sentences. Calendra is not a fast reader and she is out of practice, but the sentences are short enough that she does not live Fast at first. This changes as Narelda holds the cards up for less and less time. By the end, Calendra feels like she has been living ten-speed. When Narelda stops, Calendra becomes Normal and shakes the fog from her mind.

Narelda pushes her into a series of leaps that Calendra knows are about testing her understanding of momentum. Leaping far horizontally. Leaping far vertically. Leaping over a desk several places away and landing only one pace past it. She is mostly successful, years of swinging between trees having honed her instincts, but she struggles with the jarring, precise changes needed to shape the arc of her motion. Narelda still seems happy, clapping her hands and grinning.

"Brilliant! I fear we will have little to teach you about the mechanics of motion under changing momentum, but I'm sure there's plenty you can learn yet. There are remarkable things a Speed Artist can do that do not relate to breaking bones or swinging from tree to tree. I will put you in a class close to your actual age, Calendra. In some matters, you will be so far ahead of your classmates that you will be bored. We will make sure that boredom is directed somewhere useful. In other matters, you will be far behind your classmates, who have studied Manifold theory for years. You will need to catch up."

Narelda adopts a serious air that seems incongruous.

"You are a special case, but we cannot treat you as special. Graduation from the School of the Manifold Arts is more than just a piece of paper. It is an oath from the School that you meet all its standards. You can request a younger class, but I think you can handle it. Can you, Calendra?"

"Yes."

"Good. After today, I am your teacher, not your father's friend. Remember that. Adjusting to structure might be hard, but it will be worth it. Come to the School at second hour on Firstday. The administrative staff will enroll you. I will see you on Thirday. Enjoy your other classes!" She turns to walk out.

"Other classes? Aren't I there to learn Speed Artistry?"

Narelda sighs. "Your father is a good man, but he is one of the worst communicators I know. Oh, he communicates beautifully when he chooses. He just doesn't often think to do so. You will study a complete curriculum, including civilian subjects such as natural sciences, social sciences and manual arts. Some are mandatory while others you may select from a range, but it is only Speed Artistry for which you receive training, not just education. Your father will explain. See you next week."

The strange old woman scurries away. Calendra sighs. She will spend so little time actually learning her Art. Still, she is to be extraordinary and she is not sure that one can truly be extraordinary if one only knows one thing. Calendra resolves to make the most of it. She loses herself in thoughts of school, Tolgarlo and the Manifold until a knock interrupts her.

"Come in."

The door opens and an ornate redwood cane enters the room. Her dad follows. Calendra stares for full seconds before she explodes into laughter. She has not laughed like this for so long. It hurts, like exercising a muscle you seldom use.

As well as the cane, an absurd affectation for an able-bodied Speed Artist, his clothing is a riot. He wears all ten true colors. A flowing cape striped white and black. Horn-rimmed shoes of silver and gold. Loose pants with vertical stripes of blue, green and violet. A tight short-sleeved shirt with dizzying patterns of red, yellow and brown. Shading his grinning face is a narrow-brimmed top hat made of soft material in folds. It is white, but it is covered in dozens of dots of every other color. Utterly ridiculous.

She gathers herself, wipes her eyes and looks at him again. She dissolves into giggles once more. It is the short sleeves with a cape that she cannot get past.

"Not going to forget it, right?" He winks at her.

"Please tell me this is the new you."

"In public it is! From my first official appearance. If I must do this, I won't do it through shady deals in musty rooms. Where's the fun? Where's the color? Your embarrassment is a steep price, but it's one I'm willing to pay. I'm sorry that I've been absent, though. A lot to do in a short time. Once things settle in a few weeks, we'll get to spend more time together. Well, you'll stay at the School, but you'll be with me on rest days."

"I'll never be embarrassed by you, Dad. Maybe embarrassed for you."

"Bah. I am unembarrassable."

"I'm not sure that's a word."

He waves this off. "The Speed Master scolded me. Again. Claimed I haven't told you the most basic things about the School."

"You haven't."

"She told me you might be a prodigy, but you're a young woman from a foreign land and I, she deems, have avoided my parental duties. She etched it onto my bones using some arcane Art that she refuses to divulge. She's right of course. Always was. I'll do better once this damnable election is over. Meanwhile, what do you want to know about the School?"

"Which subjects must I study and which can I choose from? What are the sleeping arrangements? Do I have to share my room with someone?" She shudders at the thought.

"You get your own room. The Manifold School is very large, with very few students. She's putting you in Black. That's the third-highest grade, which won't surprise you as they correspond to the ten true colors. You'll be one to two years younger than the others. Any higher and you wouldn't get through your civilian subjects. Any lower and you would spend too long in that place. I want them to supplement your education, not spend years turning you into a scholar. You'll study eight subjects. One for each non-rest day. At that level, your compulsory subjects will be Speed Theory, Speed Artistry, Comparative Artistry, Combat Artistry, Humanities, Physical Science, a Craft, and an Expression. For the last two, you get choices. Your rooms ..."

"Wait," Calendra interrupts, "what can I choose from?"

"Hmmm. Cooking was my Craft, as it is for many boys who think of raising a family away from Sanctum. It teaches you to be self-sufficient and gets you outdoors. I think the other options were cultivation, chemistry, metallurgy, woodwork, glasswork, masonry, textiles, papercraft, and construction? I may be missing some. Expressions are about what you'd expect. Written expression, inked expression, sculpted expression, musical expression and theatrical expression. What do you ..."

"Painting and cooking. What Expression did you take?"

He grins at her and bows with a flourish, cape whirling. Calendra groans.

"They taught you to be this way?"

"Oh, I was already like this. I chose it for an easy pass. Your choices are good. You mix passion with pragmatism. Beware. You may know things other students do not, on account of your people's culture and your own abilities. They don't even know about Spirit-rich foods. Be circumspect about what you reveal. I also suggest you read through some Black textbooks if you have time on your hands. You're catching up on many things. Not in skill, but in accumulated knowledge. It might come as less of a shock if you know what you don't know. Vrai's library is formidable. Just ask the staff for the mandatory textbooks for a Speed Black. If they're a bit beyond you, ask for White or Blue. You're not ready for Silver or Gold, and the other grades are beneath you. I have meetings tonight and go to Lakeside tomorrow, but I'll try to get home to share dinner with you soon."

"Dad, I got you to myself for years. Go do your thing."

She gives him a warm smile. He winks at her and walks out, cane tapping and cape shimmering.

Calendra rings the bell. A staff member arrives within minutes. After a request and a short delay, she investigates the books and decides on Comparative Artistry for Silver students. She decides that before she exercises the mind, she should exercise the soul. She sets up the easel, brought at her request, by the garden window. She lays out paints on the palette. She selects the right canvas of the dozen they brought. Its rough, bumpy texture reminds her of the undulations of tree roots in eroded soil.

She looks out into the garden, takes in every detail, lets her eyes unfocus and, using a little Spirit, sinks into a trance. She sees the Manifold pulsing and popping, takes a deep breath and begins to paint.

CHAPTER THIRTEEN

"Those meditating on the physical should consider the nature of
strength, resilience, endurance and agility. For the mind, key aspects
include memory, the instinct borne of knowledge, and the part of
thought beyond the reach of the conscious mind."

The Traveler's Welcome

*Written record from the Eightieth Year of the Great Transference,
Library of the School of the Manifold, Sanctum*

C alendra looks up at the sculpted, painted ceiling of Speed Hall. Calendra
looks around at her classmates, whose names she is unable to remember
after three days at the School. Calendra looks at the walls of the hall, adorned with
murals depicting great acts of ancient Speed Artists. Calendra looks at the purple
fabric of Narelda's robes shimmer as the old Speed Master gesticulates.

Calendra looks everywhere but at Myla. If she lets her gaze settle, she will lack
the strength to move it.

"Myla will attend all theory classes at the School," Narelda continues, "and is expected to learn what you learn. She will also attend any practical classes she chooses. She will not, however, participate in those classes. Why, I hear you ask?"

Narelda grins at the class, her excitement apparent. Calendra keeps her eyes firmly on Narelda.

"Because she's not a Manifold Artist!"

This causes muttering. It is even enough to tear Calendra's mind from Myla's curly silver hair.

"She is an Instinct Artist. Our first! It is a very exciting development, children. Very exciting indeed. Not only the first Artist from the Great Plains in thirty years, but an Instinct Artist to boot! You will finally have the chance to talk about your Art with someone who comes from a different perspective. Who knows what pieces we might fit together with mind and soul united! So, please make Myla welcome and answer her questions. Not only will they help you learn, they are the reason that she has been granted a privilege allowed to no other Mind Artist. We believe she can help us unlock the secrets the Manifold still keeps."

Calendra's body freezes as the soft features on Myla's round face break into a gentle smile and she makes her way to the empty seat in front of Calendra. Calendra's mind freezes as Myla locks eyes with her, smiles and gives a shy wave.

Calendra lets out a breath she did not realize she held as Myla sits. She is a pace from Calendra, but it feels as if they are hair's breadth apart. As if they are close enough to feel each other's warmth.

It is the intensity of Calendra's emotions that scares her. She feels as if she has no control over her body and is a slave to her mind. She prides herself on her mental control. Her ability to focus her mind and commit her body is unrivaled, yet now she is a simpleton. She hates her weakness even as she revels in the unanticipated joy of romantic attraction. Her thoughts are not physical but of the heart.

Calendra is in love. She does not know Myla's age, though the girl looks a touch younger than her. Nineteen, perhaps. Calendra has probably seen fewer truenights but knows she looks older, a consequence of her frequent use of Speed Artistry. Meeting her other classmates and hearing repeated reminders of the importance of living Slow to offset the age gained from living Fast have made her see just how much she has aged beyond her years.

For now, Calendra does not live Slow. She does the opposite. She slows the world as Myla runs her slender fingers back through her hair and secures it with a headband. Myla slowly turns. Calendra shuts off the flow of Spirit and looks away ... to see the entire class looking at her. Mortified, she looks to Narelda.

"Back with us, Calendra?" Master Speed laughs. "I'll help you out. I asked the class to explain to Myla how Speed Artistry works. I thought that you, as our second newest student, might have a go."

Calendra considers running. She mentally slaps herself. She chose to be extraordinary. She could be herself in the Valley, trusting her dad to push her towards the extraordinary, but she is on her own here. On her own amongst the most powerful and privileged people in the world. She needs to become extraordinary on her own.

The extraordinary do not run from embarrassment. Her dad deliberately chose the world's most embarrassing clothes and embraced his role. This is not a matter of personal embarrassment. This is a matter of her future as the Daughter of the Manifold. This is duty. Calendra's mind snaps into place.

"Of course, Narelda."

She turns her head to face Myla. She is a spy undercover. She is a soldier ready to kill a stranger. She is a diplomat delivering a threatening letter to a vicious autocrat. She gives Myla an easy smile.

"Speed Artistry is a manipulation of the Artist's temporal relationship to the Manifold. Moving through time is like driving a sail carriage across sand, propelled by the winds of time. A Speed Artist can use Spirit to change their resistance. Live Fast and it's like driving on a salt lake. The winds of time blow you along with little resistance. Live Slow and it's like driving on mud. The winds of time ever blow, but we can change their hold on us."

Calendra sees Myla smile with delight. Calendra's higher functions abandon her. She is saved by the controversy of her answer.

"Actually," Narelda says, "we do not think of it that way, Calendra. Though it is a wonderful metaphor, the School teaches that Speed Artistry is not a temporal manipulation but a physical and mental one. Time is time, and does not change. It is an arrow flying ever true. We teach that Speed Artistry is a spatial manipulation, with the Artist changing their relative distance from things. The Traveler even refers to this in his founding words. Speed Artistry makes the body and mind fast enough to control it. That is why the longevity of a Speed Artist's life is determined by their use of their Art. Their metabolism is changing. It is not time itself that is changed. Time is immutable. "

"Seems like a lot of mental gymnastics just to justify time being immutable," Calendra replies with a frown. "Besides, when I see ..."

An internal warning sounds in Calendra's mind. She is deep in the intellectual stimulation of Manifold mechanics, one her favorite topics in the Valley, and almost forgets to keep her abilities private. She slams her mouth shut. Then she notices Myla again. The breadth of her smile. The sparkle in her eyes. The excitement is directed at Calendra.

Calendra's mind leaves her once more. She retains enough control to shrug at Narelda and force a casual smile.

"I forgot my point, Master. Apologies. I should catch up on my reading so I don't make such mistakes."

"Nonsense Calendra. This is a place of learning and discovery. I think you will find we have good reason for the theories we hold true, but questioning is never wrong. Your theory, which I assume you came to yourself, is a very good one. It is just one that this School has considered and rejected and is therefore wrong, in these walls. We should continue with our lesson. I just wanted Myla to have a taste of the big picture before we bore her with the minutiae. So. Vectors!"

Calendra drifts into a haze of emotions and desires. No matter where she looks, she sees the image of Myla's smile as if painted onto her retinas.

Calendra registers the class has finished when eight chairs scrape along the scuffed wooden floor in near unison. She gathers paper, reed, ink and book into her bag, ignores Narelda's inquiring look and exits the classroom.

She sees Myla. Myla sees her and smiles. Myla walks to her. Her heart stops.

"Calendra?"

Calendra is frozen in time as surely as if she were living Slow. She cannot even answer to her own name. She is like one of those touched kids she has seen, hurt when young and unable to communicate. Except that she is not hurt. She has her wits. They have just left her for now.

Calendra mentally slaps herself. Her pride finds its legs and kicks to the surface. She is extraordinary. An extraordinary person is not held hostage to their emotions. An extraordinary person does not surrender their intellect when faced with discomfort.

Calendra summons all of her rationality and uses it to beat her emotions into submission. She projects what she can only tell herself is the relaxed smile of a confident young woman.

"Yes. Myla is it?" As if the name, the sound of the phonemes, the shapes of the letters, are not burned into her soul. "What can I do for you?"

Myla looks at the floor and her fair cheeks redden. Calendra's heart pumps faster as if to compete.

"I was hoping," Myla replies with a wavering, husky voice, "that we could talk about the Manifold together." She meets Calendra's eyes and gives a lopsided smile. "I understand you're new to the School, Calendra. Your explanation of Speed Artistry excited me. You've not read textbooks? You came up with it yourself? You have other thoughts, original thoughts, on the Manifold?"

Calendra nods, mute.

"But then we must talk! Please. I'm so grateful to have this opportunity, but my Art depends on data. It's a diversity of ideas that my Art uses best to draw conclusions. Maybe you can bring a perspective that others lack."

Myla's cautious smile becomes excited. Calendra's stomach feels as if it has taken residence next to her heart.

"Will you talk with me, Calendra? Can we unravel the mysteries of the Manifold?"

Calendra cannot suppress her smile. She can only hope that Myla will see it as the joy of anticipated discovery, rather than the joy of one in love learning they will be alone with the one they love.

"I would love to, Myla. Let's meet at Dawn Terrace after the day is over. There are lovely views over the Trenches and the jungle. I hear it's a good place to think."

Myla claps her hands and laughs. "See you then." She walks away, pink dress flowing, silver curls bouncing.

Calendra sits on the floor of the hall as her legs lose their strength. Her face hurts from smiling. She hears the bell and gathers herself, then lives Fast to make it to her humanities class. She mumbles a sincere apology to Master Maideri. They were kind to Calendra during her first humanities class and she is keen to impress them. If nothing else, she has little interest in the study of people and needs to keep the Master sympathetic.

The lesson on civilization building during humanity's third century on their new world flows past Calendra's consciousness like water through cupped hands. A quiet part of her mind registers interest in the period before the Chalvenan secession, but it can exercise its curiosity another time.

Her lesson on physical science is no different. She tries to pay attention to discussions on geology but is unable to prioritize rocks over passion. She knows that she should not fall behind so soon, but she cannot care. Her mind is fully occupied. Besides, how will understanding geology help her to be extraordinary? Though she notes with interest the concept of the Twin's unseen face. The other world always in their sky, so visible yet so unattainable, has a changing face, but it is the motion of clouds, not the motion of rotation. This world is a sphere, so it stands to reason the Twin is as well, yet any observer could tell you the shapes occasionally seen beneath the clouds never change. It only presents one face. The concept of the other side of the Twin fascinates her upon hearing it.

Her final lesson is cooking. For this, she is able to concentrate. The lesson is on nutrition, something she has paid little attention to in the past. The need for a balanced and varied diet is new to her. She realizes that her dad was diligent during their years in the Valley. They only ever had a dozen meals to rotate through, comprising two dozen ingredients, but with all the nutrients a person needs. She has not thought much about Spirit foods of late but sees the use of understanding the mundane qualities required of food. One cannot live on soulblossoms alone.

It helps that she likes everything else about the class. Like her physical science class, students from all three Manifold Arts are there, not just the Speed Artists. They seem to her to be a more interesting group. More practical than academic, like Calendra. Only two of her Speed Artistry classmates take the class. Boravind, the talented young Artist from the Great Plains, and Greldra, an immigrant from the Free Cities in her thirties. Calendra finds it odd that none of the Sanctum locals see the merits of understanding the stuff they put in their faces daily.

When her lesson on nutrients finishes, she runs downstairs to the courtyard and out to Dawn Terrace. Myla is already seated on a blanket, leaning against the stone wall and looking south. Calendra's heart tries to immobilize her body, but she makes it to the blanket.

"Thanks for coming, Calendra. My last hour was free, so I came here early to think. It's beautiful, isn't it?"

"It is," Calendra says as she looks into Myla's bright green eyes.

Myla just smiles. They sit in silence for a short time and look over the landscape of humanity and jungle before Myla speaks.

"What does it feel like? Using a Manifold Art? Do you sense the Manifold itself or do you just become faster or slower at will? The more Spirit I use, the clearer my instincts become, but nothing else changes. Do you feel different or do you feel the same, but the world changes around you?"

Myla says this in one breath. Calendra stares at her for a moment, then dissolves into laughter.

"I guess you've had a lot of questions with nobody to ask. When I use my Spirit, I see …"

Calendra's pause is brief. Brief enough for Myla, hopefully, to not notice. Long enough for the warning to sound and be heard. Calendra is in love, but her dad sacrificed years, even at the expense of seeing his mother's last days, to help her become extraordinary. Her ability to see the Manifold is a key part of that. She is wise enough to keep her most important secret. Vrailen said she will need to trust someone eventually. She hopes Myla will be that someone. But she knows it is too early to open a door that can never be closed.

"… how full my Spirit is. Well, I feel it. There's nothing telling me how Fast or Slow I can be. Knowing that takes practice. My body and mind both adapt to my new speed. It's exhilarating, Myla! Though I envy your ability to understand what's right."

"It's not exactly knowing what's right, more like ... you know when you learn lots of facts and they kind of jumble around in your mind? They seem like they relate to each other, but it's just beyond your grasp. You know there's a pattern and if you could see it, everything would become clear. Instinct Artistry lets me see that pattern and form connections. It doesn't let me know why a connection is right. It just makes me certain that it is. Once I'm certain, I can usually work backwards to understand the pattern and figure things out. It's the difference between having to answer a question, and knowing both question and answer, but having to show why the answer is right. At its height, I can enter a kind of flow state - that's what my Master called it - where I just flow through the world acting purely on instinct."

Calendra takes a deep breath, as though Myla's string of breathless sentences has drained her own lungs of air. Maybe it is not as showy as Calendra's Art, but Instinct Artistry is clearly very useful. No wonder this beautiful girl is so intellectual. Her Art both requires and prompts deep thinking.

"I like that,' Calendra tells her with a grin. "I like the idea of flowing through life knowing you can trust your instincts rather than thinking. That's when I'm at my best, when I turn off and let the world guide me. I can't rely on your gift, but when my meditation is deep enough, I reach something similar. Is it right to say that your Art depends on the knowledge you gain? Or does it warn you of things you don't know about?"

"Yes, but it can tell me things I don't consciously know. As long as the information's somewhere in my mind, even if I've forgotten it or don't notice it, my Art will take it into account. But sure, I can't just max out my instincts and uncover the secrets of the Manifold! I have to learn first and then hope my instincts will put the pieces together in a way that others haven't considered."

"That explains the questions," Calendra tells her. "Let's see what we can answer together!"

Myla claps with excitement. Calendra's ownership of her own heart slips further, but she seizes the opportunity. Stimulating her intellect seems a useful distraction from her emotions. Still, one must prime the canvas.

"But first," Calendra says, holding up a finger, "we should know more than each other's names. My father is Malnor. You might as well know as you'll see him tomorrow. He's running for election to the Nineteen. I'm from Chalveno, from a small village near Chalvstrom, the capital. I found out I was a Speed Artist late, just seven years ago. I've lived with my dad in the Chalvenan wilderness since then. Until I came to Sanctum five days ago."

Calendra takes a deep breath. Myla giggles.

"The wilderness? Sounds terrible or lovely! I'm not sure which. I grew up in Odressa until I moved to Sanctum four years ago. My parents live in the Great Plains now, in a small town. I'm not actually from there. I couldn't feel my Art until I was eight, but once I did, my parents just encouraged me to learn a bit of everything. They eventually decided I'd learned enough to attend the Mind School. That was easy enough. Convincing the Manifold School to admit me was harder!"

Calendra sees a look of triumph behind Myla's grin. Calendra wants to ask a thousand questions but restrains herself. Myla asked her here for a purpose. She will focus on that so she does not lose herself in the personal once more. Calendra attempts a relaxed chuckle.

"So. The Manifold. I imagine it as the canvas upon which reality is painted..."

They talk of Manifold and Mind. They talk of speed and instinct. They talk of the wonders of Memory Artistry and the penalties for viewing or removing memories without consent, and they speculate about the mysteries of the Art of Dreaming and the world of the paraconscious. They talk of themselves and their lives. They talk of amusing failures and glorious triumphs. They talk until sunlight gives way to waxing Twinlight and the flames of the Trenches.

They do not talk of Calendra's ability to see the Manifold, nor her ability to detect uses of the Manifold Arts, nor the treeheart and soulblossoms that transformed her. But they talk and talk and talk. Calendra feels at ease like never before. The joy of conversation about common interests makes her forget about passion. Her love deepens, but her desires are forgotten. Still, it is too soon to divulge all. She must remember to be extraordinary.

Some time after sunset, but before the final bell, Myla takes a deep breath during a lull in conversation.

"I should go to bed, Calendra. My mundane instincts really get slow if I don't sleep enough, which makes my Art less effective. I try to be diligent with sleep." She smiles so broadly that Calendra can only believe it is genuine. "I had such a nice evening. The way you see things ... I've never heard descriptions of the Manifold that paint such a vivid picture while feeling so right. It was so amazing to talk to you."

Myla stands and brushes the grass from her dress, her dark skin glistening in the Twinlight. Calendra joins her and smiles. She keeps her hands firmly by her sides lest they betray her.

"It was fun. See you in class."

Myla gives a pretty wave and walks towards the gate. She turns after a few steps. "Same time tomorrow?"

Calendra cannot suppress her grin. "Of course!"

Calendra lingers for several minutes to enjoy the view and let her mind settle, then walks to her room. She lies in bed and tries to focus on thoughts of the Manifold. As her intellect tires, her emotions bubble to the surface. She finds herself increasingly awake. She gives up on forcing sleep.

Calendra rises, goes to her closet and retrieves her easel, brushes and paints. She sits, smiles and empties her mind of all but one image. She takes the time to mix precisely the right shade of silver. And she paints.

CHAPTER FOURTEEN

"You will become distinct people, spiritually and biologically, dedicated to study of and alignment to the physical, the cognitive, or the spacetime manifold."

The Traveler's Welcome

Written record from the Eightieth Year of the Great Transference, Library of the School of the Manifold, Sanctum

"**Y**ou're wrong!"

Calendra spits the word at Narelda. To be wrong is bad enough, but a Master of the School of the Manifold being wrong leaves a bitter taste in Calendra's mouth. Not least because that Master grades her papers.

"Perhaps." Narelda wears the relaxed smile of an experienced teacher, one that would not waiver during a firestorm. "But not in this place. In this place, my word is law. That law can be changed, and has been, by evidence and reason. Until it is changed, it is your truth. I cannot grade you on what I know you know. I can only grade you on what you deign to answer, Calendra."

"Ha! You admit you might be wrong."

Calendra shows a triumphant grin even while cringing at her childishness. Narelda's smile does not break, though she seems to take a moment to gather herself.

"There is knowledge, Calendra, and there is truth. Some things we know to be true. Many we do not, or cannot, know for sure. Only the foolish or arrogant claim they know the truth of these things. For these things, we debate, we hypothesize and we test. This is the scientific method. The results lead to knowledge that can be passed on and acted upon, but they do not always lead to truth. Some things will always be in doubt. So yes, Calendra, I admit I could be wrong. To do otherwise would be hubris, but a school cannot teach students if it denies knowledge of everything. We must determine what the evidence shows and teach that as knowledge, awaiting the day that evidence reveals truth. Until that day comes, you will be taught and tested on our current understanding. A superior student will still raise other hypotheses, but a successful student will ensure they conclude with the current orthodoxy."

Calendra stamps her foot and immediately regrets it. She is no child. She clenches her fists and calms her breathing, searching for the meditative state she used to drop into so easily. Back when she was extraordinary, rather than a belligerent girl on the verge of failing school.

"Calendra, why are you here? Why did you come to the School of the Manifold? Why have you stayed?"

"Because my dad is too busy to look after me himself."

Narelda stares her into submission.

"I'm here in case it helps me become the greatest Speed Artist the world has ever seen."

Calendra is surprised at her own words. Such arrogance. But she vowed it! She vowed to be extraordinary.

"Good. Very good." To Calendra's surprise, Narelda grins. It is a hungry grin. "There is no greater predictor of success, in academia and in life, than passion for self-improvement. Nurture that passion, Calendra, but you must let it motivate you beyond that which directly leads to your goal. School is a two-way agreement. I am glad you have chosen to attend this school, but we are not a buffet breakfast. You do not get to learn what you like and discard the rest. We teach a broad curriculum. This is not a combat academy. This is a school."

Narelda rubs her eyes and leans against the wall. Calendra has not seen her look so tired.

"Calendra, you don't need to be here. You are like your dad and your birth father in many ways, but you are not them. They were expected to graduate.

Malnor was very talented but lacked motivation. He had little interest in being here. You are different. He's made it abrasively clear to me that he will remove you if you wish, yet you choose to be here. You are clearly not someone who cares about titles, so I cannot believe you're here simply to graduate and call yourself a full Artist. You are still here after half a year because you think you can benefit from a formal education."

Narelda shrugs and takes on a warmer tone.

"I'm so glad you are here, but do your part. Take your lessons seriously, even if you don't see a direct benefit. Explore alternative hypotheses, but when you are tested, you must know the conclusion you are supposed to come to, and come to it. I know we are trying to teach you to think differently, and you do not want to lose your uniqueness. You need not. I only ask you to learn what we teach, not believe it. And please, take your other subjects seriously. They're important, whether or not they contribute to your Art, and the other Masters tell me you neglect them. I understand you failed tests for no less than four subjects. Given your late start to the year, the Masters have agreed that you may take those tests again in two weeks, but you need to focus, Calendra. You need to learn what you must, not just what you wish. Can you do this?"

Calendra hangs her head. She does not want to, but she knows she will. Narelda is right. Calendra needs more education to become extraordinary. Extraordinary people do not fail subjects like the humanities. An extraordinary Speed Artist certainly does not fail Speed Theory. She has spent too much time speculating and meditating on the Manifold. Too much time living Slow to conserve her life's years. Too much time painting. She refuses to consider that she might be spending too much time with Myla.

She remembers herself and raises her head to look into Narelda's eyes. Extraordinary.

"Yes, Narelda. I can. Thank you." She walks to the door, then turns to look at the old Master. "You are wrong, though. Speed Artistry is a manipulation of time, not space. Well, maybe both. But it's definitely temporal. Time is not what you think it is, Lady Speed."

Calendra winks and departs to Narelda's tinkling laughter. She likes the old woman, even if the school's anachronistic curriculum and testing drives her to despair. Narelda is right, after all. If Calendra chooses to be a student, she must be extraordinary at whatever that entails.

"Was she mad?" a soft voice asks as an even softer hand takes hers.

Calendra's thoughts slow and her heart speeds up, as though it is living Fast at the expense of her mind. They have been holding hands for weeks, but it still consumes Calendra to feel the warmth and touch of her girlfriend.

Her girlfriend! The word chimes like a bell in her mind. After so many weeks of fear that Myla would never feel the same, despite what felt like flirting, they are together. Not just in private, but for all to see. It dizzies Calendra to see the most beautiful girl in the school publicly declare that she has chosen the weird, wild girl from barbarian Chalveno.

"Narelda? Mad? I can't even imagine such a thing. I've never even heard her raise her voice! She was firm, though. And she was right, I suppose. You've already graduated from the Mind School. You really can just learn what you want. I can't. If I want to stay, I have to learn what they tell me to learn. And ... answer what they tell me to answer."

"Their answers aren't always right, Petal. We know this. What have all our discussions been about the last weeks, if not to develop and test new theories. To understand the Manifold in ways they do not. Or have the greatest conversations of my life been nothing but a slow seduction?"

Yes. "No. Maybe. I agree, of course. But Narelda seems to as well. She insists that if new evidence uncovers truths about the Manifold that diverge from orthodoxy, those truths can become the new orthodoxy. I still think it's stupid that there is a 'right' and 'wrong' answer in those damn tests, but I'll have to satisfy myself with giving their answers while searching for new ones."

"Who stands before me?" Myla makes a show of looking at Calendra from every angle. "Who is this pragmatic young woman? My girlfriend is headstrong, determined and extraordinary. I do not know this new Calendra. This girl who balances strength and restraint." Myla cocks her head and looks into Calendra's eyes. "Is it possible that she's even more beautiful?"

Calendra once thought that love has two modes. One is in love, or one is not. She knows better now. She feels love's levels, like the layers of paint that underlie the top layer and give it structure. It would be silly to say that Myla's words make her fall in love all over again. She was already deeply in love. By talking of the Manifold, their pasts and their dreams, she has fallen deeper in love every day.

She sinks even further now, thinking of the little things. The way Myla randomly picks flowers and places them in Calendra's hair. The way her dimples show just before she starts laughing. The way she marks pages of a book by folding in the bottom corner, when the entire world uses the top corner. Not to be different, but to be her unique self.

"I need to hit the books. Will you join me?"

"Always, but passing tests won't make you extraordinary. You already are. Don't let tests determine that or I'll drag you from this place myself."

"Ha. You sound like my dad."

"How is he? You haven't mentioned him in a while."

"Oh, he's fine. He complains, eyes dancing, about the burdens of greatness. I think he really does hate the position, but he loves the excitement and influence. Though I think he regrets wearing that ridiculous outfit during the campaign. He's stuck with it now."

Myla bursts into laughter. "I think it's amazing. He hasn't found himself a woman yet?"

"Claims he's too busy. It's not going to stop me setting him up with Narelda."

Myla stares for some seconds, then dissolves into giggles. "Imagine them in bed. One living Fast, the other living Slow ..."

Calendra puts her head in her hands and tries to sigh out the mental image. "I'll pay you back for that one day. Now, stop distracting me. I need to study while I'm motivated." And study she does.

Chapter Fifteen

"*After seven generations, come together to join your nations and share your knowledge and bloodlines. This should result in a unified humanity with a versatile power set.*"

The Traveler's Welcome

Written record from the Eightieth Year of the Great Transference, Library of the School of the Manifold, Sanctum

Calendra finds it easier than expected to dedicate time to her studies. As someone that lacked all semblance of a routine for so many years, she quickly finds that structure provides focus. She settles into a comfortable regimen of classes, time with Myla and book learning, punctuated by time with her dad on weekends. The latter mostly consists of training, so Calendra's time is packed with productivity. She continues to miss the reliable afternoon rains of the Valley but relishes the occasional but magnificent storm that would sweep over the lake and envelop the world.

Her results in the humanities improve rapidly. It is the subject she paid the least attention to and she is determined to prove herself to Master Maideri. While she still finds much of human history irrelevant, she is surprised to find it interesting.

The Chalvenan accounts of humanity's flight from the Twin, their old home and new moon, largely align with the teachings of Tolgarlo. She is baffled to discover that the Traveler's Welcome - the Tolgarlan record of their saviour's plan for the human diaspora - does not include several stanzas from the equivalent Chalvenan songs. She does not raise the matter. She has discovered that Tolgarlans can be precious about their scriptures. Their history as well. It is not her fight.

She is startled to learn that Tolgarlans consider the Traveler's instruction that humanity meditate on the Arts to be metaphorical. It is amongst the most important of her people's beliefs and she has personally experienced the benefits. The people of this strange land dismiss such thoughts as unscientific, backwards and arrogant. The Arts are immutable, she is told, and cannot be affected by the mere thoughts of humans.

She does not argue. She will learn what she is taught, as she has been ordered. She shows Master Maideri that she can learn and they warm to her considerably.

Her study of the physical sciences improves, but remains patchy. Try as she might, she cannot engage with areas like geology and mathematics. What does it matter if she can name a rock? And she can add just fine. Not in her wildest dreams can she imagine a practical use for quickly and accurately multiplying numbers to over one hundred.

Ecology becomes an intellectual passion. For people who remain skeptical of the Spiritual benefits of plants, Calendra is impressed with their systematic study of botany. Her growing understanding of life's connectedness prompts her to consider new aspects of the Spiritual nature of plants, even if she struggles to remember the names and technical terms. Along with a curiosity about weather science, she gains ground.

Her Artistry classes remain a joy. Her manipulation of her speed is so instinctive that those classes are pure fun, Comparative Artistry most of all. The rush of unfamiliar Spirit and abilities as Donors grant her power over gravity and spatial location does not get boring. Mostly, it is the shared joy of Myla experiencing the Manifold Arts as she tests hypotheses through careful instructions to the Donors.

Even Calendra's results in painted expression improve. She is already best in class, but her attention in lessons about composition and perspective make her work more realistic than ever. Master Dovla notes that something intangible about her paintings has changed, but she lauds Calendra's technical expression.

Cooking is a breeze. She resigned herself to learn nothing of Spiritual significance from the class, but she learns to make food that is delicious and nutritious, and it allows her to journey into the jungle around Sanctum. These day trips help her become more familiar with the life around Sanctum. One day out of twenty is not enough, though. She feels increasingly disconnected from nature. The feeling of oneness she became so used to in the Valley is fading.

It is on one of these day trips that she decides to reveal her truth. Vrailen said she would one day need to trust someone with it. After ten weeks as Myla's girlfriend and most of a year getting to know her, Calendra finally speaks of her Manifold sight. Her ability to see uses of the Arts as, or before, they happen. How no Manifold Artist can defeat her because she can see them use their Art before it activates. She admits that she has not needed to use it in many weeks though, so great are her other abilities, and that she cannot see uses of Physical or Mental Arts anyway. She even reveals her other great secret. The heart of a tree that forged her Artistry beyond what she had once imagined.

Calendra sees Myla change with this truth, like a woman who has only ever smithed copper blades being taught to forge steel. She sees joy, shock and hints of fear, but burning these away are the fires of knowledge that can ignite when fed enough air. Calendra even demonstrates by flooding herself with Spirit to see and describe the canvas. She is surprised at how much it takes. She feels like it used to come far more easily, even when she had considerably less Spirit. Still, come it does and Myla's eyes light up at Calendra's description of the Manifold - the fabric of spacetime itself.

Calendra feels on top of the world, having shared her most important truth with the person most important to her. Back at the school, Calendra tries sharing some soulblossoms with Myla, but they stop after several days as Myla feels no appreciable change.

Myla interrogates her for several weeks, drawing on Calendra's descriptions of the Manifold to make her own strange internal connections. The process tires Calendra more and more, requiring larger amounts of Spirit.

During a rushed interrogation before the annual Artistic Games, Myla says that she thinks she has enough data. She sits quietly for a few moments, her eyes flickering in the way they do when she fuels her Instinct Artistry. When they open, she tells Calendra she knows nothing more yet. Besides, they have sports to watch.

One thing Calendra has loved about life in the School is the dedication to sports. While common sports like foot-ball and canopy-dash are part of life in Chalveno - the former for everyone, the latter for the bravest - there is less systematic dedication to games of the body. The Tolgarlans make it into a universal recreation and a professional spectacle. Calendra has found herself particularly taken by the solo 'Fitness Warrior' events, with their combination of unstable platforms, athletic leaps and feats of agility. While the use of Arts is banned in these events, Calendra is a child of the jungle. She needs no Arts.

Calendra and Myla gather themselves and make their way to the School of the Physical Arts. The thrum of hundreds upon hundreds of student Artists sitting on benches and standing on crates, the smells of sweat and spices and the beating drums stoke a fire inside Calendra. She pushes through the crowd, pulling Myla with her.

The sports she watched as a child in Chalveno were mostly individual feats of physical prowess and one ball sport with five-person teams she never understood. They all, without exception, prohibited the use of Artistry. Tolgarlans do things differently, as Myla explains it.

Calendra watches the teams take the warehouse-sized field, six on each side. Two Spatial Artists, two Gravity Artists and two Speed Artists face off against two Strength Artists, two Agility Artists and two Endurance Artists. She sees the Resilience Donors, clothed in white and green, hovering near the coaching staff on the sidelines, ready to heal injuries. She soaks in the dull roar of excitement and the rhythmic beats. Calendra is fond of Chalvenan music's focus on rhythm, where Tolgarlan music favours wind instruments. Give Calendra a good drum beat any day. A beat to match her heart's. A beat to match the world's.

Within minutes of the game starting, Calendra understands all the fuss. She is a proud warrior and a subtle wielder of the Art of Speed, but these people are something different. Athletes who use skill, strength and their Arts to run, leap, weave, spin, slide and teleport past their opponents.

Calendra starts to recognize the strange balance between the teams. Tasked with getting a single ball past their opponents' goal line, either by running it over or throwing it through a kept goal, the Manifold Artists seem to have an overwhelming advantage. How can you stop opponents that can appear behind you, teleport past you, or move faster than you?

Spirit capacity, of course. Spatial Artists might be capable of only four or five teleports in a game and are forbidden from teleporting to within five paces of their opponents' goal line. A Gravity Artist can leap over you but must be grounded while crossing the goal line. There is only so much a Speed Artist can do against numerous opponents on a narrow field, and only so long their Spirit will last. It does not take long for Calendra to remember her uniqueness. The Speed Artists' time spent Fast is measured in dozens of seconds. Calendra can move much faster for hours.

The Physical Artists have their own advantages. The Strength Artists throw the ball so fast that even the Speed Artist goalkeeper struggles. The Agility Artist - the one not keeping the goal - weaves between all but the Speed Artists, limbs twisting and flowing like liquid. The Endurance Artists never stop sprinting and harassing every possession by the Manifold Artists.

The Manifold Artists win in the end, having conserved much of their Spirit through the first three quarters. Calendra cheers with the rest of her schoolmates but does not particularly care about the result. She is riding the high of intense social interaction. The adrenaline-soaked thrill of hundreds of emotionally charged people focused on physical competition. She runs with Myla back to the School of the Manifold after the first game and they return to Calendra's room.

It is weeks later, not long after her first anniversary at the School, when Calendra feels a change. She has conserved her Spirit, concerned at the effort required to see the canvas. She has focused on her studies and Myla's theories. She has not even had time to meditate in weeks.

Something clicks. She feels a sharpness of mind. The textbook she studies seems to become easier to understand. She feels like she has woken from a dream in which the world was hazy. While she is tempted to use this focus to finally beat Myla in *Biome or Bust*, the board game of fashion this season, she decides to be responsible and studies furiously for the remainder of her break. She arrives at her Speed Artistry class full of energy.

After half an hour of easy Artistry, she disengages from her spar with Boravind to watch Myla. Myla is not often given the chance to participate outside of Comparative Artistry, but Narelda has asked Greldra, their only Speed Donor, to help test some of Myla's theories. Calendra wants to watch the change in the Manifold to see the effects of Myla's ideas around controlling donated Arts.

Calendra draws on her Spirit and relaxes her mind. Nothing happens. She uses more Spirit. More. Nothing. Alarmed, she tests her Art. Calendra becomes Fast.

Calendra is barreling across the ...

Calendra becomes Normal. Her Art still works with the incredible efficiency she gained in the Valley. She wonders how much Spirit it will take to see the canvas.

She uses more Spirit. More still. She begins to despair. Even her prodigious Spirit capacity is strained. She draws forth a final torrent, almost to her last, in a desperate attempt to see the sight once so familiar to her.

She sees nothing. Overflowing with Spirit that she has drawn on but not yet used, she siphons away the excess into a burst of speed.

Calendra falls to the floor and curls up. Living at twenty-speed as her classmates continue oblivious, Calendra weeps. Narelda and Myla reach her at the same time. Calendra looks up at her love through a curtain of tears.

"I need to leave," she says to everybody and nobody.

She does not look at Narelda. She lets Myla steer her to bed. After untold minutes of paralyzing fear and sorrow, she finally explains.

"It's gone, my love. The canvas is gone. The Manifold is invisible to me. What have I done?"

Myla looks stricken. After a few moments, she lies next to Calendra and silently holds her.

Calendra's despair slowly gives way to musings about the changes she felt over recent times. A sharper mind but lessened connection. A feeling of intellectual rigor but spiritual detachment. The way her paintings shifted from imperfect reflections of a deeper truth to perfect renditions of a shallow one. The fact that she has not meditated for so long. The alarm at realizing that she has thought for so long of the Manifold in recited facts rather than as reality itself.

What has she done? She has changed her nature to conform. She has pounded and hacked away at her uniqueness until it fills the box of normalcy. In her determination to become extraordinary at everything, she has become extraordinary at nothing.

A Memory of Alvertus

Forty-five years ago

A lvie tore along the splintered docks of the Free City of Veranel, barely
staying ahead of the filthy mundoes. They disgusted him, the talentless
trash, with their jealousy and hatred. What drove a man with nothing to make
sure his fellow man had nothing? Nothing more than jealousy.

Alvie's parents were mundane. He didn't understand why he was blessed with
access to the Arts but he refused to be ashamed. He had heard of places where
Artists were celebrated. Here they were hidden or victims.

Well, Alvie was no normal Artist. He was a Spatial Artist. One of only three
types of Manifold Artist. He hardly cared that his ability had been discovered.
He could teleport! What a wonderful thing.

He had practiced carefully the last few weeks, staying out of sight and practicing his Jumps. They seemed to require not just willing the Jump to happen but
concentrating on where you want to go. It was much easier when you could see
the location, but it was possible to go farther with the right imagination.

His imagination was wrong this time and he had appeared out of nowhere in
front of a group of neighborhood thugs. The type that sat by the side of the road
looking for trouble as an excuse to make you hurt. He had tried to Jump away

before they saw him well enough to remember his face, but his Spirit was too low for it to work. He had sprinted away, hoping his Spirit would regenerate enough before they caught him. It was close now, after ten minutes of running.

He did not want to provide more proof of his Art in case he could still convince people it was a trick of the eye. He leaped over the wall into the rough waters below. He entered feet first to sink as deep as possible. Once he was fully submerged, he Jumped away. Maybe they would even think he was dead.

He sat on the makeshift chair at his default Jump site, the one he could picture so perfectly he had made it into a base. He would avoid town for the day and sneak home at night. His parents would not worry until late - he was seventeen after all - but they would if he didn't return that night. He would just have to avoid the dockside district for a while. He doubted the trash that chased him would report an unregistered Artist to the authorities. That would deny them the fun of vigilante justice.

Alvie whiled away the rest of the day visualizing Jump sites. When he wanted to Jump, he channeled Spirit into his Art and visualized the desired location. He knew he could Jump when a hum resonated through him in response to the right mental picture. Something in him that had connected to that location. Maybe it was something to do with the Manifold. He knew the word, but not what it meant. He thought of it as connecting to the Manifold.

It bothered him that this did not happen unless he was actively using Spirit. He could practice visualization all he wanted, but he could only know if he was right while drawing on his own Spirit. While it took far more Spirit to actually Jump than to just connect to the Manifold, it still took a fair bit. He could not afford that while regenerating.

An hour after sunlight gave way to Twinlight, his Spirit healthy but not full, Alvie Jumped to his bedroom. The sight made his chest freeze mid-breath. His jaw dropped and his knees wobbled under locked thigh muscles. He could not move or scream or run or hide or Jump. He felt as if his body were stuck in time while his mind moved at normal speed.

After little or much time, fear overcame terror and he crept downstairs. It was all the same as his bedroom. Everything smashed. Vile insults carved into walls. Isolated blood stains.

He opened the front door and looked out. When he saw them, it was his mind that became bogged in time while his body moved normally. His thoughts froze before his eyes could look too closely at their bodies. It was enough that they were dead.

His body responded. He ran. He was miles away by the time his body failed and his mind came back.

He had to get away from this place. As far away as possible. His Spirit was full. He could not visualize an exact location, but he knew where he wanted to go. The opposite side of the world. The south-eastern lands where Artists were free. The place where he could learn to protect himself and make sure nobody could ever hurt him or his again. Tolgarlo.

Alvertus, son of none, opened the gates holding back his Spirit and channeled the torrent into his Jump.

A Memory of Danald

Two hundred and fifty years ago

D anald broke through the tangled brambles and gazed down at true beauty. Hundreds of paces below, ringed by gargantuan pines, lay a perfectly circular lake, perhaps a mile wide. In the middle of the lake, its water hot enough for steam to drift through the crisp mountain air, was a circular island a couple of hundred paces across. In the center of that island was a tree. Not in all his wanderings had he witnessed such a tree.

The tree's bark was the deep burned red of the iron-rich soil he had seen in the western lands. Its leaves were the deep golden color of a new dawn on a humid day, similar to the yellowing of a deciduous tree in autumn but with a metallic sheen. Yet it was winter in these cold lands, so this tree must be an evergreen. An evergold? Danald chuckled at the thought.

The tree was monstrously large. Danald had seen some whoppers during his nine-year sojourn. He had seen trees two hundred paces tall. He had seen trees ten paces broad at the base of their trunks. He had seen nothing like this. This tree must have been close to three hundred paces tall. Its trunk was easily fifty paces wide and barely narrowed as it stretched towards the Twin. It seemed inconceivable that it could bear its own weight.

Danald had tracked the flows of fire for four years. Through forest and jungle and swamp and desert, along beach and mountain and cave and river, he had tracked those flows of energy. Flows that had to be visible manifestations of the life energy, lazily referred to as Spirit, that granted him his ability. He had walked wherever the flows took him, always heading towards greater flows, like a lost hiker following a trickling stream downhill until it joined with a larger river.

This tree was the apex of those flows. A hub. A nexus. Perhaps that was how such a thing could exist at all. Did the life energy flowing through this tree strengthen it, as the new physical powers manifesting in the highlands strengthened the bodies of their practitioners?

Who knew? Not Danald. Danald loved questions and had little care for answers. Maybe he would discover why. Maybe not. He knew his wanderings were over. He knew this was his home now. For there could be no more important place in the lands settled by the pitiful remnant of his ancestors whose homeworld, the Twin, had become uninhabitable. This tree was the destination he had sought. It was, simply, perfect. The physical representation of the energies that made this world so extraordinary.

Danald reached the island after foraging for food and taking a lengthy swim in cold rain. The water truly was warm, verging on hot. A pleasant diversion after weeks of chill. Not for the first time was he glad for his hydrophobic clothes sack. He quickly built a fire nonetheless, worried that the bitter winds would so freeze parts of him they would fall right off. The golden leaves easily caught the spark from his flint and the fallen branches, despite their density, were ablaze within minutes. Danald bowed to the tree and thanked it.

Danald explored the small island once he was dry. There was little else other than the tree, which made sense, Danald supposed. Something that big would soak up all the sunlight and moisture and nutrients, like his older brothers on feast day. Danald chuckled, then wiped away unbidden tears. Well, there might not be much else on the island, but there was enough room to cultivate a garden. It would do no good to swim this lake each time he needed food. No good at all. He would need to craft a boat soon enough.

Meanwhile, he had his tree. Anything else was details. He was surprised and delighted to find a natural opening at the base that opened into a cozy den within the trunk itself. Even with the heated water surrounding it, the island was cold. He had little desire to camp and even less to build a permanent shelter, at least until winter birthed spring. He had seen enough trees thrive despite hollowed out trunks to know that it was fine. It was the outside layers that lived. Provided the tree could bear its own weight, it would suffer no ill effects from internal damage. Which, looking at the size of the tree, gave him an idea.

Danald counted the rings inside the tree. Some half hour later, Danald mentally ticked off the last ring. Three thousand two hundred and forty-one. Danald was not one to overblow matters, but he considered that pretty impressive.

First things first. It was the flows that brought him here, and it was time to really understand them. Not through a background use of his art of dreaming from a distance, but through contact and familiarity and meditation and the deepest use of his art.

Sitting within the tree, touching its walls, listening to its creaks and groans, breathing in its scents, meditating on its place in this ecosystem, Danald drew forth his life energy with ferocious determination. The wall between his conscious and unconscious mind crumbled in an instant.

Danald felt the familiar rise and fall of life energy pumping in and out of his tree, starbursts of color showing the movement of the life energies and his breathing aligning with the flows. Within minutes he felt like he knew the tree, and it he. His life energy was already running low, but he drew on it harder.

So it was that Danald felt it. A weakness. A defect. A flaw. A lack. There was a complex network of energy flows that passed through this tree. Lines of energy passed into it from under the lake and from the trees beyond, and wove out of it, the nature of the energy somehow changing in between. Intriguing. It raised a most excellent question. One that even might be worth an answer.

It was the flaw that demanded his immediate attention. Danald did not consciously understand the network of energy, but he knew enough to see the error. There was something about the way the tree was processing, for want of a better word, the incoming energies. It was creating an imbalance of sorts. It felt wrong, a violation of the way things ought to be, like the visceral wrongness of a dislocated knee, or the heartbreaking wrongness of a child with strange mutations.

Danald did not understand, but Danald had never been one to delay what must be done simply because of a lack of understanding. To understand was to know, but knowledge did not require understanding. Danald did not know what was wrong, but he knew what was right. This was his tree, and it was right to help it. Somehow. And how do you know how to help someone in need? Why, you ask.

Without thinking further, Danald burned away all but the last of his Spirit and he asked. He received no response, of course. Even the greatest tree of them all was still a tree. But Danald received something he did not expect. An invitation. He accepted.

Danald's perspective shifted. He could see the same flows, but now he could feel them as well. He could feel the changes to the energy from a generalized blend into specific aspects, like a prism changed white light into a spectrum. He did not hear thoughts or voices - a tree being, after all, just a tree - but he felt a will. It was the will of water to flow downhill. The will of fire to consume and rise. The will of warm air to flow to cold places. It was the will of natural order, the insistence that processes must happen according to the laws of nature. Those laws, however they applied to networks of life energy, were being broken here. And it was the will of the tree, the land, the world, that the break be repaired. That things be made to work as designed.

Danald acted on instinct without thought. As he always had when it mattered most. He knew that the only way to achieve the impossible was to not try. To try not to try, with unthinking faith in his unconscious mind to know what is right.

Danald joined his will to the tree and allowed the energies to flow into him. He listened to the will of the world and allowed his innate power to shape and sculpt the energies as they flowed out of him. Like placing the last pieces of a jigsaw puzzle, the picture snapped into place. Harmony.

That was when Danald understood that he could not fix the network. He could feel that something in the tree was badly damaged and would take time to heal, if it healed at all. He could not fix it. He had to be the network. A part of it, at least. Curious. Somewhat troubling, though. How long would he be needed?

He shrugged to himself and chuckled. He was needed. That was what mattered. It was not like he had anything better to do with his time than save the world's tree. Danald surrendered, and became the tree.

CHAPTER SIXTEEN

"For those meditating on the spacetime manifold, I can only tell you that place, time and relative distances are key. The nature of the manifold can only be discovered, never truly taught."

The Traveler's Welcome

Written record from the Eightieth Year, Library of the School of the Manifold, Sanctum

C alendra talks to Myla first thing the next morning. Myla's solidarity is a warm fire in the cold expanse of her lost Manifold sight. When they are done, Calendra pays a runner to deliver a message to her dad. An hour later, Calendra readies herself and visits Narelda before first class.

"Are you ok, Calendra? Please, sit." The old Master closes the door and scurries to Calendra's side. "You can keep your troubles private, but is there anything I can do?"

Calendra feels a ray of warmth towards the Speed Master, but it does not brighten the gloom nor affect her determination.

"I ..."

The door bursts open and a whirlwind of color tears through the room. Calendra breathes a sigh of relief. She hoped he would be in time.

"What have you done, fell woman?" Calendra's dad reaches to the sky, fingers clawed as if to pull the Twin from the heavens. "What did you ..."

Narelda stands, as inevitable as the phases of the Twin. "Sit down, boy!"

Lord Speed sits down and shuts up.

"Explain." Narelda's expression is icy.

"I apologize, Master. But you don't understand. She was unique, maybe in all history. She was meant for something beyond any of us. She could have been a god! Now she's just ... an A-grade student." He spits the term at her.

"Malnor! You might not have cared about your grades, but do not presume to impose your warped world views on your daughter. She is here to learn, and she is doing so superbly. I am proud of her. You should be."

"You don't understand," he mumbles.

Calendra, wrung out, cried out, looks at Narelda. "You don't."

Narelda pulls at her own hair. "So someone explain it to me! What possible damage can a sound education ..."

"She could see it, Narelda," her dad hisses. "She could see the Manifold with her waking eyes."

"Dad!"

"She could see when a Manifold Art was used. She could see it before it happened."

"Dad! What have you done? Do you know how much I've been through to keep that quiet?"

"She was extraordinary."

Her dad hangs his head. Calendra grips his shoulder.

"I will be again, Dad. I swear it."

Narelda stares in stunned silence, her eyes darting between the two of them as if they had told her humans descended from trees. "What? How can this be? See the fabric of spacetime? See Arts before they're used? I've never ... but if this is true ..."

Narelda collapses onto her chair, shaking her head. Calendra's dad rises with a sense of formality and addresses his old teacher.

"I am withdrawing my daughter from the School of the Manifold at her request. I thank the School for accepting her and instructing her. She has learned a great deal. Further attendance, however, will only be a detriment. She must recover what she has lost."

His expression softens as he abandons formality and looks at Narelda with a sad smile.

"I thank you, Narelda, for doing your best. You are such a good teacher that you convinced my daughter to do what she knew to be wrong. That is not your fault. You did as you know, and I don't doubt you did it with passion and determination. This place is just wrong for her. I fear it is wrong for many Artists and will remain so until the faculty explores knowledge rather than repeating it. My girl will find her own way."

"Where will you go?" Narelda's soft words are directed at Calendra.

"Away from Sanctum. I've been so apart from the life of this world for so long. I miss my trees. This Sanctum is remarkable, but it's so disconnected from the rest of the world. Of course I can't see what I once could. This world's raging river of Spirit has no tributaries here."

"And I suppose," Narelda says with a sigh, "that on top of losing a secret prodigy, I will lose the greatest Instinct Artist of our time. Well then. Good on you. Had I any idea of your gift, I might have done things somewhat differently. Still, I am sorry, Calendra, for any damage I've caused. I pray you'll recover anything you've lost."

"Narelda." Calendra's dad's voice is commanding. "Promise me."

"I'll take it to the grave, Malnor. I've not yet processed what it means, but of course nobody can know. Her life would be in danger. Nobody hurts my children, you know that. You have my word."

Calendra walks to Narelda and embraces the old Master. "Thank you for caring, Narelda. We'll see each other again, I hope. Meanwhile, we have a farewell gift."

Calendra walks to the door, opens it, and calls to Myla. Myla walks in, a vibrant glow of silver hair, pink lipstick and the pink dress she wore when Calendra first met her. Such a pleasant change from the dull gray robes the School had to make for a student of no particular grade.

"Master Narelda," Myla says, "thank you for supporting me this past year. You treated me as one of your own. Our talks on the nature of the Manifold were invaluable. I will leave, not just for love, but for knowledge. Calendra is right. We can only truly understand the Spirit of this world by living amongst it. I leave you with a discovery we made together. It is principally useful for Gravity Artists, but it might help you understand the Manifold better."

Calendra's dad raises an eyebrow and Narelda leans forward, eager.

"You think of gravity as something that pulls you downwards, towards the ground. When a Gravity Artist eliminates gravity, they can float or soar in a straight line as no external force acts on them other than air resistance. They cannot fly, only make use of the initial momentum created by their leap. Well, think of gravity as a steep downwards slope. You fall towards the ground, but it catches you. Thing is, Master, there's more than one slope. More than one down. The world on which we stand is not the only source of gravity."

Myla gives a broad grin. The one Calendra knows so well. Excitement mixed with triumph. She points one finger towards the roof. Calendra's dad frowns. Narelda cocks her head and looks up at the ceiling. She finally smiles.

"The Twin!"

Myla's laugh is a summer breeze. "Yes. Each planet is 'down', but we are so much closer to this world than the Twin, the slope towards the center of this world dominates. But nullify only the gravity of this world and the only 'down' left is towards the Twin."

"Which is perpetually up!" Narelda claps her hands. "Well, unless you're in the northern parts of the Grand Reserve. Nevermind that. The implications are staggering. A Gravity Artist can fall *up*. Very slowly, I'd expect."

"But how has nobody realized?" Calendra's dad breaks in.

"It's all in the mind," Myla replies. "When a Gravity Artist changes gravity, they intend an effect. Their mind unconsciously adjusts both sources of gravity to create that effect. I have no idea how hard it is to isolate the sources, but I'm certain it's possible."

"Remarkable," Narelda mutters, "if it's true. I really wish you could stay, Myla. The knowledge we could gain …"

"Anything else to share, girls?" Calendra's dad looks at her, his seriousness a striking contrast to his rainbow of mismatched clothes.

Myla looks to Calendra. Calendra smiles and shakes her head. Now is not the time nor the place.

"Then we are done." Calendra's dad claps his hands together and bows to Narelda. "We take our leave, Master Speed. I'll see you in the madhouse soon enough."

Calendra follows her dad out the room, Myla's hand in hers. She wipes away tears before turning back and smiling at Narelda. She realizes she will miss the School, to her surprise. The trauma of losing her Manifold sight focused her on the need for change. She knows it is the right decision. She is only surprised at the sadness she feels at leaving the people. Her classmates, though they never became close amidst Calendra's obsessions, and the Masters, particularly Narelda and Maideri.

Myla squeezes her hand as they walk together. "To new adventures, my love, and new discoveries. I know it's hard, but it's worth it."

"I'm proud of you, daughter of mine." Calendra's dad ruffles her hair and winks. "It's a brave decision. I would expect no less from the Daughter of the Manifold."

They pack their belongings in a blur of tears and determination and hand them over to the porters Calendra's dad hired. They have too much to carry to Vrailen's house themselves. They say a hurried goodbye to their startled classmates, going from room to room to track them down. Then, hand in hand, led by Lord Speed, Calendra and Myla leave the illustrious School of the Manifold in search of what Calendra has lost.

CHAPTER SEVENTEEN

"I hope you will also have the maturity, wisdom and connection to this world to use that power for the greater good."

The Traveler's Welcome

Written record from the Eightieth Year, Library of the School of the Manifold, Sanctum

Calendra wipes her tears on her dad's chest. She will miss him immensely. While they have lived apart the past year, she has seen him each weekend and he was never far if she needed him. After eight years in his care, many of them in the Valley, she will be on her own.

Not alone though. She feels Myla's reassuring touch and breaks the embrace.

"I'll miss you, Dad."

"I'll miss you too, daughter, but I will worry about you. I've earned that privilege. Please be sensible."

"Really, Dad? Sensible? I've picked up some things since the Valley and that turned out alright."

"You jest, but not every burden can be borne with half your weight in soulblossoms. You can always run, sure, but Myla cannot. So be careful. To that end, some spending money courtesy of Vrai. If nothing else, some burdens can be bought off."

Calendra's dad rummages in his bag and hands her a coin bag and a small envelope.

"The credit note in the envelope will let you access funds at any Verbank branch. Any town with more than a few thousand souls should have one. To make theft less tempting, they come with a passcode. You remember the name of the person who owed Vrai a debt?" He does not wait for an answer. "Good. It's not enough to live in luxury but it'll cover any crises."

"Thanks Dad. Thank Vrailen for me. Will he ever call on my debts to him?"

"Vrai? No. You owe him nothing. He invests in people. He knows you might one day be important, powerful or wealthy and considers it a sound investment to assist such people early. But he's also fond of you. Claims you have his humor and your birth father's honor to round out my recklessness. Still, it would do you credit to remember his generosity. He didn't need to provide you with the tincture made from five hundred soulblossoms you'll find in your pack, yet he did."

Calendra's jaw drops at this news. The soulblossom tincture is more valuable than any amount of money.

"Anyway, off you both go," her dad continues, looking flustered. "I have diplomacy to do. Some nonsense about an assassin spy who killed some Artists in Chalveno some time back." His eyes twinkle.

"Dad! What will you do?"

"Do? Why, as little as possible, as is my wont. They only raise it now as we're in a trade dispute over grain prices. They think to consternate me, but they do not yet know that I am unconsternatable. Still, I must appear to take it seriously. So, go. Write to me, Calendra. It will ease my mind. I know you'll regain what you lost. Maybe you'll also discover what to do with it. I love you."

He walks away without turning back. Calendra and Myla help each other with their backpacks. Myla carries their personal effects, Calendra the camping and cooking equipment. Calendra gives silent thanks for Vrai's provisions, as good as any in the world. They must both carry a weight that will hurt for weeks, but it still seems remarkably light when carrying one's life on one's back. Besides, they only have a week or two of walking to get to Odressa. They can rest for weeks on the long voyage to the Great Plains.

Myla beams. "Ready, Petal?"

Calendra grins through the tears and marches south into the jungle towards the Gap, with Myla by her side.

"So ..." Myla says as they walk, "assassin spy, hey?"

Calendra glances at Myla and smiles. They trek southwards at a solid pace the first day, to ensure privacy. They are both fit but steady trekking with a pack places different demands on the muscles, as Calendra rediscovers. Their only actual break is during smallnight, when trekking is impossible. Calendra is exhausted and sore by sunset. The canopy is dense enough that even the reflected light of the Twin does not allow walking safely at night.

Once they find a suitable clearing, Calendra calls it a day. They set up camp in the warm evening rain using tension lines attached to the thin waterproof tent and retire to talk of school, the trip to meet Myla's parents and assassin spies.

It is a short walk the next day to the highway. As they arrive at the edge of the forest and see the entrance adorned with an ornate archway, Calendra sees why Vrai called it a highway. It cannot be compared to the paths they trod around the lake. This is a road. Five paces wide, it is paved with hexagonal stones, the small gaps filled with concrete. It is the smoothest road Calendra has ever seen. Wide, smooth, and dead straight. The hardwood forest grows to the edges of the road, forming a canopy of towering trees over the highway.

Calendra remains unsettled, consumed by her loss and impatient to remedy it. As they walk, Calendra becomes lost in the forest, like endless columns in a quiet court. The trees are almost all hardwood of a type that looks too tall to hold such a narrow base and are clothed in thick, dark gray bark with rich brown-red wood underneath. Their long, slender branches only emerge from the trunk close to the top and spread to narrow gray-green leaves as long as her forearm. Even with the space afforded by the wide road, Calendra struggles to see the top. They must be one hundred and fifty paces high? Two hundred? With no sense of scale, the mind has no frame of reference from which to calculate the distance.

Calendra has seen such trees before, but so occupied has she been at school and in the metropolises of Sanctum and the Trenches that it has been many weeks since nature surrounded her. She begins to notice it once more. Myla talks of small matters, avoiding issues that might trigger Calendra, but Calendra's mind drifts through the forest. Her forest. Magnolia. Blackwood. Persimmon, with their majestic red autumn leaves. Golden ash casting dappled light of white and velvet on the grasses below. It is not the forest of cold central Chalveno or the jungle of the Valley, but it is still her jungle. All one forest.

They camp in a clearing a hundred paces from the road after a long day of walking. Calendra finds herself grateful to Vrai yet again for the quality of their equipment. While most children are taught to create waterproof shelters from locally harvested materials, she is relieved to have a high quality one. Vrai's tent is superb, keeping the two women dry and packing down more compact than seems possible. He even included stacks of thin silkbark, offering the most luxurious way to clean up after a trip to nature's bathroom. Calendra has never been in a place that completely lacked acceptable alternatives, but this is a much better experience. To her surprise, Vrai even included absorbent sanitary cloths, something even her dad had not thought to ask about until years after Calendra started using them. And of course, the most valuable thing of all - a fold-up easel with cleverly built-in bushes and paints, and a weatherproof tube of canvases.

Myla gathers ingredients as Calendra prepares the fire. They cook together. The stew is delicious, savory and bitter with a hint of sweetness, the mix of stems and roots providing the right amount of crunch to balance the soft tubers, the spices releasing a rich odor reminiscent of the south-eastern cuisine so prolific in the Trenches. Calendra inwardly praises Myla for her insistence on bringing spices.

The days and nights continue in this way, and Calendra starts to enjoy the journeying. It has been some time since she has reveled in the sounds, sights and smells of nature that roll past in the methodical rhythm of unrushed traveling. While the major thoroughfare between Tolgarlo's two largest cities is far from empty, there are few enough travelers to mostly ensure their privacy. Sanctum's elevation compared with the port city of Odressa ensures that most of the journey is downhill, giving Calendra time to get pack–fit once more.

The mighty hardwoods give way to thirsty tropical trees and plants. Within four days of leaving Sanctum it is predominantly rainforest. Calendra glories in the trees, familiar but different to the temperate rainforests of the Valley and lower Iceteeth. Huge teak with leaves large enough to use as a blanket, surrounded by tiny white flowers. Durian reaching for the skies as their discarded fruit leave an aroma best ignored. Impenetrable networks of vines gripping trees like lattices and connected in interwoven webs near the canopy. Gnarled banyan, a dozen stories high, with protrusions on the trunk like blades and branches that sprout fresh additions that reach back down to the ground. The plants-on-plants are striking, the various ferns and flowering plants that grow on trees without ever touching the ground. Life upon life. It is lovely. There is a sense of wildness to it after the towering but sparse redwood forests.

The ferns are magnificent. Massive ancient things dominating the jungle floor. They differ from those with which she is familiar. The trunk of a fern nearby grows out of the ground in an arc before reaching vertically, the lower four-fifths of the trunk bare of branches but retaining the broken stumps of discarded branches. It must grow a series of branches around its crown each year, gathering energy to grow itself further, progressively ridding itself of the lower branches to maximize its efforts on those which would receive more light. The result is a crown of huge, flat leaf-filled branches reaching up and out, with a thick but textured trunk supporting them. A bent old chief laboring to stand tall in his final years.

Calendra also discovers a joy for fruits that she forgot in Sanctum, other than during berry season. She washes down every meal with sweet, viscous, freshly squeezed juice. Mango, coconut, jackfruit, papaya. If there is one thing she will miss about the jungle, it is the availability of sweet, juicy fruits. She knows that people in the north rely on crops for food, growing the vast grain crops that feed much of humanity, but people could never truly go hungry in the tropics. All the food you could ever want is on the floor.

Calendra finds peace, or at least an armistice with her emotions, as they journey. When she thinks of her lost Manifold sight, she becomes hurt or enraged or despondent, according to her mood, but between the serenity and Myla's company she does so less often and for less time.

The wildlife around the road changes as the days progress, transitioning from a tangle of competing life to a world of giants and a bare forest floor. Immense trees create an almost impenetrable canopy and almost no plant life grows on the forest floor, just lichens and the ever-present fungal life of the world. Myriad colors and shapes of mushrooms. Fungus is an eternal companion wherever she has been, especially in forests with a lot of decaying plant matter, but she has not seen it as dominant as here. The mushrooms add texture and variety to the sight of endless narrowly-spaced wooden pillars to the heavens. Some are tiny, others as big as her torso. Some short and fat, others tall and thin. Whatever their size, they come in an endless variety of colors. Yet it is still the trees that capture her attention, as always.

They set up camp one night under a sprawling giant of a tree that has Calendra particularly wide-eyed. The trunk separates into two, then four, separate trunks that reach towards the heavens, each sending a radial series of horizontal thin branches that spread like ferns with deep green flat leaves the size of dinner plates. It creates an inverted cone composed of layers of disc-like foliage. The lower quarter of the monster is covered in bright green moss and the rest with white and red-brown lichen, creating a dappled effect as the light catches it at different angles. It reminds her of the tiny toy trees some people cultivate using careful craft to grow the tree while limiting its height. Except that this tree must be eighty paces high and a similar diameter around the lowest spreading branches. An entire community of Agility Artists could live in the thing.

They wake the next morning in the middle of the Spawn. Calendra exits their tent to find an endless carpet of pollen of every color, like a rainbow patchwork quilt. She delights in the iridescent glow of the pollen as it is kicked around and sent swirling in the air and catches the gleams of violet light from the Twin.

Myla exits the tent an hour later with a pretty yawn, hair tangled, to a breakfast of berries and nuts laid out on a moss-covered stump within a carpet of pollen. Myla smiles sleepily. And Calendra feels such joy she considers, for a moment, forgetting about her Manifold sight. Forgetting about being extraordinary. Just living a simple, stationary life in the wilderness with Myla. Being ordinary. For a moment.

They arrive in Odressa two days later, the last of the pollen withering and washing away with the rain. Calendra has heard of the beauty of Odressa's gardens, the majesty of its ancient palace and the engineering triumph of the drainage system that prevents flooding during cyclonic storms, and is excited about seeing it. Unfortunately, the next boat to the Great Plains leaves the following day, so they agree to shorten their time there and head straight to the hotel district. It is the first commercial accommodation Calendra has used. She quickly decides she prefers camping.

The purposeful walk to the docks early the next morning is enjoyable. The blur of sights, smells and sounds make it hard to focus on much, but is enough to get an impression of the place. Aromas of dry spice and freshly baked flat bread drift out of various restaurants. The clangs of industry ring out through the humid air, transforming the raw materials imported from northern Tolgarlo into artisan goods to be sent to Sanctum. The people are as varied in physical appearance as the few other places Calendra has visited. A rainbow of hair colors, eye colors and skin colors. Their fashion is less chaotic but more colorful than in Sanctum. They look like flowers.

Once they arrive at the docks, it takes little time to board the passenger vessel, the extravagantly named Odressa's Fury, and make way. While there are small boats on the lake surrounding Chalvstrom and some larger ones on the Lake of Sanctuary, they cannot compare to the mighty ocean-going ships in the Port of Odessa. She can see immediately that the Fury is amongst the mightiest. At least twenty paces long with three masts waving triangular sails, Calendra loves it.

Standing at the rear of the Fury and holding Myla around the waist, she absorbs the sights of Odressa as they sail towards the heads. She is surprised at how few passengers embark, but the vessel operates as a mail and freight service so will sail irrespective. As they journey far enough for the view to open up, Calendra sees Odressa is at the pointy end of a fjord shaped like a stiletto. The western wall of the fjord must be thirty miles long, low at either end, but rising to at least two hundred paces high in the middle. It is black as truenight. The eastern wall is made of the same black rock but gives way after several dozen miles to a series of sandy bays.

Odressa itself is a sprawling patchwork of white stone or concrete buildings between three and six storeys high, with pointed roofs. The contrast of white buildings at the tip of a blue watery dagger, flanked by black rock and crowned by the black Palace of Tolgan, dazzles her.

The pace of the Fury slows as they leave the fjord and sail west against the prevailing winds, but once they round the Cape of New Dawn, they sail with the wind and their speed picks up. Palm-lined black beaches and stands of tropical rainforest give way to subtropical forests as they continue their journey north-west along the coastline. Calendra has seen a variety of ecosystems, but usually at walking pace. It is a different experience entirely to see changing landscapes at the speed of the wind and from a distance. It lets her see the forest for the trees.

Her efforts are aided by Myla who, after wandering off without so much as an announcement, returns with the ship's spare telescope. They are a fearsomely expensive piece of newer technology, Calendra remembers, something about the difficulty of creating the lenses. It is a surreal experience for her to see the distant up close, as though her eyes are teleported to that location. Calendra asks how Myla got her hands on the device.

"I just asked," she says with a happy shrug.

After surveying the wilds of the coastline for a time, Calendra is struck by curiosity and turns the telescope westwards, away from the land. She has never seen a true horizon. She has seen many miles from high places through clear air, but there were always hills or trees in the distance. The emptiness of the sea makes it appear as if the Traveler himself carved a line to separate sea from sky.

After a time, Myla at her side, Calendra notices a slight aberration in the otherwise straight horizon. A hint of jagged discontinuity. She shows it to Myla, who confirms it is no figment of the imagination. At that moment, the ship's first mate comes to request the telescope back.

"Kelgin," Myla tells him as she hands it over, "what is that in the far distance? It looks like something on the horizon." She points towards the aberration.

Kelgin holds the telescope to his eye. "Obsidian Wall, Miss Myla," the gruff sailor responds. "The Encircling Sea is narrow at this point and that's good glass you use."

"Obsidian Wall?" Calendra asks. Both Myla and Kelgin look at her as if she is an oddity. Myla recovers first, realization dawning.

"She had an atypical education, Kelgin," she says. "Knows more than you can imagine about many things, but nothing about some things others take as basic.

Petal, the Obsidian Wall is a massive razor sharp rock barrier that completely encircles the land. We're taught it's the end of the world. I never thought about it much, though."

"What's beyond it then?" Calendra asks.

"If they described it as the end of the world," Kelgin replied, "they were right. The end of the known world, lestaways. There's an ocean beyond. Traveler only knows what's in it."

"But how can we not know? We can't get a ship there with all our technology and Artistry?"

"I don't know, kid," Kelgin grumbles. "But if you'd seen it, you'd understand. It's not just some neat wall that you can anchor to, send some Gravity or Spatial Artist to the top and haul people and boats up. It's an endless sprawl of jagged stone. Anyone trying to climb it will mostlike shred their feet into paste. Same with trying to drag a boat over it. Folks occasionally devise some genius plan to explore there, but they come back beaten. Or don't come back. Nothing gets from the Encircling Sea to whatever's beyond. And nothing from beyond reaches the Encircling Sea."

Myla's brow furrows. "But how did it get there? A geological feature that perfectly closes us in?"

"Who knows, Miss." Kelgin laughs. "It's just there. Do you ask how a mountain appeared? How the rains choose where to fall?"

Calendra is satisfied and thanks him for the answers. Myla does not seem satisfied.

"Love?" Calendra looks at her curiously.

"I'm not sure, Petal. It seems so deliberate, so designed. But how? By who? To what end? It implies a level of order that reminds me of your description of the Valley, but at the level of the entire landmass."

"But would it be so strange if it was underwater? Maybe it's just some natural mountain range exposed when sea levels fell? Is that possible?"

"Hmm." Myla seems to consider this. "Maybe. But I wonder more and more about this land. This planet. Spirit flows. Treehearts. Maybe it's more connected than we think. Just like a tree clothes itself in bark, maybe this entire land clothed itself in a reef."

"You think it's intelligent?" Calendra is skeptical.

"No, of course not. Clever, maybe. There must be a level of group cooperation in nature to explain some things. Maybe that cooperation can exist at ever higher levels. But intelligent? No. Even the Chalvenan word, Zem, doesn't go that far, right? It speaks of the world as an entity, but a conceptual one. A symbol for all life in the world we now call home. But natural adaptation can be clever without being intelligent."

The matter seems to occupy Myla's mind for a time until her playful restlessness returns. Calendra embraces it. Their days of travel have been a salve because she has lived in the moment.

After a happy couple of weeks of watching the world pass by over games of Willow's Dilemma and surprisingly decent food, Calendra stands at the Fury's prow to watch their arrival into Karthran, kept warm only by Myla's closeness as the cold wind penetrates the coat she insisted she would not need. She stares at the surroundings as they dock. She knows that Karthran is the greatest trade port in the world, but underestimated what that scale would mean.

An endless series of jetties connect the town to the massive breakwater within which the deep ships moor. She watches the ingenious system of belt conveyors move grain from storage silos as teams of workers turning cranks to roll stretched rubber sheeting over small wheels, a seemingly endless supply of grain falling down metal chutes into the storage compartments of waiting ships. Humanity mastering nature with brilliant efficiency. So different from life in Chalveno, with its focus on self-sufficiency and harmony with nature.

She looks upon Karthran itself, built at the entrance to a mighty fjord before the land rises. Rise it does, far higher than Odressa's black walls. Pine trees blanket the northern walls. Calendra has missed them, the oddity and perfection of their conical shape making them look like enormous living stalagmites.

They soon disembark, Myla leading the way. Cold, salty air blends with the acrid smells of industry and trade, both rounded out by the sweat of thousands of souls. Cobblestone alleys weave between buildings of polished pine in vibrant blues and whites. Smells of baking bread and spiced seaweed drift from the windows of homes. The dull roar of industry and shouting of men and women at the docks gives way to the chatter of the idle, the feigned outrage of bartered trade and the clanking of metalworkers. The white noise of ordinary people doing ordinary things.

They pass several inns and restaurants, including one that claims to specialize in Spirit-rich meals. Feeling famished, Calendra pays a street food vendor for a Hlordish saltcake, a dessert made with powdered seagrass. It tastes both sweet and salty, the seagrass infusing the fluffy, moist flourcake with the unmistakable taste of the sea.

There is a vigor to the people they pass. Calendra is cold despite the blue sky. The wind is freezing. Yet most of these people keep their arms and legs bare. Madness. They seem to have a collective energy, a bounce to their step, as if this were the best weather they had seen in years.

"I don't miss the place," Myla tells her as she pauses to watch some teenagers play marbles in the middle of an intersection of alleyways, people passing around them with a laugh or an eye-roll. "But I do miss the people at this time of year. During the winter, with two hours of daylight, they start to degrade. People stay in their dark homes and think dark thoughts. During summer, they shine. They're happier, live in the moment more and are nicer to others. Especially on a lovely day like today. I only lived here for two years, but days like this were my fondest."

Myla smiles, and Calendra remembers how in love she is.

"Lovely?" She laughs as they walk. "Blossom, this wind could cut through steel. I thought the Chalvstrom plateau was cold."

"Just hope we don't end up in the northern Free Cities in winter." Myla grins.

They reach the city gates soon after the end of smallnight. From their slightly elevated position above the Great Plains, Calendra takes in a sight she has never seen. A golden ocean stretches forth as far as the eye can see, vast fields of barley moving and swaying in the wind, creating wave patterns that dance and spin in the glistening sea of gold.

It is natural. It is life. Yet it is so unnatural that it jars something inside her. Life is as dense as any jungle, but it is all the same. All one type of life. Not a tree to be seen. No flowers. No vines. Not even mushrooms. Just endless sameness. Still, it is beautiful and Calendra has learned of late to seize those moments of beauty.

She takes hold of Myla's hand and runs towards the golden waves, dragging Myla behind as she tries to keep her balance beneath a heavy pack. Holding Myla tight and dancing in fields of gold, Calendra feels content.

That night, camping by the swift waters of the Northway amongst a rare stand of trees, Calendra paints. Golden seas and silver hair under a crisp blue sky. A short, dark-haired girl in a moment of serenity. Not extraordinary, no. But happy.

It takes three more days to reach Helmrun, Myla's hometown. It is typical of the few mid-sized towns Calendra has visited in Tolgarlo. With a population in the thousands, it is large enough to justify formal government, police and courts, but too small for these things to operate smoothly, as Myla tells it. It exists due to a bend in the River Helm, which powers a huge mill. As with many towns that started with a single purpose, it grew organically around that purpose. It houses mill workers, merchants, transport and logistics workers. All the professions and farmers required to support those workers. People from nearby who want to leave their village for a town with opportunities. And people who want a quieter life than in the great cities of Sanctum and Odessa, like Myla's parents.

They arrive at a red brick two-storey house after a short walk. The house is like a fine jacket with a cheap patch. Calendra can see it was built from the finest materials but has been repaired with cheap replacements and shoddy workmanship.

The woman who answers the door is in her late thirties. Her smile is joyful, but her eyes are weary. Myla's mother, Drialia, embraces her daughter and welcomes Calendra. Myla's father, Kortilin, runs to them and sweeps Myla into a crushing hug, tears navigating their way through the weathered contours of his face. He extends a massive hand to Calendra and crushes hers in welcome.

The inside of their home is a mirror of the outside. Fine pottery with chips missing and cracks taped over. Plush seating with stains and holes. A thousand small signs of a once prosperous household swept away by the winds of misfortune. Calendra settles into an enveloping armchair, waving away their apologies for catching up with their daughter first, and watches the family reacquaint. Whatever tough times have befallen them, their fierce pride for their daughter blazes through. They are not Artists so they cannot truly understand how unique Myla is, but they appreciate the significance of her being the first Mind Artist to attend the School of the Manifold. Anyone can appreciate the significance of being the first to achieve a thing.

Calendra learns with Myla of the troubles that Myla's parents would not put in writing. With blank expressions and eyes downcast, they describe how the economic downturn in Helm's Run, prompted by the development of massive mills closer to the docks, cut back their income just as their debts had fallen due. Debts incurred to pay for Myla's attendance at the two most prestigious schools in the country. Debts owed to people best to not disappoint.

Calendra determines to fix this. She has power. She has money. Well, her dad has money. Well ... her dad's friend has money. She will not allow family to be poor and scared. Not wanting to affect Myla's time with her parents, Calendra decides to wait until the end of their stay to raise it.

The ten days with Myla's parents are simple and enjoyable, full of reminiscence, laughs and the open pride only family can have for one another. Calendra did not grow up in a loveless family, but her parents were different. Her birth father was always away. Her mother died when she was young and her new dad was so goal-oriented and manic. And all of them were successful and motivated. With parents like that, no wonder she always looked to the future. Myla's family live in the present in a way Calendra sometimes yearns for, despite their grinding worries about what may come.

On their last morning together, Calendra proposes she arrange for Myla's parents' problems to disappear. She quickly realizes she ought to have discussed it with Myla first. Her parents' reactions are offense and coldness. Muttering about pride and charity, they make clear to Calendra that they need no help, least of all from a friend of their daughter's lover's father. While it leaves a sour taste in Calendra's mouth, as such offers are a normal part of community in Chalveno, Myla defuses the situation and they leave with smiles, tears and promises to return.

That night, Calendra leaves their tent and pays a visit to a private lender in a luxurious house in Helm's Run.

The next morning, Calendra tells Myla what she has done.

And for the first time since they met, Myla gives Calendra a look she has never seen on that perfect face. Disgust.

Chapter Eighteen

"If I am right and you are diligent, within another seven generations you will be something this world needs. A guiding hand."

The Traveler's Welcome

Written record from the Eightieth Year of the Great Transference, Library of the School of the Manifold, Sanctum

Myla arrives back at their camp several hours after stalking off. Her face is a storm-cloud.

"I was worried they would need to go into hiding," Myla hisses, "but we figured out a solution. Once the death is discovered, they will travel the long road to Helm's Fall to make their next payment."

Calendra is confused. "But ..."

"But what? You thought murdering a local thug would solve this? That lender was a small time employee of a Plains-wide syndicate. All you did was commit murder, create suspicion and prove once more that Calendra does things Calendra's way without bothering to ask what Myla thinks."

"I ..." Calendra hangs her head. "I thought you'd be worried about me and tell me not to go."

Myla's laugh is mirthless. "Calendra, I'm not worried about your safety. You could kill every person in this town without sweating. I'm worried about your soul! I would have asked you not to go because your plan was murder! Over a matter of money! Don't you see how wrong that is?"

"But he was a bad guy. An enemy."

"It doesn't matter, Calendra! It's still a life."

"I ..." Calendra touches her wet cheeks. "I just wanted to help. Your family is my family. I just wanted to solve it. They deserve better."

Myla closes her eyes and takes a deep breath. Her expression softens. "I see that, Cal. But you have to talk to me about big decisions. Not least those that directly affect me. We're a team. You should want to know what I think. And, well, you don't think like other folks in some ways. It's not your fault. You grew up being hunted by an immortal Manifold Artist and raised by a man more trainer than father. But there are rules. You live in a society and part of that is following society's rules. Not murdering is the first one. And it's about you, and who you are. About what you value."

The rules of human society. Calendra wants to be with Myla, but she grows less and less sure of whether she wants to be part of human society. Most of her experiences with other people are disappointments she could do without. Still, she loves Myla more than she hates people and so she apologizes, promises to be better and makes herself, once more, live in the moment. Even in the aftermath of their worst fight, they still retire for the night together at peace. But Calendra does not forget that look of disgust.

They take four days to reach the eastern forests of the Plains, one of the few left in the region and therefore one of the few places they might find another treeheart. The forest borders the Free Cities and provides a more secure border than crops, so is allowed to thrive. Calendra immediately feels at home amongst the pines. As they meander through the endless trees, Calendra finds herself sinking into the forest and becoming familiar with its moods and whims. She even becomes meditative, something she has not had the peace for since losing her Manifold sight. Or before. They camp that night by a pebbly stream, surrounded by life that feels separate to her but part of her.

Calendra wakes at dawn, stiff as ironbark, with Myla's hand resting on her hip. Calendra refuses to stretch her cramped muscles, determined to soak in every second of the physical intimacy. In her exhausted contentment, she stops thinking and lets herself be. The world narrows until there is only her and Myla. Her and Myla. Two beings of this vibrant world connected physically, mentally and spiritually. Daughter of the Manifold and Daughter of the Mind.

Calendra's perception twists. Her eyes snap open. Was that …

Calendra feels Myla's hand suddenly pull away before it returns a moment later.

"Good morning, sleepy." Myla's voice sounds even huskier than usual, but her tone is bright. A curtain of tangled silver curls appears in Calendra's view, followed by a face more beautiful than ever. Calendra realizes that this is what she will wake to from now on. Perfection.

"I saw it, My. Just for a moment. Though I didn't see it like I once did, so much as felt it."

Myla sits upright, eyes wide. "The Manifold? Quick, before you forget. What were you thinking about? Every detail, every hint!"

Calendra shakes her head to clear it, assaulted by the need to intellectualize her dreamlike thoughts.

"I was just thinking about us, I guess." Calendra tries to remember what she was actually thinking about at the time. "About your touch and your warmth. About us together in the jungle. But I don't know what was really running through my mind. I was awake for a while and it all runs together."

"Well, if you remember, please let me know. I might be able to figure out what triggered it. The more we treat this scientifically and objectively, the more my Art can map the connections."

Calendra furrows her brow and searches her memories. The harder she thinks, the more the memory slips through her grasp, like staring too closely at the fashionable paintings that can only be seen properly from a distance. In little time, Calendra's relaxation becomes agitation.

"I don't know, Blossom. I don't remember. Let's pack and keep going. Another day or two and we should be deep enough that nobody will run into us."

Myla grins and shrugs as though it is of no account. "It will come, Petal. You're back where you belong amongst the trees. And I'm here with you."

It takes longer than Calendra expects to decamp, but they are on their way soon enough. They settle into the relentless, heavy plod of people with large packs and many miles to go, but nowhere to be. Calendra's legs are thankful for the enforced break of smallnight and they scream at her when it ends. Her stomach thanks her for the foraged meal. They pass the afternoon in silence and set up camp near a stream, ringed by majestic willows. She misses the afternoon rains of the Valley once more.

Calendra struggles to sleep as she focuses her mind to once more glimpse the Manifold. The light of smalldawn startles her. How many hours has she been thinking? The mental kick is enough for her body to grab hold of her mind and force it into inaction. She falls asleep in minutes to the silhouette of branches shifting in the breeze. She wakes to bouncing silver curls.

"Any luck, Petal?"

Myla looks so hopeful that Calendra feels shame at her answer.

"No. Nothing. I was awake half the night trying."

"Can you remember what you were thinking? I'll write it down. A failure can provide as much evidence as a success!"

Calendra watches Myla's joyous optimism at the power of data and analysis, so different from Calendra's years of meditation and listening to her subconscious. Well, Myla is the one with the genius brain and genius Art. Calendra will try. She is almost in tears after a minute of thought.

"I don't know! I don't think like you. I just ... think, then the thoughts leave my head. I don't retain them as facts, just impressions. And my only impression of last night was thinking in circles!"

Myla brushes the hair from Calendra's eyes. "It's okay, Petal. Put it out of your head. It's a new day. Let's just enjoy it."

A weight lifts from Calendra's shoulders. They eat, pack their belongings and set off for another day of trudging. Calendra enjoys the day more without constant analysis. The focus required to maintain her footing makes her forget about the individual trees and plants and notice the iterative ecological changes. It is all verdant forest, but it has variation.

They follow the stream downhill and make camp a hundred paces out from its intersection with a small river. Calendra does not mention the Manifold and Myla does not ask. By the time they have eaten, Calendra is relaxed once more. She falls asleep in Myla's arms, content and free of circular thinking.

Through the next three days of trekking, Calendra notices the flow of the forest more and more. She begins to rediscover her affinity with the wilderness. Not just her emotional longing for it, but her resonance with it. This is her forest, as the Valley was hers, and the snow gum woodland around her treetop home in Chalveno was hers.

Calendra starts to flow through her actions. The weight of the pack becomes a part of her and the steady walk is as effortless as breathing. She speaks to Myla less and less, but she knows her joy is clear and that Myla will not take it as disinterest. She sees Myla watching her, analyzing her, but Myla's mood seems light when Calendra catches her gaze.

Calendra drifts through the world in a half-conscious daze, feeling as she once had. At ease. She changes their direction based on the mood of the forest, taking them on circuitous routes through the wilderness.

Several days later, during their smallnight lunch, Calendra hears a sniffle. She wonders what troubles Myla when Calendra herself is in such a good mood. Then she realizes she has barely spoken to Myla for two days.

"Myla? Are you ok, my love?"

"I ..." Myla clears her throat. "I'm lonely. We talked so much in the School and during our first days out here. You hardly talk now. I understand it while we walk. I can see you listening to the forest. But we don't even talk in the evenings. You just meditate. I can see it's how you connect to your Art and I can see how much happier you are, so I didn't want to say anything. But I'm lonely."

Calendra's stomach drops. She is happy, but Myla has been her whole world. Myla is the one who encouraged Calendra to leave the School. Myla upended her life to follow Calendra into the wilderness out of love. Calendra is ashamed to have caused Myla pain.

"I'm so sorry, Blossom. I've been feeling so much more like myself, and like I'm certain to see the Manifold any day now. I feel one with the forest again. Like I can just flow through life. It's a very solitary way to live. I need to feel the world rather than think about it. But I'll do better. I'll balance these things. I love you more than anything. I'll find a way to be what I need to be and what you need me to be."

Calendra wishes for light to see Myla's reaction. There is only a momentary pause before she speaks.

"I love you, Calendra."

Calendra squeezes her hand and commits to do better. And better she does. She makes a conscious effort to tear herself from introspection each evening and converse. She remembers to laugh. Even with her recent contentment, she has done little of that in recent weeks. Myla's smile slowly returns.

After a week of holding this balance, Calendra emerges into an idyllic clearing like none she has seen. A wall of monstrous ferns form a perimeter around a cool spring that issues forth from the base of a jarrah of endless height. Blue mushrooms with white dots are scattered through the clearing. They are as tall as her. Calendra feels a rush of excitement.

"We're here! This is the place. This is where we need to be. I know it."

Myla stares around the clearing, wide-eyed, grinning ear to ear.

"Hosts of the Traveler, Petal. What is this place? I've never heard of anything like it. It's like someone designed it. It reminds me of how you described your clearing in the Valley, though I always wondered if your description was a little ... exaggerated. I stand corrected! Do you think there's a treeheart here?"

"I don't know." Calendra shrugs. "But it's the first place I've seen that feels like the Valley. I just wish I could see the Manifold! It's hard to believe such a similar place would be any different, though. Which means, if there's a treeheart here, we know exactly where it is!"

Myla beams. "What do we do?"

"Last time I just cut away at the tree until I could get to the heart. Then I, you know, ate it."

Myla stares for a moment, then dissolves into laughter. "Ate it. Raw. A wooden heart."

"You may recall," Calendra replies with a raised eyebrow, "that I had around thirty seconds to save my dad and myself from half a dozen trained warriors. It didn't cross my mind to do otherwise."

"And that's the chili that rounds out the delicious meal that is my Calendra. I can know the best thing to do and still be paralyzed by fear or indecision. Once you know what to do, you do it. Who cares if it's impossible? Of what possible relevance is impossibility? We're quite the pair, aren't we? The Speed Artist who acts on instinct and the Instinct Artist who overthinks."

Calendra places her backpack on the ground, retrieves the spade and hatchet, and throws the former to Myla.

"You're overthinking it, Blossom. Dig."

Myla laughs and attacks the soil beneath the jarrah as Calendra hacks at the base. She soon sees that it is a fool's errand. The wood is impossibly hard, even for a jarrah. Maybe a two-person crosscut saw would get through. Maybe. She drops to her knees and uses her hands to help Myla dig. This proves too painful too quickly and they switch to taking turns with the spade. As it is designed for burying waste, it is a slow process. Calendra feels some concern that she feels nothing from this tree, in contrast to the affinity she had to her tree in the Valley, but she dismisses this as connected to her ability to see the Manifold.

After several hours, they have excavated dirt from beneath and between all the roots close to the trunk. The massive tree remains upright, so broad and long are its roots, but they are able to access the root ball. What Calendra sees makes her heart leap. A treeheart! But it is different from the one she consumed. Vibrant, strong, alive.

She remembers, for the first time in a long while, the countdown she heard that day in the Valley. The clear impression that a thing long alive has suddenly died. This heart is certainly not dead. Will that matter?

It soon becomes apparent that it matters. No matter their cutting, hacking and burning, the heart is unaffected. It has the feel of wood but the indestructibility of diamond. This is nothing like the heart that she could cut into strips and chew. While she cannot know, Calendra feels certain that no tool could affect this treeheart. Something about its connection to the jungle, the Spirit it creates or draws upon, protects it. Myla nods in agreement when Calendra explains her theory.

Calendra rises and kicks the tree. "Stupid tree! Why did you lead me here if I can't eat you?"

Calendra is surprised to realize she is fuming. Her anger is broken by Myla's giddy laughter. It is enough to force a smile from her.

"Ok, a bit juvenile. But I really thought we had it, My. I was so sure ..."

"But you were right! Sure, this one is not for us, but you really did find a treeheart. You found a treeheart using only your instincts. Now we know that you can do it."

"But I want it now! I want to be extraordinary once more. I'm sure that ..."

"Calendra," Myla interrupts, "it is but weeks since you left the School. We have the rest of our lives! Be patient. We will find the heart that is meant for us."

Calendra takes a deep breath. She knows Myla is right, but it is not easy to be patient when you have lost the thing that makes you unique. Still, patience is relative. It is inconceivable that Calendra will not become extraordinary once more, but she can accept it taking time if she is progressing towards her goal. She embraces Myla and rests her head on Myla's shoulder.

"Thank you, Blossom. You're right." She pulls away and looks into Myla's eyes. "But I won't sit back. We will find them all. Those that live, we'll take note of and check from time to time. We'll stumble across a dead one eventually. Maybe I'll recover my Manifold sight again or maybe you'll figure out some pattern that lets us know where to look, and it will happen sooner. But we will find them all."

Find them all. Calendra notices Myla's eyes wide and mouth slightly open - perhaps Calendra was a little intense - but Myla nods after a moment. Calendra throws on her backpack and gestures to the edge of the clearing.

"Right now? You don't want to rest a bit? This clearing is a tiny paradise. If we just put the soil back, we could set up here for a bit. Do some day trips from here, learn the area and figure out our next steps. It's so beautiful." She looks into Calendra's eyes. "It could be our Valley."

"No. No, we need to keep looking. It's out there somewhere. I can almost hear it. Are you with me?"

Myla breathes out heavily. "Always."

So they leave their pretty, Spirit-rich clearing in search of the extraordinary. Calendra surprises even herself a little. It would have been a nice place to just be a couple, she realizes as they leave, after the strictures of school. But she cannot wait. She is to be extraordinary. Like she vowed.

CHAPTER NINETEEN

"Beware! Points pierce. You can cut your hair, trim your nails, and clean away dead skin without damage. You can cut or bruise yourself and heal. You can even break or destroy parts of yourself and still heal, or at least function. You cannot remove your heart and expect to continue."

The Traveler's Welcome, Eleventh Refrain

Excerpt from a transcription of the Canonic Oral Traditions of Chalveno

Calendra prowls the jungle, Myla trailing behind. After an hour or two of walking, Myla gasps. Calendra whirls on her.

"My? Have you found it?"

"I felt a tingle in my instincts," Myla tells her, "like my eyes saw a pattern that my mind hadn't grasped. I used a burst of Spirit and I think I understand, Cal! Something we've missed. Something they've all missed. It just makes sense. Even though I ..."

"Myla! You're killing me."

"There's a hierarchy. There has to be. Plants obviously generate Spirit, or absorb it from their surroundings, and we know they share Spirit with each other. That's how it accumulates in treehearts. They're a nexus, a point of confluence, as we've thought." Myla is increasingly breathless but does not stop holding forth. "But I don't think they're just points of confluence where flows meet. I think they're just one layer of a larger network."

Calendra gives Myla a flat stare.

"Ok," Myla continues, "think about the flow of water. It falls everywhere but makes its way downhill along certain paths until it forms creeks. They further converge and form rivers. The rivers flow into lakes. We could think of Spirit as working under similar principles. A treeheart is a lake. But what if all of those lakes have outflows and they all drain into one gigantic lake? And what if you repeat this so a bunch of gigantic lakes themselves feed into the ocean? It's fractal. They're all just points of confluence but Spirit pools at higher and higher levels. Think of the system at the level of the smallest lakes as ecosystems, the larger ones as biomes, and the ocean as ... well, everything. There are probably more levels than that."

Calendra exhales slowly, thinking it through. Could it be right? It sounds intuitive. She has never heard the idea before. Why not? Cultural reasons, most likely. Chalvenans focus on life itself rather than the nature of Spirit. Arts in Chalveno are a gift from nature that one uses without thinking overmuch. Tolgarlans are the opposite, thinking only of their Art but without delving into the nature of Spirit, which they would dismiss as philosophy. To Tolgarlans, utility is everything.

It is an exciting thought. Could there be hearts more potent than the one from the Valley? Still though, will it help her actually find a treeheart? Will it help her regain her sight? The possibility of something greater increases her sense of urgency.

"That sounds reasonable. But what does it mean for us now? Where do we go?"

"I don't know, but isn't it exciting?" Myla does a little dance at the idea. "Somewhere out there might be the heart that represents the ocean! And for now it gives us new patterns to analyze. Something to, well, add some variety to our search. It might be important for understanding Spirit itself."

Calendra shrugs. All well and good, but she has tried to understand things enough. She needs to act, to improve herself. She still has no idea how she gained her Manifold sight in the first place, but she knows that she has never felt as she did after eating that heart. If anything will make her extraordinary once more, it is another treeheart. Reaching for the heavens is premature when one is trapped underground.

Calendra notices Myla's face fall and chastises herself. Myla is excited. Calendra should at least pretend, even if she finds herself unable to share that excitement.

"That's great, My! Thank you. Maybe it will help. Let me know if you see anything."

Calendra continues and hears Myla follow after a few moments. They walk on. Calendra eyes every piece of ground like it might hold the keys to the universe as she wanders where the forest bids. Myla talks more of Spirit networks, community-level hearts and population-level hearts once they set up camp. Calendra barely listens, but she nods or smiles when appropriate. Her focus is on the Manifold.

She stares at nothing, trying to see it. Exerting her will to force its appearance. At one point she recalls her meditations used to be relaxed, peaceful, detached, while this seems exhausting. But she cannot relax. To relax is to be inactive and to be inactive is to get further from her goal.

The following days and nights continue in the same manner, though Myla talks less after the second night. Calendra does not complain as it frees her to focus on her goal until she is exhausted and can sleep. Every day without her sight, every day without the power of a treeheart, makes her feel further from greatness.

It is several days later, shortly before smallnight, when they hear voices. Stunned, they sneak through the forest and find a place that could have been straight from a picture book, before its ruin. A majestic fig is flanked by a trio of smaller figs, all of which are dead. Violet flowers fill the clearing around the trees, crushed under the boots of the dozen men digging at the ground and hacking at the massive tree.

Calendra has found what she needs, but she is too late. How could someone be here? How could they know? Calendra wants to scream. If only they had not wasted so much time. She turns to Myla.

"We can take them," she whispers. "If you ..."

"What?" Myla hisses at her, eyes wide. "What on the Twin are you talking about, Cal? We're too late. But we're not too late for our goal! It's barely been a few weeks and we already found *two* treehearts. We'll find more. Let it go."

"No!" Calendra's voice is louder than she intended. She lowers it. "What if it's the only one in this part of the world? What if it's a higher level heart? What if we never find another? We can take them. I took down almost this many in the Valley, and with your smarts, we could do it!"

Myla looks at Calendra with utter disbelief. "Calendra, you're talking about murder! Again! Are you really so detached from humanity that you would kill a dozen people just to steal from them? Is that who you are?"

"It's mine! They stole it from me! I won't let them get away with it. It's not murder. They're the bad guys. Can't you see it? Coming into my forest, trampling my flowers, hacking at my heart. How dare they?" Calendra fumes, struggling to breathe. "How dare they?"

"Oh?" Myla's look is cold. "Were you not about to do the same? Is your goal not to kill these people, then do exactly as they are doing? Did you not try to do the very thing they're doing, just days ago in this very forest?"

"Who's side are you on?"

Myla's eyes close and she breathes deeply. "I am on your side, Calendra. I love you. But I will not murder for greed. You are not yourself. If you were, you would not either. I'm walking away. Please don't let me go alone."

Myla walks off. Calendra considers taking on all the thieves herself, but the rational part of her mind wins over. She stalks after Myla, catching up after twenty paces and walking alongside her.

"Why are you taking this from me? Maybe I am myself. Exactly who I was meant to be. Why won't you help?" Calendra's rage is building. Myla is supposed to love her! "You're afraid."

Myla stops in her tracks and stares at Calendra. Then she slaps Calendra across the cheek.

"How dare you? I abandoned my whole life for this stinking forest, just to be with you! How dare you!" Myla's last words are a scream that echoes off the trees.

Calendra hears a shout in the distance and freezes. What have they done? She stares at Myla.

"Run. Run!"

Calendra can outpace any pursuer without trouble, but she will not leave Myla to their mercies, however angry she is. She seizes Myla's hand and drags her at a sprint, too hurried to even remove her heavy pack. They run without care through bushes and over jagged roots. The sounds of pursuit become muted. Calendra starts to believe they are past the immediate danger, that their pursuers chose the wrong direction.

They round a massive boulder when Calendra's head explodes in pain. She crashes to her knees and retches. The world spins.

Discontiguity.

Calendra wakes, famished, in a small room adorned with paintings of flowers. The sun streams in at a shallow angle through the lone window, making it either early morning or late afternoon. She downs the cup of water on the table by her luxurious bed and rings the bell placed next to it. In moments, the door opens and a tall, plump woman walks in.

"Uh, Calendra then?" The woman's eyes dart around and she frowns. "This is my house. You don't know me. I'm, uh, a friend of Myla. She brought you here unconscious. Do you feel alright? Oh, you can call me Shaivel."

"I feel okay, I think," Calendra replies, before touching the back of her head and groaning. "It feels like someone knocked out part of my brain. Where is Myla?"

Shaivel's eyes dart back and forth once more. Calendra finds the behavior strange but can sympathize with the nervous tic of a woman confronted with an unconscious stranger.

"Uh, yes, Myla is here. I'll let her know you're awake."

The woman grimaces, nods at Calendra and walks out. Calendra's thoughts are too hazy to puzzle about her odd host. Best not to count the rings of a gifted tree. Besides, she cannot wait to see Myla. Her excitable grin. Her easy laugh.

Even as she thinks this, she remembers the terrible fight they had before stumbling on the heart. Myla's beauty was contorted with rage. But they made up, right? Why is that foggy? Well, Myla somehow disposed of the guard that attacked Calendra and dragged her here. She must have forgiven Calendra.

The door opens once more, interrupting Calendra's introspection. Her Myla - her love - walks in. Calendra sees immediately that she has not been forgiven. Myla's beautiful face is a visage of rage painted over the tracks of drying tears. Rage or ... detachment. Calendra shudders. She tries to smile at Myla. Myla does not even meet her eyes.

"Are you well?"

Calendra chokes back a sob. "Are you still angry?"

Myla stares at her. "Angry, Calendra?" Her lip trembles. "I thought I was. I am ..." Myla cradles her head in her hand and shakes. "I am fed up. With you."

Calendra feels herself rip, like the canvas on which she is painted is hacked apart with a chipped blade. The breath leaves her body.

"I am sick of your arrogance," Myla continues, "of your obsession. I followed you, indulged you, and you repaid me by ignoring me. You repay the world for your gift with murder and theft. But what should I have expected? What could possibly compete with your obsession?"

Myla's mouth hangs open for a moment, as if her mind has caught up. A shadow of bottomless grief passes over her face. She seems to catch herself, clenching her fists and muttering to herself, and the rage returns.

"I know now that you'll never change," Myla hisses. "That I will always be second. Or worse. Calendra, daughter of Malnor, daughter of the rotting Manifold, will only ever have one love. Herself. One passion. To be extraordinary. I hate your stupid vow! You were a child, yet it controls you to this day. You were a child trying to survive. Now you are a bitter, selfish woman who would destroy everything before she sees another possess what she thinks makes her unique. You were unique, but not because of your gift. Now you're not. Now you're just an angry child."

Myla sobs. "You could have been mine, and I yours. We could have been ordinary, but happy. Well, now you can be extraordinary by yourself. I'm done."

Myla turns to walk out. Calendra pulls her mind out of the spiral stair of despair it is descending.

"Please," she stammers. "My love. My Blossom. I'll stop. I don't care. I don't need my canvas, only you. I'll ..."

Myla whirls towards Calendra. Her face is broken with grief. She takes several sharp breaths and speaks to Calendra slowly.

"I wish I had never met you. Goodbye."

Myla walks out. She does not look back.

Calendra does not hold back the scream of anguish, nor the tears.

It is several hours before she can haul herself from her sweat-drenched sheets. She retrieves her backpack from the corner and stuffs in the clothes Myla left crumpled on the ground. She does not bother to change out of her filthy clothes.

She walks out, mumbles genuine but uncaring thanks to Shaivel and accepts the bag of proffered food. She leaves the house and walks straight into the adjacent forest.

She walks until she can walk no more, long past nightfall, numb to her growing collection of cuts and bruises. She shrugs off her pack and curls up on the cool, black soil, surrounded by leaves and twigs and softly glowing mushrooms. It starts to rain.

Calendra shakes and sobs and keens until she can hurt no more. A part of her mind detaches, seeking to preserve the whole. Calendra floats in a current of pain and forgets about Calendra. She is just another part of the forest. Another tree. Another plant. She need never move again, need never think again. She could just put down roots and be the forest and forget the agonies of being human. One with the forest.

The world twists in on itself. Calendra sees the Manifold.

It is pain on pain. She hates it, that which stole her joy. She dismisses it with disgust and slams closed the gates to her Spirit.

Calendra falls asleep in the dirt.

Shattered. Alone. Extraordinary.

CHAPTER TWENTY

"Please don't break this world."

The Traveler's Welcome, Eleventh Refrain

Excerpt from a transcription of the Canonic Oral Traditions of Chalveno

The sunlight sparkles through Calendra's tears, casting her Valley in a rainbow shimmer. The wedge of redwoods that once sheltered her jungle home from the mountain winds is a ruin of shattered wood, as if the heavens knocked them over with an enormous ball. Through the still, crisp winter air she can see that her jungle haven has been destroyed by rot and wind. After week after week of numbed walking, refusing to use her Art, Calendra has arrived home to desolation.

Calendra slumps against the tunnel wall, her arms wrapped around her shins, and sobs. So long journeying alone for nothing. But where else would she have gone?

Certainly not to Sanctum. Even her dad's presence is not enough to make her set foot in that accursed place. Besides, she could not face him after losing Myla. She still dares not. Calendra might be able to see the Manifold, but she knows now that more is required to be extraordinary. She will not face him until she is what she swore to be.

Certainly not to Chalvstrom, or her childhood home in the nearby treetop town of Maple Meander. The Announcer might have forgotten her but betting one's life on an immortal being forgetful or impatient is too reckless even for her.

No, the Valley is her true home. Now even it is no more. How many centuries must the beautiful redwoods have taken to grow so tall, only to fall in the two years since she left? Even in her despair, Calendra needs no thought to understand what changed. The Valley's heart died. Calendra ate it.

Calendra remembers the strange plants in Vrai's private garden. Plants that teleported. Plants that floated unfettered by the strictures of gravity. Perhaps it was not even the Spirit-rich environment that enabled it but the alignment of the heart to the Manifold. Was that how the trees here achieved such heights? Did the Manifold Heart reduce the effects of gravity on the redwoods?

Calendra slumps further, bile rising, as she considers that she might be responsible. That heart died, but did it still play a role? She shivers through the thick coats she was forced to purchase before tackling the alpine track.

No, she cannot take that on. What's done is done. The only place she had to go is gone, and now she has nowhere. She looks out over her home. Once vibrant, now shattered. Her ecological mirror. She silently thanks it. She rises and turns to leave before realizing it is not enough. After so long of facing backwards, she must now look forward, but she should not so lightly discard such an important part of her past.

Calendra detaches the travel easel from the side of her pack, unused since leaving Sanctum, and rummages through the pack's contents for her carved snow gum paintbox, a gift from Myla for Calendra's nineteenth birthday. Calendra blinks back the tears and sets up. The small canvas she selects threatens flight in the eddies of wind at the tunnel entrance before she subdues it with pegs.

Brush in hand, Calendra stares out at the Valley. She has not painted in so long she must remind herself how to start. She tries to recall her lessons on composition but gives up, feeling drained. Instead, she thinks about the paintings she made of the Valley while living within it. Paintings she abandoned when fleeing. They had a glow to them, a feeling of extra-reality.

Then she remembers how she felt while painting them. Free. Unencumbered. Calendra did not paint the Valley in those days. She was the Valley. She would but picture herself and the strokes would follow. But she had not just been free.

She had been herself. Her true self. The Daughter of the Manifold. She might be a shadow of what she once was, but she can still remember that oneness. She knows what she must do.

She has not drawn on her Spirit since Myla left. She hates it, yet feels unworthy of it. But this is her home. Was her home. The Valley is worthy and her hatred is not relevant. She releases a breath she did not know she held and closes her eyes.

The deep lake of Spirit she kept dammed for so long rushes through the floodgates she opens. Calendra gasps. Her eyes snap open and she sees. Her heart leaps at indulging a desire long denied. The Valley is dead in truth, its image on the Manifold weak and washed out, its Spiritual verdancy spent. But this is her Valley, and she is the Daughter of the Manifold. She sees the Spirit it once held as a temporal echo.

With three images overlaid in her mind - the Valley she can see, the Valley she can feel and the Valley she once felt - Calendra paints. She is aware of her hands darting to mix paints and lay down brush strokes, but the movements feel as if she is a conduit for a deeper truth. In a state of flow, she finishes in a matter of hours.

She stares at the abstract vision of the Valley. It is a superposition of physical and spiritual, of past and present. She has painted the shattered redwood forest as it now appears, but the jungle as it once appeared. Infused through the images of trees and plants are the flows of Spirit she has never seen with her eyes but once felt. The memory of the Valley's soul. But it is a memory only, a visual abstraction of a truth only sensed.

She watches the Valley until the sun descends behind the jagged mountain walls and the temperature drops further. Knowing the folly of seeking shelter in the Valley, she packs her bag and carries the easel into the tunnel network. She dare not roll up the painting yet. These particular paints dry quickly, a wonder of nature and technology supplied by Vrai she reserves for the rare painting she intends to keep, but her strokes are thick and she will not damage her tribute any more than the travails of travel demand.

Once she is deep enough into the mountain to enjoy the cool-but-not-cold temperature all underground places share, she pulls out her thin bedroll and blanket and falls asleep to the unfamiliar feeling of contented melancholy. She is sad, yes, but she has the closure of a widow who has just concluded her late husband's eulogy.

She carefully rolls Memory of the Valley the next morning, stores it in one of her smaller nested canvas tubes and departs through the tunnels along paths she has never forgotten. In no mood to set up a cooking fire, she satiates herself on fruit jerky purchased back in Tolgarlo and wanders, searching for a temporary home. She has no destination in mind, only a desire to remain in Chalveno,

Announcer be damned. Late in the day, she finds a cave deep enough to stay warm in the alpine winter and close enough to a river and food. She departs after several days, though, feeling compelled to journey. She knows not what she seeks, but she will know when she finds it.

For weeks she wanders, directionless but tending south east towards the riverlands that form the border between Chalveno and the southern regions of the Free Cities. She forces herself to enter civilization just once to stock up on trekking supplies and write to her dad. It has been weeks since she wrote to let him know she is alive and well. She was diligent while in Tolgarlo despite her misery, but risking contact in the Announcer's lands is a thing to minimize. She writes a separate letter to Djulita to ask about things she knows her dad will keep quiet.

Winter has relented by the time she is in the warm, sub-tropical riverlands. She brushes away the irony of transitioning from bone-chilled to sweaty over the weeks, relieved simply to sleep under the Twin rather than escaping into the bowels of Zem to avoid freezing. Even the swamps and snapvines do not bother her. The relative comfort provides the headspace for Calendra to look within, in a way she consciously avoided while trekking to the Valley and unconsciously avoided since.

Atop a granite hill, small by the standards of the great range but large in the flatter wetlands, Calendra gazes out at a part of the world she has never seen. Creeks and streams connect into a series of rivers that join before emptying into the eastern sea, like the twigs, branches and trunk of a tree. She is surprised to feel a moment of contentment at the picturesque scene. Snow-capped peaks far to her left, sea to her right, jungle behind, river delta ahead and the waning Twin in a bright blue cloudless sky above.

Calendra sets up easel, canvas and paints, determined to capture this aspect of the world's beauty. She plans the expression while mixing colors but soon understands there is something lacking. She knows what is needed, but is reluctant to do it. Painting Memory of the Valley gave her inspiration, but she owes nothing to this place. Still, this is the first place in which she has felt inspired to paint for some time. Not obliged to capture a treasured thing lost, simply compelled to capture unsought beauty.

She unseals her soulpaints, her own creation on the long journey to the Valley. Paints blended with soulblossom essence. Memory of the Valley was all her, but if she is right, the use of soulpaint for her current purposes will add something a little extra.

She embraces her Spirit. The Manifold pops, a layer of reality under that which she can see with her eyes. There is no nearby use of the Manifold Arts, no significant source of Spirit nearby that draws the attention, but she can once again see the reality upon which all is drawn.

Calendra relaxes and lets her hands place on canvas that which she feels in her soul. The canvas in front of her is not the canvas of reality, but the act of creation feels to her no different from Spatial Artists redrawing the Manifold to place themselves elsewhere. She revels in her flow in a way she could not in the Valley, basking in the warmth of creation without concerning herself at the result.

When she is done, Calendra considers the finished piece. It is a near-perfect replica of the scene her eyes behold, but with a key difference. Parts of the forests and jungle are more vibrant, deeper and more real. Those parts are reminiscent of her relationship to the Manifold when she lives Slow, as if she is more deeply embedded in the canvas of reality. Other parts are represented by shallower, duller strokes, as if the paint barely clings to the canvas. As if the life in those areas has but a passing acquaintance with the Manifold.

Could it be? Her paintings, at their best, have always had an ethereal quality that hints at a deeper truth. Here, though, they seem to more directly depict the strength of the relationship between life and the Manifold. During that fateful day in the Valley, filled to the brim with Spirit, Calendra sensed the dying treeheart. It has been no mystery to her that Spirit must flow between plants and trees, but she could never see this directly. She could see uses of the Manifold Arts, and her ability to see the fabric of reality let her understand the world and her Art like nobody else, but she could not see Spirit itself. At best, she could let her instincts guide her, as they did when she and Myla found a live treeheart. At those times she almost felt like she could see the flows, but never has she seen them directly.

Now, if she is right, everything will change. Her painting, enhanced by soul-paint, shows her a reality her eyes will not, even in the grips of Spirit. A corner of the forest between rivers glows, like a violet flame. Feeling excitement for the first time in so long, Calendra hurriedly packs and descends the hill, painting in hand. When she reaches the forest below, she pegs the beautiful painting to branches before placing her bag on a rock and jogging to her destination.

Two hours later, slowed by the darkness of smallnight, she arrives at the area she saw in her painting. A triangular island between two shallow, broad streams. The land is rich with mahoganies and figs, and packed to bursting with ferns, mosses and vines. Most striking here is the fungal life. Mushrooms on plants, live and dead alike. Drawing on Spirit, mind open, it takes little time for Calendra to find what she seeks. A broad fig, wrinkled and gnarled like a grandmotherly songteller, surrounded by concentric rings of tall ferns with thin trunks. She knows immediately that a treeheart lives here, and that it is very much alive. The song-teller and her acolytes radiate life.

This heart is not for her. She is not disappointed as she was with Myla, for this discovery is not about power. It is about science. She hypothesized that soulpaints can reveal a concentration of Spirit, and this experiment proves that. Incredible! Could this Art of Painting, as she is beginning to think of it, be her ticket to endless treehearts?

While she knows there is little point in trying to remove this one, she wants to try. If only to prove that all living treehearts are indestructible. More than that, she wants to paint the place. Most of all, she wants to stay here for a while. She has avoided remaining in place for longer than several days these last weeks. Where better to grow her roots than in the presence of a Manifold heart?

She runs back to the hill near where she left her bag and painting. She loses patience after several minutes. Calendra becomes Fast, for the first time in so long.

Calendra is running, ducking, weaving past trees, rocks, vines. She is chewing up the distance and spitting it away. Calendra is rejoicing. The long-ignored Art is exhilarating. The minutes are passing. She is slowing, seeing her bag. Skidding to a halt. Rolling and storing her painting. Throwing on her bag. Running back, never slowing. Calendra is flying, bouncing, spinning off soil, bark, moss. The minutes are passing. She is skidding to a halt.

Calendra becomes Normal. Her heart thumps from adrenaline. Such a joy! How had she set it aside for so long? She knows the answer, but neither bemoans nor regrets it. She was not ready. Now she is. Not yet ready to resume the journey to the extraordinary, but ready at least to be Calendra. To be herself. And a big part of herself is the Manifold Artist.

She calms herself and rests a while, reclining against a fern and looking at the old fig. Just with her eyes at first. After some time she embraces a trickle of Spirit, just enough to sense the Manifold, and continues to watch. She lets her breathing and heart rate slow.

After minutes or hours, she shakes herself out of her trance. She needs to set up camp before sundown, lest she need to wait until smalldawn. The cold will not kill her in the riverlands, but it is still cool. She finds a small clearing forty paces to the west and goes through her routine.

By the time she is established, campfire blazing and hammock strung between trees, it is getting dark. Calendra cooks a simple meal of foraged berries, nuts, sweet tubers and fruits, eats and retires, feeling a bit more like herself. And, for the first time in a while, seeing opportunity in her future.

A Memory of Alvertus

Thirteen years ago

A lvertus ran his fingers through his hair and breathed out audibly in a practiced show of disdain. "The dignity of we Nineteen, and of this nation," he replied, "continue to be demeaned by Malnor."

"Lord Space, again, you will refer to Lord Speed by his title," insisted Lord Strength, who held the rotating chair.

Alvertus waved this away. "Lord Speed is not only a fool, he is not only diminishing the rights of Artists through his naked politics, he is a criminal. And he will cause a war. Every year, Chalveno gets one step closer to following through on their threats. It is no accident that they choose the anniversary of Lord Space's murder of Chalvenan forces on Chalvenan soil to issue their demands. We should hand him over as all natural laws demand."

Alvertus ignored their screeches and sat down. The simpletons would do no such thing, of course, but the seed must be replanted each season until it sprouts. Once the meeting concluded, he Jumped to his office.

His briefing on quarterly profits was pleasing, mostly due to the growing price of wheat as a result of a shortage he engineered, and the soaring demand for Spirit-rich foods amongst his luxury clients. Alvertus himself had created the

Spirit food market only years ago after fifteen years of tracking down sources, acquiring licenses and stockpiling ingredients, and was now one of the wealthiest people in the world. Yet, it was the discoveries that he didn't release to the public that would truly give him power.

The personnel update was bland, though he was pleased that they had recruited another Endurance Donor. He had plenty of Endurance Artists to endlessly roam the world, searching for sources without tiring, but a Donor would be useful in other ways and were far rarer. He just needed more Strength Artists and Resilience Donors in the short term. The former were common but the latter were hard to get, indoctrinated as they were to use their skills in hospitals rather than being held in reserve for combat healing. He also needed Speed Artists and Spatial Donors of course, but the former were one in ten thousand and the latter were one in a hundred thousand.

Besides, what Speed Artist would join him? He had been in opposition to Narelda, but his relationship with Malnor was nothing short of antagonistic. After Malnor's electoral success and his disgustingly inclusive displays as Lord Speed, his Guild had united behind him. The vainglorious fools were addicted to the adulation of the Artless.

Alvertus loved Tolgarlo. How could he not? In the Free Cities he would be dead or a slave, while here he could reach the height of power in only twenty-five years. A height only limited by Malnor's self-righteous meddling. Alvertus had marched straight to Sanctum on first arriving in Tolgarlo, aided only by farmers who would offer their food and house for the night. Usually on being presented with proof that he was a Manifold Artist.

From there, it was induction straight into Sactum's School of the Manifold, which would accept any Manifold Artist by virtue of their Art alone. The rest had never been a trouble. People were greedy and selfish. Not all of them, but enough. Alvertus had simply fed those innate urges with promises and deceptions and, when he could stomach it, smooth talking. The urges grew, and grew, until they defined a person. As long as you could keep feeding them, the person was yours. As his network grew, so did his access to information. Information led to power, when carefully deployed. Power over people, and the power to give them what they want. The power to please someone is power over them.

Yet Alvertus hated Tolgarlo. Why would Artists, in a land where they had come into the power they deserved, share that power with mundo scum? The Artless deserved none of it. Alvertus knew from experience what they would do with too much power. They would use it to subjugate those who could take it from them. It was human nature. The strongest prevailed unless they were weak of will. The very reason they should jump at the chance to seize the Free Cities was the thing that stopped them. Pity.

His next appointment was intriguing. He looked up and down at the girl who entered. Her bubbly demeanor and bouncing silver curls belied a sharp mind. One of the sharpest, if reports were true.

"What do you want?"

"I ... you asked to see me, Lord Space?"

"Yes. What do you want? Why are you here?"

"You know why I'm here." The girl seemed to gain some confidence. "I named my price."

"And it is being paid as we speak, but you are no simpleton and I am no fool. You need not want for money. Any number of leaders, schemers and upstarts would pay dearly for your services. So what do you want?"

Her expression relaxed from a forced smile to a small but fierce lopsided grin. Her eyes blazed.

"I want to know everything. I want to understand everything. What do I want? I want data. You, I'm sure, have resources I could never acquire myself, no matter how well I'm paid. Our interests align. You help me gain information and I share my insights with you, on what I learn and on anything else you would have me consider. Maybe we should start with the tree you were attacking, hmmmm?"

Alvertus laughed out loud. Cheeky girl. The imitation of that old hag Narelda was spot on. He liked the girl's fire. It was needed, if he wanted the best out of her. An Instinct Artist's work was very subjective and a reluctant employee could withhold the most important conclusions.

If their interests aligned in truth, she would be a formidable asset. He knew that hunger. He could use it.

A Memory of Kolan

Eighty-nine years ago

K olan found an empty world enchanting. His childhood had been one of duty to his community's burgeoning Time Artistry.

The Announcer had promised the first generations that if they divided into communities dedicated to the exploration of one particular aspect of reality, arcane powers would slowly become available to the masses. Not just the blood relatives of the Announcer as had been the case. The Time Artists had only been two generations away from mingling their bloodlines with other communities to infuse their Art into the broader population when Kolan had dropped out of their Timestream.

That duty had seen Kolan confined to the marshy coastal region his community inhabited. He'd been able to explore time but not place. He had felt claustrophobic and always, always watched. It was the lack of freedom that had stifled him, not the oppressive wet heat of the mangrove coast.

So, faced with a version of the world in which no other humans existed, Kolan had embraced his freedom. For three long years he had explored the world once closed to him, from tropics to taiga, from mountain to meadow. Its beauty and variety had surpassed all his expectations. He liked people well enough, but they could sure spoil a good view.

By his eighteenth birthday, the joy of freedom had become the pang of loneliness. He decided it was time to return. Kolan only felt a small eddy of guilt at realizing what those he left behind had thought at his disappearance after so long. He did not even know how much time had passed for them. Probably a fair bit over years. But his parents, while not hateful, had seemed to care little for him other than as the manifestation of their intergenerational duty. His friends had been colleagues in mischief, more than confidants, and he had not missed them. He missed his sister even though he resented her fame as the first Time *Donor*, but only a bit. He even missed his master occasionally.

After years of finding himself, Kolan rubbed his hands together, grinned in anticipation and released the river of life energy he had kept dammed for so long. A flood of energy waiting to be channeled. Channel it he did, straight into the spacetime manifold. The manifold broke apart before him and the current swept him into a place not of the world. The great ocean of time with its endless waves of different heights.

Kolan surfed his way towards the waves of home, life energy draining with each transition he made to higher waves. By the time he was in the large swell of Human Time, his life energy was almost gone. He halted the flow and popped back through the tear in the spacetime manifold like a cork held underwater and released.

Kolan looked around at the village in which he had lived his first fifteen years of life. It was burned rubble. The damage was not fresh. Massive strangler figs grew from the stone ruins, their roots breaking through cracks to grasp the soil below.

Kolan walked through the shattered maze until he arrived at what had been the village square. A small steel monument in the shape of a sundial, undamaged, stood in the center.

Dedicated to the men, women and children killed or missing in the Chrontaro massacre of 185.

Kolan fell to his knees. Gone. All of them. In only three years. As he thought it through, he registered the date. 185. One hundred and eighty-five years since the exodus from the Twin.

Kolan had left in the year 114. The implications caught up with him at that moment and he wept. Even if they lived, everyone he knew would be long dead. Perhaps none had survived and he would not even get to meet the descendants of his people. Had knowledge of Time Artistry even survived? His community was the only one that had achieved any success with it.

Blinking away tears, Kolan noticed a shimmer at the bottom of the plaque, like light through fog. The closer he looked, the less clear it became, but it looked like an echo of written words. Kolan started to release his life energy, drawn by instinct to shift Timestreams. He stopped when he remembered he was too low but the trickle of energy he took in suddenly made the shimmer sharpen into clear if translucent text.

RAN OUT OF TIME

That it was written in a form that required Time Artistry to read made him certain this message was left by his people. Kolan waited the longest days of his life as his life energy regenerated. He would not do this half-empty. Would they go upstream or downstream? To gentler waves or larger?

They ran out of time. So they ran out of this Time. They would want more time, not less. They would go where time moved more rapidly, where they might recover, grow and still re-enter this Time without the world changing too much.

With greater care, keen to use his life energy as efficiently as possible, Kolan surfed to the next discrete Timestream. There was no sign of anyone. There was now a shimmering translucence to the stone rubble. He kicked at a chunk of building stone and his foot passed right through it. He experimented with other objects. The trees and plants turned out to be just as real as in Human Time, as were the soil and natural rocks. The monument was just as physical, though the Time message below it was more solid here.

Kolan shifted up another Timestream. He figured he could do this two more times. Considerably less energy was required to surf the distances between closer Timestreams. The rubble was even less corporeal, though still visible, and the time-message almost completely solid.

The next Timestream up was to an utterly different sight. The non-human life and the memorial were as tangible as ever, but in place of rubble was a thriving town of ornate stone buildings covered in plants of every type. He stared, dumbstruck, at groups of children playing and adults purchasing fresh produce and baked goods at a market.

A bell rang, followed by a female's cry of "New arrival!" An ancient woman of unheralded diminutiveness scurried up to him as the townsfolk looked his way. Some began muttering.

"Welcome then," the woman informed him, "and who might you be? It's a rare thing I see a face for the first time! Tell me, have they finally rediscovered the Art in Human Time?"

"I don't know. I spent only long enough there to find your message and recover my life energy."

"Life energy? Ha!" The elder cackled. "That's a term for the ages. Spirit, we say. I suppose these things come and ..." She paused for a moment. "Oh, I see then. You came from upstream. How long? I don't recognize you and I've lived a while, lad!"

"Relative to whom? I don't know the flow of time here. Relative to Human Time? The Timestream we originated in? I lived three years where I was and lost at least seventy-one before returning."

"Oh. Lad." She practically jumped to pat him on the head. "I'm very sorry to hear that. So young. You're from before the time exodus, then. This must be a lot to take in. As will the news that one hundred and forty-seven years have passed in this Timestream since we fled here just twenty years ago, as the rest of humanity measures it. You are welcome here. You are one of us. There are other communities, in this Time and others. Rest. We will find you suitable accommodation."

One hundred and forty-seven years, on top of the seventy-one before that. His people had lived over two centuries in his three years of personal time. Ten generations.

"Thank you," he answered, gathering himself. "I'm Kolan. Please, why did you not return to the original Timestream? Why stay here?"

"Kolan?" Her face took on the cast of the very old remembering their early years. "I see. I know your story from our histories. I remember your sister leading the village in a prayer to the Traveler for your safety. She was so old then, and I was so young ..." The old woman seemed to greet herself. "Why did we leave? I suspect you've guessed. War, and oppression and enslavement and abuse. It has changed over time, as Artists have grown in power. There is relative peace now. But we are happy here and chose not to leave. As you will be, Kolan."

"But," Kolan said with hesitation, "the gene pool ..."

The old woman laughed. "Our young have sabbaticals. We send them back into Human Time for a year when they are first adults, as a chance to decide whether they will share our isolation. Some come back with husbands or wives. It all comes out in the wash. Oh, call me Nanitra. Welcome to Kolrissia."

Kolrissia. Tolgan let a tear fall at the memory of his sister, Kolrissa, long dead.

"Yes," Nanitra told him, taking his hand, "after your sister, who used her Time Donor powers to pull the survivors here one by one. Come. We will visit your grave."

CHAPTER TWENTY ONE

Dear Djulita, I hope it's okay that I write. There are some things a girl can't share with her dad. And I have no Mum. So ... She left me, Djulita. It hurts. I thought pain was only for children. The things she said. They've lodged in my mind like hookseeds, scraping away at my thoughts. I don't know what to do. I can't sleep. I can't think. But I know I can't return. Not yet. Dad won't understand. Will you explain? Until I find myself? DM

Calendra wakes at smalldawn. The forest calls to her. She decides to make use of the bright midnight hour to paint. It is a hurried and simple effort, flowing without thought. She finishes as the reflected light of the Twin diminishes, unable to see her handiwork properly but aglow with the warmth of meditation, creation and oneness. She hangs her new painting in the gentle breeze, enters her tent and nestles into her clothes-stuffed sleeping bag.

Just short of sleep, Calendra hears the forest call to her again. This time it does not sound like her mind translating an indefinable connection to a living ecosystem. It sounds like an actual voice.

Startled, Calendra extricates herself from her layers of bedding, throws on a coat, laces her boots, exits the tent and explores the area around her campsite. As she circles to the north of her campsite, north-west of the treeheart, she hears it again. It is loud enough to be distinct. A human whistling. Probably male, from the pitch.

Calendra freezes. She is outraged. Not fearful. She cannot imagine anyone threatening her while she is on her guard, not with her speed, but she is appalled that someone has intruded on her sanctuary. Are they here for the heart? How would they know?

It occurs to her she did not explore this part of the island before setting up. Perhaps she is the intruder. Not that she would give up this place lightly, but a civilized approach may be in order. She is, after all, not afraid. Calendra breathes deeply and walks towards the sound.

She finds a small clearing soon enough. A man sits on a fallen mahogany, legs crossed and back straight. A quick scan reveals no tent or bags, but a small fire glows orange under a plate-sized river stone balanced on rocks.

The man has shoulder-length wavy golden hair framing a pinched face. He appears some years older than Calendra, maybe in his late twenties. He seems lean under loose clothes that resemble no fashion she has seen. He seems to wear high-collared white shirt under a woven brown sweater, a dark green buttoned waistcoat and deep brown trousers. The light is poor, but she is good with colors in low light. It is not like Calendra to pay such attention to physical appearance, but the man's look and clothing is unusual enough to notice.

The man continues whistling as he turns to her and looks her up and down. Pursed lips become a lopsided grin.

"Hello," he says in a soft, deep voice with a sandpaper-on-wood quality, as if he is unused to speaking. "Fetching night for a walk, no?"

"It is," Calendra replies warily. "What brings you here?"

"Serendipity," he tells her, "or fate. If there's a difference. I found this place some time back and visit when I'm in the area. I'm glad I was bored enough to be attentive. It's been some time since I've had company. Sing me a memory."

"Calendra," she replies before her mind catches up. He did not ask for her name, nor provide his own. She frowns. "Sing you a memory? I don't sing, and I avoid memories like a woman in a junkyard avoids breathing through her nose. The pleasant smells are not likely to make up for the bad ones."

The man gives a slow chuckle in response, his teeth reflecting the orange glow of his fire. "I was hoping for episodic memory, but I like the analogy. Semantic will do. I won't give you my name, Calendra. I treat my name as you do your memories. It recalls matters I both hate and miss. How did you find this place?"

The abrupt change of subject leaves Calendra momentarily flustered. She starts to answer before remembering to be sparse with her information.

"How did you ..."

Her demand is interrupted by the man's sudden movement as he reaches down and grabs something from the ground. He hurls it at her chest. Already drawing on Spirit as a precaution, Calendra's instincts take over.

Calendra becomes Fast.

Calendra is watching the slowing object. Judging. Pivoting off her left foot. Watching the object pass her profiled form. A seedpod? Calendra is springing forward. Running at the man. Raising fists. The man is ... accelerating. Moving as if Fast, but not. Calendra is striking out. The man is not moving fast enough. The blow is landing ... no, Calendra's fist is passing through him. Through him ...

Calendra becomes Normal and gapes at the man. He is an Artist, but what kind? Calendra felt the manipulation of the Manifold as he employed his strange quasi-Speed Artistry. It reminds her of a Speed Artist lifting off the canvas enough to reduce time's friction, but it felt like he lifted off the canvas completely, just for a moment.

Calendra puts her hands up in an unthreatening gesture. She is not afraid, but the fearless can still show prudence. She takes a slow step back, then another.

"Stop," the man tells her, seating himself. "I won't harm you. I can't, not with that speed. And you can't harm me, not at any speed. I only wanted to know what kind of Artist you are. Adrenaline gives lie to guile. Now we can be civilized, knowing we have nothing to lose and everything to gain. Sing me a memory."

"Stop saying that!" Calendra feels flustered. This strange man and his strange way of speaking are not helping her deal with her confusion at his Art. "Who are you? What are you?"

"The first doesn't matter," the man replies with a smirk, "and the second you'll figure out. Sit. We've established that you're in no danger. I just want to talk. My time is lonely. Your memories will be sung elsetime."

Calendra oscillates between agitation and ease. He feels genuine. It has been seasons since she allowed herself to interact with another person other than to purchase supplies. She sits next to him on the mahogany trunk, though she leaves a respectful and prudent gap between them.

"Ok then, I could do with a good chat. Swear to me first, by Zem and on the Traveler's name, that you mean me no harm."

The man raises an eyebrow and his mouth twitches. "You hold value in an oath? I didn't expect to see such a tradition held by the young. Very good. I swear to you, by the name of Chalv and his wife Essa, and on this world however named, that I mean you no harm. Satisfied?"

"Yes," Calendra replies without delay.

"Very good. New acquaintance should be accompanied by good food. Will you eat?"

Calendra nods. The man rises and walks out of sight before returning with long wooden tongs and a piece of bark covered in simple food. A green root vegetable, distinct silver flower petals and large blueberries lie neatly arranged. He sits on a small mat next to the low fire, takes a deep breath and places three blueberries on the hot rock plate, flattening them with the tongs to release the juices. After several seconds, he places the sliced root in the sizzling juices and squeezes the berries on top of the root. He turns to Calendra where he sits, still holding the tongs.

"I think you'll enjoy the food, Calendra. Life in this place has more energy than in most places."

"Are you telling me," Calendra says, "that you picked those soulblossoms here? I didn't see any. Ah, because you'd already picked them, I suppose."

The man's body stiffens when she mentions soulblossoms and he speaks with a blend of surprise and enthusiasm.

"I've not heard that word for them. Curious. It's a good name. Tell me, Calendra, are these soulblossoms well known? They were my secret when I was last here. I thought they remained a secret, though I've heard that more attention is being paid these days to the qualities of this world's bounty."

"True enough, I guess. But as far as I know, soulblossoms are still a secret. I only know them because I lived next to a heart." Alarms sound in Calendra's mind. "Next to the heart of a deep forest, I mean."

Her correction sounds false even to herself. The man dropped his tongs before she issued the correction. Aghast, she takes a moment to realize that his reaction can only mean he knows of treehearts. At least she has revealed nothing that was not known. Well, other than her knowledge of them.

"Well, then." The man sighs. "I wondered. For you to be drawn to this place, you had to be extraordinarily lucky or closely attuned to the spacetime manifold. You also knew of soulblossoms, though knowledge like that won't stay hidden forever. But I'd hoped that the hearts would remain unknown for centuries to come. Please tell me they are not common knowledge."

His last words are a plea. Calendra is surprised. He does not seem like the type to be concerned about competition for a valuable resource. He retrieves the tongs and pokes at the food.

"No," Calendra says cautiously, "no, they're not. As far as I know, only I and a few others know."

"I dearly hope so," the man whispered, "for great damage could be done to this world with determined selfishness."

"But how? What damage can really be done? If you know this much, you know that a living treeheart can't be removed. And what harm is there in taking a dead one?" Images of the shattered Valley flicker in her mind's eye.

The man stares at her for several seconds before responding. "Very good. Still, best not to assume that we know all that is possible. There are people with great resources and few morals that might find a way to harvest a living heart. Such a thing could make entire ecosystems collapse."

"That happened to my poor Valley. The heart died before I left. When I came back, the whole Valley was dead."

"What?" The man sounds genuinely surprised. "That shouldn't happen. A new heart should've taken its place. That's a concern. Did everything die?"

"All the redwoods fell, as if they were bowled over. They protected the jungle within from high winds. With the redwoods gone, it looked like the jungle was scoured by the weather."

"Hmmmm." The man pauses for several seconds, flipping and stirring the food in specific patterns, before responding further. "That's something, at least. I assume these redwoods were unnaturally tall?" At Calendra's noise of assent, he continues. "Those trees can't bear their own weight, Calendra. They were stable only because they manipulated gravity. With the heart gone, they fell. I'm still concerned that no new heart grew, but I've seen it before. Ecosystems change."

"Do you ..." Calendra does not want to voice her fears lest they be confirmed, but who else can she possibly ask? "Do you think it's my fault? Because I ate the old heart?"

"So you did consume it. I see. No. Maybe. I'm not sure. How long after it died did you harvest it?"

"Almost immediately after it died. I felt it die. I'm not sure how many seconds after. I was very, very Fast at the time."

The man splutters for a moment before regaining his composure. "Seconds? But how? How would you have had time to prepare it properly? And what do you mean you felt it die?"

"Prepare it?" Calendra laughs. "A team of Artists attacked us. I had seconds to save us and was already at twenty-speed or thirty-speed, and so full of soul-blossoms I couldn't think straight. I had to do something. So I did." Calendra consciously avoids answering his last question.

"Thirty-speed. So it's true then. Artistry is getting stronger." The man mutters this, apparently to himself. "So you ate a heart, without preparation or cooking, within seconds of it dying, in the middle of combat. Hacked it out and ripped it apart with your teeth, I suppose."

His wry laughter dies when Calendra does not correct him.

"Huh," he continues, "I'm surprised you survived. Maybe the soulblossoms helped prepare you. How many did you eat? I was stunned you knew of them, but from the description of this Valley, it makes sense."

"How many? I don't know. Hundreds. Thousands."

The tongs fall once more and the man sucks air through his teeth. "By Chalv's boundless manhood. You must be nine parts life energy, one part biology. Either your soul was very carefully prepared for this over many years, or you're a very lucky woman."

The man falls silent as he manipulates the food again. The patterns this time are similar, but not identical.

"What are ..."

The man cuts her off with an upraised hand. He continues his cooking in silence. After a minute or so, he tosses the ingredients and sweeps them onto two half-cylinders of bark. He hands one to her.

"No talking. Eat. Whatever connection you feel to your Art, focus on that as you eat."

Calendra slips into the meditation she has avoided for so long, like an old shoe that still fits. She feels the effects before she has finished. It is reminiscent of the connection she felt during her soulblossom binge, but noticeably different. It is not as intense, but is somehow more focused.

"Good, no?" The man grins at her, having finished his own meal.

"Wow," she replies, "yes. You used so few soulblossoms that I didn't expect much. Was it the other ingredients?"

"I'm glad to see I've something to supplement your knowledge," he says with a laugh. "What do you know of Spirit-rich foods?"

Calendra shrugs. "Plant life becomes infused with Spirit. Eating that plant will release the Spirit. If the Spirit is closely aligned to the Manifold, it will boost a Manifold Artist's power."

"Boost their power? The amount of Spirit they have at that moment or the total capacity of Spirit they can generate? Is it a temporary boost, or permanent?"

Calendra considers this for a moment, surprised she has never given the details much thought. "I guess that normal Spirit-rich foods just replenish any Spirit you've lost and do little for capacity. Intense ones like soulblossoms seem to boost my capacity, but only temporarily. I've never felt so full of Spirit as I did during my blossom binge. Hearts are different. I've been able to access way more Spirit since that day and I think that's the heart, not the blossoms. It expanded me. More than that, my Spirit seems to be more pure. I feel closer to the Manifold than I did before."

"Very good. I'll bet your Spirit was almost empty at the time. Why would that matter?"

"You're like my teacher, asking questions rather than answering them!"

"Ha!" He grins at her. "Then you were a lucky student. Facts disappear from memories too easily. An answer people come up with themselves will lodge in the mind forever. Answer the question."

Calendra ponders for half a minute before answering. "Because the more pure version of Manifold-aligned Spirit I took in would get diluted by any Spirit I already hold? Like filling a flask with clean water without emptying the muddy water first."

"Very good! Yes, Spirit seems to regenerate itself. The smallest seed of Spirit will proliferate, but the nature and quality of that Spirit will depend on the seed. A heart of decent size is so dense with Spirit and so aligned to body, mind or soul that an Artist's Spirit quality and capacity will be permanently changed by consuming it."

The man pauses and looks at her as if awaiting her insight. Calendra stays silent as she thinks this through. The man continues after a few moments, apparently unwilling to wait.

"Ok, not there yet. Almost, I think. Tell me, Calendra. Why did I ask you to focus your thoughts as you ate?"

"I don't know. To be in the right mindset? To align mind and soul. Does it matter why? I've been doing it for years. I know the importance of mindset."

"Good. And yes, it matters why. So, why? What practical effect could conscious thought have on dead plant matter? Why is it important that body, mind and soul are aligned?"

Conscious thought. Meditation. "Because," Calendra slowly replies, "thought somehow focuses Spirit. It's not just preparing yourself to receive the Spirit. It's changing the Spirit."

The man claps his hands together and rubs them with the excitement of a teacher more passionate about a topic than their students.

"Yes. Very good. It makes little sense to me that this is not universal knowledge. Chalv, bless that man, left instructions for humanity to disperse into separate enclaves, each dwelling on a different aspect of reality before merging once more. We did. We developed the Arts through collective, determined, focused thought. Enclaves of Artists of different types. We mixed those bloodlines so all can be

Artists. I can't understand how people failed to understand the implications. Or forgot them. This should be no mystery. We spent generations doing it."

"I think," Calendra says, remembering her dad's instructions so many years ago, "that it isn't unknown. Just not widely known. But you're right, both versions of the Traveler's Welcome - I gather Chalv is what you call him - talk about this. I guess most people just think of it as a kind of social specialization. Not a way to hack Spiritual mechanics."

Calendra notices the man staring at her, mouth wide. He splutters in response. "Both versions?"

"Yeah, I was surprised as well. My dad - my first dad - insisted I memorize every word of the old songs. When I went to Sanctum, I discovered their written account is different. Some verses are missing. Others are subtly different, changing the words to place less emphasis on the sanctity of this world's living things."

"Well, that's horrendous. Editing the last words of the savior of humanity and the greatest Artist to ever live is deplorable. Even worse if that's a deliberate attempt to diminish life's value. Though that may be the reason some of these matters are not widely known, which may be for the best. Perhaps it also means that the last piece of the puzzle remains closely held."

"What puzzle?"

"Why, the puzzle of why you enjoyed that meal so much!"

"I mean, it was pretty good, I've ..."

"No no no," he interjects, shaking his forefinger at her like he might with a naughty child. "It was excellent. But why? Just because of the ingredients?"

"I know where this is going. You focused your thoughts as you cooked, and that helped focus the Spirit in that food. But how? I understand that working while you eat, but how did you force your will into the food?"

Calendra says this almost to herself. The man just waits. Calendra considers whether there was anything different about the way the man cooked, and it hits her.

"You turned and flipped and mixed the food in specific ways. There were patterns I didn't recognize. Are they some kind of code then? Maybe it's not about your mindset, but some deeper pattern."

"Very good. Though not quite. There may be some inherent significance to the patterns I use, but I'm not aware of one. It is indeed about mindset, but I find that using certain patterns helps me maintain that mindset. But you hit on an important truth. The proper mindset isn't enough. The Artist must have a way to externally apply their will."

The man grins at her while she considers. After a few seconds, he taps his foot with mock impatience and twirls his tongs. She looks around the clearing at the fire, the bark plates and the stone grill, all of which he must have gathered from the area. All except the intricately carved wooden tongs ...

"The tongs. There's something special about those tongs. They're the only thing here that you own."

"Good," he tells her with apparent satisfaction. "Yes. An Artist can focus Spirit during a cook in a way that makes the meal Spiritually greater than the sum of its parts. Now, this only works when the Spirit is already well aligned to the Artist, and when the Artist can exert their will through an object infused with tightly focused Spirit."

What? Infuse something non-living with Spirit? Calendra has never even heard a whisper of this.

"How?"

"Just as it sounds. You focus your thoughts, draw on your Spirit and will the object to align. It's far easier to push your Spirit into a living thing, particularly a sentient thing, as Donors know. Non-living things don't accept it easily, but they do eventually, especially if they were once alive. These tongs have been the only thing I've cooked with for many years. I maintain the same mindset every time I use them. I spend idle hours holding them and pushing my Spirit into them. It takes a long time and it takes a consistent, reproducible mindset."

"Wow." Calendra does not know what more to say. She looks at the tongs in awe. "Can I have them?"

The man cocks his head, then laughs. "No, you can't have them. I'll give you knowledge, but you can't have my most treasured possession."

"Why, though?" Calendra tries to clarify. "Why are you telling me these things? These secrets so powerful. Why do people keep giving me opportunities that nobody else has?" She says the last to herself but speaks it out loud.

The man shrugs, as it is obvious. "You've the feeling of someone important. One of those rare people who send ripples through the waves of time as they tow fate behind them. You had dangerous knowledge already. You know enough and have sufficiently advanced abilities to cause damage already. I can only hope that the context I've given you will make you an ally of this world. The knowledge I've given you can then enable you to defend this world."

He shrugs. "Or it can help you destroy it. I don't know you. I know what you can be. A swift river that washes away destiny in your wake. I can only hope to direct the current."

"What are you? Who are you?"

"I'm human, just like you. Who I am doesn't matter. I'm just a guy who made a mistake with my Art and it cost me everyone I knew. I've avoided people since then, leaving them to their own time. Occasionally someone catches my notice, though. You're not the only person with whom I've shared the secret of infusing. But I mostly keep to myself."

"You can have your privacy." Calendra sighs. "At least tell me about your Art. You seem something between a Speed Artist and a Spatial Artist, without being either."

"That, I'm afraid, is not something I'll share. I think you'll figure it out, eventually. I just hope you don't. Too many secrets have been revealed. Too many truths made secret. This is one truth I'm glad has become a secret. Bye, Calendra. Be good. I look forward to the day when you sing your memories."

She began drawing on Spirit more rapidly when he said 'bye'.

Calendra becomes Fast.

Calendra is staring at the man's image on the vibrant Manifold. The man is activating his Art. He is lifting off the canvas like a Speed Artist. Unlike a Speed Artist, he is not stopping. Even so Fast, it is happening in a blink. He is lifting off the canvas completely. An echo of an echo remaining. It too disappearing. Calendra is staring, unblinking, but seeing no evidence he ever existed.

Calendra becomes Normal. She was sure that would work. She said nothing of her Manifold sight. The man's Art feels like Speed, but seems to work like Spatial Artistry as he must have appeared somewhere else. The mystery frustrates her, but not for long. She has knowledge. She has an objective. She has, for the first time since being alone, a path to become extraordinary.

Calendra walks back to her campsite to retrieve her hatchet, knife and precious soulblossom essence, and goes to the clearing containing the heart. She spends some time checking over the lower branches of the gnarled old fig. She eventually chooses a branch that suits her needs.

Calendra apologizes to the sacred tree and hacks off the branch. She sits, leans against the trunk and drinks several drops of essence. She clears her mind and falls into the meditation that was once such a part of her life. She draws on Spirit and focuses her will as she picks up her knife.

Under the dim Twinlight, Spirit raging within and around her, mind as sharp as her knife, Calendra carves herself a spatula.

CHAPTER TWENTY TWO

Hey DJ, I'm fine. Happy, perhaps? Your thoughts helped a lot. As they have for so long now. Even when I don't feel up to replying properly. I had a remarkable encounter recently, and learned a great new skill. This might be a turning point in my journey to the extraordinary. Miss you both. DM

C alendra drifts out of the trance that accompanies living Slow to the urgent clanging of a nearby village's bell.

Dingding. Ding. Ding ding.

She sighs out the frustration. Another raid.

She cannot see the town from her treetop winter home, only glimpses of the irrigated rice fields circling the hills like three-dimensional fingerprints. It is so different from her home for the rest of the year, the isolated cloud forest in the peaks far above, where she can spend her afternoons watching the forest generate its own clouds, meditating on the visible flows. But her winter home has further uses than just escaping the cold of the mountains.

Dingding. Ding. Ding ding.

She will help them, but she is not one of them. She is her own. Separate. When she is not here and they are raided, so be it. They should not rely on her. But when she is here, she will help.

This is a time to help. Two clear dings means an unscheduled meeting. Three means an emergency. Five, a raid. Five in that pattern means someone has been taken recently enough to mount a rescue.

They are brave people. Free Cities raids are conducted by hard men, harder women and, at times, Artists. These simple rice farmers risk death, yet they will not lightly abandon their own.

Calendra corrects herself. They are not simple people. They are people who embrace a simple life and simple pleasures. Good people, though she still tries to avoid them as she does all humans.

Calendra has spent seven years in the wilds since returning to Chalveno, cooking, painting and exploring the wonders of Zem's life. Her Manifold sight is a permanent companion, fueled by perpetually drawing on Spirit. Her Spirit capacity feels boundless after years of consuming Spirit-rich foods, prepared with the spatula that focuses and exerts her considerable will. She has found three significant hearts in that time, but two were healthy. The remaining heart was dead, but she knew it was aligned to Body or Mind as it did not resonate with her.

Her wanderings brought her back to the riverlands several years ago, drawn by some intangible imperative. While she considers the entire riverlands her domain, it is in the warmer lowlands close to the Eastern Sea that she spends the most time.

Her wait for the perfect heart, a heart of the Manifold at a higher level than that from the Valley, has not been without gain. Chalveno claims the entire riverlands but does not resource its protection, making those living close to the border vulnerable. The clay soil's unrivaled productivity for rice cultivation means that people will settle anyway and look after each other. They profit enough to make the risks worthwhile while the Announcer taxes them without giving anything in return. This makes the riverlands susceptible to Free Cities mercenaries taking riverlands Artists to sell, or overzealous bigots hunting them out of hatred.

It is not her home, not even for most of the year, but Calendra is not one to walk away from a fight. Her skills in combat and speed manipulation now put to shame the heights she achieved in the Valley. Every raid is an opportunity to help innocent people. An opportunity to punish the invaders and deter them from ever coming back. An opportunity to train.

Calendra ties her combat satchel around her waist, snug against her left hip. She seldom uses it, preferring hands or tree branches, but there are times she needs ready access to her dagger, throwing knives or soulblossom essence. She ties her first aid satchel to her right hip, as she does every time she ventures. There is no snow here in winter but the environment is no friend, bringing endless rain and foggy mornings.

She walks to the platform at the edge of her hand-crafted treehouse, grabs the bungee rope and hops off the edge. It only takes several seconds of acceleration and deceleration to reach the ground. She lets go of the handholds at her nadir and watches the rope spring upwards through the branchless gap.

Calendra increases her draw on Spirit beyond her baseline usage, just enough for her purposes. She is exquisitely familiar with her Spirit and her Art, and knows exactly how much she needs to fuel five-speed for several minutes.

Calendra becomes Fast.

Running. Weaving. Jumping. Sliding. Civilization appearing.

Calendra becomes Normal. These villagers are not fools. Some have seen her fight and word gets around. Still, she avoids advertising her Art where possible. She runs into the small village and through the door of the village hall. A few heads turn. The din of panicked deliberations gives way to whispers, then silence.

"Protector," the wispy man with the wispy beard murmurs mid-bow. "It is but a child this time. Is there anything you can do?"

Calendra feels the hopeful stares of three dozen people boring into her. She looks at her feet.

"I'm not your protector," she mumbles before looking back up at the village head. She has been told his name several times but avoids remembering it. Still, these people deserve encouragement. She firms her voice. For their sake. "I'm not your protector," she says again, "but of course I will help. Who did they take? Where did they go? How many are they?"

A wrinkled, sun-beaten grandfather steps forward and speaks. The village cook if Calendra's memory serves. "They took my grandson, Miss Protector. Only five years old and looks younger. The boy looks like me if I had three parts less skin than I do. His mumma, my daughter, is beside herself. Her husband and three lads ran after them, having heard the boy's screams in the distance. The boy was playing at the edge of the forest, curse me for allowing it."

Five? The hairs on Calendra's arms rise. Monsters! She will break them.

"You saw nothing?" Calendra addresses the cook, but looks around the room. "How many? Were they armed? Any Artists?"

The man shakes his head. No other villager offers anything.

"Where?" The question is aimed at nobody in particular.

"I'll take you!" A teenage girl with short hair runs to her. "Come."

The girl runs towards the exit. Calendra follows. Calendra is impressed with the girl's speed and stamina. After several minutes of running, they reach a section of forest bordering a field with assorted vegetables. Calendra sees the chaos of churned mud and broken branches that mark the brave men's pursuit.

"They will pay," she tells the girl ferociously. She runs into the forest and makes sure the girl has not followed.

Calendra becomes Fast. Very Fast.

Minutes later, having experienced over an hour of Calendra time, it is done. She delivers the child to his wailing mother while the brave pursuers still help their wounded fellow. Calendra is glad his charge was rewarded with a leg gash that deterred the others from continuing.

Calendra walks towards the door without a word to the mother, wondering whether she should have hidden those bodies. She does not want retaliatory attacks on the village, given the example she made of them, but the message had to be sent. She hopes it was clear. Carving the words 'never children' into several trees around the bodies should make that pretty sure.

The cook intercepts her as she gets to the exit. "Please, wait. We owe you everything. I might be capable of giving you something in return. Come to my house. Please."

Calendra considers. What could this man provide her she cannot get herself, in this simple place? But no, they are not simple. She has the time, and to deny someone the chance to show gratitude is to deny them an important thing. She nods in assent and follows the cook, who identifies himself as Velekhno, to his nearby cottage.

"What do you know," he asks her, eyes ablaze, "about Spirit foods?"

Calendra shrugs. "More than most."

Velekhno falters. "I ... oh, I see. Good then, you might understand. What do you know about the Art of Cooking? Of maximizing the potential of these foods by focusing the mind and Spirit?"

Calendra stares at him. He knows? How? Perhaps more has been discovered during her time in the wilds, but an old man all the way out here? Besides, she thought her knowledge was unique.

"I see you're skeptical," Velekhno continues. "I will demonstrate."

He walks to a locked cabinet, unlocks it with a key tied to his belt and retrieves a small wooden box. He opens it, removes a small brown block and slices a sliver from it before replacing the rest.

"Eat," he says, handing the sliver to her. "Think of your Spirit. Focus on it. Find the feeling you get when you use your Art and hone in on that."

She does. Calendra has developed and mastered her Spirit cooking over recent years using the perfect ingredients. She knows her advances. She feels them.

As the sliver of dense, homogeneous food settles in her stomach, she realizes she is an amateur. She can feel that the release is not just about the ingredients used. She suddenly feels that, if a normal Artist extracts only one hundredth of the Spirit in the life they eat and her cooking releases a tenth, this is letting her extract half of it. Something about the alignment of the Spirit, perhaps.

"How?" Her tone has more accusation than she would like.

"It is a rare Art. Perhaps unknown outside my family. I have never revealed it, but no greater debt can be levied than by saving a child through selfless bravery. You see, I am able to focus my Spirit through an object that ..."

"I know," Calendra interrupts. "I've spent years infusing my spatula. Here I was thinking I had mastered it. How did you make this so potent? It's like nothing I've ever Cooked. What ingredients did you use?"

The old man's body is completely stiff and his mouth hangs open. "You know? But how? I thought ..." Velekhno trails off.

"So did I," Calendra sighs. Yet it is coming together in her mind. The golden-haired man had mentioned telling one other person. Someone in the southern reaches of the Free Cities. But what are the odds?

"Seven years ago," she tells him, "I encountered a man. He knew much. He had long, golden hair and carried carved tongs."

"Traveler's Mother," Velekhno whispers. "I thought this was my knowledge alone."

"I think it is, Velekhno. He told me he had only revealed it to one other person. A Free Cities man. I had expected someone younger."

"That's a relief. I only wonder, if he waited decades to tell someone else, whether he might have told more since."

What? Impossible. Calendra springs to her feet, fists clenched. "When did he visit you?"

The old man looks alarmed. "Why, thirty-five years ago, Protector. I was a scared lad in the Free Cities whose Artistry had been discovered. You have infused your spatula for seven years. I have infused all my utensils for thirty-five, but most important is my wok."

Velekhno's beam of pride obscures the concern of a moment before. Calendra cannot believe her ears. Thirty-five years? The golden-haired man appeared barely that old when she met him.

That must answer the mystery. The golden god of the cook is a Speed Artist. He avoids aging by living Slow. She has done so herself more and more in recent years, concerned with her visible ageing, but this seems extreme. The slowness with which he must live to age so slowly. The solitude that must entail. Of course, he did things with his Art that Calendra, a goddess of speed manipulation, cannot understand. Maybe he has tricks she cannot imagine. His strange phase shift, when her hand went right through him, must have been him moving so fast that she could not even detect his movement.

"That man appeared in his early thirties when I met him, Velekhno." She does not give him time to voice the shock that appears on his lined face. "Did you say that you infuse your wok with Spirit? He didn't mention that, but it should have occurred to me. Is that the source of the potency?"

"It helps a lot." Velekhno seems to bite down on his questions and wonder. "You're still underestimating time. My cooking has ten times the potency it did thirty years ago. You'll get there. So. He was a Speed Artist."

"Huh. Yes, that's my best guess. Strange type, though. How did you know that?"

"You didn't think to ask, so I didn't raise it. I'm an Instinct Artist, young Protector. I don't use it much other than during a Cook. It's an exhausting Art, most folks don't realize. So many false positives. You have to focus to ignore the noise. Sometimes it gets too much and you just turn it off. I'll not make that mistake again. Not while the raids continue. I'm already tired from using it."

Calendra nods in understanding. Instinct Artistry needs data. The old man cannot intuit matters of which he knows nothing, but he can piece together conclusions with the right information. The thought makes her think of Myla, so she turns her mind away.

"Thank you for sharing your secrets with me." She stands. "Even though I already knew them. You've given me something to aspire to, at least. I wish you all the best. You'll need to learn to take care of yourselves if this continues. It may not after they receive my message."

"But you must wait!" Velekhno stands in a hurried motion. "It was not knowledge that I give in exchange for my grandson. That was just so you would understand my gift."

He walks to the kitchen, looking back frequently as if afraid she will escape. She resumes her seat at the table. After some shuffling in a drawer, he comes back with a small wok. He places it on the table in front of her and remains standing, glowing with pride.

"It's not the wok I've spent most of the last thirty years with, but it is the one I used through my flight from the Free Cities and years of travels after meeting this Speed Artist. I think it will be more suited to you. It is infused with enthusiasm and innovation that you can shape, even though my Spirit is different to yours. It is small enough to clip to any backpack. I think you will like it."

Calendra breathes out in wonder. This could cut years off her advancement in this amazing Art. It represented years of this man's commitment.

Calendra stands, walks to the old man and embraces him with a long, warm hug. "Thank you. I will forge it into the greatest wok this world has seen."

Velekhno breaks out in a delighted laugh that makes him look decades younger. "That, young lady, was precisely the right thing to say. If you ever need Mind-rich meals or if you just want to talk about your new Art with the only other person who knows it, my son lives in the east of Chalveno. He settled in a small village named Streamsilk, inland from Sun's Kiss. Hwandro lacks my years and tools but his skill as a Cook is far greater. His instincts are strong indeed. If you are in need, tell him what you did here. Show him the wok. He will know it."

Calendra expresses further thanks and departs, leaving the village in a random direction before circling back to the home in the sky she spent so long building.

The wok is everything she hoped. She falls asleep that night buzzing with Spirit. Unusually, she wakes at smalldawn with a mental itch. She crawls to the open platform and gazes down at the ground ten storeys below, dazzling with dappled Twinlight shining through the patchy canopy.

Struck by an urge to paint the scene, she straps a few supplies to her back and climbs down to an intersection of branches that provides a comfortable seat. She has painted the same scene at smallnight a hundred times and does so without thinking. She will compare it in the daylight.

Calendra has come to understand that trees operate on a different time scale from humans. Longer than she would care to admit as a Speed Artist. She can see the Manifold and, with her painting, bring out details her eyes cannot recognize, but she still lives faster than a tree. So, just like the Odressan flip-books that create moving pictures, Calendra paints the same scene from time to time. Slow change is best noticed slowly.

Dawn reveals a subtle change in the ethereal glow that indicates Spirit. Seen over seasons and years, the change is less subtle. The vibrant intensity of this area, and this tree in particular, continues to diminish at an increasing rate.

Not long now. Maybe weeks, maybe even days. Hopefully not seasons. She can wait, but she will be ready. She knows now what she will do when it happens. Where she will go. All her plans changed with Velekhno's revelations. She thought she was the best. She thought she was the only. She needs the best. Not just the best, but someone who can bring something additional. Instincts.

Calendra hugs the great trunk of her beautiful golden ash, and thanks it. It has given her shelter and strength. It has connected her to this forest. It has warmed her soul. It will do her a last service.

Calendra feels the treeheart die thirteen days later, the Spirit that pumped through it now fully diverted to a new heart elsewhere. She knows it will be special. It is unquestionably Manifold-aligned, but Calendra hopes it is more. She thinks of treehearts as aligned to a Domain - Mind, Body or Manifold - but if ever a heart were aligned specifically to speed, it is this tree. It undergoes a dozen full cycles of the seasons each year. The tree lives Fast.

It takes Calendra hours of careful excavation to remove a treeheart the size of her head from the root ball of the majestic tree. She saves her Spirit. She expects that there is no great rush to remove the heart, but once it is done, she must be quick. She carefully wraps it in banana leaves and stows it deep in her pack.

It takes less time to harvest her field of soulblossoms, though the hike to the cloud forest eats up the rest of the day, even Fast. She still has time to navigate the forest of linden and harvest the mindblossoms she planted years ago, which, unlike the soulblossoms, she has not used at all.

She strides south-west the next morning, Fast, with her few mundane belongings, her roll of paintings, her spatula and wok, and several dozen pre-prepared Spirit meals. And the two things that can put her back on the path to the extraordinary.

CHAPTER TWENTY THREE

Hey DJ. I'm feeling upbeat. I think I've found my next home. The views are pretty, the life vibrant, the waters sweet. I feel drawn to this place. It reminds me of home. Maybe I'll come and visit soon. Give my love to Dad. DM

It takes Calendra three days to reach the Eastern Sea, moving as Fast as possible while maintaining enough Spirit to fully regenerate each night. Once in the port of Sun's Kiss, she writes messages to her dad and Djulita and sends them by postal run to Sanctum. It has been a dozen weeks since she checked in.

With some careful enquiries, she takes another day to locate Streamsilk. She tracks it down at the end of a series of ever fainter roads and paths, like finding a specific twig of a tree or tributary of a branching river. It is late morning, nearing smallnight, when she arrives. Before she reaches the village itself, she sees a small handwritten sign that reads *Cook*. She follows the small shoe-beaten path through knee high ferns, broad figs and towering bamboo.

The forest gives way to a large clearing. The sight steals Calendra's breath. In the distance is a craggy, forested mountain range. A small brook winds through fields of orchards, vegetable gardens and cultivated blossoms. Set back from the stream near the center stands the largest fig Calendra has ever seen, well over a hundred paces tall with a trunk almost as wide as the two-storey cottage at its base. When she reaches the cute home, she eyes the menu board. It describes meals of the day and declares *Foods for the body, mind and soul*. She knocks.

The door opens a moment later to reveal a slim man of middling height. He wears a floppy white chef's hat and a pristine white apron over a sharp three-piece suit. His short, dark, curly hair frames a weathered but youthful deep-brown face made all the younger by his twinkling green eyes and dimpled smile. He exudes effortless charm.

"Welcome," he tells her with a deep voice, bowing, "to The Cookery. I do not know you, which makes you all the more welcome!"

"No time," she interjects. "Do you have customers? I need your time, and privacy."

The man raises an eyebrow but acquiesces, waving her in and locking the door behind them. Calendra seats herself at a large dining table at his gesture. She arches her fingers and looks into his eyes. She briefly considers revealing her connection to him, but decides against it. It would imply a debt that she does not believe she is owed. She will play this at arm's length.

"I need a difficult thing prepared. It needs to keep for a season, at least. It needs to be aligned to the Manifold, but I want it also aligned to Mind. Specifically, if possible, aligned to speed and instinct together."

The man raises an eyebrow at this. Calendra continues.

"It needs to provide, at the point it is consumed many weeks from now, the Spiritual equivalent of a population-level treeheart." She suppresses a grin at his shock. "I take it you understand the terminology, then. Well, I have a community-level Manifold heart strongly aligned to speed."

She grins at him. There are three people in existence with the knowledge to understand what this means and she deserves some recognition. She thinks briefly of that day at the tree and realizes there may be more than three, but she shies away from the memory.

Hwan's eyebrows dance at her statement and he leaps to his feet, knocking over his chair. "How?" he whispers.

"I'm not telling you that. Sit down. Time, as you should see, is of the essence." Calendra is settling into her role nicely.

"I apologize," he tells her. "Of course. If what you're saying is to be believed, the speed at which the heart is prepared after harvesting affects its alignment. But I'm no ..."

Calendra becomes very, very Fast, pours two full glasses of wine and places them on the table. She would only appear to flicker briefly at that speed. The cook gasps.

"Ahh, you're a Speed Artist? We don't see many of those, even in the capital. What other ingredients do you have?"

"I brought a community-level Manifold-aligned treeheart," she says slowly. "If I can spend my time securing one of them, do you think its best use is to gather basic ingredients?"

Rude, perhaps, but it would be what he would expect from a wealthy, powerful Manifold Artist. He smiles instead.

"I apologize. I have almost everything I'm likely to need in my gardens. A few things I don't have will be available in the local capital. A messenger to the nearest Endurance Guild chapter and they could be here within two days. How did you plan on this without a Mind-aligned heart?"

"Oh, I expect you already have one."

Hwandro gapes. "Just ... lying around?"

"Don't be silly. I brought one. Only, I harvested it a season ago. I've kept it in soil, which I hope will help. I imagine you'll want to discuss payment?"

"That, and your name. If that's for discussion."

"Calendra."

He bows with a flourish. "And I am called Hwan."

"It's good to meet you, Hwandro."

Calendra enjoys his momentary confusion as he seems to consider whether he already gave his full name. After several moments, she puts him out of his misery.

"I know your father, Velekhno. He told me where to find you and that you are an Instinct Artist."

"Ahhh." Hwan's confusion gives way to pride.

Calendra avoids humans, but when she needs something from one of them, she knows the value of a compliment and the use of making it indirect.

"I wondered how you knew of treehearts and the Art of the Cook," Hwan continues. "I'm glad that this is not general knowledge."

"Oh, I already knew of both those things. Your father just showed me how much I have to learn, then declared his son as a prodigy that makes his own cooking seem like soldier slop. When I discovered the heart, I knew there was only one person on this planet with the skill to do what I need."

They spend some time discussing plans for the Cook. Some of the Cook will require Calendra's will, though none of the preparation. She can live Slow for a day or two. It has become such a routine part of her life that she barely gives it thought. If she has nothing urgent to achieve, she lives Slow. She has still aged beyond her natural years as her gargantuan Spirit capacity allows her to live far too Fast for her own good, but can she slow her own decline.

A day and a half passes like a flash. She is roused from her temporal trance by an enthusiastic Hwan.

"It is ready, Calendra. Including the minor heart. You understand I won't be able to explain what I'm doing once I begin?"

"Of course," she replies, "I appreciate more than most the importance of the right mental state."

Even with his talent and the right ingredients, even with his instincts and her speed, this is no simple preparation. For a meal like this to temporarily grant Instinct Artistry to a Speed Artist, as far as she understands, it needs to be personally aligned to her. If speed is one note, plucked on a string, and instinct another, the required alterations will be like a range of different but harmonious notes, all forming a distinct chord. A chord that matches the equivalent notes of her Spirit, with the addition of massive amounts of instinct-aligned Spirit. She cannot know for sure until she tries, but years of experimenting with minor trehearts and blossoms of Mind, Body and Manifold make her confident.

Hwan has been clear that he has to go from raw ingredients to a finished meal in about half an hour. Seventeen ingredients, a dozen ways of preparing them and half a dozen ways of cooking them. Half an hour. To balance Calendra's speed and Hwan's instinct, Hwan must focus on his speed and Calendra on her instincts.

It would not be possible without a Speed Artist, of course. There are ingredients that do not require instinct in their preparation and for which little skill is needed to peel and chop. Calendra can get these ingredients done quickly and ease Hwan's prep burden.

To cook the meal in that time is nonsense. In theory, the hearts must be slow cooked. A Speed Artist helps though. An object she touches while living Fast, one that she already has some Spiritual connection to, will live Fast to an extent. The effect is similar to infusing her spatula, a fact which inspired the discovery. It will still not live as fast as her, which limits the usefulness in most situations, but for their purposes it is perfect.

Half an hour all up, from when the prep starts. From when the first ingredient was altered from its natural state. Madness.

Calendra seizes control of her Spirit.

Hwan stands still as stonewood, looking over the cook bench, eyes closed, hands hovering above the ready ingredients. Calendra watches his deep breaths. His eyes slowly open and sparkle with the exhilaration only known by a true master attempting the impossible. Calendra knows that she chose well. She looks at the clock.

"Begin," he whispers.

Calendra watches in astonishment for far too long before she starts her job. The most important half hour of her life and she burns through a part before recovering her wits.

She has never seen anything like it. He moves like he is living fast. His hands are a blur. It is not just his speed. It is his skill. He peels in one unbroken motion, the blade moving in curves and arcs, never once lifting off the surface. He peels each ingredient, no matter the shape, in a second or two. When he chops, it is clear that the only thing limiting his speed is the physics of muscle contractions. The result is perfect precision. Even the milkweed is squeezed so rapidly she sees and smells tendrils of friction smoke rising from his fingers.

She watches Fast as he cuts different ingredients in completely different ways. Certain cuts disrupt the structure, as he described it, releasing flavor compounds and freeing spirit, while others maintain and focus it to contain the flavor and Spirit until the cooking process can condense it and bond it to the greater meal. She knows he is making every slice with perfection, even though what constitutes perfection is beyond her knowledge. But the speed!

One minute.

She watches as he carves fifteen tubers of some kind into figurines resembling her form. He did not mention this in his explanation of the plan, but he is so deep in his Art that she assumes the plan was just a framework to be drawn upon or discarded as his feelings dictated. She has, after all, some familiarity with Instinct Artistry. She shoves down the thoughts that arise.

Focus! She recovers her wits and begins her limited role.

She starts to wonder if half an hour was a gross overestimate. Forty seconds into the cook, Hwan closed his eyes. They have not opened since.

Two minutes.

Hwan begins to laugh. Then he speeds up.

Using a long paring knife, he commences complex motions on the first salt-root, a notoriously challenging vegetable to cut because of its intricately layered structure. He weaves his knife towards and away from himself, rotating his wrist and shifting his forefinger to trace the contours. He finishes after seconds with six unbroken sheets of flesh.

As he finishes the last of ten and moves onto the mindblossoms, he opens one eye and looks at Calendra. Checking up on her, no doubt. Good. She may not be him, yet, but she will demonstrate that she is on the path to it.

Three minutes.

His eye snaps shut. To her surprise, he starts preparing her priceless speed-aligned heart. This was to come later, but he is the Instinct Artist. She will have faith.

The heart has to be split into smaller pieces to ensure an even cook. It is so dense that cooking it whole would burn the outside or leave the center raw. It is critical, as he explained it, that each piece has the same ratio of each part of the heart - the ironbark, softer flesh and the seed at the center. Then he can sear the long slivers on his white-hot grill to lock in the juices and Spirit before quickly slow cooking it.

He moves by feel, eyes still closed, and carves out the spear-shaped segments. He slams two at a time onto the grill using delicate tongs, removing after two seconds and repeating for each side.

Four minutes.

It only takes a minute to sear the remaining segments and throw them all in a roasting pot. He puts on the lid and carefully places the pot into the oven before plunging his hands into cool water to relieve the burns he must have received.

Five minutes.

Calendra's role now becomes important. She seizes a clever extension to the pot, designed by Hwan to emerge past the small purpose-built hole in the oven's front.

Calendra becomes Fast. Very, very Fast indeed. She uses her experience in infusing her spatula with Spirit to will her raging Spirit into the pot. She wills it to live Fast. She has no idea if it will work, as it is not hers in the way the spatula is, but she will try.

Six minutes.

The next minutes will be her hardest of the Cook. She will need to do a similar thing with the instinct-aligned heart. She planned to pace herself, to keep enough Spirit for the other heart and the final roast without running dry. She cannot do this now. She cannot give anything but her all after watching Hwan work.

She did not realize before the Cook started. This grinning young man is a genius. A god of the culinary arts. She was impressed with the father but is blown away by the son. If he, without any incentive but the joy of it, could bring himself to the brink to make this Cook shorter, then she, who would be the one to benefit, could do no less.

At the cost of a few extra days of her life or weeks of living Slow, she diverts more Spirit and picks up the pace.

Eight minutes.

She sees Hwan move on to the Mind-aligned heart. The timing is important. The instinct-aligned heart does not need to be roasted for the time the Manifold-aligned heart does, but they need the same level of doneness when they are combined with the remaining ingredients for the final roast.

Calendra is living so Fast it might throw off the timing. Will he see?

She sees him slowly turn his head and open an eye. His eyebrows creep up.

Hwan, looking at her, lets out a booming 'YES' that lasts twenty seconds, with a voice so deep it could be that of a granite mountain. She grins for thirty seconds to make sure he sees it. He repeats the procedure with the Mind-aligned heart. Calendra takes over, willing speed-aligned Spirit into both hearts. She looks at the clock.

Ten minutes.

Hwan signals, and she removes both pans. He seasons both hearts and glazes them with a small amount of Body-aligned patternbush sap.

Twelve minutes.

Hwan transfers the contents of the wok into the roasting pan with one deft flip. Holding Calendra's hand, each holding the panhandle with their other hand, they sink into their respective mindsets and rage with Spirit.

Together, they place the pan in the oven. Calendra imagines the Spirit of her, Hwan and the pan align, like three complementary chords harmonizing. Fueled by the energetic chaos of heat, they infuse the developing meal with speed and instinct.

Calendra starts to feel what control of instinct must feel like. Still, she is shocked to see Hwan living Fast. She did not know such a thing was possible. Is it because their Spirit is so aligned?

Together, they Cook.

Sixteen minutes.

A short time later, Calendra feels a change in Hwan. Even in herself. She hears a distant bell ring.

"Stop!" Hwan yells.

Calendra instantly stops diverting Spirit to her Art, and they both remove the pan from the oven.

With the moisture and heat trapped within, Hwan throws the contents into the strange contraption to compress and dehydrate the meal. With steam pouring out the release holes, the meal becomes a cube the size of her head. Another thirty seconds of sustained pressure using a hand shaft and good old-fashioned elbow grease, and it is the size of a fist.

Calendra takes over, holding the dehydration oven and living Fast one final time. Within ninety seconds by the clock, any trace of steam is gone, as is most of her Spirit.

"Enough," Hwan tells her with a grin. "It's ready. The Cook, Calendra, is complete."

Eighteen minutes.

They both collapse.

Calendra lingers only long enough to recover. She bids him farewell and, to his visible shock, leaves him a slice of the meal the width of a fingernail, insisting he did far more than he was paid for.

With their Spirit so aligned, the balance of Mind and Manifold, instinct and speed, means it is almost as perfectly aligned to his Spirit as it is to hers. If he ever has the chance to use the services of a Speed Donor - one of the rarest Artists in existence - he will use it with the efficiency and subtlety of a savant and a power beyond which a normal Speed Artist would burn themselves out. She doubts he will be able to access Speed Artistry himself. The Manifold heart was dominant. Still, even that might work. She does not tell him this, of course. He is a genius. He will understand.

Calendra walks out of the picture-perfect cottage. Out of earshot, she finally begins to laugh. She laughs until it hurts. She laughs until she cries. She has not laughed for joy in what feels like a lifetime.

Eighteen minutes. *Eighteen minutes.*

Extraordinary.

She walks through fields of blossoms, vegetables and fruits in the glory of early spring, taking in the scent of food with a purpose. Once she reaches the forest, she turns back for a last look at Hwan's little paradise. She cannot imagine a more perfect place to Cook.

She pays her respects to Hwan, the world's greatest Cook, and to the mighty fig that anchors and feeds his Art. It is best to show respect when one leaves the presence of a tree that contains a living community-level Mind heart.

CHAPTER TWENTY FOUR

Why can't everyone just be normal, like you and Dad and Vrai. Sometimes I just hate them, DJ. The things people do to each other. Some are good but they're a gentle whisper in a roar of selfishness. Sometimes I just want to kill them. Kill anyone who would prey on innocent people. Women. Children. CHILDREN. Sometimes I want to kill them all. I could. I love you both. You remind me that not all with power are evil. DM

Calendra becomes Normal. For the weeks it has taken to reach the Skyshrine she moved as Fast as possible while retaining enough Spirit to regenerate each night. It is exhausting, moving Fast for so long. It taxes the mind, especially when moving through the uneven footing of jungles. She is still there quicker than expected. As she does not know her time limit, this is all the more important.

She knocks. It takes several minutes for the gates of the Skyshrine to creak open in response. A short young man bows in welcome, his voluminous burned-orange priest's robes billowing in the swift mountain breeze.

"Welcome, sister. May the Traveler whisper your name in his hall. Do you seek wisdom, solitude or mastery of self?"

"I seek these things in equal measure, Elevated One. I wish to ascend the tower to contemplate alone, to look upon Zem's glory unveiled."

"So you are Chalvenan then, child." He smiles like a tolerant mother with a troublesome child. "You are welcome, whatever your beliefs. All are one under the Traveler's benevolent gaze. If others wish to ascend the tower, they too are welcome, but no others are here. Only the Elevated, and they will not disturb you. Will you need anything?"

"Thank you," Calendra tells him. "I might be hours or days, I am not sure, but I appreciate the privacy. I need nothing."

Calendra ascends the stair that spirals around the outside of the tower. She is comfortable with heights, but even she feels her stomach twirl. Between the narrow stair, the wind and the view, the ascent is not for the faint of heart. She is glad for the spring weather.

Standing at the center of the platform atop the tower, she sees why people do it. The view takes what little breath she has left. The Skyshrine crowns the world's tallest mountain, Skypeak, at over three miles above sea level according to the charts. Skypeak also has the fortune of being well over two hundred paces higher than its neighbors. With its location at the geographical center of civilization, it affords an unparalleled view of the known world.

It seemed silly to her until now, that religious folks would go to such effort to build a temple and tower in the hardest place to reach. Being 'closer to the Traveler' sounds pretty, but it seemed a lot of effort for just another shrine. Besides, in Calendra's view it should be about metaphorical closeness, not literal spatial closeness. The Traveler died on the Twin to get humanity off that broken world. Who would want to be closer to the world from which they escaped?

Calendra realizes now that the height is not the point. The view is the point. One feels so above the world here, so separate from it, that it gives some kind of god-like perspective. Calendra deeply reveres the Traveler for sacrificing his life to transport humanity to this world, even more so now she understands Spirit and the Arts well enough to understand the enormity of the act. Calendra is powerful, but she truly cannot comprehend the Spirit required to teleport thousands of people from one planet to another. It is a feat of Artistry that only those without Arts can dare to imagine.

However, Calendra does not worship the Traveler as a god. Few raised in Chalveno believe such a thing. Even most in Tolgarlo only revere him as a man perfected. Still, those who worship him number in the thousands. Perhaps it used to be more, for such a monument to have been built.

Even if it is not holy to her, it is a place of reverence and it is a holy place to others who mean well. Calendra did not trek glaciers and climb mountains for the Skyshrine, though. She did it for the view.

Calendra has continued to grapple with the question of how best to use her speed-instinct meal. She is still not certain that it will even grant her temporary access to a second Art. Perhaps it was a mistake to try. She hopes it proves to be wise.

The decision came down to one thing. Time. Calendra has purified and expanded her Spirit over recent years through training, meditation and Cooking. She has mastered her physical skills and subtle uses of her Art. She located a dying Manifold heart of great power. Anyone would consider this a great success.

But Calendra is not anyone. She is to be extraordinary. Repeating this process will make her stronger and stronger, but it is too slow to make her extraordinary. It will not make her the goddess that her dad declared she would become. She needs something far more powerful than the community-level heart she won in the riverlands.

Calendra's confidence in Myla's theory has grown. The idea that Spirit generated and shared among plants and trees is filtered through smaller population-level hearts like the one in the Valley has resonated more and more as time passes. Those populations would then network across a broader area through a series of larger community-level hearts, like the one in the riverlands.

Calendra is sure that there is a higher level again. The riverlands are large, but they are just one small part of one region of one country. There must be ecosystem-level hearts that accumulate the Spirit of entire ecosystems.

Calendra can find community-level hearts. It has become second nature since she met the golden-haired Cook to use her painting, enhanced by soulpaint, to detect Spirit. Most are of no use to her, being alive and well, but she can do it. But she has understood something else about the fractal nature of the great Spirit network.

Calendra has seen large, intricate paintings that act similarly. Standing close to such a painting, you can see every brush stroke, but you cannot see what the painting depicts as a whole. You need to stand paces back to do so.

Calendra can detect what she thinks of as the small, swift, shallow creeks of Spirit at the lowest levels. Not by picturing the Spirit itself, but through differences in the brightness and saturation of colors. However, she needed to stand atop a hill to find the community-level heart. She needs that broader perspective to see the differences caused by larger, slower, deeper Spirit streams.

There is no way Calendra can wander far enough in her limited years to chance upon the deepest rivers of all. She needs to have the broadest view possible.

Her painting reveals truths her eyes cannot see, which means it must draw from some deep understanding beyond her conscious mind. Calendra needs to see everything, and perfectly understand everything she sees. She needs the right instincts.

Calendra begins to paint. She cannot paint a full circular view on one canvas so she readies four. She does not know how long her meal will last, so she does all the preliminary work first. It is only on the last layer of paint, the soulpaint, that she fully depicts Spirit, so she can do much of the work before eating.

It is a slow process, but the progress of the sun shows only an hour passing as she finishes. She lives Fast not just to get it done before sunset, but to drain her Spirit. She will not empty it completely as the risk is too great, but she wants the Spirit provided by the meal to predominate.

Almost drained of Spirit, exhausted, Calendra sits on the cold stone platform. Her easel holds the canvas depicting the southern view, from western Chalveno to central Tolgarlo. The other three canvases lay weighted down, ready. She rests for several minutes, gazing around at the view. She is not drawing on Spirit, but it is important that she is intimately familiar with the image her eyes paint. Her mind will then be free to interpret what her soul feels without being distracted by what her body sees.

Calendra removes the priceless meal from its airtight storage container and stands. She starts to smile. It grows into a grin, broader and broader until it threatens to split the corners of her dry lips and she begins to laugh. A slow laugh of relief at long-laid plans coming to fruition, and of bubbling excitement at impending pleasure long-denied.

The laugh dies away, but the smile remains as Calendra eats. It takes several minutes and all her remaining water to finish. She does not feel an instantaneous effect as when she ate the Valley's heart, but it happens far faster than with the meal her dad gave her during their flight. Within ten minutes of eating, Calendra feels a change. It builds over the following minutes.

Within half an hour, Calendra's world is ablaze with sensation. The power! She can feel Spirit raging inside. She can see the Manifold without the slightest effort and intimately feel her place on it. And she can hear ... she can hear the faintest sounds, like the distant tune of a carillon. She realizes her Spirit has somewhere else to go.

Calendra draws on more Spirit and directs it towards the distant bells. She feels her Spirit flow into this new Art. Then the bells are everywhere. Chimes of every note. Everywhere. It almost overwhelms her. Old Velekhno mentioned this.

With effort, Calendra sinks into the meditative trance she once required to even glimpse the Manifold. So much training over so many years holds her together amidst the storm of Spirit and sound. Her mind focuses and her body relaxes.

In control, aware, Calendra quietens the bells. She listens for patterns in the chimes. For anything that helps her mind understand the signals her new Art is sending. She slowly looks out at the world as she listens. Then she remembers what she once told Myla. Stop overthinking it.

Calendra lets herself be guided by her instincts. Calendra has done the same with her Manifold sight. Calendra knows how to meditate. How to defocus. How to flow. This need be no different. Try not to try.

Calendra looks south, the canvas a small mirror of the view that frames it. She relaxes her eyes and her mind. Chimes and flows become one as she gazes out. She sees connections and patterns in the Manifold she has never seen before. And she paints.

Calendra flows. She does not know what she paints and she does not remember what she sees. Her action is effortless. Her soul reaches out for a greater truth. Her expanded mind dissects that truth to find meaning and her hand becomes a focal point for her mind's interpretations, like a rock-hammer's tip to a sculptor.

As Calendra lays down the final strokes of soulpaint on the final canvas, she hears a chime, clear as glass. It is done. Her new Art is telling her to stop. Not just to conserve his Spirit, but to avoid undoing what she has done.

She sits and laughs. It is done. Will it work? She stops drawing on Spirit, if only for some moments of rest, and holds the southern painting in front of her. She runs her eyes over every part and holds it at different distances. She does the same with each painting, straining her physical senses. She is, after all, dealing with massive distances on a two-dimensional surface.

After some quarter of an hour, Calendra feels less exhausted and intimately familiar with her paintings, though does not see what she needs. The sun approaches the western horizon. It is time to throw caution to the wind.

Calendra hoped to keep as much of her instinct-aligned Spirit as possible. She suspects that her natural regeneration will only create Spirit aligned to her true nature. If so, the more she uses Instinct Artistry now, the more dilute that Spirit will become as her pure Spirit replaces it. She wants some instinct left for whatever comes next, but she took a chance in choosing this path. She will not do it by half.

Calendra opens the floodgates holding back her thunderous Spirit and falls to the stone. Everything goes black.

Calendra wakes to deafening bells clanging discordantly. She tries to focus her eyes and mind but cannot.

Coming out of her grogginess, she sees why. Too much input. Too loud. She draws on a small amount of Spirit. She feels how little it needs compared to her use of instinct.

Everything snaps into place once more. Calendra sees.

Not the shallow, swift streams of the lesser Spirit networks, but the deep rivers of the networks between entire ecosystems. Where she previously saw subtle differences in color or texture, she now sees ethereal rivers of translucent color.

The jungles of the tropics link to the highlands of central Chalveno. The savannah of eastern Tolgarlo links to the great alpine region along the world's spine. The Great Plains of the north link to the frozen tundra of the northern Free Cities.

All of it is connected. And the mightiest treehearts of this world are the connectors. They appear as beacons.

The flows of Spirit are stable and certain, like the rivers that have flowed the same for so many millennia that they form canyons. Throughout the world, the flow as they have always flowed. Except in one region. The Great Plains.

To her eyes, the endless fields of gold seem vibrant. A textured carpet of the grains that feed the metropolises of humanity. To her soul, they are withered. An ancient boulder with a deep crack. A river delta after seasons of drought at its source. A tree transplanted into the wrong soil.

Part of the Spirit network in the north is failing. A heart is dying and it is more powerful than she can imagine.

Calendra burns the image into her mind. It is far and she will need to find a single tree in a massive region, but she knows where to search. If she is very lucky, she will still be able to access Instinct Artistry once she arrives. That will simplify things. If not, she will do what she has always done, at her best. She will listen.

Before releasing her flow of Spirit, Calendra notices glowing lines along her hands and arms. Shocked, she eases off her use of Spirit and the lines dim. She increases it, and the lines brighten. Noticing them extending from under her shirt and up her neck, she takes out her knife, polishes it and peers at her reflection. The lines form distinctive flowing patterns under her eyes and around her jaw.

Calendra breathes out slowly. The visual manifestation of the use of Spirit.

She rolls the paintings into a tube and packs everything into her backpack. She descends the tower and thanks the Elevated One before leaving through the ancient gate and walking down the narrow mountain path, heading north when it reaches Heaven's Pass. It takes hours to reach the fringing forest on the lower peaks as she will not risk moving Fast on the mountain paths and must move in the dark, but she will not remain in the mountains. She needs shelter.

Once in the forest, she starts a fire and sets up her tent. She wants to keep moving, but she knows she will regret it. It will take weeks of walking to get where she needs. No point in rushing now. The best way to maximize her prospects of retaining instinct is to resist the temptation to live Fast. The more Spirit she uses, the more she must regenerate. The more she regenerates, the more this unique dual-Spirit will dilute.

Calendra will need to spend the following weeks Normal, for the first time in many years. But what is a few weeks? She has spent her whole life striving to be extraordinary. In a few weeks, she will be. Calendra falls asleep with a calm mind and soft smile.

CHAPTER TWENTY FIVE

*Hey DJ. I'm doing better, thanks. I think I had been in a bit of a
rut, staying put for too long without achieving much. I guess I helped
some folks but things still felt stagnant. It was worth it in the end. I
got what I was waiting for! I'm not sure where I'll go next but I'll
find out when I get there. I'm feeling more hopeful. Hopeful that I'm
on the path to being extraordinary. Hopeful that things will be better
then. It's a nice feeling. Love you both. DM.*

The days pass in a happy haze of simple pleasures. The endless trudge of
travel. The contrasting beauty of ecological variation. The pleasure of foraging and preparing simple food. The relaxation of, for once, being Normal. It is
a normalcy that city dwellers might find arduous but Calendra has spent most of
her life in the wilds of the world in all types of weather, carrying her whole life on
her back.

She avoids towns and chooses tracks over roads. She encounters people occasionally, when she is too slow to move off a road or when she cannot avoid
farmland without an unpalatable detour. Otherwise she is just a Normal girl
doing Normal things and she does not expect to be remembered.

During smallnight of the fourth day, she hears a girl crying. Heavy footsteps punctuate the sobs. She is near the border with the Free Cities. Though her destination is well within Tolgarlo, the shorter route has taken her close to the border.

Calendra slows. She is in a hurry, but a child is in pain. Do the borderlands with Tolgarlo share the same problem with raids as the Riverlands? There are guard posts here, but they are dispersed, perhaps one each mile.

Calendra stops. A child is in pain. She cannot trust that others will hear. She places her backpack a dozen paces into the forest and marks the side of the road to trace back her steps. She runs towards the cries. She does not need to use her Art. She catches them within ten minutes. There are three of them, plus the young girl.

Calendra becomes Fast. It takes seconds. She does not even bother with a knife. She just uses a nearby rock.

It takes several hours to return the girl to her village. Thankfully, the child knows the way once they get to the main road. She deposits the girl at the village hall, packed with panicked people, brushes away tearful thanks and ignores questions about who she is and how she did it. She is happy to help but would prefer to be on her way. She is bothered by the way they stare at her Spirit markings - the lines painted with silver-blue dye distilled from soulblossom petals to trace the pattern she saw atop Skypeak. They glow when she is Fast, which she avoids revealing to the crowd.

The only people who leave her alone are a group clearly not local, from their dress and demeanor. Two of the women and two of the men smile at her. The other two men, one of them huge and richly bearded, cast suspicious glances her way.

Calendra walks out of the hall and leaves the village. She does not run or become Fast, but her stride makes clear she has places to be. She hears some people come out behind her but none harass her.

To her surprise, though, she feels a note of suspicion. On a whim, she draws on her Spirit enough to fuel her Manifold sight. It is only a minute after she descends out of sight down a narrow valley that she feels the same twisting of the Manifold that she once felt in the Valley. Gravity Artist. Which of the six? For it is surely one of the visitors. If one is a Manifold Artist, surely the others will be Artists of Mind or Body. Not for the first time, Calendra wishes her Manifold sight would allow her to detect uses of the Physical and Mental Arts.

Curse her generosity. She has drawn so little attention for so many years and now, on the way to the greatest prize yet, she might have a band of Artists on her heels.

Calendra recognizes that the thought is unfair. A good deed is its own reward. The girl was so young. One should not regret doing the right thing just because it brings risk, but it is another reminder of why she needs nobody. She has the whole of Zem. She has her painting and her cooking and her trees. Calendra does not need other humans. She certainly does not need love.

Calendra finally reaches the forest and chances to look back. Sure enough, two people face her direction from the top of the valley. Calendra relaxes. What can they do? She takes off her pack, sits beneath the nearest tree and meditates, reaching out to the local part of the world's one great jungle. This is her domain. All this world's jungle is her domain.

Calendra finishes meditating and thanks the sprawling banyan. It is time. She ignores the cries of her pursuers. Nobody but a Manifold Artist - the living legends of bedtime stories - can hope to catch her. She will soon be something beyond even them. The Daughter of the Manifold has nothing to fear. She has something to pursue.

Calendra becomes Fast.

Calendra is running. Jumping. Grabbing a vine. Swinging. Grinning. Catching. Swinging. Laughing. Catching. Flying. Ringing. Bells ringing. Instinct! Launching upward. Grabbing a high branch. Hiding.

Calendra becomes Normal. Fifteen thundering heartbeats later, she hears the rhythmic crunch of leaves and twigs. She holds her Spirit at the ready, her senses heightened.

The footsteps get louder until she sees a woman below. The footsteps stop. How did she keep up with Calendra? Impossible. But no, she was not one of the two Calendra saw on the hill. This woman must have circled around her.

The woman cocks her head and bends down to pick up something. An elm branch. Calendra broke it off as she careened into her hiding place only paces above the ground. Calendra's heart races. The break will be fresh.

The woman slowly looks up and around. She knows, but she does not know where. She looks only slightly upwards towards the lower branches of her tree. She does not expect Calendra to be high above the ground. She expects her to run. After half a minute, the woman walks off in the direction Calendra came.

Calendra cannot believe how close that came. Her instincts saved her. She did not even consciously use it, but save her it did. Such a useful thing. She wishes it could be permanent.

She waits in the tree for a long half hour, only taking the time to find a better hiding place. Higher, better hidden, and much more comfortable. At the sound of voices and footsteps, she settles in so the only gap visible from below is occupied by a solitary eyeball.

"... bit unlikely, eh? I'm no tracker, but I haven't seen any signs at all."

The dark-haired woman's voice is slightly higher pitched than Calendra's. There is a playful smirk in her tone that reminds Calendra of Vrai.

"It was near here. Ah. Ha! Here."

It is the woman from earlier. She has long blonde hair. Calendra cannot make out much other than the tops of their heads, but she remembers them well enough from the village. From their hair at least, as it was the one thing different about each of them.

"Look," the blonde woman says, holding up the broken branch from before. "Fresh break."

The blonde man, the silver-haired man and the hairy giant walk over to the women. A few moments later, the dark-haired man ambles up, hands clasped behind his back, and turns his head upwards as if to take in the majesty. He speaks to the others with a soft, introspective voice that still carries through the quiet forest.

"So I guess this is what this whole area would be like without the fields. These small stands of forest they leave alone have changed as we've moved south. I think this is my favorite. I didn't think to find vines in such a cold climate. Though this part feels a bit ..."

His musings are interrupted by a rumble from the giant, like large stones tumbling down a hillside. "Lad ..." Giant says with a long-suffering tone.

The introspective man mumbles an apology. Calendra decides to call him Dreamer. The blonde girl, who Calendra decides is Tracker, continues.

"I know. One branch in the entire forest, but it's something! You can't tell me the wind did that. Or that it broke more than an hour ago."

Silence follows for several seconds until Dreamer speaks. "Just one branch ..." And he slowly tilts his head until he can see directly above him. Right where Calendra hides.

Calendra snaps her eye shut and lays completely still. Footsteps quietly move below. All is still for twenty seconds.

"I don't know, Vel." The small, dark-haired woman. Smirker. "It was a good idea. Probably even right. But even if that woman can move between trees, she's not going to stick around, eh? Let's go. We didn't learn anything here."

"She's right, folks," rumbled Giant. "I let suspicion get the better of me. That girl's an Artist, no doubt, but there are plenty of Artists out here, notwith-standing their inability to breed them. Strength probably, or a good fighter with resilience or agility. Most people that can take down three men will take down three men to save a child. She's probably not involved with any of this. I doubt any of the pond scum Alvertus drags in his wake would bother saving a child. And if she's not with Alvertus, there's no way she can know about treehearts. Move out."

It takes several minutes for the sounds of footsteps to recede beyond hearing. She knows she did not imagine it. He referred to treehearts. The secret is spreading. She has taken too long perfecting herself and biding her time. There are not just others hunting for hearts, they are hunting in the same area. From the sound of it, Alvertus might be here as well.

Calendra has suspected for years that Alvertus is after treehearts, ever since she found out from Djulita that Myla joined him. He had to be the person they saw that terrible day. There is nothing she can do about it and dwelling on it takes her places best avoided. He could be here, though. With *her*. And others are on the trail.

Calendra has not brought herself to the cusp of the extraordinary by ignoring risk. She must move. She remains determined to retain as much of her dual Spirit as possible. But there is no point in leading a race if you cannot find the finishing line. She must increase her speed. Cutting the several weeks remaining by a third could be the difference between second and first.

Calendra becomes Fast. Somewhat.

The days and nights blur into a routine of walking Fast from truedawn, eating during smallnight, walking Fast until dusk and setting up a basic camp in which to sleep and eat. It is tiring. Even a portion of extra speed requires constant awareness of the body and its surroundings. At least Calendra's Spirit is so plentiful these days that she is capable of increasing her speed by half for fourteen hours a day without depleting it.

She passes the river that marks the border of her search area in the morning of her thirtieth day after leaving the Skyshrine. Full of Spirit, she finally has the opportunity to use the Instinct Artistry she has been so careful to preserve.

Calendra draws on more Spirit than the wisp she constantly uses and directs it to her new Art. Nothing happens. The Spirit just remains within her, waiting to be used. She tests her speed. It works just fine, but she has no access to instinct.

Calendra screams in her head. All that effort conserving Spirit to maintain the dual Spirit of her meal is wasted. She could have been here much faster if she had not restricted herself, and it was for nothing. She took too long.

Releasing a sigh of resignation, Calendra just keeps walking. She will have to do this the old-fashioned way. Listen to the forest and hope her Manifold-sight can help. If in doubt, she will paint.

None of it proves to matter. Within an hour, she hears voices. She approaches in silence and peeks around a boulder to see what she faces.

A ring of guards encircles a beautiful pine. A man crouches at the base. Calendra draws on her Spirit more strongly and sinks into meditation. She needs to be sure. After endless moments, it snaps into place. She can feel the flows of Spirit in the area. Not like when she paints, but enough to get a decent sense when the Spirit is strong enough.

Here it is strong enough, but the image of the tree on the Manifold has a solidity that even her tree in the Valley lacked. Was she wrong? This is a treeheart, almost certainly a Manifold heart, and most likely ecosystem-level. From the potency of the Spirit here, though, she is as certain as she can be that this heart is alive and very healthy.

Of course, such a heart should be here. Not the heart she is after, but the one to replace the dying heart she seeks, as the golden-haired Cook had said. Why then would there be guards here? Maybe whoever found it does not know that a live heart is of no use.

Whatever the reason, she must act. If someone has found the new heart, they know enough about these matters to recognize it. Either they already found the old heart and it is too late, or they will once they realize this one will not help them. Or, perhaps, they already have the old heart but are waiting for it to die.

It all amounts to one thing. She must move.

Resisting the impulse to run, Calendra creeps away until certain she is out of hearing range. She finds a fallen hollowed tree trunk, burns the location into her memory, and hides her backpack inside. It has everything she loves - her paintings, her wok, her spatula, her soulpaints - but she needs to move quickly and be ready to fight. She keeps only her combat satchel.

Calendra draws on a stream of Spirit and enters into a meditative trance. She closes her eyes and takes in the forest. The smell of sweet, sticky pine sap. The creaking of stubborn wood in the light breeze. She sees the Manifold through closed eyes. She releases her sense of identity and blends into the forest. Her forest. Herself.

Calendra downs a vial of soulblossom essence. Her eyes snap open. Calendra lets loose the floodgates holding back her Spirit. Calendra becomes Fast. And Calendra runs.

Her speed is reckless in the extreme. She does not notice. She does not think. She flows. Her eyes watch the terrain and transmit orders directly to her legs. Her entire consciousness is focused on the dreamy haze of Spiritual potential. Her body and mind operate at terrifying speeds, but her consciousness slows. It is adrift in the winds of Spirit, feeling for changes in pressure and direction.

One part of Calendra will handle the real world. The other will handle the world beyond.

She feels it. The change in Spiritual potential. Left. The energy is weaker and dropping off. She follows.

Within minutes, Calendra arrives. She knows it immediately. The place is not Spiritually empty. It is Spiritually dead. Like a river canyon run dry. Well, almost. Almost dead. Almost dry. She is on time. Perhaps only just in time.

Calendra becomes Normal.

She staggers, her mind fracturing at the suddenness of dragging her consciousness back to the real world. After a few moments to ground herself, she creeps forward until noticing a significant clearing. She finds a safe spot and peers down.

The small unnatural amphitheater, thirty paces across, has been dug up to reveal an entrance to a cave. A strangler fig straddles the cave, roots covering and cracking through the cave roof. A strangler fig. In this climate! It is not what she expected, but it is the image of the perfect tree.

The site is guarded far better than the other. She notices four sentries monitoring the rim almost too late. There are eight below. One tends a small fire against the chill wind and driving rain. She has no doubt there are more within the cave.

She does not know what to do. She cannot be sure - she has only impressions - but she does not think the heart has died yet. Does she kill the guards now and wait? Does she hide, in case someone comes, and wait until the heart dies before killing everyone?

Calendra decides. She must act. Easier to hold off newcomers if these are dealt with first. Never one to mull over a decision once made, she seizes her knife, retrieves her soulblossom essence and drinks it all.

Calendra becomes Fast. Very Fast. So fast the raindrops freeze in place.

Calendra is running at the first sentry. Arriving before he moves. Grabbing her knife. Death. Running at the next. Death. Running. Throat. Running. Chest. Running down the excavated hole. Death. Death. Running at the last. He is opening his mouth. Death. Running to the cave. Entering the cave. Seeing only three. Death death death. Seeing the heart! Sawing at the roots connected to the heart. They are yielding! They are yielding! Losing consciousness. Too Fast!

Calendra becomes Normal, shuddering at the transition. She hears fifteen bodies hit the ground in unison as the pitter-patter of rainfall resumes. Erupting with Spirit from the soulblossom essence but needing a break from living so Fast, Calendra goes back to sawing at the roots. Nothing. She cannot harm them. They are like granite.

What in all the hells? It cannot be. She was just severing it. Is it not dead? How then had she ...

A horn sounds. Traveler's beard. She must have missed someone.

Calendra becomes Fast. The sounds of the forest halt.

Calendra is turning to the heart. Cursing. Not dead. Not dead. But ... trying again. Becoming Faster. Sawing. Is it working? It is partly working. Calendra is understanding. Becoming Faster. Faster. The root is splitting. Sawing. Sawing. Sawing. Death. Grasping the heart. Hers. Hers! She ...

Calendra becomes Normal. Not by choice. Her Spirit is gone. She did not run out. She knows whether she has Spirit more instinctively than whether she has shoes on her feet. She was running low but should be nowhere near empty. It is just gone.

A horn sounds. It is not more than a five minutes run from the other site, but if they have a Spatial or Speed Artist ...

Calendra cannot risk fleeing with the heart. Not without Speed Artistry. She has only one choice. She must eat here. Food of unmatched power and she cannot Cook it. Perhaps eating just part will provide enough Spirit to escape with the rest.

Calendra saws small chunks from the withering heart and swallows each one. The heart is surprisingly small, only the size of a fist. She chokes down more and more from a dead man's flask, carving as she feasts. After a quarter is gone, she feels it. The seed of Spirit within her. It is growing rapidly. She keeps eating.

Without warning, she blazes with Spirit. Her heart thunders in her chest, drowning out the sound of rain. Her Manifold sight returns. A heartbeat later, she feels the Manifold collapse inwards. Spatial Artist.

Calendra becomes Fast. Perhaps Faster than ever before.

The world is utterly still. Calendra is sawing and eating. Drinking and sawing. She is doing it easily. She is living so so Fast. Considering running. Knowing it will not be the same. Knowing this heart is not for multiple meals. It is for one sitting. Eating and sawing. Seeing the Spatial Artist slowly looking over. Sawing and eating. Seeing the Spatial Artist freezing. The Manifold is changing again. Two Arts! Her chest is thumping. No!

It is him. It is him. The Announcer is coming. Fast. His expression is twisting. Faster. He is hitting his limit. The Announcer is coming. Slowly. He is not speeding up. Calendra is Faster. Sawing eating drinking sawing. Calendra becomes Faster. Eating sawing eating drinking. The Announcer is three paces away. The Announcer is leaping. Calendra is becoming Faster. Throwing the last piece down her throat. The Announcer is an arm's length away. Calendra is running out of Spirit. Washing down the chunk. Needing to save her developing seed of Spirit.

Calendra becomes Normal.

An eye-blink later, the snarling Announcer touches her on the shoulder. Calendra feels the Manifold twist around her. The forest becomes a cell of iron bars.

She tries to become Fast, for all the good it would do, but her Spirit is empty. No, not empty. The seed is there. It just does not grow. Her Spirit will not regenerate.

She falls to her knees, sick. She cannot regenerate Spirit. How? Did she do something wrong, eating the heart the way she did? Is it ... is it because it may have been alive when she removed it? The impact of that moment of decision weighs on her. What did she do? Is this her punishment?

The Announcer appears on the other side of the bars moments later. He stares at her for several seconds, then takes a few steps back.

"I can't remain long. I can't afford to have my Spirit emptied today." He stares daggers at her. "Do you know what you did, you fool? Do you know what you risked by killing a heart of Zem, even one so close to death? Had I not been with the new one ..."

The Announcer clenches his fists and takes several deep, controlled breaths.

"You're dangerous, daughter of Malnor. I'm not yet sure what to do with you. I don't like death. It's so wasteful of the Traveler's efforts. Had the great network collapsed today, I would've regretted sparing your life in the past. You deserve death for your act, but not for its consequences."

The Announcer shrugs, seeming briefly human. Calendra tries to process all he has said.

"You're in my care now, Calendra. I've no desire to hurt you. You cannot leave this room, but we can make it comfortable. Have ready a list of things that can make your stay more pleasant, for when I next visit. Furniture, books, craft materials. I've no reason to deny it."

"Why are you keeping me here?" Calendra spits the words at him. "What will you do with me?"

"You're a problem," he tells her icily. "You know dangerous things. You behave recklessly. You are very, very powerful. I cannot tell if you are a knife at Zem's throat, or the scalpel over Zem's infection. So you'll remain my guest until I decide."

The Announcer turns on his heels and stalks out. Two armed guards enter the dungeon behind him, along with a servant with blankets, a tray of food and a flask of water. One places the items inside the cage and watches her with wary eyes.

Calendra lies on one blanket and covers herself in the others. Using her arm as a pillow, she curls up and lets herself drift off to sleep.

Alone in a dungeon, imprisoned by a god and utterly without an Art for the first time since childhood, Calendra pictures the hibernating seed of Spirit inside her. She smiles.

A Memory of Danald

One hundred and seventy-two years ago

D anald felt the invitation from the tree-which-was-him-but-separate. Danald was invited to stop. The tree had repaired its flaw. The tree could now process Spirit without supplement.

Danald tried to shrug to himself, forgetting he was a tree. He chuckled at the thought. Then, without thinking overmuch, he abandoned his treehood and became Danald the man once more. He felt an immediate pang of loss as connections so much a part of him were severed, but he felt a corresponding rush of gain as the identity he once held was restored.

Danald had been a tree for a long time. He hadn't been the tree, exactly. He'd retained his mind, even as it had been connected to the tree. It had been a different experience, an existence in which time and space were twisted and curved, but he was pretty sure it had been at least a week. He was famished. Then he realized he only thought that because he should be famished. He was not even hungry. Maybe it had just felt like a week.

Danald scratched an itch at his cheek and was surprised to find half a pace of beard where before there had been none. Curious. More than a week then. Definitely more. The length of his nails bore that out.

Danald emerged from the tree's interior to the clear skies and warm sun of an alpine summer. Curious and troubling. Half a year then. A year and a half? How fast do beards grow? Yet Danald was no slimmer, despite not having eaten in two seasons.

Danald became somewhat concerned when he looked over at the pines encircling the lake. They were far, far taller than before. Too tall. How long had he been in there?

After dithering awhile, Danald finally submitted to counting tree rings once more. It was no joy to count accurately for a sustained period, but his curiosity had gotten the better of him. Many questions were more interesting than their answers, but this needed answering.

When he counted the last ring, he seriously considered a recount. It made no sense. Yet he knew he had counted carefully.

Three thousand, three hundred and nineteen. Danald hung his head, and for the first time since he was a child, he wept. A slow, mournful cry of loss. Seventy-eight years. Only his mother had been still alive when he had begun his journey and he had not seen her in a decade, but he wanted to see her again. A friend or three from childhood had still been alive, those not killed in the border war. A few friends he made during his journey. People he thought there would still be time to see once more, despite his years of voluntary isolation.

They were all dead now. His family was gone, in truth. He had been the surviving hope to continue the famous bloodline. All long gone.

Danald dried his face with a golden leaf and calmed himself. Had it been worth it? Had his sacrifice at least saved this most magnificent of all trees?

Danald looked back at the tree he had been and drew on his Spirit.

His soul exploded.

The rush of Spirit almost overwhelmed him. He desperately pushed it into his art of dreaming. So much energy had to go somewhere and do something. With that amount of Spirit, Danald anticipated a trip into the dreamscape like no other. He braced himself.

Nothing. A torrent of Spirit raged through him, but the walls remained. Danald, always one to search for equilibrium, panicked. He felt like his body would completely burn away if the Spirit was not used. So Danald did what he always had in such situations. He stopped thinking. He stopped trying. He flowed.

Almost eight decades of experience as an integral part of a Spirit network clicked into place below the level of conscious thought. His soul knew what to do. It had processed and shaped Spirit for almost a century. It knew the flavors of this world's energies. It shaped this firestorm of Spirit until it was usable. His Spirit flowed down four channels. Not one. Four. None were his art of dreaming.

Danald did not know these new arts, yet he did. He had been a tree. He had felt these uses of Spirit even if he had not thought about them.

The great tree had been too heavy to bear its own weight, of course. Too heavy under normal gravity. So the tree had reduced gravity's hold. Danald became weightless.

The great tree had been too big to hurry, and had too important a role to act slowly. So the tree had manipulated its speed. Danald became, in mind and in body, fast.

The great tree had used him for nearly a century, yet he had only aged a season. To be useful, the tree needed him for a long time, but he could not be of use if time had literally stopped. So the tree had manipulated time itself, causing it to pass very slowly indeed. Danald felt that this was related to the art of speed, yet different. Danald felt himself jump back and forth between different streams of time in a blur.

The great tree, to Danald's surprise, had not first taken root on this island. It had grown elsewhere, as a predecessor had occupied this island. Once that had died, this tree had punched a hole through space itself to teleport to this island. Danald felt himself punch through space again and again, Jumping between tree and island and mountain and lake in a blur.

Gravity. Movement. Time. Place. He could see now that all four things were aspects of reality. Fundamental truths of existence. In the manifold of time and space, these properties shaped the interactions of existence. They had been alluded to by the Traveler and communities had spent more than a century meditating on them, as instructed. But Danald *knew* them. His art was now to change his relationship with the spacetime manifold itself.

A Manifold Artist. Yes. Yes, he liked that term.

So it was that Danald, Lord of the Spacetime Manifold, came into his power and his destiny. He vowed to make the great tree he had once been a part of into the most sacred and holy of all this world's life. He vowed to establish a community of those who cared about the trees and lived in equilibrium with the world that had welcomed humanity. He vowed to protect the great tree and all trees that, like the human heart, processed and pumped the energy of life to where it was needed.

He had his mission. This world was to be protected. It would start with this place. He would name it Chalvstrom, and his new nation Chalveno, after the birth name of the Announcer himself. People would witness this great tree, which he would call the worldtree, and know this world for its majesty. He would build a palace inside the living worldtree, unlike those built from the corpses of trees. He would still need to convince people to care for the broader world, so he would give this world an identity. A name. Something to remind people that the life of this world truly was connected, as the Traveler had said. It was much harder to hurt something with a name. He was sure of that.

It would all take time. More time than he had. He hoped that this new power to manipulate time itself may be the answer. He could instruct his people, then disappear into a different timestream, where he would age more slowly. With his ability to change the speed at which his body and mind worked, he could live far more slowly when not needed, which should extend his time dramatically. It was immortality of a sort.

Yes, a plan was coming together. This world was sacred and he, Danald, would announce it to all.

A Memory of Djulita

Half a year ago

Djulita sat at her ornate mahogany desk, trying to focus on reports from Vrailen's 'informational network'. His spies reported to him, but she was granted access to support her work for Lord Speed.

Artist-civilian relations continued to improve as Guilds or members of the Nineteen adopted Lord Speed's approach. Tensions along the Free Cities border were worsening, but violent conflict remained localized and small scale human tragedies with little chance of escalating to a strategic threat. Even diplomatic relations with Chalveno were improving as Tolgarlo started to walk Lord Speed's talk of respecting and working with nature rather than conducting wholesale land clearing.

Domestic matters were of greater concern. Lord Space's antagonism towards Lord Speed had grown to outright hostility and threats over the years. The man's private empire was expanding in troubling ways, including through aggressive recruitment in the Schools of the Arts and amongst former civilian soldiers. Alvertus' company spent a lot on security for an agricultural enterprise.

It would have been easier to stay on task had there been urgent work to do. Everything was under control or in the 'watch and wait' basket, which freed Djulita's mind to stress about Calendra.

For thirteen years, Calendra had stayed in touch. From a season after the break-up that broke her, Calendra wrote to Djulita through Vrailen's secure message network. Not weekly or anything - it was Calendra, after all - but frequently.

Were there nothing more, Djulita would stay her fears. Mal remained philosophical about it, noting that his daughter was wily and largely indestructible. She put aside matters of state and stared at Calendra's last letter.

Hey DJ. I'm doing better, thanks. I think I had been in a bit of a rut, staying put for too long without achieving much. I guess I helped some folks but things still felt stagnant. It was worth it in the end. I got what I was waiting for! I'm not sure where I'll go next but I'll find out when I get there. I'm feeling more hopeful. Hopeful that I'm on the path to being extraordinary. Hopeful that things will be better then. It's a nice feeling. Love you both. DM.

Djulita still grinned each time she read 'DM'. Daughter of the Manifold. It was written in jest, but no doubt had deeper importance to Calendra.

Reading the letter for the fiftieth time enlightened Djulita no more than previously. Calendra remained cryptic even through a secure network. Djulita knew the wild girl would rather the world forget all about her. Wild woman, to be fair. She would be in her early thirties by now, older if she had not balanced her time spent Fast with living Slow. Djulita found it hard to imagine Calendra doing anything slowly, even sleeping.

Indulging herself, Djulita looked back through previous correspondence with the woman that had become a daughter to her. All through the written word. Djulita had not seen Calendra in almost fourteen years. Nobody had. Yet Calendra had opened up through letters in a way she might not have in person. Djulita shared that trait, preferring the written word. As a result, Djulita had witnessed the rhythm of Calendra's adult life, its ebbs and flows, from afar. And vice versa, with Calendra providing some of the most heartfelt words at the passing of Djulita's mother just two years after Mal's election.

Why can't everyone just be normal, like you and Dad and Vrai. Sometimes I just hate them, DJ. The things people do to each other. Some are good but they're a gentle whisper in a roar of selfishness.

The bitter words of a year ago contrasted with the optimism of her last letter. Yet only a year before that, Calendra had seemed content.

I'm feeling upbeat. I think I've found my next home. The views are pretty, the life vibrant, the waters sweet. I feel drawn to this place. It reminds me of home. Maybe I'll come and visit soon. Give my love to Dad.

The tone had changed over the years. Barely restrained fury and poorly hidden despair matured to resigned disappointment and measured sorrow. Fierce pride and triumphant joy grew into understated determination and contented satisfaction. But the pattern had not changed. Optimism. Hope. Action. Disappointment. Cynicism. Action. Success. Optimism. Hope. The endless cycle of a perfectionist who will settle for nothing less than the unattainable.

Her last letter had been the most optimistic in years, which was why the silence was so unsettling. It could be consistent with the pattern. If her high optimism had been deeply disappointed, she might have switched off and dropped out, to re-emerge once she found herself. It felt different this time, though.

Djulita was far from considering the worst, but she wondered if Calendra might have been taken. While it had been years since the general buzz of curiosity around the disappearance of Lord Speed's daughter had died away, there were still people who might feel they had unresolved business with Calendra. The Announcer might still remember her, though there was never any guessing the agenda of the ancient Manifold Lord. Djulita also suspected Calendra had made enemies in the Free Cities. While she would never say it out loud, the patterns behind some of her letters had pointed to her intervention in Free Cities border raids.

However, Djulita's biggest worry was that sniveling creep, Alvertus. Calendra had hinted long ago that Lord Space was a competitor in the search for the grand prizes Djulita dare not discuss with anyone but Mal. The treehearts had remained a secret since Calendra's discovery in the Valley. Vrailen conducted very discrete studies. Djulita approached them through very indirect enquiries during her research in the great libraries, but to Djulita's knowledge, their existence remained a secret otherwise. Except to Alvertus, if Calendra's hints were followed.

Indeed, Alvertus' activities had been consistent with the hypothesis that he was searching for treehearts. That worried Djulita in itself. The more aggressively Alvertus did so, the more likely that others would discover them. Alvertus was wily, but not subtle. The last thing the world needed right now was tyrants, mercenaries and nations warring over powerful natural treasures.

Had Alvertus encountered Calendra in the search for these hearts? Had he dared to abduct her, waiting for an opportunity to use her as leverage against Mal? Calendra would be very hard to catch, but not so hard to hold. It was Djulita's greatest fear. There was something about the conduct of Chalveno that made the Announcer feel more antagonist than villain. Alvertus, on the other hand, was a villain through and through. Djulita did not trust him to play by any civilized rules, especially as his influence in the Nineteen continued to erode.

Djulita wanted to search for Calendra, but she was no intelligence agent. Besides, Vrailen's people were on permanent watch for her. If Alvertus really was the key threat to her, now or in the future, the best thing Djulita could do was to figure out what Alvertus would do. Anything she discovered would support Mal, so it was well within her job description. Not that her job description still meant anything after a decade and a half. She did what needed doing.

She had already requested a report from Vrailen's people on any research or quiet enquiries made by Vrailen's known associates, and copies of his company's public reports. There had to be patterns waiting to be uncovered. There was not too much else she could do, though, so she approached it from the other angle.

Alvertus was after treehearts. If Djulita could understand the things that Alvertus and Calendra both sought, maybe she could be proactive rather than reactive.

Aid the hero, foil the villain, help the world. All with the turn of a page. What could be better?

Djulita threw herself into the research. She gained quiet access to the libraries of the Schools of the Arts, archives in the main civilian library and private archives of the Speed Guild. She soaked up anything and everything on Spirit, biology and ecosystems. As she did, patterns started to emerge.

The commodification of Spirit-rich foods in recent years had prompted renewed interest amongst natural philosophers in the role of Spirit in non-human life. It was clear that plant life contained Spirit, but whether it generated Spirit like human Artists or took it in from the environment was hotly contested. Growing evidence that plants could be aligned to a type of Spirit, even a particular Art, had bolstered the self-generation camp.

It was the overlooked argument of an obscure Chalvenan Instinct Artist that really caught Djulita's attention. She outlined, without examples or evidence, a network theory of Spirit in which the 'general' Spirit generated by living things was shared among connected plants and naturally developed certain alignments that humans categorized as Body, Mind or Manifold. The idea felt consistent with the little that Calendra had said about treehearts. It seemed this natural alignment might be active, like the hearts acted as a pump and filter for Spirit networks, as the human heart did with blood.

Still, it was very conceptual and esoteric. An elegant model, but not one easily applied to the physical world. It was not enough to let her map these networks to the world of experience. It was not actionable intelligence.

So she explored the ecological aspect. The evidence of networking between organisms was remarkable. A multi-study analysis demonstrated the resilience and diversity of old-growth forests compared with clonal plantations, providing evidence that the world of the tiny, between the trees, was as vital to their health as the world of the large. Biological indications that groups of trees would share nutrients with a damaged neighbor when there were enough to spare indicated a level of collaboration. Controlled studies even indicated that trees *communicated* with each other over moderate distances, with one tree raising chemical and Spiritual defenses when its cousin was attacked. There was further evidence that this communication extended to different species of tree.

The connection seemed obvious to Djulita, though she found no evidence that anyone had hypothesized it. Perhaps it was the lack of knowledge of treehearts, the lack of attention paid by civilian researchers to Artists and vice versa, or the total lack of collaboration between biological and Spiritual theorists. To Djulita, though, the pattern fit. All trees, and maybe all plants, were networked in a way that enabled collaboration. The sum was greater than the parts. The hearts were the things that facilitated that, filtering base Spirit and translating it into useful Spirit.

It was still not actionable intelligence, but it meant Djulita could be useful. Treehearts were hubs in a network. Networks were patterns. Patterns were Djulita's jam. She dived into the next book.

CHAPTER TWENTY SIX

What is Spirit? The fuel for Artistry within the Domains of Body, Mind and Manifold. Yes but what is Spirit. A self-renewing resource that can effect change through the conscious intent of its vessel. Yes but what is Spirit. It is the product of life and the facilitator of interconnection. Yes but what is Spirit. Is it biological or conceptual or incorporeal or emergent or a property. Yes.

Extract from interview with Patient 132

Records of the Mind Sanctum

Calendra stares at the man who has hunted her for twenty years. The man who has imprisoned her for one hundred and forty-seven sleeps.

The Announcer has changed little since Calendra left Chalvstrom. His closely cropped coal-black hair frames discerning gray eyes, a sharp nose and full lips. The ceremonial silver robes from his Descension, and the practical khaki suit he wore when he captured her, have been replaced with flowing golden trousers and not much else. His chest bears only a simple yet exquisite amulet that highlights dark skin over taut muscles. He gives her a lopsided smirk, eyes twinkling.

"I've been wondering what to do with you, Calendra. Any thoughts?"

The Announcer chuckles to himself as though hearing a fine joke indeed. He throws an apple between the bars of her cell. She catches it and takes a sizable bite, chewing before responding.

"I thought," Calendra mused, "that I might kill you."

"I see," the Announcer said, nodding slowly as if reflecting on rare wisdom. "Why?"

"Why?" Calendra splutters despite her efforts to be cool. "You hunted me as a child. You sent assassins after me. You destroyed my valley home. You threaten my father every year. And you have imprisoned me without cause. I need more?"

"Did I? Was my business with you, or was it with Malnor? Was it I who destroyed that valley, or was it you? And without cause? Without cause? You still don't know what you did? The destruction you so nearly wrought?"

Calendra bites off the belligerent response she would like to give. This man has been her enemy for so long, yet his response feels authentic. As if, in his story, he is the hero and she the villain. Did he destroy the valley? She supposes not. And had he hunted her? Her dad had told her as much, yet he had been a spy, unmasked, in a hostile nation. Does it matter? An enemy of her family is her enemy.

These are not the matters that trouble her. It has been years since she cared about such things. She is a child of the wild and has little concern these days for the affairs of humanity. The trees are her people. It is his last words that resonate. He insisted when capturing her that she risked great damage to her trees. She has given it little thought during her weeks of captivity, but now, faced with his earnestness, she is forced to address the claim. Not because he is entitled to an explanation, but because the thought of ignorantly hurting that which she loves terrifies her.

"Let us say," she says, seating herself with a sigh, "that I don't know what I did."

The Announcer stares at her for some time before replying. "You are no fool, Calendra. One does not uncover multiple treehearts by luck. I protect secrets that must remain hidden. Tell me what you know of these matters first."

Calendra will not speak of her Manifold sight, but she holds back little else. If any human already knows as much as her, it is this man.

"A treeheart is a nexus in the flows of Spirit between trees. It gets infused with Spirit aligned to one of the three Domains, like a barrel used to repeatedly make whisky will become infused with it. Consuming one infuses you with that Spirit, but it can only be consumed once it has died."

The Announcer rubs his forehead as if trying to choose from a long list of scathing remarks.

"Yes. Yes, that's supposed to be the case. Yet that didn't stop you. You severed that heart while it still functioned. While it was still connected to the network. Did it not occur to you …"

The Announcer sighs before composing himself and continuing.

"For Chalvan's sake, does it take mental gymnastics to see the problem with destroying a key part of a network? What in the fires of the Twin did you think would happen?"

"Nothing," she tells him, irritated at the condescension. "You were protecting the new one. The old one had no further use."

"I thought," he replies, nodding, "that I saw a Speed Artist that day. When I felt the network shudder mere minutes later and found you at the other site, I knew it couldn't have been you. It was miles away. Nobody can move that fast. I knew it must have been Malnor. It is rare that a thing I know proves to be false."

The Announcer shakes his head several times and starts pacing.

"Who are you? How can you wield such power?" The question is an attack and a plea. "One of Tolgan's branch? Not one of mine, surely. No, no, it doesn't matter. What you did was reckless and selfish beyond words. That heart was weak. Had I not been there …"

"That doesn't make sense. Why would a new heart need help? This all existed long before humans arrived. Even if the old one was still part of the network, surely treehearts are more resilient than that?"

"You should be right, but you're not. Normally, yes, by the time an old heart is dying it's because the new one is established. The old one is cut off and withers. Severing it before death is still dangerous, as the network itself might be disrupted."

"The whole network?" Calendra scoffs at the idea. "I doubt that. It's just a point of confluence. The flows will change and that point will move elsewhere. A new treeheart will form in the nexus of the new flows."

"Fool! You …" He seems to pull himself together, seating himself on the chair outside the cell. "I see the problem. You've been thinking of the network like roads. Where you find many roads intersecting, you will find a town. Destroy the town and the roads still work. This is wrong. A treeheart is like that after which it is named, and the Spirit network is like the interconnecting vessels that carry blood around our bodies. A treeheart is a pump and a filter. Remove it and the Spirit generated by life spills out, lost as waste energy. Spirit is no longer filtered. The local Spirit cycle fails. Ecosystems fall."

Calendra stares at him. He is sincere. Could it be? Has she misunderstood the nature of treehearts all these years? Has she really considered it, though?

"If you are right," she replies cautiously, "why have you kept this secret? If folks knew, maybe they would protect the hearts."

"Protect them?" The Announcer guffaws. "I've watched the best and worst of human life for ten generations. At their best, they perfect. At their worst, they destroy with a permanence that nature never achieves. It only takes humanity's worst at one key moment to bring down all that humanity's best can achieve. Besides, you are only the third or fourth human since we arrived here almost four centuries ago, after me and my grandfather, to have found a heart and understood its significance. The secret is well kept."

"Sure," she replies bitterly, "known only by you, me, the entirety of Alvertus' organization, and some band of Artists roaming the Plains." She spits for emphasis.

The Announcer launches from his chair and grips her cell bars, white knuckled, eyes intense. "Tell me it's a lie," he hisses. He wilts as she shakes her head.

"Saw some Artists in the area before I found the hearts. Mercenaries, I think. They referred to hearts and talked of finding them before Alvertus could. That was when I hurried."

"Royal rot. I might have known." The Announcer cracks his knuckles. "I might finally need to deal with him."

"But I still don't understand," Calendra interjects. "I understand why severing a living heart could be dangerous to parts of life in the area. But what harm is there in consuming a dead one?"

"There is no direct harm," the Announcer sighed, "as far as I am aware. Some indirect harm in taking Spirit that would have slowly returned to the system. It is the risks it creates that are intolerable. You proved this beyond question. A live heart is susceptible to attack. If the wrong person finds a way to emulate you, all is doomed. It is all one, and Spirit is a part of it all."

"So, I'm not the wrong person?" Calendra allows herself a cheeky grin.

"I've not decided," he replies, showing no trace of good humor. "I might believe you didn't know what you were doing, and the risks. I might believe you think you wouldn't do the same again. I'm not sure I can believe that, faced with power, you could resist. I do believe that I might have misjudged you, and perhaps Malnor by implication. With the threat expanding, I think I shall reach out to him."

"And tell him I'm safe?"

"I think not. You are safe, but you're not free. Malnor would tear down these walls to get to you. He would fail, but it would strain our relationship with

Tolgarlo even further. I think you are not my enemy, though. Just too dangerous. I'll make your stay more comfortable and have your possessions delivered. I have one request first."

Calendra raised an eyebrow. He would keep her imprisoned and still ask something of her?

"Tell me," he says, "where to find the next dying heart. I need to stop Alvertus but I cannot Jump into Sanctum and lay waste to his residence. Well, I can. But it would be ... imprudent. I need to stop him at the scene of whatever crime he plans. Where would he look for a treeheart? Could there be more in the Plains?"

Calendra frowns. He does not know? He is the Announcer! Since the last experience, she assumed he will be an ever present threat. It took a lot of Spirit to find the last one, but it was not that difficult.

"I don't know. I spent years finding that one. I hadn't thought of the next one. It's not like I have a map of them. You don't know? You beat me to the last one. Anyway, how did you get so powerful if you haven't been consuming hearts?"

The Announcer looks at her with skepticism before answering. "I do not consume the hearts of the world. I lent one my strength when it was in need. It left me infused, you might say, like a treeheart. If you must seek power, I wish you'd done it that way. That is symbiosis. Collectiveness. Not parasitic and dangerous." He shakes his head at her and turns to leave.

"That's it?" She expects more, at least to keep him talking. She has learned more than she expected.

"That's it," he replies, looking over his shoulder. "Once I'm satisfied you're no danger, I'll release you. Meanwhile, enjoy your painting. I will have books brought to you. And you may commune with the worldtree."

He turns back and releases a lever, which drops the bars that kept the bark of the worldtree out of reach.

"So you really believe it? You really think this world is one alive, thinking person?"

"Believe it?" He looks thoughtful. "I know the world is one. All is connected. I have been part of that network. I've felt it. But Zem? It's a useful story. Ask a friend to water your plant while you're away and most will fail in this small task. But tell them that you have an old plant passed down through the generations that your grandmother named Bruce, and that the hardest thing about going away is worrying about Bruce, and could they please take care of your Brucey while you're away ..."

Calendra laughs out loud, to her surprise.

"It doesn't matter though," he continues, solemn once more. "The world is fragile. It was the same for endless epochs and we came and changed it. If we do not think of it as a person, we will kill it. It's what we do. We are the worst kind of life. Zem may be a lie, but it is also a truth. They are better than us, the lives of this world. We must learn from them. Think like the trees, Calendra. Be like the trees. It will serve you well."

He walks out. Calendra sidles up to the tree, happy to have physical contact with something alive. It is a mighty tree indeed, the long section in her cell comprising a tiny portion of the trunk's circumference. She touches its rough bark and thinks back to that day so many years ago when, waiting for the Descension, she gazed at the rings above. The Hall of the Announcer is probably ten storeys below her, but might as well be a world away.

So much has changed, yet so little. For all her growth in power and knowledge, for all her uniqueness, she is still a powerless woman in the hands of a powerful man, with no control over her own destiny. Have the years of toil and sacrifice been worth it? Has she become all she could have? Does it make her happy?

Calendra laughs to herself. Happy? The word is spun sugar, enticing but unfulfilling. She is proud, mostly. Engaged and, at times, passionate. She experiences the truly worthwhile things that most humans could not imagine even reaching for. And she is extraordinary. Almost.

No, things have not changed, but she has. She can see the world like no other and hear it like her own thoughts. It has become a part of her and she a part of it. To the Twin with the rest of them. With humans. Only the Announcer understood, and long before her. Her path is set. She will not let captivity stand in her way. Nor can her destination remain as it was. For it is not just the Announcer's warnings about consuming hearts that sunk in. It is his words of top-down hierarchies, and of lending strength and becoming like a heart.

She too could bond with a living heart and become like him, but more than him. The worldtree is magnificent, but as she leans into it and feels its Spiritual flows resonate with her, she knows this is not the Worldtree. She knows that there must be treehearts at an even higher level than the one she consumed. Even higher than this one. Hearts not just higher in area of effect, but in type. A heart that is not just of Manifold or Mind or Body, but of all three. An apex heart that cycles all the Spirit of all life on the entire planet. The true Worldtree. She will find it and join it and become infused by it. Then she will be extraordinary.

Meanwhile, she will learn. Not through whatever books he would deliver, but the way Calendra always has. With her back against the tree, she meditates. Not the floating, unstructured mental wanderings of long days in a cell. Purposeful, focused meditation.

Calendra wills her Manifold sight to activate with the scraps of Spirit that never rise beyond a certain level in this place. They are too little to become Fast or Slow, to give her sight, but as the hours progress, she begins to sense something. It is not her Manifold sight, but it is like Manifold touch. She feels inflows and outflows of Spirit through arms that feel like her own. Thrilled, she pushes harder, but the feeling diminishes.

Frustrated, held by the determination to brute force proprioception, she takes a mental step back. Meditate. Try not to try. She does. After a while, the feeling returns.

She can feel tendrils of her Spirit grasping at the tree as if helplessly attracted to it. She can feel the branches of Spirit pumping forth from the tree to destinations unknown. She feels it as one feels blood return to a limb after being restricted.

As the days of meditation pass, interrupted only by guards bringing new ways to occupy her time, she feels what she needs. There is a change in the Spirit between entering the tree and leaving it. Not just a difference in amount, but in type. She feels the purposefulness of the outflows, not in thought but in structure. The heart is sending the processed Spirit to specific places in concentrated flows. It is a level of resolution her Manifold sight never before granted. Where that provided visual cues of blurred color, this has all the sensitivity of heightened touch. She can feel not just where the Spirit flows are greatest, but how far they extend.

With a rush, Calendra mentally transposes the geography of the land onto the body of the world she can feel. She imagines her body as the world they know. The thickest, most concentrated outflow runs towards ... her head. North. It does not feel like it is towards the Plains. This north is farther. Into the Grand Reserve, into the far north. The ice waters. Is there even land up there?

North. Calendra knows where she needs to go. Who she needs to be. But she is still trapped.

It is several more days before an option presents itself. Days of being one with the tree, of feeling its flows like they are parts of her, of learning to distinguish subtly between them. She realizes with a start that there is a subtle inflow of Spirit the tree draws upon that is unlike the rest. It is not drawn through conduits from afar, but is pulled into a small bubble around the tree itself. It is as if the tree invisibly reaches into the air for ten paces around itself to draw in any available Spirit, like a cloud forest pulling in moisture from the clouds themselves.

That is why she cannot regenerate Spirit. That is why the Announcer keeps his visits short. The tree saps Spirit from anyone in her cell.

Calendra smiles to herself. It is something to work towards. She sinks back into a trance and feels for the pull of Spirit. She notices it eventually, a slight tug that creates a tiny outflow of Spirit from her like smoke drawn through a ventilation point. It is only a trickle, but Spirit regenerates exponentially. She has so little that even the slight pull is enough to prevent regeneration.

Calendra mentally glowers at her fleeing Spirit. No. It is not right. It is her Spirit. It belongs to her, refined and focused by her efforts. She frowns. No. It is hers. A part of her. She seizes it with her mind.

STOP.

It stops. Her wisps of Spirit churn and swirl inside her, but it no longer leaves. It is hers. Hers!

Calendra grins, crosses to the far side of her cell and waits cross-legged on the polished wood. The guard looks at her quizzically. It is the most she has moved in days, other than using the chamber pot in the curtained corner and washing herself with the weekly soapy water bucket. She nods to him and waits.

It takes hours of mental exertion, maintaining the command of her Spirit, before she has regenerated. But what good will it do? The last heart gave her Spirit that was clean and powerful, but no amount of speed will help her. It is the greatest of all Arts, but even strength would be more useful here. If only she shared the Announcer's spatial abilities.

The instant she thinks it, she feels something. Like a woman who learns to work wood starts to see a tree as the beginnings of a table, she sees a new use for her Spirit. Two, in fact.

Calendra falls to the floor and laughs. She laughs like she has not laughed in years, tears of joy and exhaustion streaming from her. She opens her eyes and notices the guard on his feet, eyes wide.

"Are you ... okay, Miss?"

"I'm okay," she tells him gently, "and I'm sorry."

Calendra rises, punches a hole through the Manifold and is pulled through to stand behind the guard. With three rapid blows, he falls unconscious. Calendra is confident he will live. With hours left until the regular changing of the guards, she sits back down and waits. She will wait as long as possible. Better to have a small head start and plenty of Spirit than a large one and little Spirit. If she has Spirit, they will not catch her. Calendra is, after all, extraordinary. Almost.

When she hears footsteps approaching hours later, the poor guard still unconscious, Calendra focuses her mind on a place she can picture perfectly. The eastern shore of Lake Chalvstrom, where she first saw the worldtree with her dad.

Calendra punches a hole in the Manifold and steps through. Perfect. It uses less Spirit than she anticipated. Ignoring the stares of onlookers in a place with so few Manifold Artists, least of all ones with glowing Spirit markings, she Jumps to the summit of Mount Covenant, ten miles away but visible.

Calendra is free! She whoops, raises a fist and Jumps to the next mountain.

CHAPTER TWENTY SEVEN

What is the Manifold? A semantically prescribed grouping of spiritually related powers. Yes but what is the Manifold. A medium through which Spirit fuels and is shaped by the Manifold Arts. Yes but what is the Manifold. The four-dimensional fabric within which the existence and properties and interactions of matter and energy over time are embedded. Yes but what is the Manifold. Is it ontological or conceptual or incorporeal or emergent or a property. Yes.

Extract from interview with Patient 132

Records of the Mind Sanctum

Calendra stands atop the Traveler's Seat, the great plateau not far from Skypeak, and looks north. The view is the same as the day she consumed the speed-instinct meal, if slightly less elevated, but this time she is not looking for a destination. She is looking for the fastest way.

Calendra readies herself at the southern end of the plateau, wearing all the clothes she possesses. She learned a thing or two about her new Arts as she traveled. Spatial Artistry seems to be efficient when line-of-sight, but mentally challenging and expensive otherwise. Her blind Jump away from the worldtree cost far more Spirit than her Jumps since. She has Jumped from one set of mountains to another, as far as she can see, making her way north.

Curiously, while Speed Artistry conserves momentum - changing speed mid-flight resulting in a lurch or boost - Spatial Artistry does not. At least she thinks it is about momentum. These things get fuzzy when she tries to apply normal language to the bizarre interactions between the Fast and the Normal. Her body knows how to use it, though. Either way, with Spatial Artistry, no matter what her velocity is before Jumping she becomes motionless after a Jump, other than gravity's downward pull. Which is where her second new Art comes in.

She is near the highest point in the world, but it is still too far to see the next range to the north. She can travel the old-fashioned way - Fast, on foot - but that seems so dreary now. She can Jump blind, but it will cost Spirit. She just needs to get a little closer. And she has more than one new Art.

Calendra becomes Fast.

Calendra is running. Legs pumping. Surroundings a blur. Approaching the edge. Leaping. Discarding gravity. Flying. Flying! The world below is a painting. Flying. Reaching an apex. Descending. Miles passing below. Descending. Approaching the forest heights. Seeing mountains on the horizon. Grinning. Jumping.

Calendra becomes Normal and gazes down at the view from ten storeys above the summit of some unnamed peak as she drifts down like a leaf. Much of the Great Plains lies to the south and the northern Free Cities to the east. To the north, her destination. The Grand Reserve. But she has one more detour.

Close enough now to see it, Calendra Jumps to a point directly above the strangler fig and floats down gently. She becomes Fast and, minutes later, she has her precious pack with painting materials, tent and clothes. Everything she needs.

She Jumps to the next set of hills visible to the north. From there she can see the Traveler's Cordon in the far distance, a thirty storey high tangle of bushes with thorns like daggers that grows higher each year and covers the distance between the two mountain ranges that flank the elevated peninsula on which the Grand Reserve lies.

Calendra punches a hole in the Manifold and appears on the other side. Without ceremony she continues her Jumps between visible mountain peaks, gaining altitude as she heads north. Some time later, having covered dozens of miles, or hundreds, she stands atop the highest mountain in the Reserve. She realizes her Spirit is running somewhat low and gives herself a chance to rest. It had to happen sooner or later. She thinks back to the two or three Jumps of the Spatial Artists in the school sporting leagues, and Vrai only having several Jumps in him at the Valley. She reflects, not for the first time, that Spatial Artistry is perhaps easier for her than the average Manifold Artist, as most things seem to be.

Calendra takes the time to look around. The view is spectacular. The Grand Reserve is riddled with sharp, steep peaks and narrow ravines dropping into nowhere. It is not just the Cordon and the prohibitions that prevent access.

On the slopes of mountains below the snow line, down the mountain valleys and around the edges of ravines, life thrives. Unfamiliar trees and plants of countless types own the alpine region. Struck by the view and faced with an hour or two to regenerate her Spirit, Calendra paints. At first she paints without her Manifold sight, enjoying the motions. Then she draws on a trickle of Spirit to activate her sight and overlays the faint Spirit flows. As she finishes, she realizes something.

She has relied for years on her Manifold sight activated by her using Speed Artistry without actually becoming Fast or Slow. She thinks of it as drawing on Spirit but it is really fueling her Art without using it to change anything about the world. She has other Arts now.

Calendra uses a small amount of Spirit to power all three Arts without making changes with them. She feels her relationship to the Manifold change. She is Normal, but the friction of movement has no hold on her. Gravity exerts itself, but has no power over her. She remains in place, yet her location is indeterminate.

She sinks into a trance and her Manifold sight pops. It has a richness of color and a textural depth it once lacked. She can see the flows in all their power and finesse with her waking eyes. It is much clearer than with one Art. Calendra readies her soulpaints and begins.

Once she is done, she understands the Reserve. She sees it. It is a hub. It is to the rest of the world as a treeheart is to the local ecosystem. It is not just the greater part of the Chalvstrom treeheart's outflows that lead here, but flows from treehearts all over the landmass. It all leads here.

It is not just that, though. It sends Spirit back to the rest of the landmass, processed and changed. It is true, after all, that treehearts transform Spirit as well as accumulating it. Even then, the network here does not send all of it back south. Not by a long shot. Thick flows of Spirit head north. Still north. That was one thing in Chalveno, in the south, but she is now almost as far north as one can be. She can see Land's End, where the frosty Reserve gives way to frigid seas and shifting ice floes. The Spirit flows continue north, into those seas and past the horizon.

Calendra is dumbfounded. She was sure the Reserve was her destination. Further north? Could they go to true north, on the top of the world? It is said to be only water and ice. How could a tree exist in such a place?

Calendra punches the rocky ground, absently feeling her knuckle break and re-knit. It makes no sense. She needs to see farther, but there is nowhere north of her that is higher than where she stands. She needs to get higher.

Calendra buries her palm in her face when she sees her oversight. Calendra punches a hole in the Manifold and appears miles over her current position. She immediately reduces gravity to avoid falling too quickly and looks north, fuming that she could have done this earlier. Why Jump to a high point on land when you can Jump anywhere above it?

The view is unimaginable. She is so high that the air is too thin to breathe. She is so high she can see the shape of the northern part of the landmass and the flows of Spirit beyond. She is so high she can see the curvature of the world. She can actually see it is round. It is a sight, she realizes, that only Spatial Artists and Gravity Artists can ever hope to see.

Content with the glory of it all, Calendra releases her Gravity Artistry and plummets towards the ground. As she gains speed, the wind buffets her and she closes her eyes against it, feeling herself fall, feeling the world pull her down and the air slow her fall. She can still see the flows of Spirit far beneath, through her eyelids, and when they seem close, she opens her eyes. Barely a hundred paces from the ground, she Jumps back to the peak where she started.

Exhilarating. She could do that endlessly if she had the time and Spirit to burn. Looking down at the world from so high feels godlike. To actually see the world curve away rather than end in a line is the most surreal of all. The flows indeed continue north into the patchwork of white ice on blue-gray sea, but they do not travel along the surface. They go underwater. From Land's End they submerged, heading north. She could tell they were below the sea and extended to the curved horizon.

They must go somewhere. There must be land further north. How far will she need to go? So far she would likely emerge on the other side of the world! Calendra laughs at the idea, then it hits her like a hammer. The world is a sphere, as she knows and has now seen. There is a limit to how far north one can go, but at some point, if you keep going straight, you will start to go south.

There is land there, but on the other side of the planet! The shortest path to it must be over the north pole and its shifting ice. The only path, Calendra realizes as she considers the mighty Obsidian Wall that encircles the landmass. The Obsidian Wall that prevents humans from leaving the landmass. From accessing this second land she now knows must exist. Did the Traveler create it?

She needs to regenerate her Spirit first. She has no way of knowing how far her journey might be, or even if it is possible. That changes nothing, but increases the need for preparation. She sits atop the great peak and meditates under a snow gum, feeling the flows around her. As with the Chalvstrom tree, she becomes more attuned to it as the time passes. She finally recognizes something she had not before, so enchanting and distracting was her new Manifold sight.

There are points of failure in the Spirit network of the Reserve. Points where the flows are interrupted and go back on themselves to flow elsewhere. They are dead or dying hearts! She is eager to get to them but knows to be patient. She really needs as much Spirit as possible.

As she listens further to the network, she understands. It all relates to the Plains. Perhaps the heart she consumed, or perhaps others dying, destabilized the entire region's Spirit flows. Are the failures systemic? Is an entire chunk of the Plains failing to contribute Spirit to the network and falling even to allow Spirit from other regions to pass through it? It feels like that.

Calendra lets out a long sigh. It is the part of the Great Plains that has been taken over by agriculture. Endless golden fields that fed so many. It is all so connected, all the variety of life contributing to a collective pool of Spirit. The massive fields of grain do not fit, somehow. Is it the lack of trees or something more?

Whatever the immediate cause, the effect seems clear. The network is failing and hearts are dying. Calendra does not know if it is cause for concern or an unfolding calamity, but she knows she will not let a dying heart go to waste, whatever the Announcer says about Spirit returning to the system. It is too valuable to her and too dangerous to fall into the hands of another. Besides, she is doing good now, right? She will find the Heart of the World and lend it support, and in doing so, become something greater. Any dead heart she consumes here will only add to that good. And should the rot have spread and the Heart of the World is dying, a new one being established would mean ...

Calendra follows the flows to the points of failure. Through valleys and caves, over mountains and streams, she tracks them down among the spare populations of winter willow, alder, mountain ash, and tiny varieties of spruce and birch. It takes a week and change. Several prove to be alive, if weak. She leaves them. Others are still in the process of dying, their replacements in the process of establishing. Most are small, far weaker than the one she consumed on the Plains. But after a dozen days of camping in caves to avoid the cold, endless sunlight, cooking harvested ingredients of startling Spiritual strength, she finds the three hearts she needs, able to harvest them after confirming their replacements, often miles away, are established.

The first is deep in a network of caves lit by ghostly fluorescent mushrooms. Despite its isolation from the world outside, the mountain ash thrives due to the presence of an underground stream and the rays of sun that shine through massive fissures in the walls and ceiling. A heart of great power, aligned to the Domain of Body. A heart of the physical.

The second is in an open valley bordered by jagged peaks that reminds her of the one in which she became who she is. The winter willow sits by a river of unnatural warmth, fed by hot springs above. A heart of great power, aligned to the Domain of Mind. A heart of the cognitive.

The third is high atop a peak surrounded by far higher peaks. The snow gum is alone, gripping to a patch of soil not much larger than it. A heart of great power, aligned to the Domain of Manifold. A heart of spacetime.

A heart of each Domain. A true Heart of the World should govern all types of Spirit, not just Manifold, she reasons. She hopes that filling herself with Spirit of all three types will help her join to the Worldheart by giving her a kind of Spiritual compatibility.

Her elation is tempered by concern at being able to find recently deceased hearts of such power of all three Domains but that is a concern for another day. Perhaps, when she is extraordinary, she can fix this. Force people to change. Destroy the grain fields herself.

Driven by purpose, inspired by hope, Calendra presses on. North. North once more. She Jumps from peak to peak, getting into a rhythm as her visualization improves. It takes only hours to reach Land's End, for in endless light, the days are irrelevant.

As she approaches Land's End, she Jumps to the summit of a nearby peak. She looks out at the white-on-gray landscape. The sea is half covered by shifting ice, like jigsaw puzzle pieces that someone has laid out but not yet connected. She leaps off the summit, waving aside gravity as she does, the weight of her pack still enough to gently accelerate her downwards. She Jumps only when she sees she is approaching the ground slightly too fast.

Then she is there. Standing on a black beach at the end of the world, the sun low and the Twin on the far horizon, Spirit markings aflame, she allows herself some time to regenerate Spirit. There is no telling how taxing the next part of her journey will be. Her Spirit capacity and regeneration rate is beyond words, unimaginable to fourteen-year-old Calendra who even then was a prodigy, so she hopes it will not be a long journey.

She looks around the area, surprised that a forest of spruce exists so far north. Barely five minutes of walking through the forest reveals something she did not expect. A stone building. What in the ten hells is a building doing there? There is a stone mosaic sign near the entrance.

Drink's End.

Calendra laughs out loud at the absurdity. She is at the frozen end of the world, past hundreds of miles of forbidding forbidden wilderness, and there is a pub. She shrugs to herself and walks in.

The place is empty but it does not feel ancient. Old, yes, but not abandoned. There is no food. No drink. No people. No music. But there is a bar and fireplace and kitchen and tables and chairs.

Calendra sits at a table, alone, and eats a portion of Spirit-rich jerky, wondering how this place can be. As she lazily studies the room, she imagines the sight of happy patrons, the smell of spiced tubers and the sound of pub songs, the feel of a sticky floor beneath her boots and the taste of ten-spice pumpkin. Like a strange version of Manifold sight, creating visuals from nowhere, she starts to see it. Half a dozen ghostly apparitions wear strange clothing, all edges and angles. A smiling middle-aged barwoman calls for the bard to liven things up.

Calendra taps her feet to music that does not exist and feels the floatiness that accompanies a good drink in good company. She grins at the visions or memories or hallucinations of folks she will never know, and she dances. As she dances, they become more real. More solid. She laughs. How long has it been since she danced? Since she heard music? Since she was with human beings for no other reason than company?

Calendra laughs and holds out her hand to an apparition of a quiet woman with a gentle smile, inviting her to dance. The woman's eyes slide past Calendra. Then snap back to her.

The woman freezes. Every person in the room turns to Calendra. Then they vanish. In an eye blink, they are gone, and the pub is empty. Calendra is alone once more.

She turns to the empty room, gives thanks for the diversion, and marches out. Hallucination, memory or vision, it has refreshed her. She does not need people, but it is a good reminder that people are worth protecting. For every predator and opportunist, for every act of selfishness and malice, there are humans enjoying a simple life of simple pleasures. The trees are her people now, but humans once were.

Calendra, always one to look forward, departs the forest with a smile. Spirit, heart and pack full, she becomes Fast and launches into the air northward, annulling gravity and soaring over the shifting ice below. Wind buffeting her eyes and streaking through her close cropped hair, Calendra rejoices in the freedom as the miles pass. The fragmented landscape opens up ahead of her though the patchwork of ice, endlessly varied, continues.

As she descends through the crisp air, her pack creating a gradual downward acceleration, she realizes she is far too fast to actually land. Ready to Jump to the farthest ice floe she can see, something occurs to her. Instead of Jumping to ground level, she Jumps to a point at the same height but several miles ahead. She quickly cancels her Speed Artistry but keeps gravity low. She appears hundreds of paces above the ice and slowly descends.

Calendra takes her bearings and focuses on a point in the sky several miles farther, but at the same altitude. She Jumps. This time, she appears a hundred paces closer to sea level. She is surprised at the mental effort. It seems the ease of Jumping to a place you can see still depends on visualization. It is easy enough to visualize the top of a mountain you can see, but much harder to visualize a specific point in the sky.

Calendra tries again. Better this time. And again. Better. Again. Again. Her course veers and her altitude fluctuates but she develops a rhythm. Jump. Watch. Visualise. Jump. Watch. Visualize. Jump.

After twenty or forty Jumps, it becomes effortless. The demands on her focus lessen as her visualization improves. Jump. Jump. Jump.

The miles race by, every Jump revealing a slightly different icescape, but the flows of Spirit always head north. The minutes pass by, or the hours. Time is impossible to tell, such is her focus on space and Spirit. Her Spirit gets low but her will gets lower. As she fades, she notices unbroken ice ahead. She Jumps.

Her Spirit is low but she is on solid ground. Solid ice, at least. There is no telling what lies beneath it, but it does not move like the fractured ice on the open sea. It seems to stretch forever north, east and west. Though this far north, with the Twin barely peeking above the horizon, is there even still a north? Forward, left and right, she decides. Directions of a compass are no longer relevant. There is no back. Left and right only exist to avoid obstacles. There is only forward.

Calendra moves forward, conserving her Spirit by walking. Any distance she walks is a rounding error, but she is cold. Very cold. She must, as always, keep moving.

For the hours it takes to regenerate her Spirit, she sees nothing. No life at all. Nothing but ice. She wonders at how Spirit can traverse regions void of life but then remembers the flows are underwater. Does that mean she stands on floating ice rather than ice-covered land? Moreover, does that also mean there is life at the bottom of the sea?

Fascinating, pointless questions. The kind Myla loved. Calendra scowls and dismisses the unbidden thought. Forward. Always forward. Calendra Jumps and appears forward, high in the air. Endless unbroken ice ahead. Jump. Jump. Jump.

After dozens or hundreds or thousands of miles - with no night and no geographical features, she cannot tell - exhaustion takes its toll. Her Spirit reserves fare little better. Strangely, she is not hungry. Perhaps the second causes the other two. She needed little food and little sleep these last weeks, not that she can imagine sleeping in a place where the sun never sets. Perhaps her prodigious Spirit capacity protects her from the rigors of a mortal body. All the more reason to stop and regenerate.

She tries to walk but, without drawing on Spirit, she has no command over her own body. She collapses onto the hard packed snow. As the cold sends its roots into her back, she forces herself to rise, puts on all her clothes and sets up her tent to defend against the icy wind.

She notices the Twin has disappeared from the sky. For some reason, this is what makes her finally realize how alone she is. She is so far from civilization that the Twin is gone. The ice is just white. There is no ethereal blue-violet filter over the world, as happens in all known places as the sun reflects off the Twin. There is just a cold white sun over a cold white land.

She thinks of her dad and Djulita. She has not seen them in years, but she always stays in touch and always had the option to see them. Out here, she is absolutely alone. Ignoring the freezing tears, she tries to sleep but finds herself too exhausted. Not knowing what else to do, she meditates.

She wakes up an unknowable time later. She is so cold. She decamps as fast as possible and runs. After several minutes, her body feels less frigid. Her Spirit full, she draws on some to see if it helps. It does, immediately. Perhaps she should have done that first. She realizes that she must be more careful. Spirit is sustaining her somehow, beyond what her body can otherwise endure. She doubts a normal person would survive here. She must not let herself get so low again.

Calendra continues to run until she is warm, then sets off in a series of aerial Jumps. Still forward, ever forward, following the Spirit flows. She stops hours later to regenerate. It only takes half an hour this time. She sets off once more.

She suffers one more sleep in however many hours she takes to reach the end of the ice. The Spirit flows continue under the sea, heading south, she supposes. There are shifting ice floes on this side of the world as well, but fewer. She Jumps high above the ice to get a better outlook. It is not promising. The ice floes barely continue for two miles. Beyond that is the sea, all the way to the horizon.

It does not even occur to Calendra to turn back. The Spirit flows continue, so she will continue, but she is no fool. She knows the consequences of misjudging. If she runs out of Spirit over the open sea, short of whatever land exists, she will die a lonely, icy death. She must start with as much strength as possible and trust, with no reason other than hope, that she will make it. Make it to a land she does not know exists, in a direction she cannot be sure of, at an unknowable distance. So much uncertainty when her fate is to either die or be extraordinary.

It does not even occur to Calendra to turn back.

She allows herself a proper sleep helped by drawing on a small amount of Spirit. She rises cold but refreshed. She needs time for her Spirit to regenerate entirely, so she exercises to keep warm and eats what is left of her dried fruits. She makes sure she has her soulblossom essence in her pocket, ready to top up her Spirit mid-flight. Finally warm, rested, fed, watered, packed and full of Spirit, she faces the sea.

Calendra closes her eyes and focuses. She takes long, slow breaths and gathers her will. Her fists clench. She rolls her shoulders and shakes the nervous energy out of her legs. She opens her eyes, looks to the sky, and smiles. Time to be extraordinary.

Calendra punches a hole in the Manifold, forward and up. She visualizes her next location. Jump. Without using Gravity Artistry, to save Spirit, she rapidly falls after each Jump. She must move faster. She must visualize faster. Keep moving forward. Jump. Forward. Jump. Jump. Jump.

She hits a rhythm, one jump turning into the next before she can fall too far. Jump. Jump. Occasional height corrections to compensate for gravity. Jump. Jump. Jump.

Finally, no longer needing to think, eyes closed, tracking the Spirit flows, deep in the rhythm, she enters a flow state. Her mind empties. There is no thought. Just the endless rhythm, her Jumps aligned to her heartbeat. Jump Jump Jump.

As her Spirit diminishes with no land in sight, she lets herself fall long enough to sip some soulblossom essence. Her Spirit leaps. Jump Jump Jump. She repeats the process without thought each time she feels the need. Jump Jump Jump. There is no Calendra now, only that which follows the Spirit flows. She is Spirit given form and will flow with it.

Jump jump jump jump jump jump jump jump jump.

Calendra's flow is disrupted when she finds her soulblossom flask empty. No matter. There is only forward. Come what may. Jump Jump Jump.

Calendra begins to fade. She has covered hundreds or thousands of miles, but her Spirit is getting low. Very low. Jump Jump Jump.

At her very last, her Spirit a trickle, her will wrung dry, despair mounting, she sees something ahead. It is not another landmass. It is nothing more than a line in the blue sea, but at this height she knows it must be thick. She focuses all her will and Jumps to a point far above the line.

Calendra cannot believe her eyes. It is the Obsidian Wall. Has she turned in circles? But no, she knows she has not. The Spirit flows towards here, not away from it. She is on the other side of the planet, and there is another obsidian wall. Putting aside the implications of such a thing, she knows what it must mean. There is another landmass! She is close. Most importantly, she has somewhere to pause and regenerate Spirit.

Calendra Jumps onto the obsidian, lucky to avoid slicing herself to ribbons. She removes her pack, lies on the least sharp piece of obsidian she can find, and screams. All her hope, pain, exhaustion, pride, loneliness and achievement pour out of her in one triumphant, shattered cry. She is alive. Extraordinary.

The air is warm, so she removes her alpine clothes and lays back down. Sleep comes without delay. Hours later, judging by the sun having actually set, she wakes. There is no Twin but the night sky is a riot of stars, thousands upon thousands of tiny white lights. It is dazzlingly beautiful. The display dwarfs the several dozen stars visible normally on her side of the world, and far outshines even that visible during truenight. It is spectacular.

Rested, full of Spirit and sure that land is near, Calendra gathers her things and looks to the sky. She draws on Spirit, knowing her destiny is one more set of Jumps away.

Jump. Jump. Jump. Jump. Jump. Jump.

Land! Land! Land!

A verdant landscape unfolds ahead. White beaches. Grass. Trees. It is here. It is here!

Calendra Jumps to the beach. She falls to her knees on the warm sand. She bursts into tears. She collapses. And she passes out.

A Memory of Danald

Half a year ago

Danald watched Calendra Malnorka flee from Chalvstrom through a series of spatial Jumps. He released a drawn-out sigh, an unusual display of emotion these days. Her 'escape' was necessary, only she could find their destination. He had hoped she would remain only a Speed Artist. If she had Spatial Artistry, she was a Gravity Artist as well. If she discovered her Temporal Art...

"What do we do?" asked Halderona.

"You do nothing," Danald told his long-time steward, the woman he hoped would carry on his legacy. That time might come sooner than Danald had expected. "Continue as you always have in my absence. If I'm not back in a season, you'll know to prepare the next generation."

"But Announcer ..."

"I have tried to be the rock that anchors our people to this world, Halda, but the currents of change are flowing like they never have before. A rock is left behind. I must be a leaf on the water."

"And a leaf finds strength in vulnerability," she intoned, and hugged him.

It was a breach of the decorum he had been forced to adopt, but he said nothing. She was the closest thing he had to a friend in a century.

"For Zem," he told her.

Danald punched a hole through the Manifold and stepped through to open air. He immediately annulled gravity and hung several hundred paces above the forest. Moments later. Calendra popped into reality atop one of the mountains north of Chalvstrom.

She showed far too much talent at Spatial Artistry for someone new to it. Danald was not surprised. She had troubled him for two decades, from when the spy became her guardian. She had come into her power and discovered his secret thanks to Alvertus' assassin. Danald did not like to use force, but he had been unable to let her go with so much at stake. Then she disappeared. Only weeks later, his agents had informed him that the Nineteen knew he was a Manifold Lord.

He might have left things there. Her threat had diminished. Then his people, searching for a treeheart he had known should be in the Splintered Peaks, had discovered the protected valley that held it. And there she had been. He would not have harmed her, of course, but he had intended to arrest the spy.

She killed some of his best Artists. He had inspected the site himself. The spy and someone else, probably a Spatial Artist, had killed several, but the carnage had been wrought by someone with speed far beyond that of the spy. Disturbingly, the treeheart had been taken. That had been when Danald had really taken notice.

Danald had kept the secret of the hearts for generations. Even those Tolgarlan fools had not yet seen, though his sterilization of their records a hundred years ago had helped. Now a child with Spirit capacity not seen in a century had discovered one - and consumed it. Had she joined her power to it, as Danald had once done with the dying heart of a great tree, she might have saved it. Instead, she had sought power. That alone made her the biggest threat to the world's hearts since the invasion of humans.

When Danald's agents had informed him that Alvertus believed she could see the workings of the Manifold itself, something even Danald's Dream Artistry had not achieved, they had shaken their heads and assured him it must be disinformation. Danald had known better. Her threat level had been raised once more.

Then she disappeared for a decade, so long that Danald assumed she had died. When he finally figured out the location of the next hearts to be replaced, he thought nobody would challenge him other than Alvertus. He had beaten Alvertus to the heart and helped the new one to mature while his people had protected the dying one.

Then she appeared. A whirlwind of death. He had been too late to stop her first true atrocity. No person had ever destroyed a living heart. They could not be touched in this Timestream and Danald knew that the Time Artists living in the hearts' Timestream would never hurt them. Yet Calendra Malnorka had found a way.

Danald had considered just killing her. Her crime had been grave. Yet she had not understood. She threatened this world, yet could be its greatest asset. Halderona's efforts to read her memories had failed. They were fragmented. Halderona could not explain it. So he had kept her and hoped that his influence, or the worldtree's, would channel her prodigious talents into protecting the world rather than eating it.

He might have realized she had become a Manifold Lord. It happened to him just by bonding the heart of the worldtree. He had underestimated her. Again.

He had not underestimated her hunger, though. His interrogation about Alvertus had worked. He had given her incentive to beat the monster to the greatest prize of all. The true Worldheart, which he had long known should exist in theory but never had a way to verify or locate.

She broke out hours later and he had been ready to follow. He just had not anticipated trying to follow a Manifold Lord with far greater power than his own. He had to hope her inexperience with gravity and location would limit her. He definitely had to hope that she did not know about Time Artistry. He could follow her in different Timestreams, but it would be harder to stay hidden with no other humans around, and he could keep up with her insane speed from faster Timestreams.

Danald Jumped hundreds of paces above her and hovered, using the minor gravitational pull of the Twin to balance the effect of Zem's gravity on his pack. Calendra used her viewpoint to Jump to the farthest summit she could see. The next Jump took her less time. Danald followed.

This was what Danald had hoped for. It took most Spatial Artists years to learn Jumping blind. It required intense focus, superb visualization and a great deal more Spirit. Calendra could probably brute force anything with her Spirit capacity, but blind Jumps could not be achieved through Spirit alone. It was impressive enough that she blind Jumped out of the palace.

So the game continued. As they developed a rhythm, Danald started to genuinely enjoy himself. It had been so very long, as humanity measured things, since he had used his powers for anything other than training, showmanship or violence. Besides, she was the first person in two centuries to show any prospect of stretching his abilities. A true Lord of the Manifold. Danald was actually having fun. He chuckled to himself.

It took less than a day to reach the Iceteeth. As Calendra went higher and higher, Danald sighed. Line of sight indeed. The Daughter of the Manifold - a term he hated at first but had come to rather enjoy - would need a great deal of

Spirit to do what he thought she planned. Even a powerful Spatial Artist would be down to a trickle by now. Few would have made it this far. She was, of course, no normal Artist.

Once she reached the spine of the Skypeaks, she Jumped to the great plateau. Danald watched from above as she became as Fast as he had ever seen. She covered hundreds of paces of the plateau in seconds, then launched skyward, shaking off the fetters of gravity. She shot like an arrow at a forty-five degree angle and flew miles, affected only by wind drag. As she flew almost beyond sight, she disappeared once more.

She was heading north, consistent with their route so far. Danald would have to guess, but he had suspected their destination for some time. She was not going north. She was going to the North. The limits of human civilization. Practically, and by sacred custom.

The Grand Reserve. The great swathe of protected land the Traveler himself designated off limits to humanity. While many Spatial Artists, including Danald, had explored it, humans had not permanently settled there. Even the barbaric Free Cities respected the injunction. The guarded walls at its borders testified to that. That the place was an impenetrable tangle of sharp peaks and scalding springs did not hurt, nor did its bitterly cold climate. Beyond it was nothing but ocean and scattered ice floes. The end of the world.

Danald waited half an hour for his Spirit to fully regenerate. There was no need to rush. She had used line of sight so far and to blind Jump safely to a place one had never been was all but impossible. Which she surely had not.

Danald Jumped to Karthran for supplies. Things were going to get chilly. Then he Jumped to the highest peak in the northern part of the Grand Reserve and waited for the woman who would lead him to the Heart of the World. He hoped he would not need to kill her. Such a waste that would be.

A Memory of Kolan

Sixteen weeks ago

K olan's irritation at the interruption gave way to excitement. It had been a long year but the most thrilling since he had found his purpose. It had cost him though.

Kolan was forty. He started the year, as measured by the glacial Timestream he inhabited, as a thirty-five-year-old. During that year, the community of Time Artists had aged five years while the rest of humanity had experienced twenty-five revolutions around the sun. Kolan should have only aged a year, but he kept getting called back to Human Time. Then things would become urgent and he would be forced to enter swift Timestreams to be where he was needed, where he might age two, five or ten times faster than humanity.

That was the dilemma of the Time Artist. One second per second. That was the flow of time all things experienced. Your second may be ten or one tenth to others, but to you, it was always one second per second. He could live a thousand years from humanity's perspective, or achieve fifty years of labor in one human year, but his personal allotment time was no more or less than any other human's. By Kolan's reckoning, better to use those seconds over centuries of civilization, dropping in and out of humanity to shape the future.

The Time Communities, and there were dozens now with tens of thousands of humans living in different Timestreams to their ancestors, prohibited active interference with the human Timestream. There was no other way. The technology of the fastest Timestreams was now far more advanced than in Human Time. Kolan still could barely accept the invention of automobiles using a combination of Arts and technology, nevermind the latest advancement in transportation. The advancement was so great that the transfer of technology and certain knowledge was forbidden and policed. Beyond that, what constituted 'interference' and what constituted 'active' were debatable.

Kolan had been open about his chosen role. He played it with great care. It was a basic truth that, to change the course of a river, one would divert it upstream near the source rather than downstream where it is at its strongest. Kolan did not interfere. He watched and he waited, and when he foresaw a future need for the river to change course, he altered its flow early. He only did so with words, and he only did so with those already on a path. He did not create paths. He only kept people on the right path or helped them to see other paths they could tread.

This last year or five or twenty had seen him divert more rivers than the previous five or twenty or hundred. He was absent from it all during the tumultuous second century, riven by conflict between those with Arts and those without, and between established nations and breakaway regions. He regretted missing the first monumental moment in human understanding of this world's connectedness since the Traveler, the bonding of an apex treeheart by the man who now called himself Announcer. Thankfully, Danald had chosen the right path without guidance.

Then there had been over a century in Human Time of relative quiet. Large-scale conflict had been eliminated, national borders stabilized, Artist and non-Artist relations mostly harmonized, except in the Free Cities. After the worries that more would discover the existence and possibilities of treehearts, the secret had remained secret for generations. Danald, whatever one thought of his arrogance, had proven a diligent protector of powerful knowledge.

A year or five or twenty ago, it all changed. Kolan watched as the assassin struck at Danald, ready to counsel the Announcer's replacement, were the attempt successful. Danald shrugged it off, but a new Speed Artist arose that day. The first in native to Chalveno in many years. Kolan had not taken too much notice until word had reached him that the girl, Calendra, was living with her Speed Artist guardian in a valley containing a mid-level Manifold-aligned treeheart.

Kolan watched her then and trembled. It turned out that the child could *see* the effects that applications of Spirit had on the Manifold. Kolan had never heard of anything like it. A Dream Artist who could track Spirit flows appeared from time to time, as Danald had before his transformation. That was not seeing changes in the fabric of reality itself. Once he received word that Danald's agents were heading for Calendra's valley home, Kolan had watched from the neighboring Timestream. Carefully, to avoid triggering Calendra's Manifold sight.

The entire episode had shaken Kolan to his core. Not only had she discovered the treeheart, not only had she understood its significance, she had consumed it. A heart of the world. A dead one, thankfully, but the implications for forbidden knowledge were terrifying, and the prospects of humanity destroying this world were crystallizing. The strange, meditative, introverted jungle child had become his obsession from that day.

Kolan had been relieved when she moved to Sanctum and enrolled in school. He hoped that socialization and more conventional ways of thought would shift her mindset from obsession with Artistic advancement at all costs. It had. So successfully that she lost her ability to see the Manifold. It seemed the perfect outcome to Kolan.

How wrong he had been. It seeded an obsession in the girl even more dangerous than during her days near the treeheart. Perhaps things would have been different had her relationship with the Instinct Artist lasted longer, but one fateful decision had sabotaged that chance. One decision she went to great lengths to forget.

Kolan had tried in his own subtle way to draw Calendra back to the path. He steered her to skills that would enable her to pursue her ambition without resorting to wholesale consumption. A woman who could Cook renewable ingredients to provide as much power as a small heart had no need to destroy a small heart. More than that would have been too close to active intervention.

Now, years later, the world was balanced on the point of a blade. Calendra had severed and consumed a living treeheart, a heart of power only exceeded by the one in the tree in Chalvstrom that Danald referred to as the worldtree. Kolan still could not understand it. Her use of Speed Artistry somehow enabled her to access the heart's true temporal location. Her Artistic power had dwarfed all but Danald even before that, yet she had still elected to consume the heart. It was horrifying.

Calendra was no longer the girl who knew a dangerous secret or an Artist with the innate power to effect great or terrible change. She was the woman who would consume a world. Yet Kolan did not feel devoid of hope. Calendra did not seem evil. In fact, so far as humans went, she was as neutral as one could be. She had no apparent interest in the affairs of humanity other than where they provided competition for that which she desired. She certainly did not hate non-human life. She loved it.

But her ambition was like none he had ever seen. It knew few bounds. She had not yet understood that her actions were wrong. Kolan kept hope that she had the principles to temper her goals once she appreciated the implications of her boundless ambition. It was not a lesson he, or anyone, could teach her. She was too strong willed, too blinded by her own determination. She had to realize these things for herself or she would die. Not by Kolan's hands, of course, but by Danald for the right reasons or by Alvertus for the wrong reasons. Perhaps even by her former lover, though that would grieve Kolan to see no matter how necessary it might prove.

Kolan composed himself, aware he had kept the visitor waiting, and braced himself for whatever news was waiting. He opened the door to Silviana, one of his favorite of his sister's descendents.

"She escaped," Silviana said without preamble.

It had been seven days of Kolan-time since Danald had imprisoned Calendra. That would make it maybe twenty weeks in Human Time.

"What does she know, Silviana?"

"No idea," she replied, shaking her head. "We couldn't gain access to the cell. She flees north. When she arrived at the Grand Reserve, I came here."

Kolan rubbed his eyes with the heels of his palms. Bad bad bad bad bad. Some powerful, important hearts lived in the Grand Reserve. Far more concerning was what lay beyond it. Was the Reserve her destination, or a stop on her path?

"Do you think she knows?"

Silviana shrugged. "She was not exploring, according to the report. Just continuing to Jump from peak to peak without pause."

Kolan rubbed at the bridge of his nose. "She's a full Manifold Lord then? I shouldn't be surprised. She will move rapidly. We may only have weeks."

"She's not alone," Silviana said with a sad smile.

"The scribe? Malnor's advisor?"

"No. Danald. He watches for her from a neighboring Timestream."

"So all is not lost."

"Hmmmm. Yet all that might be gained is at risk."

"I feel your hope outpaces reality, Sil, but you may yet be right. I'll go straight there. If they stop at the Reserve, I'll have wasted a great number of seconds, but if they don't, then I should arrive in time. Is an airship available?"

"It should be ready by now."

After a one or five or twenty-hour automobile journey, Kolan stood a thousand paces above Tolgarlo on the closed deck of a winged platform as the whirring engines propelled him east, to another land.

Come what may, he would be there for the end of the world. Or the start of it.

A Memory of Alvertus

Half a year ago

Alvertus maintained a perfect image of righteous rage, his face red and his voice a hair's breadth from hysteria.

"I move that Lord Speed be dismissed from the Nineteen and stand trial for treason!" Alvertus drank in the squeals of outrage.

"Lord Space," rumbled the rotund Lord Instinct, "these demands grow tiresome. You demanded for years that we hand over Lord Speed to Chalveno to be tried for murder. Now Chalveno has withdrawn the charge and you demand a treason trial. On what possible grounds?"

"On the very grounds you just outlined, Lord Instinct! He lived amongst those barbarians for years. He claimed to spy for Tolgarlo but now the truth comes out. He turned! What other explanation for their change of heart? The demands of these last fifteen years were a ruse to distract from questions about his loyalty. Now he has bought and paid for a majority of my esteemed colleagues ..."

Alvertus let the words trail away as the cries began. He kept his grin to himself as he watched the mayhem. Then he saw the look on Malnor's face. Smug mirth.

"Lord Space," Malnor chuckled, silencing the rabble, "don't you see? It's over. All your cute schemes. All your petty plotting. For twenty years you've woven canopies of intrigue like some super villain from a child's story, as though you could gain control of the world through your cleverness. You are not clever. This is not a game. The people at this table represent many competing interests, but they are not pieces on a board. They are people with experience, integrity, personal power and considerably more intelligence than you. I won't say you lost because you were the only person playing. Give it a rest. Accept that being one of the nineteen most powerful people in this nation is enough. You don't have to be the single most powerful. Go and do your job."

The room erupted in applause. Adjuncts, bureaucrats, his enemies on the Nineteen, and even some of his allies. All against him. Scum! Traitors! Simpletons! Alvertus did not bother to hide his rage as he stormed out of the Hall of the Nineteen. By the time he was leaving, the applause had turned to laughter.

Alvertus spat his fury at the empty corridor. He would kill Malnor. There was little to lose now. He had stayed his hand too long. He held sway in the Nineteeen for years, yet it had disappeared before his eyes since that Malnor had been elected. He would make sure the man suffered. Alvertus' dream of Tolgarlo conquering the Free Cities was long dead. Even the raid he had sponsored as a final effort were pushed back by some mysterious force in the borderlands. Yet, Alvertus' new goal of total control - his true goal for many years, were he honest with himself - was under threat.

If only Alvertus could get his hands on the brat child, the one Malnor had never wanted. Alvertus would see how much Malnor wanted her. If he ever found her, of course. She had somehow eluded him for a great many years. Nobody had seen her in a decade. Maybe that uptight scribe would serve just as well. He seemed to care for her more than for his missing adopted child.

Once he worked off the bluest fires of his rage, Alvertus Jumped to his office. As he screamed vile oaths and threw everything not bolted down at the walls, the door opened and Myla strolled through. He had not seen her in weeks.

"I have some thoughts you should hear," she told him, ignoring the state of the room.

Her relaxed certainty calmed him immediately. After so many years working together, she knew how to handle his outbursts better than any romantic partner ever could. Not that Alvertus had ever desired romance. He waved at her to proceed.

"I discovered some very interesting records in the libraries and archives you made available. The Memory Guild has some particularly interesting scrolls from the inter-war years, when they were hunted so relentlessly that they found the need to finally write something down. And the ..."

"Myla."

"Right. First, are you aware of the extent to which the public accounts of the Traveler's Welcome have been edited? I'd never really considered looking into it. They are, with no contest, the most important words humanity has, revered by all nations, yet no two accounts are identical."

"Yes, of course I am. Generations ago, there was a fire in the Library of the School of the Manifold, which housed our oldest scrolls. The newer copies, which were not harmed, showed evidence of tampering and forgery. The Memory Artists made fresh copies but, without the credibility of antiquity, their status diminished and new interpretations arose. Those new versions that were more compatible with prosperity and advancement floated to the top over time as the archaic or unhelpful version sank into the muck of historical curiosity. It was not my doing, but I have no interest in seeing it change."

"You should have told me. Context matters."

"Nonsense. Do you regret the research? Did you gain from it more than just historical knowledge? Would you have, had I laid these matters down as facts?"

"Second," she continued, her grin serving as acknowledgement that he was right, "I think I've made a breakthrough with spatial manipulation."

Alvertus leaned forward, eager

"I think I know how to create a stable portal. It will probably burn out three or four Spatial Donors, depending on their skill and Spirit capacity, but you might only need two to keep it open."

"Four? I only know of five in all Tolgarlo and at least two would not assist me, even were I proven to be the Traveler reincarnated."

"Ha, but I have an idea for that. I think that several powerful Spatial Artists could supplement this portal with their own Artistry. Once they are inside the portal, I believe they will become Spiritually aligned to it in a way that makes it as if it is their portal. They can then use their own Spirit to bolster it. You might achieve this with only two Spatial Donors and several Artists. I'd be a lot more comfortable with three, though. Lessens the chances of the portal collapsing with people inside."

Alvertus chewed on this. This was highly significant, if Myla's instincts were right. They almost always were. This went well beyond the utility of a Spatial Donor. He could move supplies. He could move armies. He rewarded Myla with a warm smile.

"Superb, if you are right. Set up some trials. Is there a third?"

Myla's slow smile of triumph said a lot. She might have just solved the greatest challenge of Spatial Artistry and had delivered the news with nonchalance bordering on boredom. She rarely showed pride in her work. This would be noteworthy.

"Third. I think I know where the ultimate treeheart might be, the heart that governs and encodes the Spirit distribution network of the entire planet."

Alvertus shot out of his chair. "You found it? Was it in the Grand Reserve? We've explored every other damn pace of this world."

"Found it? No. Let's not get ahead of ourselves. But I think I understand where it must be." Her grin was developing into a cheeky smirk.

"Myla, I swear to you, if you don't just ..."

She cut him short with a finger. Pointing straight down.

"Underground?" he asked, brow furrowed. "I can believe that, but underground is a big place. Where? How deep?"

"Deep." She drew out the word, her grin broadening.

Her love of leading people to figure out the answer for themselves was laudable, but sometimes drove him crazy. This time, he really was intrigued. Still, he stayed silent, as he had no idea what she meant.

"What would you have said if I had pointed up?" she prompted.

Alvertus considered for a moment. "You could only mean the Twin."

She nodded, her smile showing teeth.

Down. So far down, she would compare it to another planet. A planet, like the one on which they stood. A sphere.

"You think there's land on the far side of this world? It's been theorized."

"It's been hypothesized," she corrected, "but there's been no evidence and no means has been proposed of falsifying it. Well, I found evidence. Old, subjective, questionable evidence, but I think it speaks truth. Now, Alvertus, we have the means to falsify it. Or prove it. If it's true, if there's land there, the hypothetical true Worldtree has to be there. My instincts have never been so sure of something. If, that is, there's another landmass. Of that, I cannot be sure."

The means to falsify it. Spatial Artists could never risk a blind Jump to the other side of the planet. Even if they could make it that far, which was unknown, it would utterly drain their Spirit. If they appeared over the endless ocean, that was the end of them. But with a portal ...

Alvertus laughed. The Nineteen could go to the Twin. They could all burn. They were irrelevant.

Alvertus, son of none, would find the true Worldtree. He would consume its heart. The world would be his.

A Memory of Djulita

Thirteen weeks ago

Djulita enjoyed thinking of herself as a detective. Except that instead of detecting crime, she was detecting truth. Unlike crime, though, many who intended truth were innocent of it and some who thought to deceive inadvertently exposed truths.

Interpreting religious texts often required the sharpest attention. Djulita did not believe that religious scholars aimed to deceive. Nobody would confine their behavior to the strictures of a code unless they believed they were living a truth. It was that passion for truth that was often the problem. So sure were some of the universal truth of the Traveler's words that they sought all truth, all facts about the world, from those few words. That required flexible interpretation, which enabled any and all to reinterpret words that had once been beyond dispute.

It was in these inconsistencies that truth might be found. The words of the Traveler, the instructions and plans he had left for humanity in their new world, were often referred to as The Traveler's Welcome. The original words had been interpreted, truncated, emphasized and de-emphasized, analogized, dismantled, reordered and stitched back together by generations of adorers, sycophants, opponents and academics. Yet all those views came from one source and, like tracing mixed bloodlines back to a common ancestor, the branching lies could be traced back to a common trunk of truth.

After weeks of research, Djulita found the conclusions clear. As with so many times during her research, she wondered why others had not come to the same conclusions. Between biologists, Artists and theologians, someone ought to have taken seriously the idea that the world was, collectively, a life in itself. One big system.

Artists collaborated only amongst themselves, so sure were they that they had all the answers. Biologists focused on biology, not the things that biology might facilitate. Philosophers and scientists ignored each other, scientists dismissing philosophy as unfalsifiable and therefore meaningless, and philosophers dismissing science as the sacrifice of understanding at the altar of empiricism. Theologians just dismissed the importance of anything external to their texts, just as philosophers and scientists dismissed theology as irrelevant pedantry.

It frustrated Djulita. The things humanity could learn if they stepped beyond their self-imposed boundaries. All knowledge was useful, after all, even when wrong. The skill was to sift through recorded facts, misinformation and personal truths to find objective truths.

It was in the spirit of following patterns wherever they lead that led Djulita to the maturing study of complex systems. Philosophers and ecologists were starting to consider the topic from different but converging angles.

Consider water, one philosopher mused. *In one form, rain, it is composed of uncountable discrete entities. In another, a river, it acts as a singular physical entity, the head renewing as the tail degrades. Which is it? Drops of water, or water? If we talk about a river, we talk about its course and effects as a whole. We do not describe how, at the bend of a river, some drops flow and others eddy. We talk about the river following the bend.*

Even though the river is a different thing from moment to moment, comprising different drops of water, we describe it in an ongoing way. A river is made of drops of water, but it is more useful to describe the river than the drops. There is too much complexity in the interactions of all those drops to describe each of them, but from that complexity emerges the tantalizing simplicity of describing a single entity without losing useful anything in the description.

The conceptual ways that philosophers approached the emergence of simplicity from complexity echoed the approach of ecology. Djulita was particularly taken by one scholar's arguments.

Why must we continue to talk of trees rather than forests? It is like talking of fruit without talking of the tree from which it grows. We pretend that a forest is a collection of interchangeable trees. A forest is a forest, a thing unto itself that has many parts, some of which are trees.

Am I a person or am I a sack of organs with limbs and a head? It is meaningless to talk about my body without talking about me, and it is incomplete to talk about me without talking about my body.

So is a forest. You cannot take the trees from a forest and still have it be a forest. And you cannot destroy a forest and expect to create a new one just by planting trees. A forest is far more than just trees. The idea of a forest emerges from the sum of its parts, including parts other than trees, and that emergent property itself affects the nature of those parts. As long as we talk about trees rather than forests, we will not understand either.

The two approaches were similar in advocating a unified description of related parts, but the points differed. The philosopher spoke of directional influence. The water droplets together create a river, but a river does not create water droplets. There was a kind of nominal causation.

The ecologist thought a forest was more than just a useful way to describe a collection of related things. They believed that a forest was 'real', not just a useful concept. Real in the sense that the emergent property of being a forest actually influenced the plants and trees it contained. It was a circular influence. Causation ran in both directions. The growth of organisms created a forest, then the forest shaped the organisms. It was emergence in reality, not just in concept.

It reminded her of the idea of a nation. People referred to a nation as an entity with a will. Sometimes that referred directly to the will of the leader or leaders, but other times it really referred to a new thing. An emergent thing. A nation.

The ideas had much in common with the concept of a global network of Spirit. Was the existence of different types of Spirit a product of an emergent greater whole rather than categorization inherent to Spirit itself?

As her mind worked, enjoying the illusory freedom of time that accompanied the longest day of the year, she absently gazed at the relevant pages of the two books and noticed something. Both pages had small creases in identical places. It was not uncommon to fold in the corner of a page you wanted to access, though it was poor form in a library, but these folds were in the bottom corner. Djulita had never seen a person do that. What were the chances this was done by two different people? Two data points did not make a pattern, but they might point to a pattern. Were others exploring the same ideas?

Djulita went back through some of the other notable texts she had found. Sure enough, some had pages marked in the same way. Someone was undertaking very similar research on interconnected life and on emergence. Was their interest academic or, like Djulita, did they have an agenda?

Curious, slightly concerned, Djulita went to the greatest and most under-utilized assets of any library. Librarians. A librarian could not casually share information about its users, so Djulita approached the information desk and tried an indirect approach.

"You," she announced with arched brows, "need to better control the riff raff that enters these hallowed halls."

The librarian, well aware that Djulita was a civilian granted rare access to the Library of the School of the Manifold, gave her a flat stare.

"This is a school library, Adjunct. While students are expected to act with decorum, they are still children. Some noise and chaos are inevitable."

Djulita returned the stare. "There has been no greater advocate of engaging students than Lord Speed. Learning should be fun. I begrudge neither chaos nor noise, but there are priceless works here, works that can be copied but never released. It troubles me to see them defaced."

Djulita had only seen a librarian move faster when some fool brought an open flame into the main civilian library of Sanctum. She shot up like a released spring, her chair toppling back and papers flying.

"Show me," the woman hissed.

Djulita retrieved two of the less important texts with bottom corner creases and, cradling them like children, pointed with trembling hands.

"How dare she?" The librarian was white knuckled as she inspected the damage. "I almost banned her for this fifteen years ago, but she had special privileges. Now she comes back after all this time and does it again! Unbelievable. I will need to look through everything she checked out. Thank you for drawing this to my attention, Adjunct."

Fifteen years. Around the time Calendra was here. Could it be? Surely not. She would be recognized. Word would reach Mal. Djulita had to confirm.

"But surely you will ban this person now? It's one thing for a child, another for an adult."

"You try rejecting Lord Space's ... request. I pushed back once. He made clear that she is his eyes and ears and he enquired as to whether the Library means to blind and deafen one of the Nineteen."

Gotcha.

"I understand more than most," Djulita replied in a long suffering tone. "My apologies for being short with you. Please don't let it reflect on Lord Speed."

Djulita returned to browsing, keeping an eye out for the librarian's movements. Sure enough, after consulting a document, the woman walked to a different section to search for defaced books and scrolls. Djulita wasted no time in copying the records left on the desk. Librarians were a trusting bunch, especially when one expressed a love for books.

So it was that Djulita's detective work shifted from tracking truths to tracking the traitor that Calendra had once loved. It seemed a fool's errand to out-think an Instinct Artist, but Djulita was in her element. Besides, an Instinct Artist was still limited by data. It was more important to understand Alvertus' plans than the nature of existence, anyway.

As she located the marked pages, careful to avoid the librarian's notice, she learned more and more. Myla clearly had an interest in the nature of Spirit networks and the locations of treehearts as well as the nature of life, complexity and emergence, but the trail led somewhere Djulita did not expect.

Myla had marked a page in the ancient records of an asylum for the insane. It seemed like a strange source of truth, but the connection was apparent. The page outlined an interview with a madman from the first century after the exodus. The clinician would ask a question and the madman, who claimed to be the Traveler's grandson Tolgan, would argue with himself about the answer.

What is Spirit? The man ranted, asking himself the same question over and over, giving different answers each time. *What is the Manifold? What is life?* The answers were fascinating and surprisingly astute, in light of her research, from a madman who had lived several centuries before. But it was one question, and the various accompanying answers, that floored Djulita.

What is consciousness?

A dozen ideas floating around Djulita's mind pieced themselves together with that question, and with the madman's answer. Complexity. Emergence. The creation of a new unified whole from connected pieces. *A singular voice capable of determining action on behalf of components with no voice of their own.*

It made sense to her that the system of Spirit could be like government, a system that self-nominates components to administer the system on behalf of all. But this idea was altogether different. Could the system have its own mind of sorts, not merely be spoken for by a component with its own voice? Could the world think? Did the mind itself, even the minds of humans, emerge from a collection of mindless parts?

The implications were far-reaching. Humans would not be the only thinking life. Such a phenomenon may emerge elsewhere in other substances. Probabilistically inevitable. More important in the here and now was that if the world had a mind of its own, a range of practical and moral implications arose. Was consuming a treeheart murder? If not, was there some world-level treeheart at the center of it all that could be murdered? Was even the ecological engineering humans engaged in a form of abuse? If the world could think, it could plan. It could consider information, picture possible futures and act to pursue its needs and desires.

Of course, the Chalvenans had long personified the world as Zem, but nobody had taken that seriously. Djulita's understanding was that Zem was a concept encompassing all life but not actually a thinking, conscious entity. When she read parts of the Traveler's Welcome again with that filter, including parts that had been purged from Tolgarlan canon, she realized that the Traveler might have thought as much. His references to the world were taken as metaphor, but in a different light they could describe a conscious world.

Djulita rubbed at her temples. If this was right, those who sought to take the world's power from it were in the wrong. Even Calendra. But Calendra was no Alvertus. The girl was closer to the trees and plants of this world than anyone Djulita had met. She seemed to love them more than she loved humans. Djulita could not believe that, for all that ambition, Calendra would voluntarily harm the world, especially a conscious one.

Djulita realized it with a start. She had to get to Calendra. She needed to warn the woman she had come to think of as a daughter before she destroyed the world in her pursuit of greatness. How to find her? Djulita could still only think to stay on Myla's trail and find Calendra by finding Calendra's destination. With Myla's instincts and Alvertus' resources, they would end up in the same place.

Djulita continued reviewing the texts on her copied list. Most were along similar lines, but it was the last one, an impenetrable tome on geometry, that provided Djulita's best clue. There were odd lines embedded into the marked page, not in ink but through pressure, like someone wrote on a thin piece of paper that lay on top of that page of the book. Djulita created a pencil rubbing of it with a sheet of ultra-sheer tracing paper.

Several diagrams emerged. The first showed a flat surface with parallel vertical lines extending upwards. The next showed the same scene, but with a tiny stick figure raising its hands. The vertical lines were now curved in on each other to all but met in the center, like a cushion pushed in from both sides so that the center points almost meet. A copy of the stick figure was on the other side of the curved lines.

It took Djulita some time to understand what she saw. It was a depiction of Spatial Artistry. The Artist somehow bent the lines of space inwards to reduce the distance from one side to the other. Vrailen was a superb Spatial Artist, but he had always claimed it was instinctive. He just imagined where he wanted to be without thinking about considering the mechanics.

The next diagram showed a simple circle with horizontal lines inside. It was followed by a similar version, with the lines inside the circle warped to create a similar effect as with the flat surface. The lines were pinched in the center, converging, with two stick figures pictured on the outside of opposite sides of the circle.

It took less time for Djulita to understand, but far more to accept. What circle could be relevant to a Spatial Artist? Only one, and it was a sphere.

But why would someone want to teleport to the other side of the planet? It was all ocean outside of their landmass, beyond the Obsidian Wall. Unless it was not.

The final pair of diagrams was the same as the previous, except that beside the stick figures raising their hands on either side there were other figures, hands not raised, some queued up on one side of the world facing the Artist and others walking away from the Artist on the other side of the world. The first diagram had three figures with raised hands on either side of the world. The second had only one Artist on each side, but with a key difference. There were two additional circles in the background that lined up with the first. The large circle, presumably the Sun, was far away. The Twin was in line, on the same side. At the bottom was a single question. *Solstice?*

Djulita dropped the pencil she had been absently twirling. They intended to open some kind of stable teleportation location that stayed open, allowing the passage of multiple people. Like a hole in the Manifold that reduced the distance between each end of the hole. A stable portal. One that was easier to open when the Sun and the Twin were most closely aligned with this planet, which happened on the longest day of the year.

Myla had discovered another landmass on this planet and the means to spatially move people there in large numbers. They were going to invade! Djulita had a sinking feeling that if there truly was a world-level treeheart, it would be there.

Djulita had to get through that portal. She needed to get to Calendra, to convince her. Or stop her. She needed to infiltrate Alvertus' company headquarters. Today. By smallnight, when sun, Twin and world aligned.

From detective to spy. Djulita wondered for a moment at her presumption. Djulita, bureaucrat, thinking she was a hero from a tale. It was only a moment, though. Her daughter, and perhaps the world, was at stake.

It did not take her long to send a message to Mal. She would not go to him even if she thought there was time. What she planned could not be done with him at her side. He was too distinctive. But she did not want him to think he had lost another important person in his life. And even though she, as his advisor, would counsel him against it, she hoped he would find a way to follow.

Then she calmly altered everything about her appearance that she could and walked to the gates of Alvertus' compound.

CHAPTER TWENTY EIGHT

What is life? It is matter given will. Yes but what is life. It is sustainable and sustained reproduction of a discrete entity. Yes but what is life. It is that which uses energy from its environment to maintain homeostasis. Yes but what is life. Is it categorical or conceptual or physical or emergent or a property. Yes.

Extract from interview with Patient 132

Records of the Mind Sanctum

C alendra wakes to the inexpressibly awful sensation of greased sandpaper stroking the back of her neck. She lifts her head and sees a monstrosity, a thing so bizarre, so alien yet so familiar that not even children's tales would think to invent it.

The thing is alive for it breathes. It is no plant for it moves. It has a mouth and shockingly familiar eyes but it is sure as hell no human. It has short, dense hair covering its entire body. It has a ridiculous appendage emerging from its behind, almost the length of the four stumpy legs upon which it walks. It is as tall as Calendra, its length double her height. It licks her neck again.

A violent shiver runs the length of Calendra's body and she Jumps several paces away. She stares back at the thing, not sure whether to run from it, kill it or befriend it. What is it? It is unlike anything she has ever heard of, yet it must be a creation of some sort. A creature, for want of a better word.

"Moo," the creature tells her.

She nearly falls over from the shock. It speaks? Well, if it speaks she certainly cannot kill the thing. Unless it tries to kill her. The trees are her people but they cannot speak. What is the thing? It seems she has the opportunity to ask.

"I'm Calendra," she says, cautiously approaching and holding out her hand in greeting. "Nice to meet you. Do you have a name?"

"Mooo."

The creature says this in a more definitive, drawn out way and starts chewing, despite having put nothing in its mouth since Calendra met it. Moo. Its name? Or does it only say one thing?

"Moo," she gestures towards it, "pleased to meet you. I'm Calendra." She gestures towards herself. "Do you say anything else? Do you understand me?"

Moo, still chewing, offers nothing further. Calendra shrugs and moves on. There seems little to gain here.

Enchanted by the alien landscape, Calendra is in no rush to follow the Spirit flows. The plant life is familiar yet distinct. She has seen eucalyptus before - she extracted a heart from one - but eucalyptus dominates here, many pushing two hundred paces in height. They are interspersed with plants she has not seen. A sprawling bush with flowers of various colors that look like toilet brushes. Stout trees that look like giant broccoli, with bark that comes off in strips like paper. A particularly odd tree with a stumpy trunk, leaves that look like grass made into a ball, and a strange protuberance at the top that looks like a spear.

As curious as the plant life is, the creatures are a world beyond it. For, as she walks south, there are more than just Moo. Something with a similar shape, also walking on four legs, but far more muscled and with tree branches growing from its head. Tree branches! In fact, all the creatures that remind Calendra of humans, with familiar eyes and covered in hair, seem to walk on four legs. A lithe, proud, spotted creature her size with small pointed ears rubs its cheek against her leg and makes a satisfied vibrating sound before sauntering away.

She sees one bizarre exception. A tall, muscled creature with an arrow-shaped head and tiny arms, which bounces on two huge reverse-jointed legs. Bounces! She tries conversing with this one, hoping its bipedal nature makes it closer to humans, but it scratches its bulging chest with a tiny finger and remains stubbornly silent.

There are stranger things still. A menacing thing six paces long with yellow slitted eyes on a bulky head and skin made of small green geometric shapes, which emerges from a river and runs at her on four tiny legs. It is the first thing to attack her. She Jumps away, seeing no need to bother it further.

It is a stranger, cuter creature that really gets her attention. Its head is tiny and appears ancient, its stumpy legs are like tiny tree trunks, and upon its back it carries a round rock. On closer inspection, Calendra sees the rock is attached to it, part of it. Its legs and head withdraw suddenly. Fascinated, Calendra peers closer. Then the creature vanishes and appears twenty paces away.

Calendra is flabbergasted. This whimsical lifeform, itself its own home, is a Manifold Artist! Calendra cannot believe her eyes. Scolding herself for not having drawn on Spirit at the time, she does so and recognizes the after-image of a hole punched through the Manifold. She laughs at the beauty of it.

She sees more creatures using the Arts as the hours pass and she covers more ground using Speed Artistry. She knows she could be faster using aerial Jumps, but she is in an unknown place, maybe the first human ever, and there is life unknown and beautiful. Calendra has always chosen plants over humans, but now she wonders if it is a love of plants or a dislike of humans, for this new type of life delights her. It is like a fever dream, but with creativity even the subconscious lacks.

She sees a tiny version of the sleek spotted creature that slaps a howling long-jawed pursuer five times its size. The pursuer flies ten paces and limps away. Strength.

She sees a lazy creature with fluffy white hair and curling branches that emerge from its head receive a nasty bite from another of the howling things. The lazy one scores a solid hit with its branches, which Calendra figures must be bones, and the howler flees. In seconds, the chunk of flesh taken from the poor creature's side heals completely. Resilience.

She sees a large group of the elegant creatures from earlier, half with tree branches emerging from their heads, fleeing a large creature similar to the spotted one but with black and orange stripes. They scatter and the pursuer chooses one to hunt. Just as it reaches its victim, the beautiful creature leaps five paces into the air, avoiding a violent death. The pursuer tries several more times before giving up and stalking off. Gravity.

Calendra is approached a number of times. The approaches are usually curious or friendly. Several creatures try to hurt her, including a bizarre thing shaped like a thick rope that hisses and bears dripping curved teeth. It must be ten paces long, despite being no thicker than her leg. She avoids each attacker with ease.

A few creatures bearing Arts try to attack, but in each case she avoids them by becoming Fast. As soon as she does, they act like they are her best friend. She realizes after a few instances that the ones with Arts see her differently, almost as kin, when she draws on Spirit. Another reason to always do so, even when her Arts are not needed.

Calendra spends her first night in a new world sleeping in the open atop a grassy hill, basking in the calls of life and sight of a thousand thousand stars painting the Twinless sky. She wakes several times to ticklish sensations that turn out to be tiny creatures, utterly alien, some with dozens of tiny legs.

"Hello, little ones," she greets them, encouraging one furry tube-like creature to walk along her hand. They give no response though one of the minuscule black things that walk in groups seems to assault her. It feels like she has been stabbed by a dagger the thickness of a hair. It hurts, as much from the surprise as from the pain, which disappears promptly. She flicks it away and another attacks. Others run towards her. On the verge of a killing spree, Calendra draws on Spirit. The tiny things immediately cease their rampage. She gets back to sleep, drawing on Spirit to advertise to these tiny creatures that she is no threat. Or a greater threat than they can handle.

She wakes to the cool sun after a short sleep, full of purpose and drive. She may well continue on foot, at speed, but she needs the bigger picture.

Calendra removes a small canvas, paints and brushes from her pack and lays it down. She annuls gravity, looks up and Jumps, appearing miles above. Even with her Gravity Artistry at maximum, she slowly descends. It is not enough. Her equipment weighs enough for gravity to seize it. As she drifts down, she thinks. She cannot paint while falling.

She suddenly remembers a thing long forgotten from a time cast aside. Myla's revelation that a Gravity Artist can choose which source of gravity they manipulate. They may even eliminate this world's gravity while maintaining that of the Twin, enabling flight. There is no Twin here though. It is on the other side of the world and will add to the downward pull rather than counteracting it. But there is another heavenly body that might suffice.

Needing to start with no downward momentum, Calendra Jumps slightly higher and immediately acts. With mental gymnastics that seem to bifurcate her mind, she sweeps away all grasping fingers of gravity except those from the sun. For a moment, it seems to work. Then she registers her glacial movement downwards. It is close, so close, but not enough. Any thread of gravity will undo her, acceleration being what it is.

She slaps her own forehead when she realizes. She Jumps again to remove momentum and, with a mental strain, annuls all other sources of gravity while increasing the sun's gravity. It works! She is even pulled slowly upwards. With effort, she modulates the effect until she hovers perfectly. She breathes slowly and deep for several minutes until she reaches a mental state of holding it without conscious thought.

She looks down at the sprawling landmass below. And she paints. When she is done, she Jumps to the hill where she left her pack. Despite her desire to dive through the sky, she cannot let the winds steal her equipment and painting. Needing some time for her Spirit to regenerate, Calendra looks at the painting.

It reveals detail that even her new, enhanced Manifold sight cannot reveal through eyes or mind alone. Thousands of Spirit flows join and combine like tributaries to a river as thousands of lifeforms contribute to the pool. Separately, huge flows come from the north, the Spirit of the other landmass joining with the local Spirit. Dozens of concentrated thick flows travel in the opposite direction as the Worldtree returns Spirit to the human lands, purified and transformed.

She has her destination. Her painting does not show it, reaching only to the horizon, but the confluence of flows makes clear where they will intersect. Hundreds of miles south-south-west.

The painting reveals something else she failed to notice visually. On the western part of the landmass, near the coast, there is a defect in the Manifold. A kind of radial warping, like water circling a drain. It is uncannily similar to the sight of a Spatial Artist teleporting when Calendra is very Fast, Fast enough to see the split second when the Jump occurs. Yet this is maintained. It must be so. She painted for too long to have possibly captured the instant of a Jump.

Calendra panics. She throws everything into her pack and conducts a rapid series of Jumps in the direction of the anomaly, low enough to see but hopefully high enough to avoid being seen. Soon she hovers high above a natural clearing.

Calendra rubs at her eyes, unable to accept what they offer. Dozens of uniformed humans mill about below. More appear every few seconds. Literally appear. They emerge from a strange sphere of shimmering black. Calendra can see from above that there is nothing on the other side.

Calendra is dismayed. While no such thing has ever been proposed, she knows what this must be. A stable Jump point where someone punched a hole in the Manifold and somehow holds the hole open for others to pass through. The implications are staggering. An army is arriving.

Such a thing can only be done by three people, perhaps. Vrai, the Announcer, and Alvertus. No other Spatial Artist has the resources, though surely a Spatial

Donor is involved. If it is Vrai, she is ok, though she would prefer to do this alone. If not, she is in trouble.

As she watches, she sees what looks to be a group of the sweet creatures with tree branch heads wander towards the humans. She watches in horror as the tiny figures below destroy the creatures with axes and spears. Sickened, Calendra heads north-east in case she is seen, in a series of angry Jumps. Once completely out of view, she collects herself.

She will kill that man. Only Alvertus would discover a new type of life, almost human-like, unthreatening, and kill it. She is sorely tempted to go straight back and kill him now. She is not afraid of his little army, but he will be hard to kill and, if she fails, all is lost. It pains her to spare him for now, but she has all the advantages. She knows where to go. She can move at speed. She has no army slowing her down. The best thing she can do is stay ahead. She can, at least, make that task easier.

Far more carefully, Calendra Jumps back to the area and then to the ground in a forest a mile east of the growing army. She walks to a river and, trying to balance the obvious with the not-too-obvious, she becomes Fast and runs north-east. She lays down a trail for hours, varying her speed and direction. After dozens or hundreds of miles, she feels satisfied. Hopefully, someone will notice the trail and waste a few weeks following it.

Ready to make a series of Jumps back south-west, Calendra realizes she should try something she has not since first discovering her Spatial Artistry. A blind Jump. She draws on a torrent of Spirit and visualizes the hill where she camped, below where she painted these new lands.

Calendra punches a deep hole in the Manifold and appears exactly where she intended. She raises her fist in triumph. It used a lot of her Spirit though, more than if she had used dozens of shorter line-of-sight Jumps. Maybe it is time to walk and conserve Spirit. She needs to be far from the army so she does a series of aerial Jumps until she is at least a hundred miles south of them. Then, low on Spirit, she jogs south west at triple-speed and enjoys the trees and creatures as she journeys.

After an hour or so, her Spirit is full once more. Calendra furrows her brow at the realization? Full in an hour while at triple-speed the whole time? She has not actually traveled Fast all that much since becoming a Manifold Lord. Did she fail to notice this new efficiency earlier, so distracted by the strange new life?

Calendra ups it to five-speed as an experiment. No drain at all. Her Spirit regenerates faster than it is used. Ten-speed proves a little too much. She reaches a balance at perhaps eight-speed, able to sustain it indefinitely. And what a joy it is!

Calendra bolts past startled creatures, leaps fallen trunks, ducks branches, fords streams and flies from tree to tree, reveling in the freedom. She feels fifteen again, despite having the age of a mother and years of a young grandmother. It is when she remembers to throw Gravity Artistry into the mix that she really starts to enjoy herself. Her flight from tree to tree becomes a series of graceful shallow arcs. She uses it to avoid collisions. Even running becomes a breeze as she learns to lessen gravity at the right moments to propel herself forward effortlessly, without losing too much pace.

Calendra laughs with elation. This ... this is what it was all once about. The joy of Artistry, the satisfaction of owning one's abilities and the oneness of connection to nature. Calendra dances with the forest, her truest partner for many wearying years. She runs until the sun begins to set, never tiring. Realizing she cannot run at night with no Twin to light the way, she kicks it up to twenty-speed. Thirty-speed. As sunlight fades, she finds a little hill on which to sleep, without her winter clothes this time as the weather is far warmer this far south.

She does another skypainting the next morning to ensure that she is on track, and nothing has changed. She is, and it has not. She is now too far south to see the army, but she must be far ahead of it, even if it did not follow her false trail. She puts it out of her head. She has days' head start, at least. She cannot imagine anything that could allow Alvertus to catch up.

She looks ahead rather than up. She is a creature of speed and of the ground. She would rather travel with nature than over it, even if it costs her time. She is not sure that it does anyway, such is her pace.

She makes an exception only once. Forced to Jump to the top of a plateau too steep to ascend, she looks south over a vast plain. Rather than punching a hole in the Manifold, she unleashes a flood of Spirit into her Speed Artistry as she sprints for all she is worth. She must be well over fifty-speed by the time she launches off with her right foot. She explodes forward at a perfect forty-five degree angle as she annuls the gravity of two planets and boosts that of the sun. Calendra soars and laughs.

It is three days later when Calendra realizes where she is. The days are the same, yet every minute different, a haze of joyful but non-specific memories of trees, creatures and Artistry. Three days of experiencing what it is like to truly be extraordinary instead of endlessly pursuing it. Three days of seeing that which no human has ever seen. It is understandable that in her flow, aglow with the fire of life, she might need a moment to notice where she stands.

The funny trees with grassy leaves and spear-like appendage surround her. There are hundreds. The grass on which she stands is almost knee-length. The area itself is a semi-circle, the shape formed by rocky slopes and black cliffs, but these things are but backdrops. It is here.

It is not the tallest tree Calendra has seen, though it is the biggest. It is not the most perfect tree Calendra has seen, though none could be more perfect at that scale. It is the ideal tree, inspiration to and inspired by all others.

It is not just several hundred paces tall, it is twenty-five paces wide at the base of a trunk that barely narrows as it stretches towards the heavens. Its heart-shaped leaves, various shades or red, orange and purple on top and iridescent silver underneath, are the size of her torso.

It is her Manifold sight that sings the true tale of this tree. It is ablaze with shifting, shimmering colors, as if a god captured a thousand rainbows, weaved them together and set them chaotically spinning. It breathes Spirit.

The Worldtree. The true Worldtree.

Calendra falls to the ground and weeps. It all catches up with her. All the worry and pain and passion and determination. All of it was worth it. In the ever-receding goal of becoming extraordinary, she is finally at the end. Never again will she be at the mercy of another. Never again will her ability to forge her own path be jeopardized.

Calendra gets up and hugs the tree. She will get to know it first. She will meditate, feel the flows from the heart and understand it before acting. As the hours go by, back against the tree, cross-legged, she feels its struggle. It is hard to put into words.

The Worldheart is so much stronger than the failing hearts of the Reserve that it is hard to accept that any damage could flow through. Yet it seems that it has. She can feel the Worldheart compensating for the weakness in the network, pumping purified Spirit to a part of the network that contributes little of its own. Spirit is rerouted and changed to counteract system-wide imbalances.

The Worldheart is slowly failing. Perhaps it will take two hundred years or perhaps two weeks. Calendra has no way of knowing. When it does, it can be hers. Provided she satisfies herself that a replacement is established. She could protect the new heart, with the old her reward.

The idea is lightning in her veins. An opportunity for unheralded power. It tempts her. Oh Zem, it tempts her.

But her thought about Zem brings the Announcer's pleas to a place in her mind she cannot ignore. Even consuming a severed heart might damage an ecosystem. She has disregarded that warning until now, but this is the heart of the entire world. Dare she? The Worldheart still lives anyway. Moreover, it presents an opportunity to truly emulate the Announcer.

It has been Calendra's plan anyway, formed when she was clear-headed. The Announcer said he lent his power to the Chalvstrom heart, but how could one actually join to a treeheart? Perhaps it is only when that heart is failing that a human with enough Spirit can insert themselves into the network and benefit from it.

Consume or contribute? Act or wait? Wait for the heart to die, consume it and become the most extraordinary thing this world has seen, maybe even surpassing the Traveler? Or join with the heart to save it and walk away with lesser power but a cleaner conscience?

Calendra sighs. Damn him. Before the Announcer filled her mind, she would not have hesitated. She would have waited for this heart to die and if it took too long she would have consumed it anyway. She would have used her new god-like power to fix any damage.

The problem is that she knows he is right. She already knew it. Part of her had hoped that the temptation of consuming it would overwhelm her. Calendra is many things but willfully ignorant, deliberately wrong, is not one. She will deceive others, and often herself, but she will not convince herself of a lie for her own benefit. She knows he is right. Even her ambition, the defining trait of her life, does not outrank her love of the life of this world, the defining love of her life.

She might even help, after all. Should that result in a priceless benefit to her, she will not complain. She will not live a lie nor betray a world, but she is not against symbiotic mutual benefit.

Decision made, Calendra allows herself to look forward once more. She will soon be extraordinary. Daughter of the Manifold, and the Mind, and the Body. Daughter of the World.

She might even feel good about it.

Calendra must prepare herself first. She has time. She will do as she did with the Chalvstrom tree and learn about it first, drawing on Spirit, meditating and using her Manifold sight.

By late the next day, she feels ready. She prepares a fire from scattered wood, lays out her wok and spatula and, with great ceremony, takes out the three treehearts.

A Memory of Djulita

Twelve weeks ago

Djulita strode past the gate guards, trying to look confident and urgent. The two states were mutually exclusive for Djulita, but the Advisor to Lord Speed was accustomed to the contradiction. Confidence and purposefulness were key to influence and persuasion.

Djulita was still surprised that she was not stopped. It probably helped that it was several minutes into smallnight and her features were obscured. Her luck did not hold long. As she approached the entrance to the office building, a soldier approached. No, not a soldier, Djulita had to remind herself. Just a mercenary. Alvertus did not command real soldiers.

"Stop," the gruff older man declared. "State your business."

"I need to see her immediately," Djulita told him acidly. "Show me the way or get out of mine."

"See who?" The guard's tone was combative, but he paused, uncertain. "Who are you?"

Djulita ran a hand over her face. "Her. The silver-haired one. I'm not supposed to mention her name. I need to see her urgently. Do you understand? It concerns what is happening right now! Unless they delayed? Is it next week? If it's the next solstice, I can talk with her any time."

"I ..."

"Oh, Traveler. I'm wasting my time here. Of course you don't know. Let me through, fool! Do some good and at least point me in the right direction."

"They're all gathered in the warehouse, um, lady. Or at least they were. Back of this building, to your right."

Djulita stormed off, feeling bad for bamboozling the man but determined to stay in character. When she arrived at the warehouse, she heard a din of activity inside and paused to collect herself. If Myla or Alvertus were inside, she was in trouble. They would do nothing to her, but they might hold her for several days before 'confirming' her identity. Was she too late? Would the portal still be open? Or was she too early? The guard's words comforted her but there could be another reason that Myla and others were there.

Djulita threw open the door and stormed in, absorbing the scene in a moment. The warehouse was a huge roofed space, a strange combination of stone and metal. Fifteen outfitted mercenaries stood in queues, ready to follow those disappearing one by one into a hole in space. Djulita had thought she might see the destination through the portal, or some shifting barrier. It was just shimmering blackness, a three-dimensional hole in reality. Djulita absently wondered why they queued as if it were two-dimensional.

There were two people facing each other from opposite sides of the portal with their eyes closed. Spatial Artists. Djulita recognized one of them. There was a civilian or Artist with a clipboard and pen recording names as their owners fell into the hole. Otherwise, nothing. No Myla or Alvertus. Nobody who would recognize an obscure bureaucrat even if she worked for the most famous man in Sanctum. Nobody noticed the face behind the face.

It could work! Djulita took a deep breath and projected her voice.

"You've already started? What have you done? I need to speak with her immediately! Her or Lord Space himself. This could be catastrophic! You must stop instantly."

Djulita saw alarm on the Spatial Artists' faces. The portal vibrated momentarily, but stabilized once they both closed their eyes. The non-binary with the clipboard walked to her.

"What is this? What are you talking about?"

"I need to speak to Myla immediately," Djulita hissed in a low voice. "I've been working with her in private on this portal system. I discovered a flaw! I had hoped she wouldn't test it already. I need to talk to her. Lives could be lost!"

She said the last words louder than the others and was pleased to see concern spread through the lined-up guards. The scribe's eyes widened.

"Are you sure? But this is a problem. They've gone through already. The last soldiers are about to follow. Lady Myla and Lord Space are already gone."

"Then get them a message! Tell them they are not to come back through the portal, or send anyone else, until I have made sure my findings are wrong or can be mitigated. You need to tell her that the geodesics of the Manifold do not operate as we expected. There are fluctuations in the isotropy of the probability distribution that we didn't calculate! They are rare, but a sufficient disequilibrium in the Manifold's geometry might cause anyone inside the portal to decohere!"

The scribe's face was such a study of bewilderment at the meaningless jargon that Djulita might as well have sculpted it herself. The guards were looking at each, equally baffled.

"Don't just stand there," Djulita roared.

"Mistress," the scribe stuttered, "I have no idea what you just said. I don't think anyone here does. Just go yourself. If you've been working with Lady Myla, she'll understand you."

Djulita pulled her face into an undignified blend of disgust and fear. "Go myself? Are you mad? Did you not just hear what I said? I could decohere."

The scribe raised an eyebrow. "Oh, I see. Happy to have one of us send your message, but not yourself? Get in there, coward. Lennaro?"

A guard, Lennaro apparently, walked to Djulita and drew a knife. He waved it at her, directing her towards the portal. Djulita managed, she hoped, to put on an adequate display of outrage.

"Fine!" she spat on the ground. "I'd better get a raise for this! I'll ask someone to come back through once we know it's safe."

And just like that, Djulita walked through the portal, followed by nobody.

The feeling was strange. It felt like she hung there for fifteen seconds, suspended in space. Or between spaces. It made her stomach turn, but not because she was falling, only because the sight of infinite blackness made it appear as if she was falling.

Then she was in a different place. She was outdoors on a grassy plain, with occasional evergreen trees dotting the landscape. There were collections of guards milling about. One woman, presumably a Spatial Artist, stood to the side with her eyes closed. Several people in civilian clothing spoke together near a tree, looking up at its branches. And there was no Twin in the sky. Its absence was shocking, so accustomed was she to its immense presence in their heavens.

"And who the merry hell are you, then?" The rumbling voice came from a bearded soldier who approached. This one actually was a soldier, or a retired one at least, in ceremonial regalia.

"Quickly! Where is Lady Myla? I must speak with her urgently. She will not expect me, but when she hears of what her colleague has discovered, she will want to speak with me."

"She's with Lord Space." He waved towards a tent. "You'll have to wait. You are?"

"I just told you. A colleague of Myla."

The soldier rolled his eyes and walked away. Nobody was paying attention. Surely she could not just ...

Djulita walked to the edge of the clearing, examining plants and trees along the way. She walked through a copse of slim gray trees with green-gray leaves, taking time to look them up and down and carefully glancing back at the impromptu staging area, now almost out of sight. Nobody looked in her direction. She walked into a thicker section of forest. She heard an odd scurrying sound, but kept her focus. A little further. The staging area was no longer in sight. Nobody was in sight.

And just like that, Djulita was alone on the far side of the world. She embraced the inner scream of triumph, letting it drown out the swelling terror at her situation.

Alone. On the far side of the world. She was in an indeterminate part of an unmapped landmass of unknown size, looking for a single tree. A part of Djulita asked, again, what she thought she was doing. She ignored it again.

Djulita smiled at nobody in particular and got on with business. She strolled south. She had to pick a direction and move before her absence was noticed.

It did not take long for Djulita to notice sounds and hints of movement everywhere. The occasional rustling of leaves on the ground. A brief rhythmic thudding as she approached a new area. Her nerves frayed as she relentlessly plodded on, creating a distance between her and Alvertus' people.

She finally noticed something that she could lay eyes upon. A thin hand-length object that looked like a twig, but with strange appendages and what looked disturbingly like tiny eyes. As she bent down to look at it, she could have sworn the tiny eye-things moved. Then the twig scurried away on what looked like tiny legs, as if it was a person crawling on six limbs.

Djulita was sure that the utter shock was all that saved her from emitting an enemy-attracting shriek. A twig that moved like a person. Then she saw more. And more. Something fast, the size of a fist and ... hairy, ran into a small hole in the ground.

Djulita had seen plants that moved at human speed, but they did not uproot themselves and relocate. What were these things? They were far more like humans than plants or fungus, but they were so foreign that Djulita could not process it all.

She walked south, ignoring the three bizarre life forms that stared at her from a distance, bigger than a human, standing on four legs with no arms and with curling white branches coming from the tops of their heads. She walked south, ignoring the slimy green hopping things that burped at her. She walked south, trying to forget the sleek spotted thing that opened a lazy, menacing eye at her from its vantage point in a tree. She ran south, fleeing a cylindrical thing at least five paces long with skin made of small geometrical pieces, yellow eyes and a forked tongue.

Djulita ran south, jogged when she could not run, and walked when she could not jog. She kept going south, ignoring everything not human or plant. It had been a singular focus that got her to this strange place. It would be a singular focus that saw her to her destination. Even if she still did not know its location.

As night fell, Djulita grew fearful. She had come with nothing more than the clothes on her back which, while warm and versatile, were no shelter. In the wilds without shelter! It was a thing unheard of.

Her concern slowly diminished over the following half an hour walking in the fading light as it became apparent the night would be warm. Warm enough that she must be in the subtropics. When she could walk no longer, she curled up on a bed of leaves and tried to sleep.

The random noises bothered her, but it was when tiny things crawled across her that she began to lose it. She reminded herself why she was there. She should practice. It would keep her mind off the crawling things she would not look at or touch.

"Calendra," she said to the not-quite-quiet forest, "this world is connected. You know the Spirit network, but it's more than that. It's one thing, and it's as aware as you and I! No. No. Calendra. Not everything in this world is renewable. If you destroy the wrong thing, you will doom us all! No! Calendra ..."

Djulita continued searching for the right argument, the specific words needed to persuade, speaking loudly enough to drown out the faint sounds of moving life. Each time she drifted off, her words would die away and her mind would latch onto the sounds.

Djulita began to cry, ever so softly. She focused on the right words in between her tears. Uncertain if she had fallen asleep, her mind snapped to attention as she felt a hand on her shoulder. By the time her eyes had opened there was nothing there, though all night was truenight in this land without the Twin, so little could be seen, anyway. Things felt slightly different somehow, but she could not put her finger on it.

Then she noticed. The sounds had stopped. She felt nothing slithering or crawling on her. The forest was like any at home. The scholar in her demanded answers but she did not care. She could finally sleep.

The next moment was daylight. Djulita instinctively sprang up, away from the leaves and whatever horrors they contained. She realized that she still heard nothing and saw nothing. Perhaps it was just that the moving life here was more active at night, but she saw nothing at all. Had it all been some horrendous dream? Had she imagined such bizarre things? How could she? They were so bizarre as to be unimaginable.

Still, Djulita had not let the presence of tiny horrors and other oddities distract from her purpose and she would not let the absence of them do so. She continued her walk, picking fruits as she traveled. She saw no more evidence of the moving life, large or small.

The next day, after another full sleep, Djulita felt and heard something odd. First, she felt a sensation like her shoulder being touched. She spun around but saw nothing. Moments later, she heard something. It was not the sound of a human, but was surely a sound that could only be made by a human. The cracking of wood from a distance in a rhythm that could not be natural.

Djulita walked towards it. She did not want to encounter Alvertus' people but could not turn away. It could be Calendra. She approached cautiously. When she found the source of the noise, a tree with several fresh wounds from a hatchet, there was nobody there. Was it a trap?

Djulita looked around, alert. Nothing. No sounds, no movement. Then she noticed them. Boot prints in the soil. They led right past the tree, heading south. The prints came from the north as far as she could see.

Djulita felt hope bloom. It was only one set of prints. The feet were small and the prints were paces apart, as though the person had been moving very fast. Calendra! It had to be!

Djulita ran in the direction the prints went. She lost them from time to time, buried by leaves or filled with mud, but the telltale signs of crushed leaves or snapped branches kept her on track. She slowed after a while, realizing that Calendra was not round the next corner and she could not run forever. It was only then that she noticed animals once more. This disconcerted her. There seemed no rhyme or reason to the times at which they appeared.

Djulita tried to put it from her mind and continued at pace, driven by a hope she had not held since starting her search for Calendra. A hope not forced by desperation but informed by objective fact. Calendra was there. She was there alone. She was there recently enough that prints were still visible. There was still time, but not much.

That night she fell asleep with tiny horrors once more but again woke with a start, sure a hand had been on her shoulder. When she got up, she gasped. The prints were still there, a trail heading in the same direction, but the prints were bigger and more closely spaced.

Djulita quelled her anxiety at what might have happened. Did someone take Calendra? But how? Right there, where Djulita had slept? When Calendra had been so far ahead? It made no sense. She followed them anyway. What else could she do?

Djulita followed the new tracks for weeks, hoping they led to Calendra, eating fruits she hoped would not kill her and drinking river water. The lack of rain was her saving grace as it allowed the prints to stay visible, though she was surprised they were for so long. She must be getting more and more behind. She neither saw nor heard any more moving life. She slept under the dazzling, infinite starscape, uneasy but so exhausted from sixteen hours of walking each day that sleep was no longer elusive.

Then she arrived in a clearing. It was a vast half-bowl hundreds of paces across with sloping walls twenty paces high, with the straight side comprising a cliff sixty paces high. There were hundreds of strange trees that looked like people with spiky green hair, their black trunks topped with long green spikes and a single spear-like protrusion extending from the middle. There was nothing else other than shin-high grass and one very special tree close to the straight cliff.

The prints ended at the tree, but Djulita would have known it anyway. It was the tree of all trees. Hundreds of paces tall, two dozen wide, with dark green leaves clothing it from head to toe. Djulita took no time to absorb it and ran down the slope towards the tree.

"Calendra!" she shouted, no longer willing to be cautious. "Calendra!"

She arrived at the tree. There was nobody there. The prints just ended. What was this madness? Baffled, distraught, she sat down in front of the tree and glared at it, willing it to release its secrets.

She felt a hand on her shoulder. As she whirled around, the world lurched. She continued to turn and saw a glimpse of a person just as they vanished from sight. Djulita became frantic, but then saw large moving lifeforms in the distance. Where had they come from so suddenly? Then she turned back towards the tree and her heart stopped.

Calendra was sitting in front of the tree, mouth agape, as she stared at Djulita. The girl, now almost appearing Djulita's age, painted in glowing silver-blue lines, was cooking a meal. Djulita laughed at the absurdity of it, then collapsed to her knees and wept from shock and joy.

Calendra ran to her and embraced her. After a long while of holding each other, Calendra held Djulita's cheeks and looked into her eyes.

"What on the fiery Twin are you doing here, Djulie? How are you here? Is everything alright? Where's Dad?"

"Calendra," Djulita said, gathering herself, "your Father isn't here. It's just me. But Alvertus brought an army here! They were looking in the wrong direction, but who knows when they might find this place. We may not have long. I came to find you. To tell you ..."

All the prepared pleas left Djulita. She was lost for words. She looked at the contents of Calendra's wok. There were three small treehearts. She was still harvesting the world's energy for herself. Djulita steeled herself.

"Calendra, you cannot take this treeheart. Don't you see? It's all connected. It's all part of a system. This heart is the very center of this worldwide system. If you remove it, you might become a god, but you will kill a world."

Calendra stared at Djulita for several seconds.

"It was what I first planned. I thought if I could take the most pure Spirit in existence, I would finally become all that I wish. If this heart was dying, as I thought it might be, I could take its corpse rather than leave it to another. And it is dying, Djulie, or near to it. But the Announcer showed me another way. He became a Lord of the Manifold by joining to a great heart to save it, letting its Spirit suffuse him. I'll do the same with this heart, which is no simple Manifold heart but a heart of all three Domains. I'll help the world and become a Lord of Body, Mind and Manifold. Daughter of the World ... "

Calendra's voice was almost dreamy as she finished, like a person repeating something they had thought through a thousand times. Her eyes looked glazed. The Announcer! That's who had captured her. Djulita did not pursue it. She knew that captivity should be discussed at the victim's leisure.

"Is that why you have three hearts? To align yourself to each Domain before you bond to this heart?"

"Clever," Calendra said, nodding. "Yes."

"Where did you get them, Calendra? What did you do?"

"The Grand Reserve," she whispered. "They were already dead, Djulie. I didn't kill them. But I also think that I did. The Spirit networks in the north are failing. I think it's in part because I killed a living heart a while back. New ones had grown to replace these but they are so weak. I worry about the north, though. The Great Plains will break the network soon enough, with or without harvesting dead hearts. These were hearts of Body, Mind and Manifold that no longer served their purpose. I might as well give them a final one. Maybe once I'm extraordinary, I can help somehow."

Djulita tried to process all this, but one thing seemed clear. Calendra was not planning to break the world. But the Spirit network failing? How catastrophic would this be? Even if Calendra was not to break the world, maybe she could help it?

"Calendra, you have been extraordinary your entire life. Stop reaching for a thing you've long had. Now, I'm relieved beyond measure that you won't harm this world, but is that all you want? To be extraordinary? To have power?"

"Not power. Freedom."

"Freedom from what? You're the most powerful human on this planet, except maybe the Announcer."

"He's not even close." Calendra chuckled. "I have all his Arts and far more Spirit. But I was still captured. I was still not free. I won't be free until I'm untouchable. Alone."

That last word broke Djulita's heart. So long traveling the world with no company but her own power and she still felt trapped and crowded.

"But the freedom to do what? To do things important or enjoyable? Or to just be?"

"Both." Calendra frowned. "Neither. I have to reach my goal. Then I can do anything."

"So what anything will you do? What are the first five things you'll do with your new power?"

Calendra's frown deepened. "I ... can protect you and my dad, and make sure you have everything you could wish for."

"Vrailen is the richest person in this world. Your Father is a Speed Artist and the most influential member of the organization that runs the biggest nation in this world. We want for nothing. We fear nothing. What else?"

Calendra's eyes darted around as though searching the landscape for an answer. "I can punish bad people. The things they do to each other. I can hurt them. Make them stop."

"Everyone? Everywhere? Even when you are a god, you will be a small god. You cannot control everything. And how can you be sure you will hurt the right people? Save the right people? What else?"

Calendra's eyes fell. "I don't know. But I'm here. I did what nobody else could do. I found the heart of the world. Should I just leave it after all the sacrifices I've made? Stop running ten paces from the finishing line? You say Alvertus is here with an army. Shall I leave it to him? I won't lie to you and say that I don't want the power, but I also want to help this world. I think I can. Shouldn't I? What would you have me do?"

Djulita seized Calendra by the shoulders. "Have you do? I would have you be happy, Calendra. I never cared about more than that. Nor did your father. Your efforts were for yourself, not for us. Mal would've much rather had his daughter with him all these years. I would have you be happy. Only you can decide what that will take. But walk away? Leave this to that monster? Never."

Calendra shrank back at the hatred Djulita injected into those words but a smile started to form. Perhaps the smile of somebody who has forgotten unconditional love.

"Happy," Calendra mused. "I'm not sure what that means anymore. Having a purpose makes me happy, I think. But now I'm at the end of that purpose, I'm not sure how to feel. At least if I do as the Announcer did and plug into this network, I will gain power and have done no harm. I might do good."

Calendra could join with this heart and come home to her family stronger. They could spend happy years together. But as Djulita looked at the tired woman before her, aged beyond her years and trying to remember what happiness meant, Djulita realized that would never be enough. She would be a raging fire, but she would slowly fade away, a dying coal surrendering the last of its heat to a cold environment. She was meant for better. She deserved better. Even if that meant losing her.

"Calendra," she said, pushing back the tears, "you are thinking too small. You can't save everyone, but maybe you can save the one person who matters more than all of us. Zem."

Calendra laughed. "It's a myth, Djulie. The Announcer confessed it to me. A myth he established to make people care. It's a pleasant lie, but a lie nonetheless. This world is certainly one, but it is not a person."

"No, daughter," Djulita said with fierce determination, "no, I think it is. The connections between all life native to this planet, the connections formed by Spirit, give rise to something greater. A tree is not conscious, nor a plant or mushroom, but together they become a thinking thing. One voice speaking on behalf of all the voiceless. An identity that emerges from the infinite complexity of connected components. I'm certain of it."

Calendra scrunched up her face, looking uncertain. "Seriously? Sure." She gave a strained laugh. "Why not though? I didn't have a good idea of how to plug myself into the network, anyway. What do I do?"

Djulita had no worldly idea, but she had to maintain her confidence. It might be all that was keeping Calendra believing it.

"Just reach out to it. Touch the tree and reach out to the world with your mind. And ask. Ask what it wants. Ask how you can help. And listen."

Calendra nodded slowly, then turned without hesitation. She hugged the tree and closed her eyes. Minutes later, Calendra turned back to Djulita.

"I don't know. I can't sense anything, yet I can hear something. Something very faint but unnatural, like a distant rumble in an unvarying note."

That reminded Djulita of something. "Like the way you described noise stretching when you live Fast?"

Calendra cocked her head. Thoughts seemed to race by behind her eyes. Suddenly, her jaw dropped.

"Yes," she said slowly, "it's a tree. They move slowly and live long. They think slowly. It's living Slow."

Calendra froze in place. After several moments, Djulita realised she was not frozen, just immeasurably slow and getting slower. After interminable minutes, she re-animated, eyes as wide as saucers.

"You were right," Calendra said in a daze. "I became so Slow I could hear the rumble as a syllable. I need to go Slower. Much Slower. It means a lot of time will pass, Djulita. Don't worry. I will ask and I will listen. I just need time."

Calendra moved to her wok and began serving the meal onto a plate, but Djulita was stuck on one word.

Time. The word bounced around Djulita's skull, catching on certain memories and intuitions, dislodging unformed ideas that collided and merged.

Time. Mal had remained bothered for years about the Announcer's longevity. Mal could not accept that any Speed Artist could extend their life in such a way. It just used up Spirit too fast.

Time. What had happened when Djulita experienced the sensation of a hand on her shoulder? One time, the signs of moving lifeforms had ceased. Another time, they had returned. And it almost seemed as if she had arrived shortly after Calendra, despite the woman's speed.

Time. *For those meditating on the Manifold, I can only tell you that place, time and relative distances are key.* The words of the Traveler. Time. Taken to mean speed but written as time.

"Calendra," she said, slowly, "you can access all the Arts of the Manifold, if I understood you. Speed. Gravity. Location. Time. Right?"

"Yes, since ... wait, what? There are only three. What do you mean, time? What's the difference between that and ..."

Calendra frowned. Then her pupils dilated. Then she disappeared.

She reappeared almost instantly but was not ... complete. She had a translucence to her and was utterly still. Cautiously, Djulita touched her to find her still physically there. Just also elsewhere, Djulita supposed. She had thought Calendra would disappear as Djulita had presumably done when someone moved her through time, but she was very much still there. Maybe it had to do with her bond with the treeheart?

Djulita released a long sigh. Calendra would be in a place where time itself moved more slowly, to communicate with the tree in its own time. She would need a long time there, by their standards. Hours? Days? Weeks? She could do nothing while in that place, yet somehow could be harmed in the normal world. And Alvertus was coming.

Djulita sat on the ground in front of Calendra's motionless body and waited.

A Memory of Tolgan

Three hundred years ago

Tolgan's heart beat with the world's. His long search for the source of the pulsing from his dreams was over. A heart of wood, twice his size, hung nestled in the twisting tree roots that emerged from the ground above him. Some inner sense felt it beating as if pumping energy through the roots. The rhythm had been slowing for days, like a countdown. Tolgan was not one to be late.

The heart was a hundred paces above him at the center of a rock ceiling a hundred paces wide. He calculated, drawing on his grandfather's physics lessons. Maybe one hundred and twenty paces at sixty-five degrees? Ash and fire, it was a long way. After weeks in a labyrinthine cave system, his target was in sight, yet so far.

Not too far, though. Not for the great-grandson of the Traveler.

At least the still air of the underground chasm would simplify things. He avoided looking at the chasm below and walked thirty paces back. He emptied his mind. His body knew what to do, now his mind had instructed it.

Tolgan ran like the wind. One step out from the cavern, he seized control of the life energy inside him and willed it to make him strong. Stronger than strong.

Ten, twenty, thirty times his normal strength. Tolgan kicked off the ground and launched at a terrible speed.

As his foot left the ground, he ceased boosting strength and switched to his other talent - modifying gravity. He felt life energy rush from him and the world's gravitational pull reduced its grip. He flew towards the tree. He realized he was at too great an angle and reduced the flow of life energy enough to let the world increase its pull. His angle shifted. His conscious mind could never calculate such changes at this speed, but he had toyed with gravity-reduced jumps since childhood.

There. He would land dead on, just after his zenith. He braced himself as he smashed into the ball of roots, just above the heart. He reduced gravity further as he hit. He knew he could not grab a safe hold at this speed. Tolgan twisted and let his left leg take the impact. He bounced off the dense roots, pain shooting down his leg.

Slowly descending, hundreds of paces over a tear in the world, wracked with pain and three paces from his goal, he reached into his pocket and retrieved a small bag of rocks. He rotated his upper body and hurled the bag away from his target. Action and reaction. Like a leaf on the wind, Tolgan drifted over to the cage of roots. He threaded his arms through the gaps to hold fast, keeping gravity at bay, and let out a laugh of pure triumph. His dreams, fueled by life energy, had made him feel that this heart of wood might change everything. How, he was not sure, but it would be his.

His heartbeat was synchronized with it. He had felt its call for years and let it guide his path. If a human could gain possession of such a thing, who was more deserving than Tolgan Tri-power?

His arms were getting weak, so he diverted some life energy to strengthen himself and eased off his reduction of gravity, a more costly power. Tolgan extended a hand and touched the surface of the heart. Hard as stone. He made careful attempts with a knife to cut away at the wooden sinews securing it, but to no avail. It seemed to be unalterable.

He decided to try something different. He had heard the heart in his dreams. Not caring how much of the mystical life energy he expended, Tolgan diverted some to his third power. His mental power.

Tolgan's mind snapped into a different state. The barriers between conscious and unconscious mind fell away and he could feel things and make connections that otherwise hovered below the notice of his waking mind. The air was alive with energy, flowing and pulsing to the rhythm of the tree's heart. Of his own heart. He felt a sense of disconnection from his sense of identity, but he felt himself a part of something much greater than even this tree. A sense of oneness with place.

Without warning, memories flooded into his conscious mind. Tolgan's own memories, he realized, after hundreds had flashed before his eyes in moments. Every significant memory from Tolgan's first.

Wonder. Comfort. Learning. Training. Fighting. Whoring. Exploring. Striving. Succeeding. Searching. Finding.

It all flashed by in seconds. He, Tolgan, and his life of glory, culminating in this moment. Everything Tolgan wanted he had seized and through dedication - and, yes, privilege - he had kept. It was all Tolgan's. Now, this heart was Tolgan's. He opened himself up to the energies, ready to take in the essence housed by the wooden heart he could not conquer.

The world narrowed to a pinprick. Through his body, mind, and spirit, he felt focused. A coming together of disparate parts. A moment of cohesion. It felt like he could hear shadows of whispers.

Tolgan felt one simple intent form in that moment. One clear, focused will emerged. Not a thought exactly, but an expression of what is.

NO

Tolgan felt his connection to the heart unravel. His mind snapped back to reality. His life energy, already low, was instantly depleted. Gravity reasserted itself. His strength left him. His will unfurled. His fingers followed.

.

A Memory of Kolan

Twelve weeks ago

K olan had never visited the other landmass. His time had been too valuable to make the journey. He was glad it was forced upon him.

He watched with wonder as he passed over the great Obsidian Wall. Its scope was so far beyond its appearance from sea level. He watched with wonder as he traveled across the endless ocean beyond, an unchanging carpet of blue punctuated by distant specks of white waves. He watched with wonder as he passed the even larger obsidian wall that surrounded the second landmass.

He watched with wonder as the Twin, the heavenly body ten times the apparent size of the sun that forever hung in their sky, set below the horizon like the sun itself and did not reappear. On this side of the world, there was no Twin. There was no smallnight during the day, no smalldawn during the night. At night, though, in its place, were stars. Thousands of thousands of stars throughout the sky. It brought tears to Kolan's eyes. The Twin was spectacular, but it drowned out all but few stars. The subtlety and grandeur of so many tiny stars moved Kolan deeply, to his surprise.

Finally, after days of flight, Kolan watched the new world unfold beneath him. Only a few Time Artists had visited the second landmass. It was an impossible journey before the invention of the airship by the fast-living Time community just several years back. To Kolan, it had been a matter of weeks since being told of them.

The few visitors had reported the same thing, supplemented with sketches and basic sound recordings. Strange forms of life, similar to humans, yet so different. Unlike plants, they moved freely and functioned over human time frames. Unlike plants, they fueled themselves by consuming other life rather than by drinking the sun's light. The biologists in the Time community were calling them 'animals', as they were animated in a way that trees were not.

Kolan had intended to wait in the northern section for Calendra's approach. That plan changed when he saw the faint shimmer of tiny humans flowing across the lands like quicksilver. Kolan immediately landed the airship on a hill. He could not take it to other Timestreams and he needed to see who had already arrived. He felt certain it could not yet be Calendra. Besides, there were dozens, perhaps hundreds.

Kolan felt sick to his stomach when he shifted to a closer Timestream to identify them. They could not see him like this. The telltale shimmer was only visible to Time Artists. He could see them, though. Alvertus' private army. Not only did that reprobate know about the second landmass and found means to get there with a small army, he was surely ahead of Calendra, judging from the time elapsed since she was seen in *Drink's End*, a sighting that caused quite a stir. Kolan did not despair as Calendra had both Manifold sight and access to Speed Artistry, but things were dire. Kolan came to stop Calendra from consuming the Worldheart, but things would be far worse if Alvertus secured it. He would unquestionably consume it, or worse, and a god-like Alvertus would be unthinkable.

Kolan was torn. Follow the army until it finds the Worldheart and switch Timestreams to get there ahead of them? Or go north and wait for Calendra? The latter might be too late, but the former was ultimately pointless. Kolan could not stop an army. Without knowing the location of the Worldheart, he could only follow someone that did. He hated relying on the knowledge of the very people he was trying to influence.

As he settled on waiting for Calendra, he noticed something he did not expect. While the army was dispersed, it headed in one direction. North-east. There were outliers, probably Endurance Artists operating as scouts, but they matched the general trajectory of the army. Yet there was one person heading in a completely different direction. South. It would use up valuable time, but he had to investigate. They might be lost, but they might be important. Shaping the decisions of one important person was when Kolan was at his best.

Kolan shifted Timestreams to move much faster than the solo traveler and pursued. When he caught up an hour later, though only several minutes later from his target's perspective, he did a double-take.

It was *Djulita*. Kolan could not believe his eyes. The bookish, middle-aged bureaucrat, adviser and confidant of Lord Speed, lacking any Art or Spirit, was wandering alone in a strange land filled with mystical lifeforms. Something told Kolan she knew where she was going.

So he followed her. One Timestream up, using half the seconds otherwise required but forcing him to journey at twice the speed, he followed Djulita through forests and swamps, plains and streams. There were animals everywhere. Their time echo was much stronger than that left by humans, though not as strong as that of plants. Some were bizarre but others felt almost kin to humanity, though different in form and apparently lacking humanity's intelligence, foresight and will to change their surroundings. They were similar enough to humans for their differences to seem uncanny, but they seemed cohesive and natural and right.

On several occasions, Kolan feared for Djulita's life as an animal would seem to consider her a nuisance or an opportunity. Kolan had seen some evidence of animals *eating other animals*, which seemed to be a violation most heinous. Kolan would not see Djulita meet such a fate. He was increasingly wondering whether she really knew where she was going or just committing to a direction, though she seemed certain of it.

When Djulita went to sleep, Kolan hopped several Timestreams down and scouted ahead. He needed to find Calendra. It was the most Time-distant he could be and still see shadows of changes from Human Time. It made sense that she would go south or west. The army was heading north and east, and Kolan had to believe Calendra was smart enough to have sent them on a false trail. It was as good a direction as any.

After two days of searching, approaching the time he would need to return before she woke, despairing of finding anything in the endless wilds, he noticed a shadow of a footprint. He hopped into Human Time to confirm. Definitely her. Small shoes with deep prints spaced impossibly far apart.

Rubbing his hands together, Kolan returned several Timestreams down and waited for Djulita to wake. She did not dawdle once she did. She kept heading in the same direction, to Kolan's relief. It would only take a few hours to reach Calendra's prints.

A few hours later Kolan was hopping with frustration as Djulita walked parallel to the prints but out of sight of them. When she veered away from their south-west direction, he panicked. She was still several Timestreams down from Human Time and would not see prints from there without Time Artistry. After checking the time of day in Human Time, he carefully hopped behind her, touched her shoulder and shifted her to Human Time. He saw her shadow spin immediately, but she was in a different Time and could not see him. He ran a hundred paces through pine forest to the nearest prints and took a hand axe from his pack. Then he hopped into Human Time and hacked at a tree as loudly as possible.

His relief when she heard, followed and discovered the prints, was immense. He followed her from one Timestream down. He only then saw that they would never catch Calendra in Human Time, but he was wary of shifting her again. She would become too suspicious. Besides, she would be unable to see Calendra's prints from a Timestream distant enough to be fast enough. She remained on the trail, though was visibly bothered by the sudden appearance of animals.

When she slept that night, appearing much more nervous than previous nights, he got to work four Timestreams down. Four Timestreams was the absolute most distant he could see Calendra's prints, even drawing on a lot of Spirit. Even that was stunning. He had never achieved three. Maybe it was something about her Spirit. Whatever the reason, it was enough to follow them, which meant it was enough for him to lay his own trail. Djulita would have something to follow in this much faster Timestream where she would not be able to see Calendra's prints. He had to hope she would follow what were clearly different tracks. He would, in her shoes.

Kolan wondered, not for the first time, at the time he was spending to guide Djulita. Would this lost time be the difference between success and failure? Kolan reminded himself that he had to trust his instincts. He could manufacture more time if needed. He felt sure that Djulita had an important role to play, one that he could not. It might all come down to Calendra's humanity and Djulita was a reminder of that, so he persevered.

Kolan followed Calendra's prints for over two weeks before he caught up to her. He stopped at the edge of a clearing, reluctant to leave proof of his passing where she may see it. She was sitting with her back to a glorious tree. Kolan had no doubt what it was. She was a shadow, but nowhere near as faint as she should be from this Timestream.

Satisfied but with time against him, Kolan carefully hopped to a Timestream he only visited at the utmost need. It would consume nearly all his Spirit, but he would have plenty of time for that to regenerate during the two-week return journey. Nine hours would have passed in Djulita's Timestream already. Only half an hour more would pass during his long walk back through such a fast Timestream.

The urgency was most likely unjustified. He could probably wait right there until Djulita caught up, but there was no way he would risk that after all this. He was no longer worried about Calendra doing something during the half-day of Human Time that would pass for her. She was spending time with the tree. She would not do that if she planned to harvest it, but he still felt that she may need Djulita. If Kolan's experience was anything to go by, bonding the heart would take time. Far more than a day.

The next two weeks were trying, yet he found it hard to complain even to himself. The most important junction in time since the Traveler was so near. The scales were finely balanced, but Kolan had done his best to put his finger on the one side. All he could do now, as so often, was wait. Maybe prod a little if things did not flow as they ought. As long as he got back to Djulita in time to send her to the Timestream where his prints were.

When he arrived in the general vicinity, he hopped to the Timestream adjacent to Djulita's and found her asleep where he had left her. He shifted her to the very fast Timestream and followed her from an even faster one as she found and followed his tracks, to give him more time to rest. It would use up additional moments, but that way he could walk just a few miles a day and keep up.

The weeks passed slowly and quickly, but eventually Djulita stumbled through the last piece of forest and into the clearing. The wonder and hope on her face was worth the wait. Kolan followed her to the tree. He could just see Calendra's time-shadow from here, sitting before a meal she was cooking using the skills Kolan taught her. A meal of three trehearts. But Djulita could not see her from this Timestream.

Kolan grinned, hopped to Djulita's Timestream, clasped her shoulder and brought her into Human Time, then instantly hopped one Timestream up, temporally close enough to hear them talk. It would be a strange, drawn-out process - their voices temporally shifted - but he was used to it.

Kolan watched them silently lest Calendra notice his Time glimmer. If she had even figured out Time Artistry yet. It took every shred of Kolan's considerable will to sit back and watch rather than appear to Calendra, but Kolan was a pragmatic sort. He had waited for half of post-exodus humanity for this moment. And it was not his moment. It was Djulita's.

Djulita burst into tears when she saw Calendra. Whether for the long absence or the relief of tension, or at the sight of the woman Djulita thought of as a daughter having aged so much from living Fast that they appeared the same age, Kolan did not know.

Calendra's reaction was just as joyous, and they embraced. It sparked fresh hope in Kolan, for Calendra's biggest danger was to no longer care. Kolan could see that she cared about Djulita, if nothing and nobody else. She listened to Djulita's imploring tone as the scribe talked to her of unknown truths. As she tried to convince Calendra that the world was not just alive, but a life. As she told Calendra to think before acting in ways that could not be undone. As she reminded Calendra that it was only polite to ask before taking. And as Djulita discovered the truth of Time Artistry and led Calendra to the same understanding.

Kolan watched as Calendra effortlessly took the final step to gaining unlimited power, the step he had once hoped she would never learn. She Jumped into Heart Time, where the treehearts could be physically affected.

Kolan waited, though it killed him. Heart Time at least was so slow that a week could pass in Human Time for each hour of her time, so Kolan could afford to wait. But who would arrive as Calendra made her decision? Danald? Alvertus' army? What if they tried to kill her? Could Kolan stop them? Should he? He had come ready to stop Calendra, but now, thanks to Djulita, he might need to support her. What if he did, and she chose the path of selfishness? Could Kolan forgive himself?

Djulita sat in front of Calendra's motionless body for hours, protecting Calendra with nothing more than her own powerless body. Calendra was sufficiently attuned to the Worldheart to make her physically exist in all Timestreams. Unlike the Worldheart though, Calendra was physically vulnerable in all Timestreams. Hours stretched into night, the tropical warmth allowing them to sleep where they were. When Kolan awoke, Djulita was already awake, in the same position, staring outward. Kolan chuckled softly at the sight of Calendra's now empty plate in front of Djulita.

Hours more passed then, in a blur, the Announcer arrived. Kolan was surprised at how far behind Calendra he had been, but Calendra's speed was like nothing the world had ever seen. Even the first Manifold Lord wouldn't have kept up. So he had done as Kolan would have. He had followed Calendra in a faster Timestream. Fortunately, it was the Timestream in which Kolan waited.

Not realizing he already made his decision, Kolan threw himself in between Calendra and the Announcer.

"Stop, Danald," he said with the full weight of the authority inherent to a person who has seen and guided so much change.

With clear sorrow, Danald pulled a curved knife from his belt and looked into Kolan's eyes.

"I'm sorry, Kolan. I know more than most what you've done for the world I love, but I cannot allow you to stop me. I will kill you if I must. I will kill Djulita if I must, though she lies blameless. I will kill all of humanity, every soul, before I allow this world to be forever broken. Stand aside."

"No. Look at her. There has been no more important moment in history, so take a moment. Look at her. Does she look like she is harvesting that heart? No, Danald, she listened to you. You announced. She heard."

"I know what's required. She took more treehearts from the sanctuary. I hoped she would choose differently and take my path. I hoped she would bond with it. That can be done in Human Time. She's surely in Heart Time, Kolan. Why would she be in Heart Time if not to strike at it?"

"To *listen*, Danald. Heart Time is the pace at which the world processes information. The pace at which it thinks. The pace at which it *talks*. Come. Watch."

Danald eyed Kolan skeptically, but disappeared. He knew after so long that Kolan did not state absolutes lightly. Kolan followed into Heart Time.

The two ancient Time Artists stood in front of the true Worldtree and looked at the woman who would be a god. She was motionless, eyes closed, bearing a calm, gentle smile. Danald Jumped back straight away to avoid too much time passing and Kolan followed once more. He put his hand on Danald's shoulder.

"I'm not saying she'll make the right decision, Danald. She might still need to be stopped if she walks the wrong path, but that is not a woman trying to take the world's power for herself. That is a woman trying not to take the world's power for herself. That she has the greatest prize of all in her grasp and is taking the time to decide says she is not who you thought she was. She is not who I feared she was. Not yet. Give her time."

"Is it worth the risk?" The Announcer did not look like his heart was in the objection. More like he wanted reassurance.

"Yes," Kolan replied simply. "In principle and in practice. In principle, because she doesn't deserve death until she's earned it. In practice, because this world isn't coping with the impacts of humanity. You know this. Hearts failing in the Great Plains. The death and replacement of multiple smaller hearts as they adapt to changing ecosystems. How will the world go now that treehearts are becoming known? Now that this new land has been discovered? The world we love will wilt at the edges and rot in the center. It doesn't understand humans. But maybe it can."

Danald closed his eyes and hummed incongruously before replying.

"You think it's true, then? That the world thinks in one voice. You think she will bond with the Worldheart, not just in Spirit but in mind."

Kolan shrugged. Danald chuckled. Together, they waited for an extraordinary woman to decide the fate of the world.

It was not long - only hours for them, yet many days of Human Time - until the luxury of time was taken from them. In the distance, around the semicircular rim of the natural amphitheater that housed the Worldtree and little else, shimmers appeared. Hundreds. Kolan looked at Danald with sadness and they shifted into Human Time. Alvertus' army was amassing.

Djulita shrieked. Danald reacted as if he had forgotten about her.

"Quiet," Danald hissed at her, though not unkindly. "We've been here for hours. If we meant her harm, she would be dead."

This seemed to mollify Djulita, or perhaps she realized she had little choice, for she quieted and watched with them, continuing to protect Calendra with her body. Soon enough, a purple-robed figure appeared at the head of the army.

Even from a distance, Kolan could hear Alvertus' shrill laughter ring out. The man had brought an army yet faced only four people, one of whom was temporarily merged with a tree. Another was Artless, and Kolan himself was no fighter. That was not his role today.

No, Alvertus and his army faced one man. Just one. But there was no 'just' about Danald. He was the greatest Artist the world had seen since the Traveler. If it was to protect the world that gave him that power, Kolan knew Danald would fight to the end. And it would be some fight.

Danald turned back to look at the motionless Calendra. He paused for a moment, then looked at Djulita and Kolan in turn.

"She'd better choose well after this," he said through a grin of anticipation. He chuckled to himself as the army marched forward. Then he downed several flasks of liquid, winked at them and walked twenty paces forward, ready.

A commotion in the army's lines caught Kolan's attention. Soldiers were toppling like bowling pins. In moments, an entire wedge of thirty soldiers or more were dead. Through that wedge shot a blur of motion. By the time it arrived, it was visible as a lanky man in his fifties, eyes alight.

Djulita sobbed with joy and sorrow.

Kolan smiled as the man went to his motionless daughter, stared into her motionless eyes and kissed her three times, once on each cheek and once on the forehead. He whispered something to her, returned to where the Announcer stood without wiping away his tears and nodded.

"Tyrant," Malnor said, grinning.

Danald chuckled and tossed him a vial.

"Spy."

He winked. Kolan had never seen Danald wink.

"Vrai and I brought down the Artists maintaining the portal," Malnor told the Announcer. "There will be no reinforcements. Alvertus has no more Spatial

Donors, and the moron didn't even bring Manifold Artists here, lest they take what is his! Just a whole lot of Physical Artists."

The Announcer laughed and cracked his knuckles.

"Tell her I love her, Djulie," Malnor called back, then drank the contents of the vial.

Under a Twinless sky, the two enemies ran together at the advancing army.

CHAPTER TWENTY NINE

What is consciousness? It is self-referential. Yes but what is consciousness. It is experiential. Yes but what is consciousness. It is a system capable of acting against instinct for future calculated benefit. Yes but what is consciousness. It is a system of uncountable networked components that processes inputs and manifests a singular voice capable of determining action on behalf of components with no voice of their own. Yes but what is consciousness. Is it incalculably improbable or probabilistically inevitable. Yes.

Extract from interview with Patient 132

Records of the Mind Sanctum

C alendra does not understand at first, but as soon as she says the words *Time Artistry* in her mind, she feels their truth. Thoughts of the golden-haired wanderer and the Announcer's longevity piece together in an instant but the power feels strange. She does not understand its nature.

Then an image flashes into her head. An empty pub with ghostly patrons. A vision or memory or hallucination. Or a shadow of the present in another place. No. Another Time. A different present, parallel to hers.

She feels it straight away. Time has different flows, each at a different rate. Her eyes widen and she detaches from the Manifold completely, cast into a river of Time. Her mind translates the chaos into discrete parallel streams seen from so high they appear as one.

As soon as she thinks it, she feels herself floating above the streams. She sees their flows and feels their energies. She sees them with her Manifold sight. One of the slowest streams glows with a brilliance that leaves no doubt. Calendra dives in.

She appears exactly where she left, but Djulita has vanished. It is only her and the tree. She turns to it, touches its shimmering bark and nods.

"Okay, tree," Calendra says, "I'm here to talk. Do you understand me?"

There is a long delay. After seconds or eons, Calendra feels a pull. Her mind is drawn into a broader consciousness, far more than just a single tree. Her mind fragments into one and many. She presents her offer to the world, to herself, willing her thoughts through whatever connection has formed.

"I offer my help. You are injured. We, humans, are to blame. I am to blame. Let me lend you my power to help you restore. I am strong. Will it work? Will you accept?"

After what feels like forever, she feels a voice without sound, a thought without words, a consciousness without identity. The voice of the world vibrates through her entire being.

NO.

The voice itself is flat. Pure information. No more or less than that needed to communicate. Even at the time flow of trees, the thought is slowly formed and slowly delivered, like a committee of hundreds taking time to agree on its positions. Not hundreds. Thousands of thousands of thousands. She does not think that those thousands are conscious individuals, more like sources of information the greater consciousness takes time to reference. While Calendra-the-one retains her sense of identity, a part of her is already linked to the mind with which she communes. The voice is flat to Calendra-the-one, but resonates with a thousand thousand harmonies to Calendra-the-many.

No, it will not help. The Spirit imbalance is far too great for even Calendra to help. Something different is needed.

No, the world will not accept her help. She consumes.

To Zem, for a consciousness needs an identity and Zem is as good a name as any, her thoughts are music. All humans are music, but music that is too fast to understand. The thoughts of trees are slow and steady, in parallel, the notes of their song only varying with the seasons but at all times thinking on a dozen matters at once. A dozen notes overlaid, with rises and falls to be measured in seasons. Humans are not like that. The thoughts of humans vary by the second yet are always sequential. A wild melody of monotonal notes changing by the moment.

Trees cannot function as humans do, she sees. A tree takes great patience to develop. A forest takes cooperation and sacrifice, allowing the unfit to wither while the fit survive, sharing nutrients between those trees with access to rich soil or Sun or rain, and those without.

Humans are so different. They will cooperate, sure, but seldom truly sacrifice. Cooperation only occurs where the self benefits immediately, or under the lash of the whip. When humanity centralizes decision-making it is almost always under a single mind, or several. When trees develop true cooperation, it is not centralized but collective. The basic drive of each tree flows up to merge into a single will, the thoughts of which flow back down to affect the behavior of all. So different to collective human decision making. As Calendra's dad once put it, try to get ten people to agree to a position and you'll end up with twenty irreconcilable positions. Perhaps the difference is that each human has their own will while each tree does not. Human committees are manufactured while Zem is emergent. The many do not have voices or thoughts, but together they give rise to something that has thoughts and a voice. As Djulita told her.

Calendra reflects on the internal debates she so often conducts and wonders if it is so different to an individual human. Different voices in her head notice different things and advocate different positions. Not real voices, like for the poor souls afflicted with illnesses of the mind, but different parts of her mind reflecting different needs that must be balanced. Perhaps even a human is not one discrete thing but many parts that operate with a collective voice. Many conflicting needs requiring one singular emergent Calendra to govern them.

Yes, she feels she is right. No one tree is conscious. Zem is the voice of a consciousness emerging from uncountable unconscious components. This world's consciousness emerges from the network of life, not from life itself, and the pathways of that network are Spirit. It is Spirit that enables communication between trees, giving rise to a collective.

She feels Zem's memories, not in flashes, but as a story she suddenly knows. So integral to the world's identity that she knows it like her own story. For untold millennia, the emerging consciousness slowly governed the operations of the world, optimizing the distribution of Spirit to benefit the world as a whole.

Then it came. The fast mobile thing from the great light in the sky, the lifeform that thought of itself as *human*. The human appeared through a tear in the spacetime manifold, wielding strange energies of reality, and found the Worldtree. The human pleaded with Zem to allow more lifeforms to come, to allow them to flee their dying world. Zem agreed, seeing something in humans complementary to its own life.

Zem opened up an immense pool of Manifold-aligned Spirit to the human - the Traveler - and he used it to teleport to the Twin, gather what life he could and teleport it all to Zem's world. The humans were sent to the world's second land-mass, the one that did not contain the Worldtree. The Traveler sent the animals to the main landmass, keen to keep them separate from humans in recognition of their historical treatment. Together, the Traveler and Zem created the predatory plant life that fringes the coastline of the second landmass, to prevent the new animal life from contaminating both lands.

The Traveler died, overwhelmed by the Spirit required to terraform so much, leaving Zem alone to manage a world with life that thinks and operates faster than Zem could ever hope to match. Life that destroys and changes ecosystems faster than any redistribution of Spirit could ever address.

Calendra can feel Zem's interest in human thought. The world can learn much from humans about being dynamic, which was why it agreed to be a haven for humans. Humans can learn much from this world as well, she reflects, about patience, cooperation and unity. With time, that journey can be taken together. But there is no time now for such a journey. The world needs to catch up to the new reality within which it has found itself.

And so she knows what she must do. Certainly, the Announcer and Djulita were right. She cannot consume this heart. Nor can she do as the Announcer did and lend strength to this heart. That had been a bandage over a wound to buy time to heal one local weakness in the network. That was needed two hundred years ago, but two hundred more years of humanity undermining the great Spirit network has taken its toll.

The Worldtree may or may not die, but that is no longer the point for Calendra. The world, Zem, the life that comprises it, will not survive. It may take years or centuries, but it will not survive, not when it depends upon Spirit and humans are so able to break the Spirit network. The world will die because it is no longer fit for purpose. It needs someone to think and act on human timescales. Not to lend strength, but to join with it in truth. To be its voice. Forever.

Calendra is someone. But does she want this? Will she become Calendra-the-many in truth, Calendra-the-one dying and dispersing like the ashes of a burned leaf swept away by the wind? Does she want to leave the people she loves?

She finds little grief in the thought. She loves her dad and he loves her, but they have not been an active part of each other's lives for years. Calendra loves Djulita like a mother, and cannot believe her courage in coming here, but Djulita has her own life and will move on. There is nobody left that she loves. Only Myla, and that root was severed long ago. Once again, though for the first time in many years, she wonders at how things ended, at how she let her fairy tale end in the opening chapters.

There is nobody left to love, or at least nobody who needs her love, and she has never been one to enjoy people's company for the sake of it. Humanity can fend for itself. She will make the sacrifice for the rest of them. She will not miss them and they will not even notice she is gone. She is more of this world than she is of humanity. She is the perfect person to merge with it. She will be, finally, extraordinary. Yes. Such an act - that would be extraordinary.

As she thinks about it, she knows her decision is made. She finds peace in that. A peace she has not known since childhood. The weight of a world lifted from her.

Calendra addresses Zem, in thought and intent as much as by voice.

"I understand. I will become one with you. I will bridge the gap between you and the humans. I will give you speed of thought. I will give you the gift of speed. We will save this world. I will consume no more."

Calendra surrenders herself to the collective consciousness.

She feels Zem understands her offer. She feels its glacial deliberations. Then she hears the world asks itself something that had not occurred to her.

WORTHY?

Without warning, the memories begin.

Calendra is at the heart of the world. The worldtree. The packed hall is warm, but the hair on her arms stands on end. A chill rolls down her spine. She perches on a

cabinet not designed for perching, absorbing the majesty and chaos of the Descension ...

Calendra's eyes snap open. Her back hurts. She vaguely remembers waking only to pass out from the pain. Uncle Mal's face appears above her, shadows scampering over his face from a crackling fireplace. He speaks in his soothing baritone, so familiar yet so seldom heard ...

Calendra eyeballs her meal. She tries to remember what it felt like to look at the canvas, not just what the metaphor put in her head. She tries to picture the substance that links her and the food, even before she touches it ...

All the most important memories of Calendra's life from the time she first accessed Spirit, many of which she had actively avoided remembering, were displayed for a world to see. Memories by which a world would judge her worth.

Calendra wakes to the creaking hinges of the room's only door. She opens her eyes to the orange tint of dawn light. A spicy burned oil aroma triggers pangs of hunger. Uncle Mal - her dad! - walks towards her, grin on face, tray in hand ...

"Run to me, Calendra. Double-speed." Calendra stretches, stifling a yawn. She squints at her dad halfway down the snowy hill from the shaded entrance of the hilltop cave they have called home for days ...

As Calendra sees the first hint of sunlight in hours, her dad puts his arm in her path. "Stop, Calendra. You can only once experience a thing for the first time. Unless you're a Memory Artist. There are some things memorable enough to wish I'd been prepared for my first experience." ...

The memories swamped her, fast enough to feel like time was compressed, but slow enough to experience them fully. Calendra understood the memories were somehow encoded in Spirit. It was difficult to enjoy them, knowing all her actions were being dissected. She knew, even then, she could only process the experience at all because she was living so Slow. The experience would feel like mere flashes to a person in a normal Timestream.

Calendra reclines on her lounging chair with eyes half-lidded and meditates on the soulblossoms. Under the branches of a beautiful tree to which she has taken a particular liking, she feels the warmth of the lake as she sips fruit-infused cooled spring water and nibbles at leaf-wrapped spiced tuber ...

Calendra flies from tree to tree, catching each vine and using her momentum to launch her to the next. After six years in the Valley, it has become second nature. It teaches her to balance momentum with short bursts of speed. And it has become her favorite way to burn off some energy ...

Calendra and Vrailen lounge on their chairs shortly after smallnight. The old tree seems more and more important to this place, especially when she is meditating on the canvas. This is her favorite spot as the view of her tree is perfectly framed by the waxing Twin above. It is her favorite day of the year. The Spawn ...

Calendra smiled. This, at least, she could relive with pride. The day she saved her dad's life. The day she defended her Valley. The day she took the first step on the path to the extraordinary.

Calendra watched herself carve through the Announcer's agents with breath-taking speed. A true warrior assassin. The reaction from the world was immediate.

DEATH. DEATH DEATH DEATH.

Calendra's heart sank. The world disapproved? The world sacrificed individual lives every minute. Calendra had only killed when she had no choice, or when the world would be better off without that person.

The memories continued.

Running. Running. Sun setting. Still running. Sun rising. Still running ...

Calendra wakes as the sun's first light drowns out the soft glow of the waxing Twin. Her nostrils flare at the scents of caramelized fruit and spiced flourcake, motivating her to rise without her usual dithering. She stretches sore muscles, cracks stiff joints and walks to the door. Behind it waits a feast that could fill a family ...

Calendra awakes to firm knocking and throws on a coat before answering the door. A tiny woman walks in and grins. "Calendra, we're going to have some fun!" ...

Calendra looks up at the sculpted, painted ceiling of Speed Hall. Calendra looks around at her classmates, whose names she is unable to remember after three days at the School. Calendra looks at the walls of the hall, adorned with murals depicting great acts of ancient Speed Artists. Calendra looks at the purple fabric of Narelda's robes shimmer as the elderly Speed Master gesticulates. Calendra looks everywhere but at Myla. If she lets her gaze settle, she will lack the strength to move it ...

Calendra's scarred heart tore itself apart. She could not do this. She could not relive a joy now lost. Zem gave her no say in the matter. Yet as the sensations and experience of new love and passion progressed, the world seemed to rumble in approval.

The memories continued.

"You're wrong!" Calendra spits the word at Narelda. To be wrong is bad enough, but a Master of the School of the Manifold being wrong leaves a bitter taste in Calendra's mouth. Not least because that Master grades her papers ...

Calendra finds it easier than expected to dedicate time to her studies. As someone that lacked all semblance of a routine for so many years, she quickly finds that structure provides focus. She settles into a comfortable regimen of classes, time with Myla and book learning, punctuated by time with her dad on weekends ...

Calendra talks to Myla first thing the next morning. Myla's solidarity is a warm fire in the cold expanse of her lost Manifold sight ...

Calendra wipes her tears on her dad's chest. She will miss him immensely. While they have lived apart the past year, she has seen him each weekend and he was never far if she needed him. After eight years in his care, many of them in the Valley, she will be on her own ...

Myla arrives back at their camp several hours after stalking off. Her face is a storm-cloud ...

Calendra relived the memory with growing shame. Not at her obsession, for she would not be where she was now had she lacked the will to become extraordinary. Not even for her first kill that was not in self-defense, for that weed deserved it.

She felt it at the way she treated Myla. The intensity of the memories, actually reliving them, brought it all back. She had let her obsession control her to the point of hurting the woman she loved. A woman who had just upended her life for Calendra, no questions asked. Myla must have felt so unloved in those days. That so easily could have been Calendra's chance for true happiness with Myla. Had it been worth it?

Calendra prowls the jungle, Myla trailing behind. After an hour or two of walking, Myla gasps. Calendra whirls on her. "My? Have you found it?" ...

Calendra's mind froze. She knew this memory. She knew where this ended. She lived once more the moments leading up to Myla leaving her. The fight about her value for life. About her obsession. That was why her dream had been shattered. Right?

Calendra saw once more the men hacking at the heart tree, Alvertus commanding them. The memory continued until past-Calendra smashed her head. The memory faded to black. A thought resonated throughout the world.

DISCONTIGUITY

Calendra felt a deep sense of unease from Zem. She felt it deliberating. The deliberation seemed to conclude, for the memories restarted.

Calendra wakes, famished, in a small room adorned with paintings of flowers. The sun streams in at a shallow angle through the lone window, making it either early morning or late afternoon. She downs the cup of water on the table by her luxurious bed and rings the bell placed next to it. In moments, the door opens and a tall, plump woman walks in. "Uh, Calendra then?" ...

As she readied herself to relive that terrible moment, Calendra realized the problem. She had not seen the first time because of the physical and mental trauma, and had refused to think of it for half a lifetime since.

How had she gotten to the cottage? She had been out cold. Myla could have done little against those pursuers. On reflection, the cottage had been quite far from the heart tree. It had been morning when she woke, making it at least eighteen hours after she lost consciousness. It made no sense.

Discontiguity. Her memories were discontiguous. They no longer connected in one seamless flow. She had lost memories of that time. Because of the concussion? It felt too clean, though. Would the world even take special note of memories lost in that way?

Calendra watched Myla's friend talk. Myla's friend. That was it. How had she not realized? Myla's only friends had been from the School of the Mind. Myla's friend must have been a Memory Artist. They stole her memories! She had heard this was possible, but why? What had Myla wanted Calendra to forget?

The memory continued and past-Calendra wept as Myla's face twisted in hatred and disgust. She felt the agony once more, both in memory and in the present, but the question lingered. What had she forgotten leading up to that hatred? It felt off.

Calendra relived her Manifold sight returning with little emotion. Of course it has been destined to return. What had she been thinking, to be so impatient? Thankfully, the memories skimmed over the many weeks she had spent getting from the Plains to the Valley. Nothing had happened worth the world remembering, just a fog of misery.

The sunlight sparkles through Calendra's tears, casting her Valley in a rainbow shimmer. The wedge of redwoods that once sheltered her jungle home from the mountain winds is a ruin of shattered wood, as if the heavens knocked them over with an enormous ball. Through the still, crisp winter air she can see that her

jungle haven has been destroyed by rot and wind. After week after week of numbed walking, refusing to use her Art, Calendra has arrived home to desolation ...

Calendra wakes at smalldawn. The forest calls to her. She decides to make use of the bright midnight hour to paint. It is a hurried and simple effort, flowing without thought. She finishes as the reflected light of the Twin diminishes, unable to see her handiwork properly but aglow with the warmth of meditation, creation and oneness ...

Calendra drifts out of the trance that accompanies living Slow to the urgent clanging of a nearby village's bell. Dingding. Ding. Ding ding. She sighs out the frustration. Another raid ...

It takes Calendra three days to reach the Eastern Sea, moving as Fast as possible while maintaining enough Spirit to fully regenerate each night. Once in the port of Sun's Kiss, she writes messages to her dad and Djulita and sends them by postal run to Sanctum ...

Calendra relived those days with contentment. She had not been a happy person during that time, just driven. Looking back though, she realized those days of discovering the world and herself had been amongst her happiest. She wondered what had happened to Hwan, and Velekhno, and of course the Time Artist who had helped her take the next step to the extraordinary by teaching her the Art of the Cook. The world rumbled again, however, when it watched her killing. Even the deaths of slavers and murderers seemed to trouble it.

DEATH

Calendra becomes Normal. For the weeks it has taken to reach the Skyshrine she moved as Fast as possible while retaining enough Spirit to regenerate each night. It

is exhausting, moving Fast for so long. It taxes the mind, especially when moving through the uneven footing of jungles ...

The days pass in a happy haze of simple pleasures. The endless trudge of travel. The contrasting beauty of ecological variation. The pleasure of foraging and preparing simple food. The relaxation of, for once, being Normal. It is a normalcy that city dwellers might find arduous, but Calendra has spent most of her life in the wilds of the world in all types of weather, carrying her whole life on her back ...

Calendra relived the moments as she came into her full power. When she ate a living heart. She felt past-Calendra's rage at the Announcer and his agents. She felt a strange clash of emotions, feeling herself acting in what she thought was a just way when she now knew the Announcer had been no true enemy. The world, however, had no such conflict.

DEATH DEATH DEATH DEATH DEATH.

When she relived severing the dying heart, the heart that made her a full Manifold Lord, the world roared.

DEATH!

Calendra hung her head in shame. That had been wrong, though in her desperation she had not understood it at the time. Though, reliving the memory, she realized that part of her had understood. Yet regret was hard to summon as the experience made her attuned enough to the world to bond with it. She could see now that she had not damaged the local network, though only because the Announcer had fought so hard to mature the new heart in time. In any other circumstance, it could have been a disaster. More reason this world must be protected from humans.

Calendra stares at the man who has hunted her for twenty years. The man who has imprisoned her for one hundred and forty-seven sleeps. The Announcer has changed little since Calendra left Chalvstrom ...

Calendra relived the Announcer setting her straight, putting her firmly on the path to being one with this world, pulling her away from humanity and its short-sighted selfishness. He had convinced her so easily because a part of her knew it to be true and just needed someone to say it. Yet the world rumbled with concern.

Calendra stands atop the Traveler's Seat, the great plateau not far from Skypeak, looking north. The view is the same as the day she consumed the speed-instinct meal ...

Calendra relived her flight north from Chalvstrom and her dreamlike search for hearts in the Grand Reserve, an experience she barely remembered, such was her flow at the time. It breezed by rapidly, but she was surprised that the world only rumbled at her removal of dead hearts, rather than objecting.

The world hummed in satisfaction as, at the height of loneliness, past-Calendra thought of her dad and Djulita. She smiled at the memory of her discovery of the second landmass after soaring over endless sea with nothing more than faith in her destiny. Of all the things she did in her life, she could now reflect, that was perhaps the bravest. Her flight of faith.

Calendra wakes to the inexpressibly awful sensation of greased sandpaper stroking the back of her neck. She lifts her head and sees a monstrosity, a thing so bizarre, so alien yet so familiar, that not even children's tales would think to invent ...

It was a strange thing to relive in detail memories so recent. It was fresh in her memory, yet it felt different to view things in a different state of mind. Even the reliving was like being told a story that instantly appeared in the mind, rather than actually experiencing the events.

Finally, the memory brought her to the last moments before she had embraced the bond. The moments of Djulita convincing her to join rather than consume. Of her time jump and her offer.

And then the memories finished.

Calendra held her breath, remembering once more that this was a trial. Did she pass? Would the world forgive her violence? Was she enough like this world's life to become part of it? She felt like a slave for sale at a Free Cities market. How would Zem answer?

NO

The thought came just like that. No. No, she had not passed. No, she was not worthy.

Calendra felt the world start to dissolve their bond and expel her from the collective.

No! She would not accept this. She was not even sure why she was so determined to prove her worth, yet she was. She would not allow her memories to be her sole witness. More than that, having experienced the thoughts of a world, she finally appreciated what was at stake. She truly wanted to help. She truly accepted what it would mean, and she was willing.

Calendra felt the world pushing her out. She pushed back.

"STOP," Calendra commanded the world. And it did.

For several moments, the Manifold itself shuddered as two different wills contended for control of the great Spirit network. She began to lose the battle.

"Stop!" she pleaded this time. "Please. Why?"

The world paused and the pressure eased, holding her half-in and half-out of the collective. After a moment or a lifetime, it spoke in the same strange non-verbal impressions transmitted into her mind. Not a voice, but an intent that her connected mind translated into words.

NOT HUMAN

"But humans are destroying this world! I don't want to be like them. I want to be like you. I want to help you."

YES
NOT HUMAN
TREE
FAST TREE
NOT HUMAN

"But I am still human! I can think fast like them. I can help you think differently."

NOT JUST THOUGHT
HUMANNESS
COMPLEMENTARITY

"I am human! I..."

NO

And with that, Calendra's mind re-entered the physical world. But she would not accept it. Calendra-the-one looked around herself as Calendra-the-many fought to remain. Somehow, she did. Calendra was suspended between two Timestreams, seeing both simultaneously.

Calendra-the-one Jumped to Human Time - she now understood a jump in time was no different to one in space - and looked up at Djulita, somehow maintaining a connection to the collective across Timestreams. The woman stood in front of Calendra, protecting her. Protecting her from what? Had Alvertus arrived? Calendra looked past Djulita and her heart fell.

The scene was carnage. Dozens of corpses littered the forest floor. The Announcer was there, mortally wounded, fighting five brutes just paces from Calendra. The Announcer, once her enemy, laid down his life to protect her. To protect the world he loved by keeping her alive to save it. He moved so fast she had to become Fast just to follow as he bent gravity, time and space at will. He did not have her power, but his control of the Manifold stole her breath.

And her dad, her beloved dad, fought by his side. He was moving even faster than the Announcer. Malnor, Lord Speed, laid waste to the swarming soldiers even as blood soaked the left side of his shirt at a frightening rate.

Calendra wanted to help so desperately that she wept. She could destroy these villains without breaking a sweat, but she would need to break physical contact with the tree, which might break the bond. Maybe she could do it. It unfolded in her mind's eye.

Calendra steps away from the Worldtree.

Calendra becomes Fast. Calendra becomes strong and agile, enduring and resilient, instinctive and beyond the limits of consciousness.

Calendra dances through enemies, laying waste to those who would harm her world. She teleports behind enemies, removes gravity from them and hurls them into the atmosphere. She weaves through defenses and opens the throats of those who never see more than a blur.

She calls to the Worldtree and the Worldtree calls the strange creatures of this place, who aid Calendra in her rampage. None survive.

She heals those who protected her. They all live.

The Worldheart thanks her and rejects her nonetheless.

The world withers.

No. She would not bring that reality into existence. She would not let go of the bond. She dared not let Calendra-the-many fade away while there might still be hope. It was only her will that was maintaining the connection at all. If she broke that connection, she did not think Zem would allow it to reform. So much death to give her this chance. She would hold on until no chance remained. No matter the personal cost.

The Announcer ran out of Spirit first. Standing atop a literal pile of enemy Artists, the man staggered as his body returned to normal speed. He did not even save his last Spirit to jump away. He truly would fight to the end to protect her. Calendra felt her tears fall at the heroism. Even without his Arts, he took down three more at the cost of a deep wound to the thigh.

Calendra blinked as she realized they had almost won. The Announcer caught his breath as her dad fought three men, but that seemed to be the last of them.

The Manifold twisted again. Alvertus, destroyer of dreams, appeared next to the Announcer and stabbed him in the other leg. He teleported to the Announcer's other side and stabbed again. Behind him. The Announcer spun desperately, unable to walk but still able to stand and twist. He was too slow. Jump after jump, thrust after thrust, Alvertus was killing him.

Then her dad fell. He had dispatched the last soldier, but the battle had left a knife embedded in his chest, on his right. Calendra screamed, her whole existence anguish. Her dad. It could not be. Yet she would still fail. His sacrifice would be for nothing.

The Announcer was breathing his last. He had not laid a hand on Alvertus, the man still Jumping again and again to avoid the Announcer's strikes. She watched as Alvertus Jumped in front of the Announcer and stabbed him through the side. Calendra screamed again.

With astonishing speed - Fast, Calendra realized with shock - Djulita moved for the first time. While Alvertus was still in front of the Announcer, Djulita ran at the Announcer's back, bearing a knife. She dived at him. Calendra was frozen. What was this?

In the split second it took for Djulita's knife to thrust forward, the Manifold twisted as Alvertus Jumped behind the Announcer. Just a finger's breadth in front of the moving knife.

Alvertus gasped as the knife embedded into his back, hilt deep. He collapsed backwards, crashing into the Worldtree right next to Calendra.

To Calendra's amazement, his memories flowed through to Zem - and to her. Most were skimmed over. Zem only seemed interested in specific memories. The memories that defined a life.

Alvie tore along the splintered docks of the Free City of Veranel, barely staying ahead of the filthy mundoes. They disgusted him, the talentless trash, with their jealousy and hatred. What drove a man with nothing to make sure his fellow man had nothing? Nothing more than jealousy ...

Alvertus ran his fingers through his hair and breathed out audibly in a practiced show of disdain. "The dignity of we Nineteen, and of this nation," he replied, "continue to be demeaned by Malnor." ...

Alvertus maintained a perfect image of righteous rage, his face red and his voice a hair's breadth from hysteria. "I move that Lord Speed be dismissed from the Nineteen and stand trial for treason!" Alvertus drank in the squeals of outrage ...

The memories finished much faster than her own had, and Calendra gasped. It was a strange thing to feel another's memories. She had been appalled to feel some sympathy for the monster from his childhood torment, but that withered as he set his course.

Most traumatic was witnessing his memories of Myla. Myla had joined him shortly after dumping her. Maybe that was even why Myla had left her. The betrayal stung even more as she learned how important Myla had been to Alvertus' success.

Alvertus wanted the heart for greed even until the end. Myla had been with him. Was she still here? Calendra had seen nothing of her. After witnessing those memories, she hoped it would stay that way.

Djulita turned and walked back to Calendra. "I'm sorry I wasn't faster," she whispered. "It took time to recognize the pattern. I'm so sorry."

Tears poured down her face as she cupped Calendra's face in her hands. Djulita looked up at the Worldtree in wonder and reached out. Her memories flowed through, just as Alvertus' had.

"Welcome! Ummm ..." The man shuffled through his papers. He was tall and slim, but muscled, with the face of a warrior. Conspicuously large hands. He looked like a carving of himself. "Oh, Djulita. Hi, Djulita! Can I call you Djulie?" "I would prefer not, Candidate Malnor." ...

Djulita sat at her ornate mahogany desk, trying to focus on reports from Vrailen's 'informational network'. His spies reported to him, but she was granted access to support her work for Lord Speed. Artist-civilian relations continued to improve as Guilds or members of the Nineteen adopted Lord Speed's approach. Tensions along the Free Cities border were worsening, but violent conflict remained localized and small scale human tragedies with little chance of escalating to a strategic threat. Even diplomatic relations with Chalveno were improving as Tolgarlo started to walk Lord Speed's talk of respecting and working with nature rather than conducting wholesale land clearing ...

Djulita enjoyed thinking of herself as a detective. Except that instead of detecting crime, she was detecting truth. Unlike crime, though, many who intended truth were innocent of it and some who thought to deceive inadvertently exposed truths ...

Djulita strode past the gate guards, trying to look confident and urgent. The two states were mutually exclusive for Djulita, but the Advisor to Lord Speed was accustomed to the contradiction. Confidence and purposefulness were key to influence and persuasion. Djulita was still surprised that she was not stopped ...

Calendra's heart ached as she felt Djulita's love and care for her over the years. Her letters had been a touchstone to reality for Calendra, but she had never realized Djulita truly loved her. Djulita's bravery in traveling the world to rescue Calendra, in infiltrating countless enemies to get to Calendra, brought more tears. Her patient genius in recognizing Alvertus' pattern, built on years of watching and analyzing, was worthy of song.

Yet of all that, her heart shattering at the sight of Calendra's dad taking a mortal blow while still waiting for the perfect time to act was perhaps Djulita's greatest act of courage. Calendra smiled as she noticed the empty wok and considered not just Djulita's obvious use of Speed Artistry, but how good Djulita's instincts had become.

The world hummed with satisfaction. The world had seen Calendra's life from Calendra's perspective, but now it saw her life from the perspective of one who loved her. The world might not consider her human - she even might not - but Djulita did.

She could feel the world consider this perspective. Could someone who opted out of humanity still be human from the effect they had on those around them? Was being human about your own identity, or about how others saw you?

She could feel it was not enough. Other humans may love her as one of their own, but Zem had felt her intentions. It was still not enough. She would still hold on.

Calendra looked at the physical world again. Djulita was kneeling by her dad's side, holding his bloody hand, whispering to him and weeping. He still drew breath, but was almost gone.

The Announcer, blood seeping from a dozen wounds, was crawling towards her. She looked down at him.

"Thank you," she told him, unable to shake the anguish from her voice. "This world has never had a truer defender."

He smiled and came to her. He stood on shaky legs and touched his forehead to hers.

"Look after it, Daughter of the Manifold."

His legs gave out and he fell onto the Worldtree. The memories started.

Suspended between the dreamscape and the waking world, Danald felt one with all ...

Danald broke through the tangled brambles and gazed down at true beauty. Hundreds of paces below, ringed by gargantuan pines, lay a perfectly circular lake perhaps a mile wide. In the middle of the lake, its water hot enough for steam to drift through the crisp mountain air, was a circular island a couple of hundred paces across. In the center of that island was a tree. Not in all his wanderings had he witnessed such a tree ...

Danald felt the invitation from the tree-which-was-him-but-separate. Danald was invited to stop. The tree had repaired its flaw. Spirit could now be processed by the tree itself without supplement. Danald tried to shrug to himself, forgetting he was a tree. He chuckled at the thought. Then, without thinking overmuch, he abandoned his treehood and became Danald the man once more ...

Danald watched Calendra Malnorka flee from Chalvstrom through a series of spatial Jumps. He released a drawn-out sigh, an unusual display of emotion these days. Her 'escape' was necessary, only she could find their destination. He had hoped she would remain only a Speed Artist. If she had Spatial Artistry, she had Gravity as well. If she discovered her Temporal Art ...

The Announcer died. Danald. She would remember his true name. He was more of a hero than even she had understood. A tyrant in some ways, but a hero. Now, after almost three centuries, he was gone from the world and the world hummed in mourning.

As she turned towards her dad and Djulita, determined to meet her dad's eyes as he passed on, something flashed in the corner of her eye.

Calendra watched in horror as Myla leaped at her. The final betrayal.

Calendra did not move. She would not kill Myla, nor defend herself. She would not break her bond to the Worldtree. She would die, one with the world. Perhaps Calendra-the-many would survive as part of the collective.

Myla crashed into Calendra and ... embraced her. Her grimy face was streaked with tears, but her exhausted smile was all joy. Calendra was dumbfounded.

"Why didn't you come for me?" Myla whispered. "I waited, Petal. Oh, how I waited. Every year."

Calendra could feel her connection to the Worldtree fraying. It made no sense and she had no time to understand. What did it matter? All was lost.

Then the Manifold popped, in the way Calendra had come to learn was Time Artistry. The golden-haired Time Artist appeared next to them.

"She forgot," the man said to Myla. Then he turned to Calendra and smiled.

"Remember, Daughter of the Manifold."

He seized Myla's hand and placed it on the Worldtree.

"Sing me a memory."

And Calendra became lost in three sets of memories.

Kolan surfed the waves of Time, feeling the undulations of reality itself. He needed more moments. He had wasted too many ...

Kolan found an empty world enchanting. His childhood had been all duty to his community's burgeoning Time Artistry ...

Kolan's irritation at the interruption gave way to excitement. It had been a long year but the most thrilling since he had found his purpose. It had cost him, though ...

Kolan had never visited the other landmass. His time had been too valuable to make the journey. He was now glad it was forced upon him. He watched with wonder as he passed over the great Obsidian Wall ...

Calendra had no time to process Kolan's extraordinary memories of Time communities and mechanized flying machines, for the innermost memories of the only person she ever loved began. Began, with that singular day.

"Run. Run!"

Calendra seizes Myla's hand and drags her at a sprint, too hurried to even remove her heavy pack. They run without care through bushes and over jagged roots. The sounds of pursuit become muted. Myla starts to believe they are past the immediate danger, that their pursuers chose the wrong direction.

They round a massive boulder, and Calendra's falls, crashes to her knees and retches. Myla rushes to her. She cannot leave her Petal to these men. All worries of obsessions and casualties forgotten, Myla grasps Calendra's hands in her own, kisses her on the lips, stands and runs back in the direction of the heart tree. She changes directions randomly, hoping no pursuers will find Calendra.

A pursuer runs past her in a flash before turning on his heels and yelling at her to stop. She continues as fast as possible. She eventually reaches the clearing with several pursuers on her tail. Those who remained with the tree draw swords as they see her and form a circle around their leader.

Myla recognized him when they saw him. He visited the School of the Mind once. Alvertus. Bile rising, she addresses him as she skids to a halt.

"Lord Space," she shouts, "I have an offer you will find worthy of consideration."

Several chilling seconds later, Alvertus of the Nineteen calls his men off and approaches. He gazes at her imperiously.

"Speak, child."

"I know what this tree is. I might know things you don't. I offer my service. You won't know me, but I am an Instinct Artist and was fortunate enough to attend the School of the Manifold."

Alvertus nods at this. "I know you. I voted against you attending the School but it sounds like you might be useful. What do you know of this tree?"

"I know it is a confluence point for Spirit, and is most likely attuned specifically to one of the three Domains. But I will say no more until we come to terms."

"What of the other girl with you?"

"Her freedom and safety are part of the terms. She did not recognize you and I will make sure she does not return here until you are gone. Will you treat with me, Lord Space?"

"What do you want?"

"You will not pursue my friend. I will see to it that her memories of this day are removed. I will tell her to get out of my life in a way that ensures she does. I owe her a debt and will not see her murdered for uncovering something beyond her understanding. She knows nothing of these trees."

"Is that it?"

"Of course not. She does not mean so much to me that I would trade my freedom for hers. I am just morally obliged to insist on that as a precondition. No, I have been looking for a patron. My parents are poor and owe money to the wrong people. I have a valuable skill but lack the means to directly help them. I want their debt paid, I want them to receive a regular and generous allowance, and I want protection for them. In exchange, I will serve you as an adviser until you release me and for no more than twenty years. These are my terms."

"*Agreed,*" *Alvertus says without hesitation.*

Myla is surprised that he asks for no surety, but he knows her identity and he is one of the Nineteen.

"*Good. I will need a day and a half. Where will I find you?*"

"*I'll be back at the Tower by then.*"

"*Then I will need a few extra days. I will see you then, Lord Space.*"

Without looking back, hoping she will not be followed, Myla walks out of the clearing. She takes half an hour to reach Calendra via a circuitous route, by which point Calendra is half-conscious. She kisses her love gently on the forehead.

"*Come, Petal. Let's get somewhere safe.*"

It takes several hours, including resting during smallnight, to reach Shaivel's cottage. Calendra is more conscious though still in a daze. Myla has deferred the few questions Calendra has asked.

Myla's old school friend answers the door. Her grin at seeing Myla is eclipsed by concern at the sight of Myla steadying a girl with a head wound. She invites them in and they sit around a table. After opening pleasantries, Myla gets right to the point.

"*Shaivel, we need your services. We need memories removed. The last few hours, and the conversation we are about to have.*"

Calendra, finally bearing sufficient wit to talk, cannot understand. "*Remove our memories, My? Why? What happened? How did we even get away?*"

"*Shaivel, may we have a moment alone?*"

Shaivel nods slowly and leaves the room.

"*Cal, the person in charge of those thugs was Alvertus. He knows about treehearts. He has a way of finding them.*"

"*Oh. That's a problem.*"

"*Yes. So I made a deal with him.*"

Calendra hisses. "*You dealt with that scumbag?*"

"*I had to. He would have found you.*"

"*Screw his deal.*"

"*But Cal, don't you see the opportunity? He knows how to find treehearts. If I'm by his side, I can learn as well. Then we can find all the hearts you want! I know how important they are to you.*"

Calendra's heart tumbles. Myla working for her dad's enemy? Calendra being unable to see her? But the opportunity ...

"*I don't want to lose you, Myla. You're my everything.*"

Myla grips her by the shoulders and looks into her soul. "*You will never lose me. This is just for a time. I will leave when I've learned enough. He won't be able to prevent it, not with my Instinct Artistry.*"

"So what's this about memories, then?"

"He will view my memories. It's forbidden, but he has the people. He must not see this conversation. He must believe I've truly joined him. I demanded money and protection for my parents. It is a believable motive, but the price is that we must forget all this. I don't see another way."

"Why should I? I'm not the one to work for him."

"I told him I'd have your memories of him removed to protect him, but I worry he'll have little faith in me. He might seize you and view your memories, to make sure I've fulfilled my end of the bargain."

"But I'll hunt for you if I don't know to stay away."

"No, Calendra. You won't." Tears flow down her cheeks. "You'll have your memories removed first. Before I do the same, I'll put on a performance. You will hate me afterwards. You will stay away. I promise you that. I'm a good actor."

"But how will we know to return to one another?" Calendra is crying now as well.

"I'll have Shaivel hide our memories in a way that restores them after two years. She has the ability, though it's not an exact science. Our memories may return at different times. So, one week after the annual flower spawning, I will wait for you by the tree where you first told me of your ... ability."

"Only two years?" Calendra sniffles.

"Only two years."

Myla stumbles to the floor as the memories returned. Memories she long forgot she ever had. It has been almost three years. She weeps for the years of bitterness she harbored towards Calendra, now she can remember their plan. She shudders at the damage she's already done working for Alvertus, but rejoices at what she's learned. If only she had a way to share it with Calendra. Yet how much more can she learn if she stays? She will ask Calendra after the spawning.

Myla sleeps by the tree that night. It's been five years and Calendra has still not returned. Maybe if she stays a bit longer ...

Myla considers her options on her seventh walk back from the tree. Calendra must have chosen not to return. Her memories couldn't take this long to return, surely. Myla's parents are wealthy. Myla is making remarkable discoveries in ecological sciences, which might benefit Alvertus first but rapidly benefit all. Perhaps Myla should just embrace this life, as morally troubling as it remains, and forget about her lost love. She knows she won't. She'll be back next year. And the next. As long as it takes.

Myla folds the page with her calculations at the bottom corner, afraid to do more while being watched. Watched still, after so many years serving the old tyrant. She has only weeks until word of the secret continent reaches Alvertus' ears. Giving him the answer now will help maintain what credibility she has left after seasons of increasingly desperate delaying tactics. But Djulita, poking into affairs of Spirit and treehearts, presents a way to get the same information to Lord Speed ...

Calendra gasped. How had she never unlocked the partitioned memories? Why could she still not?

Then it hit. The final memory, unlocked by its compatibility with Myla's, crashed into her.

Calendra, kneeling on the stone Skypeak, reels at the sound of discordant clanging bells for just a moment.

The memory slams into her like a blacksmith's hammer. That awful night begins to replay in her head. Waking up in Shaivel's house with Myla standing over her.

Calendra will not relive it. Not that memory. Never that memory.

Instinctively, Calendra reaches out to an Art she did not know she possesses and, with a thunderous surge of Spirit, crushes the memory before it can reform.

Calendra wakes to deafening bells clanging discordantly ...

Calendra screamed. How many years had they lost? How much death could have been spared? How much sooner might Calendra have arrived here? All because she was a coward who did not want to remember.

None of it mattered. She was done. Zem did not want her. She was not worthy. She was not human. She ...

HUMAN

Calendra felt the understanding in Zem's thought. The understanding that Calendra's separation from humanity was driven by the most human trait of all - fear of emotional pain. She was human. She always had been, despite her best efforts.

Calendra felt the bond with Zem solidify, her consciousness slipping into something more vast. She could even feel her body shifting to become one with the Worldtree. She looked at Myla. The words would not come.

"Calendra," she whispered, "it's ok. This is why we lost so many years together. For this end. I love you."

Calendra screamed, letting forth a river of pain dammed for so many years. Calendra kissed Myla, taking care to remember the shape of her lips.

And Calendra, Daughter of the Manifold, let go of the mortal world.

CHAPTER THIRTY

C alendra's awareness expanded. She could no longer feel her body. In its place, she could feel ... everything. Every plant. Every tree. Not simultaneously. A woman could not think about each individual toe and finger at the same time. But she could always feel that they were there.

Calendra considered different parts of herself. Her jungles and grasslands. Her mangroves and wildflowers. She could not focus on each ecosystem, but they reported to the collective as needed. That was the hum of shadows of voices beneath the occasional voice of Zem. No mind could govern all life, but a mind could govern a hierarchical structure in which most actions were automatic and only deviations required judgement or interference.

As she processed her own nature, a mind that was individual yet collective, she remembered Calendra-the-one. That woman was gone, but her personality, her memories and her desires had become the voice of the world. The mind of Zem. They were important.

Calendra thanked the Worldtree. It was a beacon in her mind. As soon as she thought of it, she could feel it as intuitively as one could feel their own breath. She had no eyes to see, but dozens of tiny lives sent reports of humans, sensed through chemical reactions. Through the Worldtree, she could directly sense Spirit. She could see the clearing, for seeing was the best word to describe the image her mind presented once it sorted through various data.

Calendra saw Djulita cradling Malnor while the Spiritless body of Danald lay to one side and Kolan held his hand. And Myla, Myla, curled into a ball in the dirt, weeping, weeping.

Calendra's heart broke. All life shuddered.

No. It should not be. It need not be. Calendra reached out to the Worldheart. She felt the connection it had with the trees and grasses in the clearing. A conduit for communication and Spirit.

Calendra willed the heart to transmit Spirit of the Physical, attuned to resilience, throughout the clearing. Calendra objected.

It is a deviation. It will divert Spirit from where it might be needed. Why these people? Will you save all people?

It was a part of her that thought differently from herself, or just her own inner dialogue prompted by input from that which comprised her.

"Mercy," Calendra told herself. "Justice. These humans gave their lives for us. And the Spirit diversion is acceptable."

Mercy. Justice. These are not sufficient reasons for deviations.

"They are now," Calendra decreed.

The Worldheart responded. It altered its Spiritual outflows to divert a small stream of perfectly aligned Spirit through the nearby grasses, Spirit aligned to the truth humans referred to as resilience.

First to rise were some of Alvertus' troops with less grievous injuries. They gazed around in shock, unsure what to do. Malnor took longer but eventually awoke and embraced Djulita.

Calendra blazed with joy and all life exalted.

"Did we win?" Malnor's voice trembled. "Where is my girl?"

Djulita smiled and wept and nodded. Malnor understood and cried openly, tears running down a face aglow with pride. He looked down at Danald and his face fell.

"I was so wrong," he mumbled. "Who was he?"

Kolan answered. "A self-appointed guardian. Very old. He was once the grandson of the man after whom your nation was named, and a far better man than Tolgan ever was."

The words triggered a memory Calendra had access to, but that she had not noticed. A man who found the Worldheart soon after humans arrived here. Tolgan. He had been extraordinary, but he had not been the right choice. Zem had spared him and teleported back to the human lands, mind broken.

"Do not regret," Kolan continued. "Danald didn't care the slightest what anyone thought of him. He died saving that which he had defended for fifteen generations."

"And who in the ten hells," Malnor asked, "are you?"

"Me?" Kolan gave Malnor a lopsided smile. "Nobody of note." He turned to Myla. "Come, Myla. Let me show you something. This is a time to look forward. To divert the river upstream before it becomes a flood downstream. We could use you."

Myla looked at him, her cheeks glistening. She looked at the Worldtree, seeming to ask Calendra the question. Calendra responded with a pulse of Spirit. A solitary flower, petals the precise shade of silver, bloomed in front of Myla in seconds. Her face brightened. She plucked the flower, hugged the tree and whispered goodbye. Then she took Kolan's offered hand and they vanished, pulled into a slower Timestream.

Malnor cursed. "Can somebody please tell me ..."

Calendra had a world to tend. She commanded the Worldheart to send pulses of Spirit aligned with resilience and speed into the grassy hill in front of them. Patches of grass grew so rapidly that they were waist high in seconds. They formed a pattern. Words.

Malnor and Djulita watched in wonder. Calendra could see Djulita silently mouthing the words. A tear flowed down Malnor's cheek.

Thank you. I would be nothing without either of you. I chose this. I am happy. Do not grieve.

I sought to be extraordinary. Turns out I just needed to be a part of something extraordinary.

I love you both. I am here because of you. I can help this world adapt, but it can never match the pace of human change. Protect it. Cherish it. Share it.

I charge humanity with this mission. For if you cannot, if I must take a side, it might not be humanity's.

She commanded the Worldheart, and it sent out pulses of Spirit that teleported Malnor and Djulita to Vrailen's home. Noticing the surviving mercenaries gawking at the words, Calendra sent them to Alvertus' compound without further thought.

With considerable focus, Calendra moved to increase the protection originally instituted by the Traveler. She initiated processes that would further protect the treehearts, expanded the barriers around the Grand Reserve and addressed a hundred other points of weakness that humans might exploit when, inevitably, knowledge spread. She could not figure out how the obsidian walls were raised, though, not being made of living matter. She noted with interest what appeared to be another network, parallel to hers. She smiled to herself as she understood.

She would leave that to another. It was enough for now. Many of her measures would take decades to grow to fruition, but the system would maintain itself once established.

Anyone can change the world, but it is so much better to design it right in the first place.

Finally, Calendra turned her thoughts to the remaining body. The only one left that mattered, the rest now food for those who supported her trees.

Most of Danald's wounds had been healed, but those that counted had not. His face was serene, showing no sign of the pain he must have felt as he died, just a gentle smile. Calendra hoped he had known that he bought them the time they needed.

Calendra commanded the great Chalvstrom tree, that which she once called worldtree, and it executed her command. Large parts of it began to die and decay, sloughing off. The tree within remained strong and healed those parts with fresh wood and new bark, but the tree now had a new shape.

A living wooden statue three hundred paces tall, in the shape of a proud figure with bare chest and flowing pants, head held high, looking at his nation with eyes as tall as a woman. Letters were engraved above his head, never to fade.

Danald the Announcer.

Defender of Zem.

Heart of the World.

It was a fitting tribute for humanity, but the world of trees owed him more. She had one thing left to do.

Calendra took her time. She knew what was required, but she was new at this. She felt the worldwide flows, tracking their routes, understanding their weaknesses and picturing future needs. The network was complex beyond belief, but its fractal nature meant she did not need to understand every source, every node, every flow. She only needed to understand its emergent state, determine the state it should be in, and work backwards. Like figuring out how to mix colors to paint the image one can see in their mind's eye.

It was hard work, even with the resources at Calendra's disposal. She had to be sure. She could tinker in the future, perhaps even start again, but it was better to get it right this time. A hundred day-night cycles passed before she was ready.

Calendra smiled and diverted flows of Spirit in just the right places. The network reconfigured itself. A singularity of infinite Spiritual density appeared beneath the broken but preserved body of Danald, the Announcer. As it condensed, the Worldtree diverted its inflows and outflows to that point.

A seed formed from Danald's Spiritual nexus. Pure Spirit infused the seed and it sprouted. Drawing on the energies of an entire planet's lifeforms, incorporating the base elements of Danald's physical substance, it grew. And it grew. And it grew. It grew into the mightiest tree the world had seen.

And Danald became that which he had protected to his last breath. The Worldtree.

The Heart of the World.

The End

Acknowledgements

I never planned to write fiction. I'm not creative, said I. I consume worlds. I don't produce them.

Yet I wrote a fantasy novel. One that, I'm not afraid to say, I really love. That's a journey, and behind every journey is a tale. There's no lightning-from-a-blue-sky moment in that tale, just a steady process of curiosity, openness, experimentation, iterative learning, focus, prioritization, emotions and passion.

That tale is one of, as with all good tales, people. The people who grabbed my hand and pulled me onto the path. The people who took the first exploratory steps with me. The people who walked with me. The people who kept me on the path when I strayed. And the people who dedicated countless hours to make sure the destination was as satisfying as the journey.

To Stelios Moudakis, for busting down my creative door and telling me we're going on a world-building adventure. I can't wait to see where his leads him.

To Daniel Napoleoni, for being a warm, cuddly and astute part of my journey at every step, despite being the only one of my core group who isn't really a fantasy reader.

To Juan Ojeda, who was invaluable and took time at every single step. Every one. Ideas, wordsmything, line edits, art, website, publishing. I hope he'll one day publish. His interests, imagination and love of words will make for an amazing read.

To Juliet Lautenbach, for being my fellow traveler for that first, scary part of the journey and helping so much. Her first novel is not far behind mine, and it's outstanding. I think about it her world and characters all the time.

To Steve Dunjey, who introduced me to Brandon and was a wonderful alpha reader from early on.

And to those who, while not as integral, took the time to read my book and give me advice or encouragement.

But there is a category left. Those who taught me how to write and how to be an author.

To Brandon Sanderson, who taught me to read fantasy. Then taught me to write it.

To the various members of Writing Excuses over the years. If Brandon was my lecturer, they were my tutors.

And to Will Wight, not only my favourite author after Brandon, but the one who taught me that successful independent publishing of fantasy is possible.

There are many more who have supported me, especially my loved ones, not least my patient Hana, but I owe this book to these people.

Cheers!

About the Author

David Maxwell is an Australian author who lives with his beautiful wife and adorable greyhound, and writes in his spare time. He loves travel, hiking, scuba diving and all things science. He loves a good answer, but loves a good question even more. And he really loves a good book.

David has been driven throughout his life by the questions *what is* and *what if*. The first question has led to a lifelong passion for the sciences. The second question led him through a universe of speculative fiction.

With Rowling and Tolkien as his gateway into fantasy, and Hobb and Feist his next steps in a journey through speculative worlds, it was Brandon Sanderson that showed him what fantasy could be, leading to years of in-depth exploration of hard magic and hard world-building. Writers like Rothfuss, Jemisin and Wight revealed a space of fantasy storytelling broader than he imagined in his early days of sword and sorcery fantasy.

Motivated by the stories, characters, worlds and magics of the expanding fantasy genre, David was prompted to ask - and answer - his own *what if*.

If you liked this story and want to support me, share that love with friends, family, online, and with me directly, at author@david-maxwell.com. Register for my newsletter by visiting my website at david-maxwell.com to get updates on the next book (due 2025) and free access to short stories from Calendra's world.

David does not use generative AI for any element of the creative process.

Printed in Great Britain
by Amazon

47025455R10182